FROM THE PAGES OF
THE GREAT ESCAPES

It is not for a single generation alone, numbering three millions—
sublime as would be that effort—that we are working. It is for
Humanity, the wide world over, not only now, but for all coming
time, and all future generations.

(from *Narrative of William W. Brown*, page 9)

During the last night that I served in slavery I did not close my eyes
a single moment. When not thinking of the future, my mind dwelt
on the past. The love of a dear mother, a dear sister, and three dear
brothers, yet living, caused me to shed many tears.

(from *Narrative of William W. Brown*, page 52)

"Let us declare through the public journals of our country, that the
question of slavery is not and shall not be open for discussion: that the
system is too deep-rooted among us, and must remain forever; that
the very moment any private individual attempts to lecture us upon
its evils and immorality, and the necessity of putting means in operation to secure us from them, in the same moment his tongue shall be
cut out and cast upon the dunghill."—*Columbia (S.C.) Telescope.*

(from *Narrative of William W. Brown*, page 74)

My book will represent, if possible, the beautiful side of the picture
of slavery. (from *Narrative of Henry Box Brown*, page 100)

A cold sweat now covered me from head to foot. Death seemed my
inevitable fate, and every moment I expected to feel the blood flowing over me, which had burst from my veins.

(from *Narrative of Henry Box Brown*, page 136)

I happened to be in the City of Philadelphia—I have told the story to the convention already, but I will tell it again—in the midst of an excitement that was caused by the arrival of a man in a box. I measured it myself; *three feet one inch long, two feet wide, and two feet six inches deep*. In that box a man was entombed for twenty seven hours.

(from *Narrative of Henry Box Brown*, page 158)

I have since learned that it was the famous Nat Turner's insurrection. Many slaves were whipped, hung, and cut down with the swords in the streets; and some that were found away from their quarters after dark, were shot; the whole city was in the utmost excitement, and the whites seemed terrified beyond measure, so true it is that the "wicked flee when no man pursueth."

(from *Narrative of the Life of Henry Box Brown*, page 185)

Thus passed my child from my presence—it was my own child—I loved it with all the fondness of a father; but things were so ordered that I could only say, farewell, and leave it to pass in its chains while I looked for the approach of another gang in which my wife was also loaded with chains.

(from *Narrative of the Life of Henry Box Brown*, pages 203–204)

It may be remembered that slavery in America is not at all confined to persons of any particular complexion; there are a very large number of slaves as white as any one.

(from *Running a Thousand Miles for Freedom*, page 225)

"Under these circumstances, it is the almost unanimous opinion of their best friends, that they should quit America as speedily as possible, and seek an asylum in England! Oh! shame, shame upon us, that Americans, whose fathers fought against Great Britain, in order to be free, should have to acknowledge this disgraceful fact!"

(from *Running a Thousand Miles for Freedom*, page 274)

In short, it is well known in England, if not all over the world, that the Americans, as a people, are notoriously mean and cruel towards all coloured persons, whether they are bond or free.

(from *Running a Thousand Miles for Freedom*, page 286)

THE
GREAT ESCAPES

Four Slave Narratives

With an Introduction and Notes by Daphne A. Brooks
with research assistance from Jeffrey Gonda

GEORGE STADE
CONSULTING EDITORIAL DIRECTOR

BARNES & NOBLE CLASSICS
NEW YORK

JB

BARNES & NOBLE CLASSICS

NEW YORK

Published by Barnes & Noble Books
122 Fifth Avenue
New York, NY 10011

www.barnesandnoble.com/classics

Narrative of William W. Brown was first published in 1847. The current text is of the enlarged, second edition of 1848. *Narrative of Henry Box Brown* was first published in 1849; and *Narrative of the Life of Henry Box Brown* was published in England in 1851. *Running a Thousand Miles for Freedom* was first published in 1860.

Published in 2007 by Barnes & Noble Classics with new Introduction, Notes, Biography, Chronology, Glossary of Names, Comments & Questions, and For Further Reading.

Introduction, Notes, Glossary of Names, and For Further Reading
Copyright © 2007 by Daphne A. Brooks.

Note on William Wells Brown, Henry Box Brown, and William and Ellen Craft, The World of *The Great Escapes*, and Comments & Questions
Copyright © 2007 by Barnes & Noble, Inc.

The Great Escapes
ISBN-13: 978-1-59308-294-9
ISBN-10: 1-59308-294-0
LC Control Number 2006940020

Produced and published in conjunction with:
Fine Creative Media, Inc.
322 Eighth Avenue
New York, NY 10001

Michael J. Fine, President and Publisher

Printed in the United States of America

QM

1 3 5 7 9 10 8 6 4 2

FIRST PRINTING

The personal histories of slaves in the pre–Civil War American South offer the modern reader a unique portrait of the African-American slave and of a nation divided over slavery, the central moral issue of the time. Slave narratives played an important role in the anti-slavery movement, individualizing the slaves and providing a window onto their lives for skeptics and galvanizing white sympathizers to action. Four remarkable examples are narratives by William Wells Brown, Henry Box Brown, and William and Ellen Craft.

William Wells Brown was born in 1814 in Lexington, Kentucky. His mother, Elizabeth, was a slave, and his father, George Higgins, was a white relative of Brown's owner. Brown's owners hired him out in different capacities; he was employed on a riverboat and as a field slave, a house slave, a typesetter for a printer, and even an assistant to a slave-trader. In 1834 Brown escaped his owner and made his way North, where he worked on a Lake Erie steamboat and conducted runaway slaves to Canada as part of the Underground Railroad; his intelligence and gift for oratory made him a sought-after lecturer for the anti-slavery movement. In 1847 he moved to Boston, where he published *Narrative of William W. Brown, A Fugitive Slave, Written by Himself*. The popular autobiography described the institution of slavery in vivid yet dispassionate detail.

Brown embarked on a lecture tour of Europe in 1849 and did not return to the United States for five years, partly to avoid the Fugitive Slave Act of 1850. His time abroad inspired *Three Years in Europe; or, Places I Have Seen and People I Have Met* (1852); he also published *Clotel* (1853), the first novel by an African American. Like Frederick Douglass, Brown served the abolition movement through his speeches and published writings; he wrote major works on black history, including *The Black Man* (1863) and *The Negro in the American Revolution* (1867). William Wells Brown spent the last decades of his life in Boston, he died in Chelsea, Massachusetts, on November 6, 1884.

Henry Box Brown was born around 1815 in Louisa County, Virginia. At age fifteen, he was separated from his family and sent to work in a Richmond tobacco factory. In Richmond, Brown married Nancy, a slave washerwoman, and the two had three children. When his wife and children were sold to a distant slaveholder, Brown, devastated, resolved to escape his bondage and in 1848 had himself mailed in a tiny wooden crate to the Anti-Slavery Society of Philadelphia. With only a jug of water, Brown survived the 300-mile, twenty-seven-hour journey. He set down his story in two books—*Narrative of Henry Box Brown, Who Escaped from Slavery Enclosed in a Box 3 Feet Long and 2 Wide* (1849) and *Narrative of the Life of Henry Box Brown* (1851)—and, in illustrated form, as a scrolling panorama called *Mirror of Slavery* (1850). For a time, Brown told his story in the service of the anti-slavery movement and proved a popular speaker. When the Fugitive Slave Act was passed in 1850, he fled to England; by 1878 he had dropped out of public view.

William and Ellen Craft were slaves in Macon County, Georgia. William was a skilled cabinetmaker, while Ellen worked as a house slave. Neither endured the brutal physical circumstances of many slaves in the American South, yet as the property of separate slaveholders, they lived in fear of separation and longed for their freedom. In 1848 they determined to escape. Ellen, whose skin was so fair she was often mistaken for a white woman, disguised herself as an invalid, wrapping herself in bandages, while William pretended to be his "master's" faithful slave. The ruse worked, and the two escaped to Philadelphia and then to Boston. There they joined the anti-slavery movement, recounting their escape before rapt audiences.

The couple's heroic actions thrust them into the public eye but also into the sights of the slaveholders they had fled. When the Fugitive Slave Act was passed in 1850 and agents arrived in Boston to retake the Crafts, the two fled to England, where they lived until after the Civil War. They retold the history of their daring escape from slavery in *Running a Thousand Miles for Freedom* (1860). Following the war, the Crafts returned to the South, settling in 1868 in Georgia, where they made their home until Ellen died in 1891. William moved to South Carolina, where he died in 1896.

TABLE OF CONTENTS

1814   William Wells Brown is born into slavery near Lexington, Kentucky.

c.1815   Henry Box Brown is born a slave on the Hermitage plantation in Louisa County, Virginia, 45 miles from Richmond.

1818   Frederick Douglass is born in Maryland.

c.1824   William Craft is born in Macon County, Georgia.

c.1826   Ellen Craft is born in Clinton, Georgia.

1831   Abolitionist William Lloyd Garrison begins publishing the anti-slavery newspaper *The Liberator*. Nat Turner leads a slave revolt in Virginia that kills about sixty whites; the rebellion is quickly crushed and Turner is hanged.

1833   William Lloyd Garrison helps organize the American Anti-Slavery Society.

1834   William Wells Brown flees to Canada with the help of a Quaker abolitionist, Wells Brown; William takes his name as his own. He marries a free black woman, finds work on a Lake Erie steamboat, and helps conduct other runaway slaves to freedom. In August, Great Britain's Abolition of Slavery Act of 1833 takes effect, ending slavery throughout the British Empire.

1835   Mark Twain, author of *The Adventures of Huckleberry Finn*, is born.

1836   William Wells Brown moves to Buffalo, New York, where he becomes involved in the anti-slavery movement. Henry Box Brown seeks permission to marry Nancy, another slave.

1837   Elijah P. Lovejoy, abolitionist and former employer of William Wells Brown, is killed by a pro-slavery mob in Illinois.

1838	Frederick Douglass escapes slavery, fleeing to New York.

1839	Abducted Africans aboard the slave ship *Amistad* revolt, killing some of their white captors and commandeering the ship; the *Amistad* is seized off the New England coast, and the slaves are jailed and tried. Poet Henry Wadsworth Longfellow publishes the Romantic novel *Hyperion*. Edgar Allan Poe publishes the story "The Fall of the House of Usher."

1841	The Supreme Court frees the *Amistad* defendants, finding that the international slave trade is illegal. James Fenimore Cooper publishes *The Deerslayer*. American philosopher Ralph Waldo Emerson publishes *Essays* (first series).

1843	William Wells Brown meets Frederick Douglass. Brown's reputation as an orator grows as he delivers anti-slavery lectures.

1845	*Narrative of the Life of Frederick Douglass, an American Slave* is published.

1846	William and Ellen Craft are married. William is a skilled cabinetmaker; Ellen, a very fair-skinned black woman, works as a house slave.

1847	William Wells Brown moves to Boston at the invitation of the Massachusetts Anti-Slavery Society; there he writes and publishes *Narrative of William W. Brown, A Fugitive Slave, Written by Himself*. Frederick Douglass begins publishing the abolitionist newspaper *The North Star*.

1848	William and Ellen Craft arrive in Philadelphia, completing a daring escape from slavery in which Ellen poses as a white, male slaveholder and William poses as her servant.

1849	The Crafts join the anti-slavery movement in Boston. When Henry Box Brown's owner sells his wife and children, Brown escapes from slavery by shipping himself in a wooden box from North Carolina to Philadelphia. *Narrative of Henry Box Brown, Who Escaped from Slavery Enclosed in a Box 3 Feet Long and 2 Wide* is published. William Wells Brown visits Europe for a lecture tour; partly because of political dangers in the United States, he remains there for five years.

1850   The Fugitive Slave Law is enacted, severely limiting the legal rights of runaway slaves. William and Ellen Craft flee to England. Henry Box Brown creates a scrolling panorama, *Mirror of Slavery*, that pictures scenes from slavery and illustrates his remarkable escape; fearing the Fugitive Slave Act, during the early 1850s Brown will take his panorama to England, where he will remain active in the anti-slavery movement. *The Narrative of Sojourner Truth: A Northern Slave*, a memoir by the former slave, abolitionist, and suffragette, is published.

1851   *Narrative of the Life of Henry Box Brown*, the second account of Brown's life and escape from slavery, is published.

1852   William Wells Brown publishes *Three Years in Europe; or, Places I Have Seen and People I Have Met*.

1853   In London, William Wells Brown publishes *Clotel; or, The President's Daughter*, a novel about the relationship of Thomas Jefferson with his slave mistress and their daughter. *Clotel* is the first novel published by an African American.

1854   The Kansas-Nebraska Act opens the territories of Kansas and Nebraska to slavery and creates a political schism from which the anti-slavery Republican Party emerges. Henry David Thoreau publishes *Walden; or, Life in the Woods*.

1855   Frederick Douglass publishes a second autobiography, *My Bondage and My Freedom*. Walt Whitman publishes the first edition of *Leaves of Grass*.

1857   The U.S. Supreme Court issues the infamous Dred Scott Decision, finding that African Americans are not citizens and that a slave does not become free upon entering a free state.

1858   Abraham Lincoln campaigns against Stephen Douglas for the U.S. Senate; Douglas wins after a series of widely reported debates. William Wells Brown writes the play *The Escape; or, A Leap for Freedom*.

1859   Abolitionist John Brown leads a raid on a federal arsenal in Virginia, intent on arming a slave revolt; his plans are thwarted, and he is tried for treason and hanged. John Stuart Mill publishes *On Liberty*.

1860   The Republican Party nominates Abraham Lincoln for president; he wins, defeating Stephen Douglas. William and Ellen Craft publish their narrative *Running a Thousand Miles for Freedom* in London.

1861   The southern states, led by South Carolina, secede from the Union, forming the Confederate States and naming Jefferson Davis their president. In April Confederate soldiers attack Fort Sumter, beginning the American Civil War. Harriet Jacobs publishes *Incidents in the Life of a Slave Girl.*

1862   On September 22 President Lincoln issues the Emancipation Proclamation, which will free the nation's nearly 4 million slaves.

1863   The Emancipation Proclamation takes effect on January 1. William Wells Brown publishes *The Black Man,* a history of African Americans.

1865   The Civil War ends on April 9 when Confederate general Robert E. Lee surrenders at Appomattox Court House. On April 15 Abraham Lincoln is assassinated by John Wilkes Booth, and Andrew Johnson becomes president. The Thirteenth Amendment to the U.S. Constitution, abolishing slavery and involuntary servitude, is ratified.

1867   William Wells Brown publishes the historical work *The Negro in the American Revolution.*

1868   The Fourteenth Amendment is ratified, granting citizenship to any person born or naturalized in the United States.

1869   William and Ellen Craft return to the United States from England, settling in Georgia. The National Woman Suffrage Association is formed by Susan B. Anthony and Elizabeth Cady Stanton.

1870   The Fifteenth Amendment is ratified, granting voting rights to people of all races.

1876   Mark Twain publishes *The Adventures of Tom Sawyer.*

1880   William Wells Brown writes the autobiography *My Southern Home.*

1883   Sojourner Truth dies in Battle Creek, Michigan.

1884   William Wells Brown dies on November 6 in Chelsea, Massachusetts. Mark Twain publishes *The Adventures of Huckleberry Finn*.

1891   Ellen Craft dies at the family's home near Savannah, Georgia.

1895   Frederick Douglass dies in Washington, D.C.

1896   William Craft dies in Charleston, South Carolina.

1936–   The Works Progress Administration (also called the
1938   Works Projects Administration; WPA) interviews former slaves from the American South, creating the first comprehensive compilation of slave narratives—more than 2,300 firsthand accounts that will be published in 1941 in 17 volumes as *Slave Narratives: A Folk History of Slavery in the United States from Interviews with Former Slaves*.

INTRODUCTION

Catch Me If You Can: The Art of Escape and Anti-Slavery Performance in the Narratives of William Wells Brown, Henry Box Brown, and William and Ellen Craft

> "Are the slaves contented and happy? Here are three
> facts . . . that sweep away all the sophistry."
> —*Frederick Douglass*[1]

> "They say that the children of the ones who could not fly
> told their children. And now, me, I have told it to you."
> —*Virginia Hamilton*[2]

Although they would circle each other in the public eye for more than a decade across two continents and through the advent and end of the Civil War, the black abolitionists and fugitive slaves William Wells Brown, Henry Box Brown, and William and Ellen Craft would cross paths on the anti-slavery podium only once in their lifetimes. On May 30, 1849, the seasoned orator and vaulting cosmopolitan William Wells Brown stood before an assembly of New England abolitionists and introduced his comrades in struggle. Already close friends and lecture tour partners with the married couple William and Ellen Craft, Wells Brown, a former Underground Railroad conductor and mentor to fellow fugitives presented the Georgia husband and wife whose story of cross-dressing masquerade and flight had made headlines from the U.S. South to Great Britain. He then turned to the novice speaker Henry Brown, who, some two months earlier, had fled a Virginia plantation for Philadelphia cloistered away in a U.S. postal package in a remarkable escape likened to biblical resurrection. Each of the Browns as well as the Crafts were already instant cultural legends in northern reformist circles where their tales of adversity in bondage joined in the chorus of fugitive testimonials that served as key weapons in the battle to end slavery. Yet all were united in distinction as architects of some of the most unusual and dramatic escapes from slavery preserved on record.

On that spring evening at Boston's Melodeon theater, the New England Anti-Slavery Convention called upon these celebrities of great escapes to not only body forth the atrocities of slavery but pointedly to object to the increasing legislation designed to capture fugitives in the North and return them to southern slaveholders. Abolitionist Edmund Quincy produced a resolution for the convention that proposed "to trample under foot any law which allows the slaveholder to hunt the fugitive slave through our borders."[3] Quincy's resolve, "to make New England . . . an asylum for the oppressed," was reaffirmed in the flesh by the appearance of these "fugitives of injustice" whose masterful subterfuge and skillful plots to obtain freedom sent a potent message to all would-be slave-catchers: The ingenuity and imaginative resistance of the fugitive slave is never to be underestimated.[4]

Certainly William Wells Brown had made such a sentiment clear in his wildly popular narrative published two years prior to his appearance in New England with the Crafts and Box Brown. The *Narrative of William Wells Brown* encapsulated the sheer moxie and determination of the enslaved by offering a detailed account of his repeated attempts to reach freedom. Wells Brown's tale of his life in slavery relates to readers his migrant trips up and down the Mississippi River as a servant to various slaveholders, as well as his subsequent escape from enslavement after early failed attempts resulted in punishment and further divisions and ruptures in his family. Escape in the Wells Brown *Narrative* depends less upon spectacular stunts and more upon a steady repetition of acts and an accretion of geographical as well as spiritual moves that build a road to freedom. By articulating the steely will of those in bondage and by reinforcing the fugitive's steadfast desire for liberty and self-making, Wells Brown's text exposes the often protracted and agonizing struggles of numerous "rebels on the plantation" whose efforts to acquire freedom were anything but surgically clean and career, and he began his rapid transmogrification into abolitionist showman.[8] Wells Brown's "jocularly termed" sobriquet for the other Brown, "Boxer," would stick, resulting in the creation of Henry "Box" Brown, the fugitive wonder whose name alone encapsulated wily escape and unusual physical and psychological stamina under duress. Having arrived in a crate "3 feet long, 2 ft 8 inches deep, and 23½ inches wide" at the office of the Anti-Slavery Society in Philadelphia in March 1849, Box Brown went on to devote himself to multiple retellings of his daring and anomalous escape, employing everything from sacred song to performance exhibition to the highly successful use of visual panoramas to recount his "boxing" odyssey. Released within four months of his first public appearance, the 1849 first edition of *Narrative of Henry Box Brown* presents a key, if controversial, account of Brown's postal flight. Heavily edited by amanuensis Charles Stearns, the initial Box Brown *Narrative* presents what was a common example of rigorous ghostwriting in the slave narrative genre that often threatened to distort and mute the discursive voices of fugitive slaves. It is included in this volume alongside the 1851 English edition of Brown's escape account. While many popular slave narratives, such as Wells Brown's, would appear in multiple editions, *Narrative of the Life of Henry Box Brown* is perhaps one of the few slave narratives literally and figuratively to engage with extra-textual mixed media produced by the fugitive author. Juxtaposing both versions of the box escape reveals the extent to which Henry Brown's sacred spirituals, public exhibitions, and visual art played critical roles in elasticizing the scope and range of how the Brown *Narrative* was written and what events were included and elided in each version of his quest for liberation. Taken together these two texts provide illuminating evidence of the slave narrative's evolution in form, particularly in the 1850s, the "age of anxious escape" for enslaved African-Americans and "urgent, perilous, uncertain 'passages'" into freedom.[9]

Each of the narratives included in this anthology articulate the specific exigencies of the anti-slavery movement as the Union lurched toward war, and each built in critical ways on the path-breaking literary strides of abolitionist luminary Frederick Douglass. Elegantly immortalized by Douglass in his 1845 *Narrative of the Life of Frederick Douglass, an American Slave*, the linear operations.[5] His *Narrative* positions his own deceptively simple flight as the gateway through which many others would pass. Moreover, Wells Brown's rapid-fire evolution from Midwestern fugitive to nine-year veteran steamboatman on Lake Erie and Underground Railroad activist in Buffalo, New York, created, as his text in part demonstrates, myriad opportunities for others, most notably the Crafts and Box Brown.

By the time that William and Ellen Craft joined Wells Brown behind the podium at the Melodeon theater they had earned their stripes as public speakers as well, having worked closely for several months with him on an abolitionist lecture tour. Within days of their escape from Macon, Georgia, to Philadelphia at the end of 1848, the senior activist had taken the young couple under his wing, and he ushered them onto the anti-slavery speaking circuit by January 24, 1849. More than any other person, Wells Brown would remain a key figure in the production of the cultural narrative that would eventually result in William Craft's *Running a Thousand Miles for Freedom* (1860). Having mastered the art of narrating his own escape both orally and discursively, Wells Brown recognized the spectacular currency of the Crafts' flight and its sheer ability to draw attention to the anti-slavery cause. With the portrait of a light-skinned Ellen dressed as a convalescing "southern gentleman" circulating throughout the 1850s, the lore of the Crafts' high-risk transformation from captive wife and husband into "white master" and "black slave" solidified the legend of their escape in public memory long before William Craft committed it to paper.[6] Some twelve years, one second flight—this time to England—several extensive U.K. lecture tours, and the birth of five children later, Craft's *Running a Thousand Miles for Freedom* was published in Great Britain and subsequently "went through two printings in as many years."[7]

Although he was the rookie of the group who gathered together on the fugitive platform at the 1849 New England Anti-Slavery Convention, Richmond, Virginia's Henry Brown would evolve into the most flamboyant, iconoclastic, entrepreneurial, and elusive figure on that stage and arguably in the history of the anti-slavery movement. A fledgling oratorical speaker who had had limited experience in the public eye as a choir singer in slavery, Brown, on that day, earned the nickname that would stick throughout his colorful movement from bondage to freedom—with unmistakable overtones of New Testament theocratic ideology—rang true to thousands of readers in the United States and abroad who viscerally and emotionally connected with Douglass's resounding account of transformation from "thing into man." Douglass effectively laid out a philosophical and existential blueprint for freedom in his *Narrative*. Though the specifics of his escape were, in the text at least, shrouded in secrecy for the purposes of leaving that route open for fellow would-be fugitives, he created a detailed account of his moral, psychological, and physical conversion that would assure him success in breaking free from captivity. Numerous fugitive authors would follow suit with their own variations on these themes.[10] Clearly indebted to Douglass's model, the Wells Brown, Craft, and Box Brown narratives each take the core principles of Douglass's text, its conversion ideology, its scathing critique of Christian slaveholders' hypocrisy, and its diligent and persistent engagement with willful and exhilarating self-creation.

Where these narratives diverge from Douglass's formidable example, however, is in their buoyant emphasis on the skillful and ingenious strategy of escape itself and the spectacular lengths to which captives would go to obtain their freedom. Each work included here celebrates the extreme craft involved in engineering escapes, and each outlines the various material and performative tools involved in organizing tacit flight. By foregrounding the escape itself, all of the texts in this anthology make plain the quotidian bravery and extraordinary artistic gifts on which these fugitives relied in order to secure their liberty. These narratives sent out pointed messages of discontent and defiance to slaveholders and slave-catchers who remained determined to hunt down fugitives in the North, and they reinforced in literary terms the living tableaux that Douglass marveled over when he appeared on stage a day later at the New England Anti-Slavery Convention. Paying tribute to Box Brown as well as the Crafts, the senior abolitionist joyously observed, " 'What an exhibition!' " Douglass must have recognized the iconic silhouette that his fellow fugitives struck on stage together, for he predicted that their sheer presence would " 'sweep away all the sophistry" of pro-slavery propaganda. Employing their literary voices to declare their steadfast opposition to slavery and to displace

specious slaveholding propaganda with "the facts" of their inge-
niously executed escapes, Wells Brown, Box Brown and the Crafts
produced slave narratives that, in turn, served as majestic forms of
flight in and of themselves.

The Double Agent: Repetition and Flight in the Narrative *of* William Wells Brown

He was "the second fugitive slave to function professionally as an
anti-slavery publicist at home and abroad," but the sheer scope and
range of his talents would help to distinguish William Wells Brown
as an instrumental figure in the development of multiple forms of
anti-slavery literature.[11] Brown was born in 1814 on a farm in the
Lexington, Kentucky, area. He was one of seven children—each with
different fathers—born to the slave woman Elizabeth, who was
owned by Dr. John Young.[12] His father was, as Brown describes in
his *Narrative*, George Higgins, "a white man, a relative of my master, and connected with some of the first families in Kentucky."[13]
Within the first few years of Brown's birth, Dr. Young had moved his
farm to the Missouri Territory in order to pursue a career in politics.
Brown subsequently spent much of his childhood and teen years
in and around St. Louis, Missouri, assuming a wide variety of
positions—as a house servant, a field hand, a tavern keeper's assistant, a printer's helper, a medical office assistant, and perhaps most
critically, as a handyman and gofer for James Walker, a Missouri
slave trader, "negro speculator, or a 'soul driver' " with whom Brown
would make multiple trips up and down the Mississippi River between St. Louis and the New Orleans slave market.[14] In the wake of
his service for Walker, Brown was returned to Dr. Young in 1832 but
was shortly thereafter put up for sale. The threat of separation from
his family influenced Brown to make one of his first major attempts
to escape slavery that ultimately failed. Although he suffered the
usual range of severe corporal punishment meted out to runaway
slaves, he remained determined to flee. In the fall of 1833 and in the
household of new owners, Brown hatched yet another escape plan
and made his way to freedom on New Year's Day 1834, traveling in
the dead of winter through Ohio from Cincinnati to Cleveland. He
was just short of twenty years old.

In addition to his autobiography, which "went through four American and five British editions before 1850," Brown would go on to publish *Clotel* (1853) in the United Kingdom, believed to be the first novel published by an African American; a semi-autobiographical drama about multiple forms of runaway flight entitled *The Escape; or, A Leap for Freedom* (1858), the first play by an African American; as well as multiple works of travel literature, black American social, cultural, and military histories, journalistic articles, and oratorical lectures.[15] In England alone he "delivered four hundred lectures to over 200,000 people" in less than two years.[16] But it was the publication of Brown's *Narrative* that marked the beginning of his prolific career in belles lettres. The completion of his popular autobiography signaled his development as an agent of the anti-slavery cause who mastered the art of flight and who then reproduced this mastery in multiple forms of media and as a mentor to others.

Brown's ascent to the realm of literary cosmopolitanism did not, however, happen overnight. It would take some thirteen years from the time of his escape for him to publish the first edition of his autobiography. During that time, he moved as frequently and as fluidly between forms of employment and social circles as he had in slavery, beginning his life in freedom as a choreman for a Cleveland family and a waiter at a local mansion house, and finally picking up work once again aboard a steamer in Detroit and later Buffalo, New York.[17] Brown developed his literacy by independently studying books and newspapers. He also took advantage of observing and immersing himself in a diverse and vibrant workplace culture aboard the steamer, where he could soak up geographical and regional knowledge and seize, while in Cleveland, opportunities to gain insight about free territories both in the United States and, on the other side of the border, in Canada as well. In the summer of 1834 he married Elizabeth (Betsey) Schooner and fathered two daughters, Clarissa and Josephine. The Browns moved to Buffalo, New York, in the summer of 1836, in part to settle into an even more extensive steamboat community and one with a black population much larger than that of Cleveland.[18] He spent much of the late 1830s and early 1840s working actively as a guide to fugitive slaves on their way "to Canada by way of both Detroit and Buffalo" and, by the time of his resettlement in western New York, had become "a practicing abolitionist." During this same period, Brown also seized upon temperance as a cause of great concern to the fugitive slave community, and he became a more prominent community speaker and activist dedicated to extolling the virtues of a disciplined life in liberty lived free of alcohol. He organized a temperance society in Buffalo with a membership of more than 500 and began to emerge as a key local figurehead in a black community perched at the critical intersections of antebellum fugitive slave cartography.[19]

The seeds of his ultimate transformation from local hero to trans-Atlantic literary and political icon were dramatically planted, however, in the summer of 1843, when the magnetic Frederick Douglass arrived in Buffalo with Reverend George Bradburn of Massachusetts. The two had come to New York with the intent of holding a series of anti-slavery meetings in local towns. Having fled from slavery in Baltimore in 1838, Douglass had already earned a name for himself as an electrifying, full-time orator for the anti-slavery movement, and during his Buffalo visit spent much of the week speaking almost daily to audiences that grew in size and that were increasingly filled with noteworthy figures. This was most likely the first time that Brown had the opportunity to hear Douglass lecture, and the experience would serve as a powerful catalyst for him as he began to dedicate himself more fully to the abolitionist cause. By August 15, 1843, he had moved from audience member at the Douglass lectures to full-time participant in the National Convention of Colored Citizens, held in Buffalo with black abolitionist leaders such as Douglass, Henry Highland Garnet, Charles Lenox Remond, and others present.[20]

In the fall of 1843, William Wells Brown became the lecture agent for the Western New York Anti-Slavery Society, and he would continue speaking in public with increasing frequency and fame throughout northeastern abolitionist circles for the next four years. In June of 1847 he sought feedback on his freshly completed *Narrative* manuscript from Anglo abolitionist Edmund Quincy, who subsequently lavished great praise on the draft. With several minor corrections and additions made by Quincy and a preface added by abolitionist Joseph C. Hathaway, the first edition of *Narrative of*

William W. Brown, A Fugitive Slave, Written By Himself was published in July 1847. It was an immediate success, with 3,000 copies sold "in less than six months from the time of its publication." Brown's narrative went through four American and five British editions before 1850. His text was surpassed in sales only by that of Douglass's *Narrative of the Life* (1845).[21]

Of the nine editions of Brown's *Narrative* that were published in the 1840s alone, the 1848 second edition released by the Boston Anti-Slavery Office is included in this anthology. With the success of the *Narrative* already affirmed in sales, the second edition makes plain the ways in which Brown had boldly developed the literary and political scope and range of his text. A reprint of the first edition, this second edition showcases the ways that "the author has been led to enlarge the work by the addition of matter which, he thinks, will add materially to its value" (p. 4). This version of the *Narrative* includes "The American Slave-Trade," an essay, written by Brown and reprinted from an 1848 issue of Maria Weston Chapman's *The Liberty Bell*, that catalogs graphic cruelties in slavery collected from various periodicals and abolitionist tracts, as well as Brown's own recollection and observations. This edition also includes the poem "The Blind Slave Boy," written by Mrs. Dr. Bailey and inspired by an incident involving a mother and slave child separated on a coffle led by the driver James Walker and witnessed by Brown (pp. 65–66). The Appendix of the second edition closes with abolitionist mixed media, including an anti-slavery essay, runaway slave newspaper ads, and excerpts from various slave codes in multiple southern states.

With its legitimizing preface from white abolitionist J. C. Hathaway and its extensive appendices, the *Narrative of William Wells Brown* resembles the classic form of the antebellum slave narrative. As Robert Stepto has argued, the slave narrative genre often depended on an "eclectic" material structure comprised of a multiplicity of "authenticating documents and strategies" designed to corroborate the voice of the author. Prefaces, letters of support, and epilogues were often appended to texts in order to confirm the "authenticity" of the author's accounts.[22] Fugitive slave writers thus depended on the veracity of supporting materials in order to corroborate their own testimonial descriptions of the peculiar institution's inhumane hardships and horrors. Following this convention, Hathaway's preface champions "the truthfulness of the picture" (p. 8) that Brown presents in his *Narrative*, and he makes what would become a common comparison between the former's autobiography and that of Douglass's seminal text published two years earlier. And according to Quincy, Brown's *Narrative* "presents a different phase of the infernal slave-system" to that of Douglass's and "gives us a glimpse of its hideous cruelties in other portions of its domain" (p. 5). The constant shifts and movements between regions and forms of service distinguished Brown's work from other texts, and gives readers a different vantage point of the slave system; it also amplifies the northern reader's comprehension of its tyrannical reach.

But to Hathaway and particularly to Edmund Quincy, Brown's *Narrative* was most notably distinct from Douglass's in its "simplicity and calmness" (p. 5). To Quincy, this was a text that would affirm the necessary portrait of the *artless* fugitive slave. For, unlike Douglass's gorgeously wrought verse, "in Brown's *Narrative* there was 'no attempt at fine writing, but only a minute account of scenes and things he saw and suffered, told with a good deal of skill and great propriety and delicacy.' "[23] If fugitives were to operate as the abolitionist movement's most precious propaganda, the belief went that they must eschew aesthetic flourishes. Nevertheless, while Brown's *Narrative* would appear to diverge from Douglass's "Protestant conversion narrative" conventions and its dense self-reflection, it is the converse elements of the text—what some critics refer to as its "antiheroic" tropes—that makes the *Narrative of William Wells Brown* a text that subtly belies its seeming simplicity and self-abnegation. In short, "Brown's willingness to focus on himself as a slave trickster and to explore the contradictions between a slave's survival ethic and the dominant morality of his time"[24] set a precedence for a different kind of slave narrative—one that in form may have appeared artless but in content underscored the utility of movement, selective expedience, and cunning as methods of radical subversion and escape. Although Brown's text lacks the powerful psychological transmogrification evident in Douglass's narrative, it instead posits the personal desire and effort to be free as a self-actualizing process in and of itself, one which will, in the sheer fact of its repetition, create a wondrous identity transformation.

The spatial politics of William Wells Brown's *Narrative* articulate the unique learned transience of its protagonist that would figure prominently in Brown's ultimate flight to freedom. As Hathaway observes in his preface, the text reinforces the ways that his "experiences in the Field, in the House, and especially on the River in the service of the slave-trader, Walker, have been such as few individuals have had" (p. 5). In fact, Paul Jefferson suggests that "Brown's Narrative may be read as travel literature, as well as autobiography" and as a narrative that "map[s the] changing spiritual and physical geographies" of its protagonist.[25] Brown's text charts his many movements *within* slavery, a kind of foreshadowing of his future life as a figure comfortable with travel and resettlement and quick to adapt to his surroundings. Although Brown was perpetually moved by his master, hired out to work for others and ordered from house to field and back, his acute ability as a writer not only to delineate the distinctions between various social, class, regional and cultural spheres but to adapt to and move fluidly through such spheres set him apart from many of his fellow fugitive authors.[26] Brown makes it clear in the first chapter of his text, for instance, that he was "a house servant—a situation preferable to that of a field hand, as I was better fed, better clothed, and not obliged to rise at the ringing of the bell" (p. 12). Yet in the same paragraph he underscores his pained familiarity with the unspeakable horrors of the plantation, how "though the field was some distance from the house," he "could hear every crack of the whip, and every groan and cry of [his] poor mother" suffering at the hands of the brutal overseer Mr. Cook (p. 12).

It is in this open climate of brutality on the plantation, so porous and ubiquitous that it dilutes the boundaries between indoors and outdoors, between "privileged" slave and abject servitude, where Brown begins to strategize his first attempted escape. With the distinctions between being inside and outside and the boundaries between being sheltered and unprotected dangerously perverted in slavery, Brown makes it plain early on in his *Narrative* that running and seeking refuge in the darkness of the woods outside of St. Louis would prove preferable to working under the drunken violence of tavern-keeper Major Freeland (p. 15). Hunted by bloodhounds, captured and tortured within hours of having fled, Brown nonetheless establishes early on in the narrative his resolve to be free and his fearless aim to refuse intransigence, to move, to strike out into the land, and to explore methods of maroonage[27] big and small.

Brown is often on the move in this text, even as he faces the reality of his everyday bondage. As an assistant to Elijah P. Lovejoy at his printing office in St. Louis, he weathers an attack "by several large boys, sons of slave-holders, who pel[t]" him "with snow-balls." He "resor[ts]" to both his fists and heels, only to receive a bloody beating from one of the boys' fathers (p. 19). In his work as an assistant to the speculator Mr. Walker, Brown would make the arduous trip by land for days and by boat to New Orleans where he served as one in a chain gang, with Walker "taking the lead" and Brown "bringing up the rear" (p. 29). In each of these instances, Brown applies a panoramic traveler's view of his experiences and environs. He exposes the surprising barbarity of slaveholding in St. Louis, captive children separated from their mothers in the no man's land on the coffle (p. 29), the obstinate resolve of haughty southern gentlemen in Vicksburg (p. 32). His picaresque odyssey no doubt shores up his confidence in confronting strange places and faces in the world far beyond the reaches of his plantation life.

Nowhere is this skill put more to the test than in his work in slavery aboard various steamers heading north and south. Brown's *Narrative* captures the unique transience of a fugitive's life, the volatile shifts, the regional displacement and resettlement. As a mobile hub moving along the Mississippi River and across multiple states, the steamer affords Brown unique exposure to northern and southern culture and the cultural quirks of various regions and their inhabitants, and it is in this setting that he begins fully to transcend the claustrophobic psychological entrapment of slavery. On board the steamboat *Missouri* from St. Louis to Galena (p. 16), afloat on the steamboat *Enterprise* (pp. 19–20), Brown finds himself in unmoored environs that present the occasion for him to contemplate "leaving . . . at some landing-place, and trying to make [his] escape to Canada . . . a place where the slave might live, be free, and be protected" (p. 20). The steamboat, more than any other location in the *Narrative of William Wells Brown*, provides the space for thinking expansively and subversively. Just as the iconic ship, with its elegant sails on the limitless sea, operates as rich metaphor in Douglass's quest to be free, so too does Brown's immersion in this high-turnover marine culture serve as a significant backdrop for him to imagine and later secure his freedom.

In this life of constant movement and floating possibility, William Wells Brown would develop and rehearse multiple modes of flight and liberation. Unlike the Box Brown and Craft escape narratives that would follow, Brown's text distills and presents a variety of escape tactics that both enable and further his own self-willed emancipation from slavery. In the *Narrative of William Wells Brown*, the acquisition of freedom is not limited to one heroic act but is the sum of many large and small gestures that repeat and reenact the fact of Brown's subjectivity. Brown offers meticulous details about his failed escapes, the second of which he launched with his mother, Elizabeth, fittingly on a stolen boat headed toward the Illinois shore (p. 39). Although he had yet to succeed at securing his freedom, Brown's second attempted flight would represent the paradigmatic perils of the fugitive slave's course northward—seeking maroonage by day in the woods and elsewhere, traveling by night with his mother and guided through darkness and gloom by the North Star (pp. 39–40). Still more, the sheer emotional despair and physical torture of being captured once again and being carried with his mother "back to the land of whips, chains and Bibles" (p. 42) heightens the poignancy of Brown's escape intent. Having covered so much ground, having "travelled towards a land of liberty" (p. 41) only to be returned to bondage, Brown emerges in the text as a protagonist who confronts the vicissitudes of fugitive life and the tenuousness of freedom with a watchful eye as well as a practical outlook on his own survival.

This pragmatism manifests itself most controversially in Brown's distinctly expedient role as a social trickster primarily invested in his own self-preservation in the *Narrative*. While traveling with Major Walker, Brown's decision to mount a savvy but nonetheless mean-spirited ruse in which he frames a free "colored man about [his] size" to take a whipping for him by proxy (p. 32) demonstrates the extent to which Brown was not above using quick-witted cunning and sacrificing fellow African Americans to escape the quotidian threat of beatings in slavery. Such a tale is a risky one to tell in the slave narrative genre, for it threatens to compromise for northern audiences the hard-earned, carefully crafted veracity of the slave narrative author. Brown's resolve to pay his victim-turned-accomplice fifty cents compensation for "receiv[ing] twenty lashes on his bare back, with the negro-whip," coupled with his shrewd performance tactics—wetting his cheeks "a little, as though [he] had been crying" (p. 34) at the stroke of a lash convey an audacious penchant for duplicity.[28] Here and elsewhere, Brown's bold wit and trickster persona rise to the surface in ways that call into question how "simple" and transparent Brown's text truly is. As a narrator, Brown even seizes the hubris to argue that his sly persona is not to his making. Rather, Brown claims that this "incident shows how it is that slavery makes its victims lying and mean; for which vices it afterwards reproaches them, and uses them as arguments to prove that they deserve no better fate" (p. 34). Escaping both a brutal whipping and the disdain of his pious abolitionist audience, Brown here simultaneously experiments with literal and discursive forms of elusion that mediate his survival in slavery and his narrative authority as a fugitive author.

Brown's adept skill at multiple forms of evasion would ultimately serve him well in his final escape effort, an endeavor with a startlingly simple beginning—he slipped off a steamer in Cincinnati, Ohio, on December 31, 1834, blended into the crowd at the shore, and headed directly for the nearby woods (p. 54). Biographer William Farrison estimates that "within four days" Brown had "traveled half of the distance from central Ohio to Cleveland," where he would initially settle in his newfound freedom.[29] With dwindling food and money along the way toward free territory, Brown in his *Narrative* nonetheless choreographs a fairly straightforward physical path out of slavery, traveling consistently by night and following the North Star as much as the weather would allow. Conversely, his flight is at its most spectacular and its most existentially daring in its articulation of willed self-making. Looking well beyond his literal escape "to a land of freedom," Brown shifts the temporality of his text from the crushing and claustrophobic present and ephemeral state of enslavement to instead affirm his legacy, his being, and his "prospects of the future." His "anxious" pursuit to (re)name himself documents a profoundly nuanced form of self-liberation common to many fugitives and yet often divorced from the physical triumph of eluding bloodhounds and outpacing slave-catchers through forests and swamps (p. 56).

Brown, however, draws multiple parallels between his effort to assume a new name and the execution of escape. "I was," he declares in the denouement to his text, "not only hunting for my liberty, but also hunting for a name; though I regarded the latter as of little consequence, if I could but gain the former. Travelling along the road, I would sometimes speak to myself, sounding my name over, by way of getting used to it" (pp. 55–56). As a child, William Wells Brown would experience early one of slavery's most egregious injustices—that of losing his name. The Youngs' adoption of an infant nephew, also called "William," resulted in their resolve to rename the youthful Brown "Sandford" (p. 55), a name that he would be "known by, not only upon [his] master's plantation, but up to the time that [he] made [his] escape (p. 55)."[30] Described by Brown as one of the "most cruel acts" in his memory, the name change would arguably shape his lifelong pursuit perpetually to reinvent himself in and through a life lived as a man of letters. In this regard, the *Narrative*'s inclusion of Brown's ceremonious renaming of himself as "William," and his decision to add "Wells Brown" to his title, in honor of the Quaker who provided him with food and shelter during his flight (p. 59), represents a masterful stroke of literary ingenuity and existential self-affirmation. Brown's *Narrative* "witnesses a double-act of self-creation. Brown invents himself both in making the escape the narrative recounts, and in recounting the escape he makes."[31] This flight is no less reinscribed once more by the fact of Wells Brown's authorial reproduction of this tale, as his literacy and discursive talents mark what scholars have argued is the necessary affirmation of humanity and the critical break from slavery in the act of writing the slave narrative itself.[32]

Brown would evolve into something of a master of repetition as his career in the international anti-slavery movement flourished in the 1840s and 1850s. By the spring of 1834 he was repeating his old job working aboard the Lake Erie steamer out of Detroit, an occupation he would ultimately keep for nine seasons. Yet even in that capacity he would reproduce, transform, perfect, and bequeath his own secrets of escape by assisting and carrying fellow fugitives to Canada "by way of both Detroit and Buffalo." By 1836 and in the midst of moving his family to Buffalo, Brown had become "a practicing abolitionist who could take just pride in the fact that he was losing none of his cases." Eventually serving as a conductor on the Underground Railroad, Brown and family transformed their Buffalo home into a critical way-station on the historical escape route, providing a significant point of shelter for those who were seeking refuge in Canada. In one of the more difficult and high-profile rescues he conducted, Brown and fellow abolitionists assisted in shepherding to safety an entire family who had been taken back into slavery.[33]

Brown's efforts to save his own family in slavery were, as he makes clear in the *Narrative*, unsuccessful. Separated at an early age from most of his relatives, Brown uses his autobiography to express a deep emotional bond and sense of loyalty to his sister (also named Elizabeth) and especially his mother. For Brown, of "all [his] relatives, mother was first, and sister next" (p. 20), and it is this profound sense of duty to family—and particularly the women in his family—which ultimately sets Brown's *Narrative* apart from major slave narratives that would come before and after his text. If, as Valerie Smith has argued, "most of the narratives by men represent the life in slavery and the escape as essentially solitary journeys," Brown's text both adheres to and undoes this trope.[34] His *Narrative*, like Douglass's, would ultimately find him successfully fleeing slavery alone, but in preparing his readers for that journey, Brown underscores the bravery and guiding wisdom of his sister and mother in ways that would foreshadow Harriet Jacobs's construction of her benevolent grandmother as a moral compass in her *Incidents in the Life of a Slave Girl*, published some fourteen years later. Like Jacobs's maternal icon, Brown's sister and mother are self-abnegating heroes who urge him to take advantage of the chance to escape and who "beseech [him] not to let us hinder you" (p. 21). While Brown's chivalric impulses and his early resolve "not to leave them in the hand of the oppressor" (p. 21) reinforce his masculinist persona in the text, he also depends on their spiritual vision and pragmatic judgment in ways that transcend other representations of fugitives and their female family members. With both a sister advising him to escape with their mother and with his own mother "counsell[ing] him to get [his] liberty" (p. 39), the women figure as Brown's two greatest mentors in imagining his flight.

That Brown initially attempted to flee with his mother by his side represents the extent to which he aimed to honor both of their wishes. Wrought with emotion and the language of sentimental literature so popular to nineteenth-century female readers and writers, the extended farewell scene between Brown and the elder Elizabeth remains one of the most intimate domestic exchanges between mother and son recorded in the fugitive slave narrative genre (p. 45). Heroic as she is self-sacrificing, Elizabeth remains a model of courageous ideals for her son in the *Narrative of William Wells Brown*. Forced to part with Brown, she instructs him: *"Do not, I pray you, weep for me"* but rather *"try to get your liberty! You will soon have no one to look after but yourself!"* (p. 45). Brown's liberty is, in short, the actualization of his mother and sister's dreams in the *Narrative*, even as these women are unable to complete the journey with him. In this regard, the text as an escape tale memorializes and pays homage to the principles of the stalwart women in Brown's life who encouraged him to locate a path to freedom. Once on that road, Brown used his *Narrative*, trans-Atlantic oratory, history, verse, drama, fiction, and song to keep expanding the width of the escape route for himself and others. William Wells Brown died in Boston, Massachusetts, on November 6, 1884, having lived a life dedicated to social, political, and cultural flight and empowerment for generations of African Americans.

Escaping the Text: Henry "Box" Brown's Concentric Flight Tales

Although he would largely gain his entrance into the public spotlight as a result of William Wells Brown, would-be protégé Henry Box Brown ended up following markedly different social, political, and cultural paths from those of the veteran activist. But on that day in May of 1849, standing beside one another on the anti-slavery platform, the two Browns seemed poised to work closely together in the years to come. Few at that point knew that their creative interests in diverse forms of media and cultural expression were in many ways imbricated. Yet it would soon become clear that both Browns held a penchant for melding spiritual and anti-slavery song, for instance. Each man was known to have invoked religious melodies during various abolitionist public appearances, and critics speculate that Wells Brown may have even contributed lyrics to one of Box Brown's popular songs.[35] Still more, each would shortly go on to create two of the most landmark visual exhibitions in the fight to end slavery.

Yet despite their similar creative interests and talents, Wells Brown and Box Brown evolved into fundamentally different cultural characters. The former would cultivate a lifelong persona as an international dignitary, a world traveler, and a prolific author. From his selection by the American Peace Society to serve as a delegate to the 1849 International Peace Congress in Paris to hundreds of lectures he delivered in the United Kingdom alone, to his post–Civil War occupation as a physician, Wells Brown was one in an increasing circle of nineteenth-century black activists who fully endorsed the merits of bourgeois activism and black community leadership, working hard to cultivate early versions of the "race man" paradigm.[36] By contrast, in the years following his singular escape, Box Brown would gradually evolve into something of a social and political conundrum in black abolitionist circles. Unlike Wells Brown and the Crafts, who would remain deeply connected to various abolitionist and philanthropic causes for the remainder of their lives in freedom, Box Brown would forge a post-escape path that would ultimately distance him from mainstream anti-slavery circles. As historian Jeffrey Ruggles speculates, his late-career, popular-cultural interests in spectacular theater and magic culture would perhaps estrange him from fellow activists of his day. Likewise, I would suggest that his performance activities would render him illegible to some contemporary historians and archivists intent on preserving a conventional narrative of black liberation tactics as well.[37]

Just three years following their New England appearance together, Wells Brown would find little favorable to say of the man to whom he had given the nickname "Boxer." In an 1852 letter to white abolitionist Wendell Phillips, he would confess that Box Brown "is a very foolish fellow, to say the least. I saw him some time since, and he had more gold and brass round his neck than would take to hang the bigest [sic] Alderman in London. And as to ruffles about the shirts, he had enough to supply any old maid with cap stuff, for half a century. He had on a green dress coat and white hat, and his whole appearance was that of a well dressed monkey."[38] In his physical dress alone, Box Brown would seemingly show no fear of appearing artful in public. For the man who would gain Atlantic world attention for having mailed himself to freedom, his flight signaled the birth of a new breed of fugitive activism and cultural expression, and it affirmed his emergence as an African-American escape artist who forged new and unpredictable roads to freedom by elasticizing, supplementing, revising, and subverting his original slave narrative in ever-expanding alternate forms.

Brown was born into slavery on the Hermitage plantation in Louisa County, Virginia, around the year 1815. He was one of eight children—sisters Jane, Martha, Mary, and Robinnet; and brothers Edward, John, and Lewis. Like Wells Brown, Box Brown spent his early teen years moving around and completing chores at the whim of masters and various overseers. He and one of his brothers were often sent out to carry grain and do work at surrounding mills by the Hermitage plantation master, John Barret, a former mayor of Richmond for several terms in the 1790s. In his old age, Barret eventually passed Brown on to his son, William Barret, the owner of a tobacco business. The senior Barret died on June 9, 1830, leaving his four sons to divide up his estate and to divide up the Brown family in particular. When he was about fifteen years old, Brown moved to William Barret's tobacco factory in Richmond, Virginia, and was separated from his mother—"her smiling look," her "fond arms"— and the rest of his family, who were sold and sent off in multiple directions.[39]

Richmond would prove to be the site of life-changing events for Henry Brown, though he was no more than a teenager when he first arrived in the factory city. There Brown made key connections, initially with his first overseer, Wilson Gregory, a black man with whom he briefly lived upon his arrival at the tobacco factory and a figure who proved useful to Brown in that he eased him into the transitions of working in a sprawling new environment.[40] Gregory was succeeded on the Barret plantation by a series of coarse overseers, one of whom Brown describes in his 1851 narrative as "one of the meanest and cruelest men that I ever knew,"[41] one who, in echoes of Douglass's description of the tyrannical overseer character

Covey, "used to rise very early in the morning" to deceive, torment, and steal from the enslaved (p. 108). Especially in the second version of his narrative, Brown makes it clear that he would find some solace from the grueling daily tortures of slavery in his church life. Having gained permission from his master to join Richmond's First Baptist Church in 1831, he became an active member of what would eventually become the First African Baptist Church choir, cultivating a singing voice that would prove prominent in his abolitionist career. Ruggles also speculates that the newly formed First African Baptist Church and its choir provided the first occasion for Brown to forge a friendship with James Caesar Anthony Smith, a local freeman who would accompany Brown on many adventures to come.[42] In the tense climate following the Nat Turner slave rebellion in Southampton County, Virginia, when anxiety over religious zealotry among the enslaved was at an all-time high, Brown and Smith would find a respite in religious song and, in time, plant the seeds of what would become the first of many of Brown's great escapes.

The exigencies of Box Brown's flight had, in the context of both versions of his *Narrative*, less to do with religious inspiration and everything to do with Brown's separation from his young family. Brown's emphasis on romance and marriage in his narratives has a slightly different emphasis to that of Wells Brown, whose text strikes a bitter tone of critique toward coerced sexual arrangements and marriage between the enslaved.[43] Box Brown too is wary of marriage, and his 1849 narrative assures that "what is well known by many people [is] that no such thing as real marriage is allowed to exist among the slaves" (p. 108). Nonetheless, his relationship with Nancy, a woman who was enslaved to Hancock Lee, a teller at the Farmer's Bank of Virginia, would lead to Brown's seeking permission to marry around 1836 and as he was nearing twenty-one years of age. The two would have four children together in slavery and, for a time, would maintain the delicate balance of remaining united as a family, with living quarters unto themselves, no small feat for the enslaved and one that would ultimately prove impossible for the Browns to sustain.[44]

Throughout his career as an anti-slavery lecturer and activist in the Northeast and abroad, Box Brown would maintain that the sale of Nancy in August 1848 and the subsequent dissolution of his family led to such psychological distress and devastation in slavery that it drove him to break free of bondage. And though the genuineness of Brown's claim about his emotional suffering as a result of this separation would be disputed in the years to come, the incident would operate in the public record of Box Brown's escape and in literary terms as a dramatic and transformative turning point in his fugitive escape odyssey.[45] The 1849 narrative makes it clear that, in the wake of this "cruel separation" from wife and children, "slavery now had no mitigating circumstances, to lessen the bitterness of its cup of woe" (p. 132). The 1851 narrative suggests as well that Brown's separation from Nancy, the woman "with whom [he] had travelled the journey of life in chains, for the space of twelve years" pushes him closer to a religious conversion that in turn strengthens his resolve to flee (p. 202). Whatever the details of Brown's relationship with Nancy or the extent to which he made a concerted effort to reunite with his wife, the loss of his family would ultimately clear a path for him to create and enact a form of escape that was both literally and figuratively one of the most solitary methods of flight. Like the journeys of other male fugitives that would go before and after him, Box Brown's narratives imagine a lone hero cut loose from cumbersome domestic configurations, one whose success in fleeing slavery in a box "mythologiz[es] rugged individuality, physical strength, and geographical mobility."[46]

Yet Brown's plot to be free was anything but a solo endeavor. Although he may have lost his family, he nonetheless benefited from the friendship, support and resources of co-choir member J. C. A. Smith, as well as an eccentric white local merchant and activist named Samuel Smith. J. C. A. Smith, a free Virginian who was said to have at one time practiced dentistry and kept a Richmond "cake shop and rendezvous for negroes," would prove to be a close, long-time collaborator with Brown, and it is thought that the black Smith most likely introduced Brown to Samuel Smith, a local storekeeper who hailed originally from Massachusetts. As Ruggles makes plain, the latter Smith's New England roots as well as his gambling troubles would render him an "outlaw" or, at the very least, an outcast of sorts in Richmond. Together, the two Smiths would work closely with Brown to mastermind the details of Brown's escape and assisted him in having made a pine box that was reportedly "3 feet long, 2 ft 8 inches deep, and 23½ inches wide" for Brown to mail himself to the Pennsylvania Anti-Slavery Society office in Philadelphia in March 1849.[47]

Entombed and in transit for more than twenty-four hours, Brown leaped almost immediately from his escape box of extreme solitude into the public eye, where he would remain off and on through the late 1870s. He was embraced and mentored initially by the white abolitionists who greeted him in the North, particularly J. Miller McKim, the "Resident Agent" of the Pennsylvania Anti-Slavery Society in Philadelphia; Lucretia and James Mott; black anti-slavery activist William Still, with whom he "spent his first two nights out of slavery": the Reverend Samuel May; and later abolitionist Joseph Ricketson in New Bedford, Massachusetts, where Brown would stay as he wended his way through the Northeast that spring before settling in Boston.[48] There, at the center of passionate abolitionist activism and large-scale political agitation to end slavery, Brown not only made his debut speaking alongside other fugitives in support of abolition, but he followed through on producing the first edition of his slave narrative at the behest of McKim and many others who thought his story particularly ripe for the telling. How to tell it would prove a challenge, in that, as Ruggles maintains, Brown, like the majority of southern slaves who were forbidden literacy, "could not read or write."[49]

Brown enlisted Charles Stearns, a Boston printer and local activist "aligned with the radical abolitionists," to serve as his amanuensis for the project, and in September 1849, after having met sometime that spring in New England, the two men published the *Narrative of Henry Box Brown* and thereafter embarked on a month-long tour to sell the book and to promote the anti-slavery cause. Critics speculate that the endeavor was a success and that "the partners sold out the first printing on their tour" together.[50] The introduction of the 1851 *Narrative* states that, having been previously published in America, "an edition of 8,000 copies sold in about two months" (p. 169). No doubt, 1849 would prove a good year to publish fugitive slave narratives, as Wells Brown's text was, for instance, already in its fourth edition that year and "some ten thousand copies had been sold. The year 1849 saw more slave narratives published than in any year before."[51] A flurry of abolitionist publications and oratorical activity developed that year in particular as activists sensed the growing efforts in Congress to negotiate with southern slaveholders in a bid to preserve a stable Union. Their instincts proved correct when, in January 1850, Virginia senator James Murray Mason introduced the Fugitive Slave Bill, a piece of legislation which in part gave slaveholders the right to hunt fugitives in free states. President Fillmore would sign the bill into law by the fall of that year. Box Brown's first narrative arrived then on the eve of new laws designed to circumscribe the movement of fugitives, and it both documents and negotiates the art of escape. Most provocatively, it in many ways documents Brown's resistance to slavery as well as a fugitive's struggle to gain voice and to break free from the restrictions of white editorial control.

At its core, the 1849 narrative is largely a tale of fugitive exceptionalism. The text constructs Box Brown's life as one of relative privilege and ease during his early years living in the immediate care of his parents and siblings and later as an urban adolescent servant with some mobility between jobs and tasks. From start to finish, Box Brown's first narrative diverges from narratives by Wells Brown and others in its insistence on avoiding descriptions of graphic violence and torture in slavery. The narrative maintains that it will not catalog "horrid inflictions of the lash upon [his] naked body," but it claims to be "the very best representation of slavery which can be given" (p. 101). Rather, it is the absence of visible blood and bruises and, in its stead, an emphasis on the emotional traumas resulting from fractured family ties and rootlessness that provides the reason to run. The spectacular run that Box Brown executes is the raison d'être of the narrative in sum here. From its lengthy title, which outlines the flight in explicit detail, to the repeated allusions to the imminent escape, the uniqueness of Brown's journey remains the centerpiece of the text. In this way, it is a narrative that favors its spectacular escape denouement over all other plot developments.

Yet this focus on Brown's "boxing" odyssey from start to finish paradoxically assures readers that the fugitive author will ultimately disappear from view, that he will return to the box of his "entombment," if only to remind white northern audiences of the "dreadful position" which he endured in a "narrow prison" postmarked to the free states. While Brown's literary figure gradually shrinks and folds into the very box of his escape in the 1849 narrative, Stearns's editorial and narrative voice conversely grow in size. As amanuensis, Stearns produces a text whose structural patterns mimic Brown's notorious confinement. The narration is littered with negations—what the author will not divulge (p. 10)—and occlusions—what evils of slavery Brown can hear but not see (p. 110). Claustrophobic in form and content, the first Box Brown narrative reinforces in literary terms the very tropes of confinement that Brown had sought to escape in his flight out of slavery. As critic James Olney has argued, Stearns "dress[es] up" Brown's story in "exotic rhetorical garments" so that "for every fact there are pages of self-conscious, self-gratifying, self-congratulatory philosophizing" by the editor. "[I]f there is any life here at all," Olney concludes, "it is the life of " Stearns who "expresse[s] it in his very own overheated and foolish prose."[52]

Book-ended by a preface and a closing essay entitled "Cure for the Evil of Slavery"—both by Charles Stearns—the 56-page narrative of the events of Brown's life are sandwiched between Stearns's occasionally maudlin and histrionic appeals to northern readers to release "human feeling" (p. 95) and, in a spectacular act of displacement, to imagine their own entrapment in lieu of Brown's. In his preface, Stearns even compares the Crafts' suffering to that of Brown in order ultimately to triangulate the fears, desires, and sympathies of his audience. Unlike the Crafts who, Stearns reminds his readers, "were not entirely helpless," Brown was "enclosed in a moving tomb, and as utterly destitute of power to control *your* movements as if death had fastened its icy arm upon *you* . . . as was the case with our friend" (p. 97, emphasis added). Stearns's shift from the third person to the second and back to the third positions Brown at the center of a conspicuous vanishing act. Here it is the reader and not Brown who faces the perils of live burial, while Brown recedes to the backdrop of the preface to his own narrative. Stearns's closing essay, a radical abolitionist appeal to create "a new government to the north," follows in the same vein. Although his polemic extends the abolitionist platform outlined in the central narrative, as do most documents appended to slave narratives, his outsized literary presence here threatens to re-box

Brown's (narrative) body altogether. In short, by attaching his own lengthy "authenticating machinery," Stearns sustains a dialogue "with white America across the text and figurative body of a silent former slave." As Olney observes, "there is precious little of Box Brown other than the representation of the box itself" that remains in the narrative.[53]

How to escape such a suffocating text? The image positioned at the close of the *Narrative of Box Brown* would perhaps provide a powerful metaphoric flight route for a fugitive author who had, as it turns out, much more up his sleeve than one edition of his narrative. Featured on the concluding page of the 1849 text, the illustrated "representation of the box," a crate with five hoops and marked for Philadelphia transit, symbolically marks the next flight in motion of Henry Box Brown. An image that "boxes" back at Stearns's editorial constrictions, the box makes plain Brown's spectacularly present absence inside his "living tomb." Brown's escape image here does (figurative) battle with Stearns's editorial control and more broadly with the abolitionist movement's emphasis on fugitive slave authenticity and transparency as the text returns to the vision of self-engineered captivity and opacity. We might think of this singular representation of the box as an object of both "resonance and wonder." Cultural critic Stephen Greenblatt defines these forms of looking as, in the case of wonder, generating a kind of arresting enchantment that draws the viewer toward that object alone, while the resonant qualities of an object stimulate the viewer to consider the historical and contextual significance of that which is on display.[54]

A kind of visual metonym, the resonant image of Brown's escape crate steers the reader away from the voice of the editor and redirects the viewer's gaze toward Brown's flight. We might think of the box placed at the end of the 1849 narrative as yet another kind of figurative flight for Brown, one that delays and disrupts the closure of his (discursive) life narrative. Placed at the close of the text, the box image generates what African-American cultural critic Hortense Spillers might read as an "*intervening, intruding* tale . . . as a *metaphor* of social and cultural management" for the enslaved in flight.[55] In this way, the *Narrative of Henry Box Brown*, perhaps more than any other fugitive slave narrative, demonstrates in form the tensions of *literary* escape. The box signifies on the history of both Brown's literal flight to freedom and the struggle that fugitive authors faced to gain free expression and narrative authority in the texts about their lives. With the escape crate prominently on display at the end of this text, the 1849 narrative suggestively, indeed resonantly, alludes to the fine line that Brown and other fugitives would walk between dependence on and autonomy from their abolitionist benefactors. By "refusing to assimilate to his literary landscape," a (re)boxed Henry Brown at text's end overturns the critical notion that "once the protagonist achieves his [literal] freedom, the nineteenth-century slave narrative terminates."[56] Rather, Brown's box would provide a bridge to what we might read as a third narrative space between abolitionist pulpit and the literary slave narrative in the form of his unique and popular moving panorama exhibition.

Box Brown was not the first black abolitionist to envision mounting a large-scale visual exhibition to combat slavery. William Wells Brown had, in 1847, published a narrative description of "panoramic views" of slavery's horrors, a pamphlet that folded autobiographical events into scenes that outlined the broader historical and cultural topography of the peculiar institution.[57] He based his project on the well-known visual entertainment form of the panorama, full-scale displays on painted canvas and precursors to modern cinema that had regained popularity in the mid-nineteenth century in England and America.[58] In the preface to the script, Wells Brown claims that the inspiration for this work grew in part out of a visit he had made to "an exhibition of a Panorama of the River Mississippi" in the autumn of 1847. "[A]mazed at the very mild manner in which the 'Peculiar Institution' of the Southern States" was represented, Wells Brown set out to organize his own painting "with as fair a representation of American Slavery as could be given upon canvass" that might "do much to disseminate truth upon this subject and hasten the downfall of the greatest evil that now stains the character of the American people."[59] He, in effect, aimed to create an escape route out of the nostalgic and ahistorical predilections of the mainstream panoramas of the day. Wells Brown would eventually mount and tour his panorama while lecturing throughout Great Britain in the early 1850s, a decade which saw the development of several notable black abolitionist visual exhibitions by, for instance, Midwest photographer James Presley Ball and fugitive Anthony Burns.[60]

Box Brown's endeavor was, however, arguably the most successful, the most controversial, and the longest-running exhibition of its kind. Having assembled a group of local Boston artists that included the New England reformist Josiah Wolcott to paint the scenes of the panorama in early 1849, he unveiled his *Mirror of Slavery* in April 1850 in Boston and subsequently took the exhibit on tour throughout the Northeast. The earliest New England presentations of *Mirror of Slavery* involved a combination of visual display that featured the moving diorama painting along with accompanying narration and historical lectures on slavery. It was an "enterprise" all the "more interesting," according to one observer, for "the whole [was] conducted by colored men." The *London Times* described the synchronicity of this performance, how "as the different views of the panorama presented themselves in succession," Brown "explained them in a kind of lecture, in which he enlarged upon the horrors of slavery, and the cruelties to which the slaves were subjected."[61] As one of the narrators of the panorama, Box Brown traded off oratorical duties with Benjamin F. Roberts, a black Boston printer and local activist who would carry out early managerial tasks in relation to the exhibit. In addition to Roberts, fellow boxing conspirator and New England transplant J. C. A. Smith joined Brown in what would turn into a long-standing business relationship on the anti-slavery lecture circuit.

Together, these men forged an alternative to the discursive slave narrative genre. With more than forty scenes documenting everything from the "African Slave Trade" to the "Seizure of Slaves" and "Modes of Confinement and Punishment," Brown's *Mirror of Slavery* represented in large-scale form the very atrocities that the original 1849 narrative declared that it would avoid. The exhibition was divided into two parts. The first half traced an epic narrative odyssey, from the capture of a "Nubian Family" and the movement away from the "Beautiful Lake and Mountain Scenery in Africa" to the "Interior of a Slave Mart" and the "Interior View of Charleston Workhouse." With a wide-roving eye, the exhibition sought to expose what was previously hidden from view in the mainstream panorama's scenes of the South. Its scene titles suggested that it aimed to burrow deep inside the peculiar institution's very edifices. By contrast, the second half of the *Mirror of Slavery* traces the cartography of fugitives who break free of bondage. Like Wells Brown before him, Box Brown included a scene of his own escape in the panorama, as well as that of the "Ellen Crafts, Escaping" and fellow fugitive author Henry Bibb.

A visual minefield that moves forward toward freedom and doubles back into slavery and the reincarceration of fugitives before finally reaching the prophetic future goal of "Universal Emancipation," Box Brown's panorama set a new standard for fugitive cultural and political expression. It broke free of the bonds of editorial control in which his original autobiography was mired, and it used the tactics of spectacular theater, Victorian popular culture, and specifically that of the moving panorama "whose truthfulness was authorized by its striking illusionism" to create a denser, richer, and more complex representational platform on which to speak out against slavery.[62] That Box Brown was able to come to life, to gain voice narrating scenes of his escape alongside outsized visual images alone was a step toward transgressing and completely rewriting the terms of how fugitive slaves would be heard as well as seen in the anti-slavery movement.

Despite such bold and creative strides, not everyone was pleased with Brown's efforts. While the *Mirror of Slavery* received kudos and played to enthusiastic northeastern audiences through the summer of 1850, Brown met his most vociferous critic upon touring with the panorama in the United Kingdom during the early 1850s. Having fled the States in the wake of a brush with slave-catchers in Providence, Rhode Island, Brown and J. C. A. Smith set sail for England, arriving in Liverpool on November 1, 1850, one month ahead of William and Ellen Craft, who would seek refuge there in the wake of increased enforcement of the Fugitive Slave law. Brown had made yet another form of flight, adding his arrival in Great Britain to a growing list of escapes—from his boxing adventure and the publication of the first edition of his narrative to the display of his panorama. In a stunt that would foreshadow his later involvement in Victorian magic culture, Brown would even restage his escape by shipping himself, with Smith in tow, from Bradford to Leeds, freeing himself from confinement like an escapologist magician before an audience who then listened to an "interesting account of his adventures" and viewed a version of the panorama. Ever the industrious activist,

Brown managed gradually to link each of his cultural forms of expression together, creating a sprawling tapestry of escape art in performance culture.[63]

As was the case in New England, Brown's work in the United Kingdom was largely well-received by clergy, journalists, and schoolchildren who flocked to the panorama in early 1852. But in March of that year, Box Brown received his harshest criticism in a review of his exhibition published in the *Wolverhampton and Staffordshire Herald* newspaper. Calling the *Mirror* "a jumbled mass of contradictions and absurdities," the author of the article ostensibly objected to an exhibition that, to him, seemed to bear little "resemblance" to popular representations of the American South and slavery. This, of course, had been precisely the aim of black abolitionist moving panoramas, but it proved too much to swallow for this particular audience member, who challenged Box Brown's credibility as a lecturer and an author in two separate articles that month. Although Brown clearly escaped the boundaries of fugitive slave cultural representation, he would, on occasion, have to face the consternation and attacks of resistant audience members. Refusing to back down from his public platform, he not only took the unusual step for a fugitive slave of suing his detractor for slander, but also continued for years to come to produce vibrant cultural work in England.[64] Along with the panorama, his gift for song would play a key role in the transformation of his original slave narrative into a markedly different English edition.[65]

Henry Box Brown would go on to deliver "more than 400 lectures in Britain and 'addressed not fewer than 200,000 persons' " throughout the 1850s and early 1860s. He was well into his first U.K. lecture and panorama tour when the "first English edition" of his narrative was released in August 1851.[66] This new text differed from the 1849 edition in multiple ways, not least of which was that it was significantly retitled *Narrative of the Life of Henry Box Brown, Written by Himself.* Absent from its title were the 1849 edition's suffocating details of the dimensions of Brown's box, as well as any mention of Charles Stearns. Although critics have continued to speculate whether Brown had either the literacy skills or the editorial control over his narrative to produce this second text, the 1851 *Narrative* represents a distinctly original intertextual cultural production. Whether literally authored by the activist or not, the *Narrative of the Life of Henry Box Brown*, unlike its predecessor, affirms and celebrates the extra-textual performative skills of its protagonist.

The prefatory material and documents appended to the 1851 narrative alone create a direct dialogue with the previous edition of Brown's autobiography, while also immediately presenting a representational extension of that text. The Manchester-issued edition includes the popular 1850 lithograph of Brown's "unboxing" from slavery, entitled the "Resurrection of Henry Box Brown, at Philadelphia." Placed on the initial page of the volume, the lithograph operates as a concatenate image to that of the final representation of the box from 1849. With head and shoulders carefully emerging from the crate, Brown appears at the center of this illustration, fully dressed and staring forward with even aplomb while abolitionist on-lookers—three white and one black—ponder the scene. In this context, the image anticipates the ways that this version of the narrative will expose rather than hide Brown's body (of work), that it will amplify the cultural productions that Brown had thus far staged as an activist.

This emphasis on intertextuality informs the fundamental structure of the *Narrative*. Although it lacks the sophistication of William Wells Brown's subsequent travel writings, which were often laced with panoramic imagery and a richly descriptive narrative eye, the English edition of Henry Box Brown's *Narrative* sustains a direct and critical dialogue with the *Mirror of Slavery*. A new preface displaces Stearns's "self-conscious, self-gratifying, self-congratulatory philosophizing" in favor of opening remarks that directly address the challenge of negotiating the void between the condition of bondage itself and its representation in narrative form.[67] The preface speculates that the ordeals which he has endured at the "lash of the whip" will "never be related, because, language is inadequate to express" such events (pp. 163–164). Brown's text struggles with the crisis in mounting visual proof of the fugitive slave's experiences. Yet in a kind of call-and-response structure, the subsequent introduction to the *Narrative* offers a solution to this problem by posing an intertextual engagement with Brown's boxing feat and his panorama.

The "Introduction" to the *Narrative of the Life of Henry Box Brown* brings together multiple letters from those who were "witnesses" to either the initial boxing "miracle" in Philadelphia or to the touring English exhibition of the panorama, and in multiple ways, it speaks back to the challenge of representing slavery accurately and vividly. James Miller McKim's letter extends the narrator's initial points concerning visual proof. McKim "confess[es]" that "if I had not myself been present at the opening of the box on its arrival, and had [I] not witnessed with my own eyes, your resurrection from your living tomb, I should have been strongly disposed to question the truth of the story" (p. 169). The latter "testimonials," as they are called here, offer responses to this problem of visual representation in anti-slavery activism by foregrounding the voices of those who witnessed the panorama. British Reverend Justin Spaulding's affirming letter describes the panorama as "almost, if not quite, a perfect fac simile of the workings of that horrible and fiendish system. The real *life-like* scenes presented in this Panorama, are admirably calculated to make an unfading impression upon the heart and memory" (p. 170). With its various letters of authentication, the 1851 text would seem at a glance to resemble the standard "eclectic" form of the slave narrative with its multiple appended documents. Yet the very intertextuality of these documents serves as proof that Brown's diverse cultural productions act as interchangeable "authenticating narratives." The 1851 edition corroborates and further contextualizes the Box Brown panorama, his boxing reenactments, and vice versa.

Aside from basic differences in form (such as the introduction of "chapters" in this edition), the English publication of the Box Brown narrative diverges most significantly from its predecessor, in its full engagement with musical performance as a strategy of renewal, transformation, and liberation for the fugitive. Performance emerges early in the text as a mark of both passive and aggressive objectification in enslavement. Brown describes the instance in which one of his "kinder" overseers, Henry Bedman, "was very fond of sacred music, and used to ask me and some of the other slaves . . . to sing for him something 'smart' . . . which we were generally as well pleased to do" (p. 186). In contrast to this coerced singing, the text again includes "the revolting case of a coloured man, who was frequently in the habit of singing" and who is later tortured for this transgression which reportedly "consumed too much time," according to the tyrannical overseer John F. Allen (p. 188). This *Narrative* critically considers the limits of performance in slavery, how it operates as a tool of the master's caprice and as a catalyst for enacting power over the enslaved.

This version of Box Brown's tale also offers evidence of the ways in which the enslaved aimed gamely to reappropriate performance from the slaveholder and transform it into a method of eclectic subterfuge and survival. A new portion of material presents a detailed account of Brown's involvement as "a member of the choir in the Affeviar church" in Richmond, Virginia (p. 205). His experiences in the choir foster several critical transformations in Brown's life. As a result of his activity in song, Brown develops an increasing resistance to Christianity and an awareness of the hypocrisy of "slave-dealing Christians" (p. 205). Brown also gradually becomes aware of the ways that sacred musical performance might also spark altruistic awakenings within individuals. The narrative outlines a choir performance that serves as a crucial turning point in the text and which ultimately alters the spiritual condition of Brown's professed "friend Dr. Smith . . . the conductor of the underground railway" (p. 205). Brown himself professedly resolves after the Christmas concert of 1848 to "no longer [be] guilty of assisting those bloody dealers in the bodies and souls of men" by "singing" or "taking part in the services of a pro-slavery church" (p. 206). The performance of sacred song here both perpetuates the regime of slavery and potentially aids in its undoing by intellectually and emotionally freeing Brown from complicity with the system. From this incident, the narrative shifts into Brown's resolution to conspire with J. C. A. Smith to box himself to the free States, finally enabling him to redeploy performance toward overtly resistant ends.

In as much as the 1849 text dilutes the power of musical performance in Brown's life, the *Narrative of the Life of Henry Box Brown* privileges singing as a consistent form of expressive empowerment for its protagonist. The English edition of the narrative returns to its originating context Box Brown's "him [sic] of thanksgiving," a musical version of Psalm 40 that he reportedly sang upon emerging from his box in Philadelphia. Previously buried in the bowels

of Stearns's 1849 preface, the text positions the hymn, as Marcus Wood points out, "in its proper context," in the 1851 text. With Brown coming out of the box singing a song of spiritual praise, the text further "replac[es] the earlier linguistically sanitized account of his experience with his own language and cultural form."[68] The *Narrative* spans, in its final pages, from the exuberance of sacred song to sly revisionist folk and ends with a transcription of one of Brown's oratorical addresses that thematically expands both. Brown's "Hymn of Thanksgiving," a spirit-filled revision of Psalm 40, takes the scripture's original supplication for deliverance and transforms that Biblical lamentation into an ecstatic affirmation of resurrection and restored humanity. The 1851 narrative includes in its denouement a version of the hymn that reconstitutes the fullness of Brown's sacred song, with many repetitions of praise and joy that are missing from the 1849 text. More still, the narrative includes "Uncle Ned," the additional song that Brown would sing during his various lectures and panorama appearances, thus once again allowing for his many cultural endeavors to engage with one another.

An "old tune" set to "new words," "Uncle Ned" affirms Brown and collaborator J. C. A. Smith's compositional and performative abilities. Brown and Smith's "Ned" deftly revises an original 1848 Stephen Foster tune which was a staple of many minstrel revues of the period in order once again to deliver Box Brown as well as the iconic figure of the black laborer from enslavement. While Foster's chorus laments the passing of an "Old Ned" character who "lay down de shubble and de hoe" to die, having weathered the severe punishment of unchecked labor with fingers "long like de cane in de brake" and "no teeth for to eat de corn cake," Brown resituates himself in his own version of the song as having "laid down the shovel and the hoe / Down in the box he did go / No more Slave work for Henry Box Brown / In the box by express he did go." His song labors, so to speak, so as to displace the decrepit corpus of the slave who has nobly worked himself to the brink of death in Foster's racial romanticist vision. Brown ironically positions himself in "Uncle Ned" as a resurrected body who, in verse, stages an altogether different kind of vanishing act to that of death. As would be the case in his panorama exhibitions and in the 1851 *Narrative*, Brown would consistently seek to reposition his own body to labor in resistance to the peculiar institution through the poetics of spectacular and eccentric performances. After touring the British Isles for more than a decade and a half, Henry "Box" Brown returned to the United States in the 1870s, with a wife and daughter, as a magician and "sleight of hand artist." Fittingly escaping from the annals of abolitionist history, Brown disappeared from public record after 1878. His date of death is unknown.[69]

To (Re)Dress Freedom: Passing and Performing Liberty in Running a Thousand Miles for Freedom

Only the "Georgia Fugitives," William and Ellen Craft, would match Box Brown in their use of deft cultural performance skills in concert with their own bodies to exact what William Wells Brown described as "one of the most interesting cases of the escape of fugitives from American slavery that have ever come before the American people."[70] Stepping into the role of mentor, (stage) manager, and abolitionist cohort within weeks of their escape to Philadelphia, Wells Brown "became the first person to put into print what is still remembered as the most famous, if not the most ingenious, escape from American slavery."[71] His "Singular Escape" article trumpeted the "novel . . . means" through which the Crafts gained their freedom, with "Ellen dressed in man's clothing, and pass[ing] as the *master*, while her husband passed as the *servant*." Brown recognized how the spectacular details of the Crafts' escape were no doubt "replete with interest," and his article, like so many that would follow about the Crafts' escape, would allude to the fascinating physical characteristics of the couple, how "Ellen is so near white, that she can pass without suspicion for a white woman" and how her "husband is much darker."[72] To be sure, bodies figure prominently in *Running a Thousand Miles for Freedom*, the Craft fugitive slave narrative published some twelve years after the couple's flight to the North. More than any other text in the genre that came before or after it, the Craft narrative would use the trope of spectacularly ambiguous bodies to not only critique the system of slavery but to critique the rigidity of racial, gender, and class categories in nineteenth-century American culture.

Ellen and William Craft met in the high cotton country of central Georgia sometime in their teens. More is known about Ellen's family and upbringing. Ellen's mother, Maria, was a slave. Born in Clinton, Georgia, in 1826, Ellen was owned by her father, a planter named James P. Smith. Ellen's ambiguous status as the offspring of her master provoked the jealousy of her mistress, a common occurrence in plantation culture. As a result, when she was eleven, Ellen was given to one of her white half-siblings, Eliza, and her husband, Robert Collins, a wealthy Macon, Georgia, entrepreneur and landholder. In the early 1840s, Ellen would meet William, a carpenter who was owned by another citizen of Macon. Little is known about the couple's "initial encounters and romance," but the Crafts reportedly sought permission from their masters to marry only to have their request initially rebuffed by Ellen's master, who "discouraged marriage between his slaves and those on adjoining plantations."[73] Because of this, the couple were forced to delay their marriage until sometime in 1846. Two years later, they began to put into motion a plan to escape to the North.

R. J. M. Blackett observes that "no other escape from slavery had been so well thought out and so precisely executed," and certainly the many varied details and nuances of their plan affirm the couple's ingenuity as a team as well as their creativity in producing mischief and subterfuge.[74] Both Crafts made use of their respective *craftsman* knowledge, privileges, and skills, which they had developed and honed in slavery. As an artisan, for instance, William was afforded great mobility to move around from job to job—a situation that resulted in access to multiple regions that supplied the necessary goods for their journey. Over time he acquired the accessories to create a "gentleman's" wardrobe for his wife to wear during their flight. Ellen, a skillful seamstress, pieced together the clothing, and both husband and wife gradually stored away for their escape funds they had acquired as privileged house servants. Together the couple rehearsed their flight personas—the "aristocratic, eccentric, yet invalid young white planter . . . Mr. Johnson" and his "loyal slave valet" William.[75]

By train, boat, and coach, the Crafts made their way north in December 1848. The journey would last four days and would begin with the couple's train ride from Macon to Savannah, continuing by steamer to Charleston and Wilmington, and on by train through Richmond, Baltimore, and Havre de Grace, Maryland. They used a ferry to cross the Susquehanna and ended their escape via a train to Philadelphia, where they were hidden by a Quaker family just outside the city. Within three weeks of their arrival in the North, the Crafts moved on to Boston, where they settled into a vibrant black activist community and where they would live their first eighteen months of freedom.[76] Once in New England, William put his carpentry skills to use and took up work as a cabinet maker, while Ellen worked as a seamstress. They fast established themselves in a black community that, as of 1848, had a population of 2,000, with four churches and multiple social associations and clubs. This politically progressive enclave would prove to be an especially protective and supportive place for the Crafts to reside in the first year and a half of their freedom since, like Box Brown, the couple would endure a close and well-publicized brush with slave-catchers in the fall of 1850 that precipitated their departure to the United Kingdom.[77]

In the first few months of their new status as fugitives though, the Crafts enjoyed a kind of celebrity that was nearly unmatched, except for the international icon Frederick Douglass. They became, as Arna Bontemps points out, "heroes, about whom speeches were made and poems written."[78] Beyond word of mouth, their celebrity was no doubt fueled and sustained by the couple's near immediate appearance on the abolitionist lecture circuit with Wells Brown. By late January and February 1849, the senior activist was presenting the Crafts before audiences in various Massachusetts cities. During those early appearances, Brown would reportedly make "a few opening remarks, after which Mr. Craft" would give "a thrilling account of their escape." Ellen Craft would join her husband and Brown on the platform, occasionally answering a few questions from the audience. Their efforts were lauded by critics who speculated that these appearances alone were to affect the "growing sympathy for the slave" which, one letter-writer predicted, was "to be more dreaded by the South than bullets and guns combined."[79]

The Crafts were forced, however, to take their lecturing and agitation overseas in late 1850, and by early December of that year, they had disembarked from the *Cambria* steamer in Liverpool, England, following in the footsteps of Henry Box Brown and J. C. A.

Smith.[80] There in the United Kingdom, and before large and sympathetic anti-slavery audiences, the Crafts would reunite with Wells Brown in order to create "one of the most renowned and influential abolitionist combinations in both America and Britain." In addition, the Crafts would become "the first husband and wife team of American slaves to manage a British tour." Through English cities such as Liverpool, Manchester, Birmingham, and Leeds, and on to ports such as Bath and Bristol, and on to Glasgow and Edinburgh, Scotland, the Crafts and Wells Brown toured together six months, and their journey importantly afforded William Craft the significant opportunity to evolve as an orator and social commentator in ways that would ultimately inform the style and content of *Running a Thousand Miles for Freedom*.[81]

Illiterate upon their escape from slavery, the Crafts quickly learned to read and write, in part by studying for three years at the Ockham School outside London under the tutelage of Lady Byron.[82] Although William was green around the edges in his earliest appearances as a public speaker, he would evolve into a "sophisticated" lecturer on a tour that gave him ample opportunity to observe Brown's savvy oratorical aesthetic and multilayered presentation style. The Wells Brown–Craft combination in Great Britain featured the display of Wells Brown's panorama and a variety of speeches. Brown and the Crafts "had by now refined their pattern. First, Brown spoke against American slavery, then William described their escape, and finally, in a tear-jerking scene, Ellen was invited onstage." Brown would occasionally "sing a song or two" at gatherings before a collection was taken up for the abolitionist cause. The tour solidified the couple's status as activists committed to promoting the anti-slavery cause while abroad. Their work with Wells Brown, for instance, reached an attention-grabbing high point when they organized a quietly effective demonstration at the 1851 World's Fair in London.[83]

The Crafts spent much of the 1850s starting a family and settling into a life in England that included participating in anti-slavery meetings and the London Emancipation Committee in West London and other abolitionist organizations, and earning a living through carpentry and sewing. They gave birth to five children while abroad—Charles Estlin Phillips, William, Brougham, Alfred, and Ellen. By the close of the decade and with twelve years of freedom and international activism behind them, William took up the task of writing and publishing their fugitive narrative in the United Kingdom. First published in 1860, Craft's narrative *Running a Thousand Miles for Freedom* would go "through two printings in as many years."[84]

Appearing more than a decade after the Browns' respective works, the Craft text arrived on the eve of the Civil War and in the midst of an English literary and cultural scene which, despite the absence of any "major slave narrative . . . since the early 1850s," remained nonetheless deeply fascinated with American slavery and, more specifically, the spectacle of racially liminal figures in American slave culture. Irish playwright Dion Boucicault had only recently completed a New York City run of his racial melodrama, *The Octoroon* (1859), a play about the tragic fate of a light-skinned slave and her star-crossed white lover on a Louisiana plantation, and he was steadily making plans in 1860 to bring his production to London's Adelphi Theatre the following year. Boucicault's play would join works such as sensation novelist Mary Elizabeth Braddon's serialized text of the same name and other subsequent "octoroon" dramas in early 1860s English popular culture, as well as a host of literary texts that obliquely alluded to heroines and minor characters with racially "suspect" pasts. Called by Jennifer Brody "mulattaroons," these cultural figures represent an "unreal, impossible ideal whose corrupted and corrupting constitution inevitably causes conflicts in narratives that attempt to promote purity."[85] Consistently, these characters prove troublesome in nineteenth-century trans-Atlantic fiction because presumably they cannot be easily integrated into literary landscapes that demanded strict racial dichotomies between black and white. "Tragic" because of her entrapment between two worlds, this stock literary figure on both sides of the Atlantic was most often forced to die in order to restore stability and order to the narratives at hand.

A provocative literary text as well as a work of aggressive abolitionism, *Running a Thousand Miles for Freedom* would trouble the waters of both the "tragic mulatta" literary genre as well as the rugged masculinist slave narrative genre by presenting a tale of a married couple who revised the trope of the light-skinned heroine and who manipulated and subverted the putative stability of identity categories in order to secure their freedom. The text in some ways resembles elements of slave narratives that came before it, especially in its insistence on emphasizing "how tentative liberty is, how the Crafts are 'free from every slavish fear' only after leaving America."[86] Divided into two parts, the narrative focuses in the first half on the details of the couple's escape and, in the second half, shifts to tracing their second flight to Nova Scotia and on to England. Like both Box Brown's allusive "illustration of the box" at the close of 1849 text and like his later two-part panorama exhibition, *Running* suggests that the road to freedom is anything but a linear route. But most distinctly, the narrative would mark something of a break from the fugitive texts produced by their one-time comrades behind the lecture pulpit. In its emphasis on a female fugitive as an equally heroic counterpart to that of her husband, the Craft narrative broke new ground in the escape narrative genre. Unlike mother Elizabeth Brown or wife Nancy Brown, women who either sacrificed themselves for the good of the men in their lives or whose sale prompted their husbands to run, Ellen Craft is, of course, a pivotal player in this fugitive text. Celebrated for her "indomitable courage and perseverance betoken," as well as her "mind of no common energy," Ellen Craft, like Harriet Jacobs, who would publish her own influential narrative a year later, emerges as a true "heroine" of fugitive culture.[87]

Nevertheless, Ellen Craft's greatest challenge in a narrative authored by her husband would be to assert her agency in a culture that consistently rendered her light-skinned body an object of both popular and prurient fascination and cultural anxiety. Lyman Allen's published letter in *The Liberator*, in which he questions whether it is even "possible that that creature [Ellen] was ever a slave?" aptly sums up the public's common and incredulous response to Craft's spectacular figure.[88] Clearly, the legend of Craft's racially phantasmagoric identity combined with her high visibility on the abolitionist lecture circuit would challenge the borders between trans-Atlantic categories of "blackness" and "whiteness." For just as fugitives were called upon to testify to slavery's horrors, Craft's body itself represented a kind of spectacular "evidence" of the public secret of racial miscegenation in slavery, what the law defined as "the crime of . . . 'intermarrying, cohabiting, or inter-breeding of persons of different races.' " What legal scholar Eva Saks would call a "miscegenous body," Ellen Craft's figure "stands for the threatening clash and conjunction" of difference between "black and white . . . owner and owned . . . property and the body" and "legal and social forms of representation itself."[89] Part of the challenge of the Craft narrative, then, would be to speak back to this popular and juridical antebellum ideology, which held that "to mix the people of one region with another was to create an un-natural type, suited to no region." *Running a Thousand Miles for Freedom* sought, in contrast, to escape the impulse merely to put Ellen Craft on display for "collective, communal amusement" and "to promote . . . pleasurable difference."[90]

The Craft narrative constructs a kind of "difference" from these popular representations of doomed "mulattaroons" and seeks instead to intervene in narrow construction of tragic, racially liminal figures. Likewise, as abolitionist literature, the text furthers the cause of black liberation politics by demonstrating the ways that the couple would work together to repossess their own bodies through meth-ods of passing, performing, and cross-dressing their way to the North. Solving the problem of corporeal possession emerges as an urgent critical concern in the very first paragraph of the narrative. Craft laments that "we could not call the bones and sinews that God gave us our own" and that any "new-born babe" of theirs might fall vulnerable to being sold.[91] Immediately, the narrative calls attention to the crisis of black subjects who do not own their own bodies, and repeatedly the text returns to the ways that slavery controls, distorts, and disfigures black flesh. "It is a fact worthy of remark," Craft's narration proclaims, "that nothing seems to give the slaveholders so much pleasure as the catching and torturing of fugitives. They had much rather take the keen and poisonous lash, and with it cut their poor trembling victims to atoms, than allow one of them to escape to a free country" (pp. 239–240).

In order to free the black body of abjection, *Running a Thousand Miles for Freedom* wages a war against supposedly fixed social, politi-cal, and juridical identity categories that bind and constrict the en-slaved. A narrative of transgression, the text poses multiple forms of "boundary crossings" that open up ways for the Crafts to reinvent their status in American culture. Moving "from the South to the North," from "woman" to "man," from "black" to "white," from "wife" to "gentleman," Ellen, accompanied by William, crosses regional, gender, racial, and class lines in an anti-slavery text that works to disrupt not only "the legal institution of slavery" but, as Ellen Weinauer notes, "the normative categories that underwrite" the legal institution of slavery as well.[92] Ellen's performative cross-dressing masquerade enacts and represents its own form of escape and freedom, a liberation from the kind of excruciating corporeal abjection described by Wells Brown, symbolically referenced in the boxing of Henry Brown, and articulated in *Running* itself. Carefully collaborating with William and piecing together an alternate identity, Ellen performs a kind of liberation that celebrates radical self-fashioning in the face of a system that aims to define the couple as objects with no agency and limited access to self-representation.

As the Crafts biographer Barbara McCaskill reminds us, the Crafts were by no means the first to escape slavery in disguise, nor were they the first husband and wife team to do so. Men "escaped slavery disguised as women, women escaped slavery concealed under masculine clothes, mothers escaped with children, and husbands ran away with wives more frequently than their enemies would have anticipated."[93] But the Crafts' plot perhaps remained "enchanting" to the masses because of the complexity of its multiple acts of social and cultural destabilization. Ellen's liminality, "black" and yet "white," a woman who was not recognized fully as such in slavery, created a rich, provocative, and paradoxical reason to run. Passing for white and as a man will hopefully, the text suggests, enable Ellen Craft to be read simultaneously as free, "black," and a woman, the latter of which was a category painfully out of reach for her in bondage. Cross-dressing is thus a means to escape the gender constrictions of slavery that barred enslaved women from the realm "true womanhood." Putative "angels of the home," middle-class white women retained the social iconography of "true women" who were celebrated for their moral fitness and piety, while black women in particular were scripted as the very opposite. Thus, in donning the clothes of a gentleman and treating her husband as property, Craft passed through perhaps the "untruest" sphere in order to seize her womanhood in the North.

The quest to be not only free but, in the case of Ellen, to become a conventionally gendered subject is perhaps the most critical and influential element of *Running a Thousand Miles for Freedom*, for it not only serves as one of the reasons for the Crafts' flight, but it also shapes and informs fundamental aspects of William Craft's narration. Throughout the text, Craft aspires to protect and enact Ellen's womanhood in a variety of ways. The very fact of his narration is in and of itself an example of how Craft's work aims to shield Ellen from a public space that she had occupied along the lecture circuit in the previous decade. Taking the lead in writing their narrative, William Craft shores up his wife's respectability by ensuring her narrative absence from this text and reinforcing her privacy and her (public) image as an "angel of the home." As was already clear from their joint activism in England and Ellen's willingness to appear with Wells Brown and Craft behind the lecture pulpit, she was hardly a conventional "true woman."[94] Nevertheless, Craft's narration carefully polices the boundaries between his "master" and his wife throughout *Running*, by making pointed use of gendered pronouns, yet all the while boldly calling attention to the social construction of such categories in language. In the emotional climax to part one of *Running*, upon reaching freedom "Mr. Johnson" transforms back into "Ellen," "burst[ing] into tears, lean[ing] upon [William], and [weeping] like a child. The reaction was fearful. So when we reached the house, she was in reality so weak and faint that she could scarcely stand alone" (p. 268). The text here works to re-situate both Crafts within the conventional realm of gender categories, as husband and wife having fled a system that refused to recognize them as such. The tension between the Craft narrative's revisionist social impulses and its adherence to mainstream social conventions remains consistent throughout the text. Yet in its emphasis on the fluid oscillation between identity categories, the narrative broke new and important ground in the fugitive slave narrative genre and, more broadly, in Atlantic world literary culture.

William Craft's narrative aesthetic represented the culmination of more than a decade of public speaking and education, and the textures of his narration clearly transcend an attendance to protecting his wife. Acerbic abolitionist language and critique permeate the

tone and style of *Running*, as when Craft, early on, deftly oscillates
between documenting the perils of slavery and expressing rage at
the rigidity of white supremacist legislation that tears slave families
apart. Craft recalls the painful separation of his sister from his
mother in one instance (p. 230) and shortly thereafter strikes a
sharp and sardonic social commentary on the absurdity of identity
categories. Boldly, Craft calls attention to the subtext of racial miscegenation hovering in the background of the narrative. "It is," he
declares, "a common practice for gentlemen (if I may call them
such), moving in the highest circles of society, to be the fathers of
children by their slaves" (p. 232). The text here brilliantly foreshad-
ows Ellen's imminent appropriation of the "gentleman's" role while
simultaneously calling into question the authenticity of southern
gentry like Thomas Jefferson, whose putative sexual liaisons with
the enslaved problematize their esteemed respectability.

Running a Thousand Miles for Freedom was perhaps in no way
more subversive, however, than in its treatment of its passing plot,
which aided in setting a precedent for other texts of its kind published in the twentieth century, such as Jessie Fauset's *Plum Bun* and
Nella Larsen's *Quicksand* and *Passing*.[95] Craft's narration resonates
with scenarios that evoke what cultural critic Amy Robinson has
called the "triangular theatre of the pass." In her influential work on
the subject, Robinson has argued that, in passing narratives, there
are always three figures involved in a given scene—the passer, the
dupe (or the person who is being fooled by the pass), and the "literate in-group member" who reads the transaction of the pass. As
such, passing is a highly spectacular and performative transaction
that involves collaboration and methods of seeing (the other).[96] The
Craft narrative reinforces this triangulation at multiple points in the
text, and at once mischievous and sardonically calls attention again
and again to the serious "joke" that the couple plays out in order to
reach freedom. Craft lets his readers in on this joke and often iden-
tifies the dupes involved in various passing transactions. At one
point, for instance, while waiting for their steamer to arrive, Ellen
invades the world of southern patriarchy, where she is treated with
high regard according to class as well as gender. William describes
the scene of the pass, how the "proprietor made me stand on one

side, while he paid my master the attention and homage he thought a gentleman of his high position merited" (p. 253). Craft mocks the landlord and his "fireeating patrons, men who would insist on the unmistakable, always evident inferiority of 'black blood' but who, unbeknownst to themselves, bow and scrape to this fugitive slave" here. As literate in-group member, William executes the most enlightened form of seeing, as he reads the seamlessness of Ellen's pass and the tractability of the dupes involved in their collaborative deception.

William Craft's trickster persona emerges fully during these key passing moments when he slips in wry asides about the ruse that he and "Mr. Johnson" are executing among hapless strangers. Placed in a train cabin "with a gentleman and his two daughters," Ellen's "Johnson" generates the most sincere and swooning of responses from a young lady who claims to have "never felt so much for a gentleman in [her] life!" William, the savvy onlooker, offers the sly aside, using "an American expression, 'they fell in love with the wrong chap' " (p. 257). Together, the Crafts perfect a triangulated spectacle of passing that extends throughout the narrative. Each plays the role of a literate in-group member, each serves as the other's protection, playing each respective role in order to serve and shelter the other in the quest to be free. Their collaboration was one of the riskiest and most creative in fugitive narrative history.

Running a Thousand Miles for Freedom seeks, in the end, to collaborate with an even broader audience as it insists on ever-expanding the ranks of its literate in-group members. Readers are, of course, from the start let in on "the joke" that "Mr. Johnson" and his valet are pulling, and the text beckons its audience to engage fully with the cultural literacy of understanding, seeing, and reading Ellen and William Craft's revisionist transgression of racial, gender, and class categories. In a sense, the Craft narrative, a late entry in the fugitive slave narrative genre, would drive home the point that all texts of this kind aimed to declare. That is, the text aims to achieve the goal of making in-group members of all its readers, to convert and convince would-be supporters to become knowledgeable about how slavery falsely naturalizes what are only seemingly fixed boundaries between freedom and enslavement, black and white, gentry and slave. This point is driven home throughout *Running*, and is most chillingly evident in Craft's warning to his (white) readers that "slavery in America is not at all confined to persons of any particular complexion" (p. 225). Better to dismantle a system now, the slyly critical narration suggests, than to risk being forced into playing the role of a fugitive too. Nine years after the publication of their narrative, the Crafts would return to their home state of Georgia in order to continue their racial uplift activities. Ellen Craft died in 1891. William Craft died five years later at his daughter's home in Charleston, South Carolina.

Conclusion: The People Could Fly

Wells Brown, Box Brown, and the Crafts would make a striking tableau on the anti-slavery podium, but none of them were content to play the role of the passive (former) slave on the block. Rather, each figure used their narratives as a means to affirm their creative agency as fugitives. Transcending mere exhibition, the Wells Brown, Box Brown, and Craft narratives underscore and affirm the rise in visibility of the aesthetically adventurous fugitive slave in the 1850s, and they buck the traditional slave narrative tenets that often sought to conflate artlessness and blackness in slave culture. Each author's unconventional narrative authority far exceeded the passive display that American abolitionist Henry C. Wright called for when he suggested that British abolitionists use the Great Exhibition of 1851 so that "the Crafts [should] stand on an auction block, Henry 'Box' Brown [should] appear with the box in which he had actually escaped from slavery, and William Wells Brown [should] show his panorama."[97] Refusing the role of appearing alongside "the whips, chains" and other relics of the slave trade, Wells Brown, Box Brown, and the Crafts choreographed and re-narrated grand escape plots that resonated in history and that evoked the wonder of audiences on both sides of the Atlantic.

In spite of all of their fame, there were some who were less than pleased with the Wells Brown, Box Brown, and Craft testimonials. By the summer of 1849, the *Pennsylvania Freeman* called attention to the popularity of the "thrilling and interesting narratives of the escape of fugitive slaves" holding the public's attention. These lectures and texts, with their "details of the bold and ingenious stratagems" seem, as the *Freeman* ominously observes, to be

> . . . inconsiderate . . . ill judged, and calculated to do serious harm.
> Flight is the slave's only hope of early freedom, and to the vast majority of the present generation, their only hope of any future deliverance. Tens of thousands . . . make the attempt to escape, but are retaken, while those who do succeed often do it through incredible hardships, and by the exercise of almost superhuman fortitude and energy. Their means of escape are very few, their field for stratagem narrow, and the exposure of those heretofore successful must necessarily make their means still fewer and that field narrower, and render their escape still more difficult or hopeless. . . . In the case of the Crafts and the Man of the Box, it is doubtless too late to begin to be cautious.[98]

True, as some critics would argue, there was something certainly impractical and self-promoting about each fugitive's detailed testimonial of escape, and the apprehension of several who attempted boxing runs provides evidence that publicity surrounding such flights created a heightened atmosphere of surveillance and made future escapes in a similar vein nearly impossible to execute undetected. Notwithstanding, the Browns and the Crafts no doubt contributed to an aesthetic legacy in American letters that preserved and documented the resourceful innovations of people who, like their ancestors in the legendary African folktale, discovered their ability to fly, and who passed on the story of their flight as a source of inspiration to all those who would come after them to imagine, create, and do the seeming impossible.[99]

Daphne A. Brooks is an associate professor of English and African-American Studies at Princeton University, where she teaches courses on African-American literature and culture, performance studies, and popular music studies. She is the author of two books: *Bodies in Dissent: Spectacular Performances of Race and Freedom, 1850–1910* (2006) and *Jeff Buckley's Grace* (Continuum, 2005).

Notes to the Introduction

1. *National Anti-Slavery Standard* (June 7, 1849).
2. Virginia Hamilton, *The People Could Fly: American Black Folktales* (New York: Knopf, 1993).
3. *National Anti-Slavery Standard* (June 7, 1849).
4. *Ibid.*
5. For a detailed study of fugitive slave resistance and escape, see John Hope Franklin, *Runaway Slaves: Rebels on the Plantation* (New York: Oxford University Press, 1999).
6. R. J. M. Blackett, "The Odyssey of William and Ellen Craft," in *Beating Against the Barriers: The Lives of Six Nineteenth-Century Afro-Americans*, edited by R. J. M. Blackett (Ithaca, NY: Cornell University Press, 1986), p. 98.
7. Blackett, p. 105.
8. Jeffrey Ruggles, *The Unboxing of Henry Brown* (Richmond: Library of Virginia Press, 2003), pp. 49, 29. Ruggles's study is the most comprehensive work to date on the life and times of Box Brown.
9. Cynthia Griffin Wolff, "Passing Beyond the Middle Passage: Henry 'Box' Brown's Translations of Slavery," *Massachusetts Review* 37:1 (1996), p. 30.
10. Frederick Douglass, *Narrative of the Life of Frederick Douglass, An American Slave* (New York: Penguin Books, 1982). For more on the development of the fugitive slave narrative as a literary genre, see William Andrews, *To Tell a Free Story: The First Century of Afro-American Autobiography, 1760–1865* (Urbana and Chicago: University of Illinois Press, 1986). See also *The Slave's Narrative*, edited by Charles T. Davis and Henry Louis Gates, Jr. (New York: Oxford University Press, 1985); Raymond Hedin, "Strategies of Form in the American Slave Narrative," *The Art of the Slave Narrative: Original Essays in Criticism and Theory*, edited by John Sekora and Darwin T. Turner (Macomb: Western Illinois University Press, 1982); and Frances Smith Foster, *Witnessing Slavery: The Development of Ante-bellum Slave Narratives* (Westport, CT: Greenwood Press, 1979).
11. Paul Jefferson, "Introduction," in *The Travels of William Wells Brown by William Wells Brown* (New York: Markus Wiener, 1991), p. 4.
12. William Edward Farrison, *William Wells Brown: Author & Reformer* (Chicago: University of Chicago Press, 1969), pp. 9, 7.
13. William Wells Brown, *Narrative of William W. Brown, A Fugitive Slave, Written by Himself*, p. 11. All subsequent references to Brown's text will be cited parenthetically unless otherwise noted. According to Farrison (p. 6), Higgins was "the son of William and Dinah (Tribble) Higgins of Fayette County."
14. Farrison, pp. 10, 20. See also "William Wells Brown," in *The Norton Anthology of African-American Literature* (New York: W. W. Norton, 1996), p. 246. See also Farrison (p. 34) for additional details regarding Brown's various forms of labor.

15. *The Norton Anthology of African-American Literature*, p. 246.

16. Blackett, p. 97.

17. Farrison, pp. 61–67.

18. Farrison, p. 69. For more on Brown's two daughters, as well as his troubled marriage to Elizabeth Schooner, see Farrison.

19. Farrison, pp. 67, 73.

20. Farrison, pp. 75, 78.

21. Farrison, pp. 113, 114.

22. Robert Stepto, "I Rose and Found My Voice: Narration, Authentication, and Authorial Control in Four Slave Narratives," in *The Slave's Narrative*, pp. 228–229.

23. Quincy as quoted in Farrison, p. 113.

24. *The Norton Anthology of African-American Literature*, p. 246.

25. Jefferson, "Introduction," p. 6.

26. Brown's subsequent literary works, the novel *Clotel* (1853) and his drama *The Escape; or, A Leap for Freedom* (1858), each make reference to well-known details of both his flight as well as the Crafts' escape. See William Wells Brown, *Clotel; or, The President's Daughter* (Armonk, NY: M. E. Sharpe, 1996); and William Wells Brown, *The Escape; or, A Leap for Freedom*, in *Black Theatre USA: Plays by African Americans, 1847 to Today* (New York: Free Press, 1996), vol. 1, pp. 37–62.

27. "Maroonage" is a term used to describe the forms of shelter that fugitive slaves often sought in swamps and forests during their escapes: See Suzette Spencer, *Stealing A Way: African Diaspora Maroon Poetics* (diss.) 2003 Mar; 63 (9), pp. 3188–3189, University of California–Berkeley, 2002. See also Richard Price, *Maroon Societies: Rebel Slave Communities in the Americas* (Garden City, NY: Anchor Press, 1973).

28. Suggesting a survivalist mentality, Brown here anticipates the moral ambiguity of various trans-Atlantic racial figures and characters who would follow him in the years to come—from Box Brown to the actress Adah Isaacs Menken. See Daphne A. Brooks, *Bodies in Dissent: Spectacular Performances of Race and Freedom, 1850–1910* (Durham, NC: Duke University Press, 2006).

29. Farrison, p. 59.

30. Wells Brown, *Narrative*, pp. 19, 52. See also Farrison, p. 13.

31. Jefferson, p. 6.

32. See Charles T. Davis and Henry Louis Gates, Jr., "Introduction: The Language of Slavery," in *The Slave's Narrative*, pp. xi–xxxiv.

33. Farrison, pp. 61–71.

34. Valerie A. Smith, " 'Loopholes of Retreat': Architecture and Ideology in Harriet Jacobs's *Incidents in the Life of a Slave Girl*," in *Reading Black, Reading Feminist: A Critical Anthology*, edited by Henry Louis Gates, Jr. (New York: Meridian, 1990), pp. 216–217. Smith cites the Crafts' narrative as an exception.

35. Each man sang hymns at the May 1849 gathering. See *The Liberator* (June 8, 1849) and the *National Anti-Slavery Standard* (June 7, 1849). Wells Brown also published a successful collection of anti-slavery hymns: See William Wells Brown, *The Anti-Slavery Harp* (Boston: B. Marsh, 1848). See also Ruggles, p. 193, footnote 39.

36. Jefferson, p. 19. Hazel V. Carby, *Race Men* (Cambridge, MA: Harvard University Press, 2000). Carby's study examines the impact of public figures such as W. E. B. DuBois and their efforts to construct "particular personal, political and social characteristics of a racialized masculinity to articulate his definition of black leadership" (p. 11).

37. Ruggles, p. 137.

38. William Wells Brown, letter to Wendell Phillips, September 1, 1852, London, England, in *Black Abolitionist Papers*, 1830–1865 [microform], edited by George E. Carter and C. Peter Ripley, Sanford, NC: Microfilming Corporation of America, 1981.

39. Ruggles, pp. 3–6. While the 1849 *Narrative* states 1816, Ruggles speculates that Brown was probably born closer to 1815. See also Henry Box Brown, *The Narrative of Henry Box Brown* (1849), p. 136; all subsequent references to this text will be cited parenthetically unless otherwise noted.

40. Ruggles, p. 6.

41. Henry Box Brown, *Narrative of the Life of Henry Box Brown* (1851), p. 187. This text will subsequently be cited parenthetically unless otherwise noted.

42. Ruggles, p. 14. For more on the First Baptist and First African Baptist churches, see Ruggles, pp. 12–14.

43. Wells Brown declares that "the more [he] thought of the trap laid by [his mistress] Mrs. Price" to get him to marry, "the more [he] determined never to marry any woman on earth until [he] should get [his] liberty" (p. 50). Wells Brown returns to this topic in his drama *The Escape*.

44. Ruggles, p. 9. For more on Nancy Brown, see Ruggles.

45. After a bitter parting, "boxing" co-conspirator and one-time traveling partner J. C. A. Smith would accuse Box Brown of, among other things, having neglected to rescue his family from slavery. See J. C. A. Smith to Editor, *Anti-Slavery Reporter*, 13 March 1854, in *The Black Abolitionist Papers*, edited by C. Peter Ripley et al., Vol. 1: *The British Isles, 1830–1865* (Chapel Hill: University of North Carolina Press, 1985), pp. 363–383. Smith wrote extensively of Brown's alleged moral dissipation in England: See J. C. A. Smith to Gerrit Smith, 6 August 1851, in *The Black Abolitionist Papers*, Vol. 1, *The British Isles, 1830–1865*, pp. 293–301.

46. V. Smith, p. 217.

47. Ruggles, pp. 14, 22–25, 29.

48. See Ruggles. See also Kathryn Grover, *The Fugitive's Gibraltar: Escaping Slaves and Abolitionism in New Bedford, Massachusetts* (Amherst: University of Massachusetts Press, 2001), pp. 202–203.

49. Ruggles, p. 59.

50. Ruggles, pp. 59, 60, 65.

51. Ruggles, p. 61.

52. James Olney, " 'I Was Born': Slave Narratives, Their Status as Autobiography and as Literature," in *The Slave's Narrative*, p. 161.

53. Stepto, p. 229; Olney, p. 161.

54. Stephen Greenblatt, "Resonance and Wonder," in *Exhibiting Cultures: The Poetics and Politics of Museum Display*, edited by Ivan Karp and Steven D. Lavine (Washington: Smithsonian Institution Press, 1991), pp. 49, 45.

55. Hortense Spillers, "Mama's Baby, Papa's Maybe: An American Grammar Book," in *African American Literary Theory: A Reader*, edited by Winston Napier (New York: New York University Press, 2000), p. 276. See also Brooks.

56. Hedin, p. 30.

57. William Wells Brown, "A Description of William Wells Brown's Original Panoramic Views of the Scenes in the Life of an American Slave, from His Birth in Slavery to His Death or His Escape to His First Home of Freedom on British Soil," in *The Black Abolitionist Papers*, Vol. 1: *The British Isles, 1830–1865*, pp. 191–224. See also Farrison, pp. 172–174.

58. For more on the history of moving panoramas, see Angela Miller, "The Panorama, the Cinema and the Emergence of the Spectacular." *Wide Angle* 18:2 (April 1996), pp. 35–69. See also Martin Meisel, *Realizations: Narrative, Pictorial, and Theatrical Arts in Nineteenth-Century England* (Princeton, NJ: Princeton University Press, 1983).

59. Wells Brown, "A Description . . . ," in *The Black Abolitionist Papers*, Vol. 1: *The British Isles, 1830–1865*, p. 191. Wells Brown had most likely viewed the popular Mississippi River panorama produced by John Banvard or one similar to Banvard's exhibition: See John Banvard, *Description of Banvard's Panorama of the Mississippi & Missouri Rivers, Extensively Known as the "Three-Mile Painting," Exhibiting a View of Country Over 3000 Miles in Length, Extending from the Mouth of the Yellow Stone to the City of New Orleans, Being by Far the Largest Picture Ever Executed By Man* (London: W. J. Golbourn, 1848).

60. Ripley (p. 217) reveals that a "number of black antislavery panoramas appeared during the 1850s." In particular, the daguerrean, photographer, and freeman James Presley Ball's 1850 panorama with its accompanying pamphlet remains one of the most ambitious black abolitionist efforts of its kind and featured the work of both the black landscape painter Robert Duncanson, as well as the lectures of Charles Lennox Remond. See Deborah Willis, ed., *J. P. Ball Daguerrean and Studio Photographer* (New York: Garland Publishing, 1993), pp. 237–301; and Joseph D. Ketner, *The Emergence of the African-American Artist: Robert S. Duncanson, 1821–1872* (Columbia: University of Missouri Press, 1993), pp. 101–104. Pease and Pease note that "Anthony Burns joined promoter H. C. Garcelon and toured the country in the late 1850s. In the evenings they showed a panorama called 'The Moving *Mirror of Slavery*' and in

the daytime peddled copies of the *Life of Anthony Burns*"; see Jane H. Pease and William H. Pease, *They Who Would Be Free: Blacks' Search for Freedom, 1830–1861* (New York: Atheneum, 1974), p. 36. While Box Brown was not alone in his decision to mount a black abolitionist panorama, his work is significant both in the ways that it signifies on his discursive narrative and in that he was apparently the first to have his project visually mounted and produced for an audience. See Allan D. Austin, "More Black Panoramas: An Addendum," *The Massachusetts Review* 37:4 (winter 1996): pp. 636–639.

61. *The London Times* (July 30, 1852).

62. Miller, p. 46.

63. *The Leeds Mercury* (May 24, 1851).

64. *London Times*, "Summer Assizes" (July 30, 1852). In a letter to Wendell Phillips, Wells Brown declared that, in spite of Box Brown's anomalous social behavior, "the editor was certainly to blame" in the case; see William Wells Brown, letter to Wendell Phillips, September 1, 1852, London, England, in *Black Abolitionist Papers*, 1830–1865 [microform], edited by George E. Carter and C. Peter Ripley, Sanford, NC: Microfilming Corporation of America, 1981.

65. For more on Henry Box Brown and subversive song, see Brooks.

66. Ruggles, pp. 120, 132. Ruggles speculates that this second text may have been written in the States.

67. Olney, p. 161.

68. Marcus Wood, " 'All Right!': *The Narrative of Henry Box Brown* as a Test Case for the Racial Prescription of Rhetoric and Semiotics." *Proceedings of the American Antiquarian Society* 107:1 (April 1997), p. 81.

69. Ruggles, p. 159; see also David Price, *Magic: A Pictorial History of Conjurers in the Theater* (New York: Cornwall Books, 1985).

70. William Wells Brown, "Singular Escape," *The Liberator* (January 12, 1849).

71. Farrison, pp. 134–135.

72. *The Liberator* (June 12, 1849).

73. Barbara McCaskill, "Introduction: William and Ellen Craft in TransAtlantic Literature and Life," in *Running a Thousand Miles for Freedom*, edited by Barbara McCaskill (Athens, GA: University of Georgia Press, 1999), p. x; and Blackett, p. 88. McCaskill and Blackett have written the most extensively on the Crafts, and McCaskill is currently completing a book manuscript on William and Ellen Craft "in the trans-Atlantic world."

74. Blackett, p. 89.

75. McCaskill, p. x.

76. McCaskill, p. xi; Blackett, p. 89. Ruggles speculates that the Crafts "resided at Lewis Hayden's house, just down the block from [Box] Brown's residence" and may have perhaps contributed his carpentry skills to the *Mirror of Slavery*. Ruggles, note 26, p. 200.

77. Blackett, pp. 90–93.

78. Arna Bontemps, *Great Slave Narratives* (Boston: Beacon Press, 1969), p. 1.

79. Lyman Allen, "William and Ellen Craft," *The Liberator* (March 2, 1849); and Viator, "The Fugitive Slaves," *The Liberator* (March 2, 1849).

80. For more on the increased pressure on the Crafts to flee the States in the wake of the Fugitive Slave law, see Blackett, p. 93. See also McCaskill, p. xiii.

81. Blackett, p. 90; McCaskill, p. xv.

82. Wells Brown, "Singular Escape"; McCaskill, p. xiv.

83. Blackett, p. 98; McCaskill, p. xv; Blackett, p. 102.

84. McCaskill, p. xv. Blackett (p. 105) maintains that William Craft is the "undisputed" sole author of the text.

85. Blackett, p. 105. Dion Boucicault, *The Octoroon* (1859), Salem, NH: Ayer, 1987. Mary Elizabeth Braddon, *The Octoroon*. New York: Optimus Printing, p. 186. W. B. Donne, *Cora; or, The Octoroon Slave of Louisiana Drama* (1861), Lord Chamberlain Play Collection, London: British Library Manuscript Reading Room. See also Jennifer Brody, *Impossible Purities: Blackness, Femininity, and Victorian Culture* (Durham, NC: Duke University Press, 1998), p. 16. Brody cites Thackeray's *Vanity Fair* as an example of a Victorian novel that manipulates the use of racially liminal female characters in the margins of the narrative.

86. McCaskill, p. xiv.

87. Harriet Jacobs, *Incidents in the Life of a Slave Girl* (1861), introduction by Jean Fagan Yellin, Cambridge, MA: Harvard University Press, 1987. Wells Brown calls Ellen Craft "truly a heroine" in "Singular Escape."

88. See Allen.

89. Eva Saks, "Representing Miscegenation Law." *Raritan* 8:2 (1988), p. 35.

90. Joel Williamson, *New People: Miscegenation and Mulattoes in the United States* (New York: New York University Press, 1984); and Rosemarie Garland Thompson, *Freakery: Cultural Spectacles of the Extraordinary Body* (New York: New York University Press), 1996.

91. *Running a Thousand Miles for Freedom; or, The Escape of William and Ellen Craft from Slavery*, p. 266. All subsequent references to this text will be cited parenthetically unless otherwise noted.

92. Ellen M. Weinauer, " 'A Most Respectable Looking Gentleman': Passing, Possession, and Transgression in *Running a Thousand Miles for Freedom*," in *Passing and the Fictions of Identity* (Durham, NC: Duke University Press, 1996), p. 38.

93. McCaskill, p. xvi.

94. African-American orator Maria Stewart was the first American woman to appear in public to deliver a formal lecture. For more on Stewart, see *Maria W. Stewart: America's First Black Woman Political Writer: Essays and Speeches*, edited by Marilyn Richardson (Bloomington: Indiana University Press, 1987).

95. Jessie Fauset, *Plum Bun* (1928; Boston: Beacon Press, 1999); and Nella Larsen, *Quicksand* (1928) and *Passing* (1929; the two novels are published together: New Brunswick, NJ: Rutgers University Press, 1986).

96. Amy Robinson, "It Takes One to Know One: Passing and Communities of Common Interest." *Critical Inquiry* 20:4 (summer 1994), pp. 715–736.
97. Blackett, p. 101.
98. *The Pennsylvania Freeman* (July 5, 1849).
99. See Hamilton.

THE GREAT ESCAPES

Four Slave Narratives

NARRATIVE

OF

WILLIAM W. BROWN

A

FUGITIVE SLAVE

WRITTEN BY HIMSELF

_____ Is there not some chosen curse,
Some hidden thunder in the stores of heaven,
Red with uncommon wrath, to blast the man
Who gains his fortune from the blood of souls?

Cowper

SECOND EDITION, ENLARGED

[1848]

NOTE TO THE SECOND EDITION

The first edition, of three thousand copies, of this little work was sold in less than six months from the time of its publication. Encouraged by the rapid sale of the first, and by a demand for a second, edition, the author has been led to enlarge the work by the addition of matter which, he thinks, will add materially to its value.

And if it shall be instrumental in helping to undo the heavy burdens, and letting the oppressed go free, he will have accomplished the great desire of his heart in publishing this work.

LETTER FROM EDMUND QUINCY, ESQ.

Dedham, July 1, 1847.

To William W. Brown

My Dear Friend:—I heartily thank you for the privilege of reading the manuscript of your Narrative. I have read it with deep interest and strong emotion. I am much mistaken if it be not greatly successful and eminently useful. It presents a different phase of the infernal slave-system from that portrayed in the admirable story of Mr. Douglass, and gives us a glimpse of its hideous cruelties in other portions of its domain.

Your opportunities of observing the workings of this accursed system have been singularly great. Your experiences in the Field, in the House, and especially on the River in the service of the slave-trader, Walker, have been such as few individuals have had;—no one, certainly, who has been competent to describe them. What I have admired, and marvelled at, in your Narrative, is the simplicity and calmness with which you describe scenes and actions which might well "move the very stones to rise and mutiny" against the National Institution which makes them possible.

You will perceive that I have made very sparing use of your flattering permission to alter what you had written. To correct a few errors, which appeared to be merely clerical ones, committed in the hurry of composition under unfavorable circumstances, and to suggest a few curtailments, is all that I have ventured to do. I should be a bold man, as well as a vain one, if I should attempt to improve your descriptions of what you have seen and suffered. Some of the scenes are not unworthy of De Foe himself.

I *trust and believe that your Narrative will have a wide circu-
lation. I am sure it deserves it. At least, a man must be differently
constituted from me, who can rise from the perusal of your
Narrative without feeling that he understands slavery better, and
hates it worse, than he ever did before.*

I *am, very faithfully and respectfully,*

Your friend,
EDMUND QUINCY

PREFACE

THE FRIENDS OF FREEDOM may well congratulate each other on the appearance of the following Narrative. It adds another volume to the rapidly increasing anti-slavery literature of the age. It has been remarked by a close observer of human nature, "Let me make the songs of a nation, and I care not who makes its laws;" and it may with equal truth be said, that, among a reading people like our own, their books will at least give character to their laws. It is an influence which goes forth noiselessly upon its mission, but fails not to find its way to many a warm heart, to kindle on the altar thereof the fires of freedom, which will one day break forth in a living flame to consume oppression.

This little book is a voice from the prison-house, unfolding the deeds of darkness which are there perpetrated. Our cause has received efficient aid from this source. The names of those who have come from thence, and battled manfully for the right, need not to be recorded here. The works of some of them are an enduring monument of praise, and their perpetual record shall be found in the grateful hearts of the redeemed bondman.

Few persons have had greater facilities for becoming acquainted with slavery, in all its horrible aspects, than WILLIAM W. BROWN. He has been behind the curtain. He has visited its secret chambers. Its iron has entered his own soul. The dearest ties of nature have been riven in his own person. A mother has been cruelly scourged before his own eyes. A father—alas! slaves have no father. A brother has been made the subject of its tender mercies. A sister has been given up to the irresponsible control of the pale-faced oppressor. This nation looks on approvingly. The American Union sanctions the deed. The constitution shields the criminals. American religion sanctifies the crime. But the tide is turning. Already, a mighty under-current is sweeping onward. The voice of warning, of remonstrance, of rebuke, of entreaty, has gone forth. Hand is linked in hand, and heart mingles with heart, in this great work of the slave's deliverance.

The convulsive throes of the monster, even now, give evidence of deep wounds.

The writer of this Narrative was hired by his master to a *"soul-driver,"* and has witnessed all the horrors of the traffic, from the buying up of human cattle in the slave-breeding states, which produced a constant scene of separating the victims from all those whom they loved, to their final sale in the southern market, to be worked up in seven years, or given over to minister to the lust of southern *Christians.*

Many harrowing scenes are graphically portrayed; and yet with that simplicity and ingenuousness which carries with it a conviction of the truthfulness of the picture.

This book will do much to unmask those who have "clothed themselves in the livery of the court of heaven" to cover up the enormity of their deeds.

During the past three years, the author has devoted his entire energies to the anti-slavery cause. Laboring under all the disabilities and disadvantages growing out of his education in slavery—subjected, as he had been from his birth, to all the wrongs and deprivations incident to his condition—he yet went forth, impelled to the work by a love of liberty—stimulated by the remembrance of his own sufferings—urged on by the consideration that a mother, brothers, and sister, were still grinding in the prison-house of bondage, in common with three millions of our Father's children—sustained by an unfaltering faith in the omnipotence of truth and the final triumph of justice—to plead the cause of the slave; and by the eloquence of earnestness carried conviction to many minds, and enlisted the sympathy and secured the cooperation of many to the cause.

His labors have been chiefly confined to Western New York, where he has secured many warm friends, by his untiring zeal, persevering energy, continued fidelity, and universal kindness.

Reader, are you an Abolitionist? What have you done for the slave? What are you doing in his behalf? What do you purpose to do? There is a great work before us! Who will be an idler now? This is the great humanitary movement of the age, swallowing up, for the time being, all other questions, comparatively speaking. The course of human events, in obedience to the unchangeable laws of our being, is fast hastening the final crisis, and

> "Have ye chosen, O my people, on whose party ye shall stand,
> Ere the Doom from its worn sandal shakes the dust
>   against our land?"

Are you a Christian? This is the carrying out of practical Christianity; and there is no other. Christianity is *practical* in its very nature and essence. It is a life, springing out of a soul imbued with its spirit. Are you a friend of the missionary cause? This is the greatest missionary enterprise of the day. Three millions of *Christian*, law-manufactured heathen are longing for the glad tidings of the gospel of freedom. Are you a friend of the Bible? Come, then, and help us to restore to these millions, whose eyes have been bored out by slavery, their sight, that they may see to read the Bible. Do you love God whom you have not seen? Then manifest that love, by restoring to your brother whom you have seen his rightful inheritance, of which he has been so long and so cruelly deprived.

It is not for a single generation alone, numbering three millions—sublime as would be that effort—that we are working. It is for Humanity, the wide world over, not only now, but for all coming time, and all future generations:—

> "For he who settles Freedom's principles,
> Writes the death-warrant of all tyranny."

It is a vast work—a glorious enterprise—worthy the unswerving devotion of the entire life-time of the great and the good.

Slaveholding and slaveholders must be rendered disreputable and odious. They must be stripped of their respectability and Christian reputation. They must be treated as "MEN-STEALERS—guilty of the highest kind of theft, and sinners of the first rank." Their more guilty accomplices in the persons of *northern apologists*, both in Church and State, must be placed in the same category. Honest men must be made to look upon their crimes with the same abhorrence

and loathing with which they regard the less guilty robber and assassin, until

> "The common damned shun their society,
> And look upon themselves as fiends less foul."

When a just estimate is placed upon the crime of slave-holding, the
work will have been accomplished, and the glorious day ushered in—

> "When man nor woman in all our wide domain,
> Shall buy, or sell, or hold, or be a slave."

J. C. HATHAWAY
Farmington, N. Y., 1847.

CHAPTER I

I WAS BORN IN Lexington, Ky. The man who stole me as soon as I was born, recorded the births of all the infants which he claimed to be born his property, in a book which he kept for that purpose. My mother's name was Elizabeth. She had seven children, viz.: Solomon, Leander, Benjamin, Joseph, Millford, Elizabeth, and myself. No two of us were children of the same father. My father's name, as I learned from my mother, was George Higgins. He was a white man, a relative of my master, and connected with some of the first families in Kentucky.

My master owned about forty slaves, twenty-five of whom were field hands. He removed from Kentucky to Missouri when I was quite young, and settled thirty or forty miles above St. Charles, on the Missouri, where, in addition to his practice as a physician, he carried on milling, merchandizing and farming. He had a large farm, the principal productions of which were tobacco and hemp. The slave cabins were situated on the back part of the farm, with the house of the overseer, whose name was Grove Cook, in their midst. He had the entire charge of the farm, and having no family, was allowed a woman to keep house for him, whose business it was to deal out the provisions for the hands.

A woman was also kept at the quarters to do the cooking for the field hands, who were summoned to their unrequited toil every morning at four o'clock, by the ringing of a bell, hung on a post near the house of the overseer. They were allowed half an hour to eat their breakfast, and get to the field. At half past four a horn was blown by the overseer, which was his signal to commence work; and every one that was not on the spot at the time, had to receive ten lashes from the negro-whip, with which the overseer always went armed. The handle was about three feet long, with the butt-end filled with lead, and the lash, six or seven feet in length, made of cow-hide, with platted wire on the end of it. This whip was put in requisition very frequently and freely, and a small offence on the part of a slave furnished an occasion for its use. During the time that Mr. Cook was overseer, I was a house servant—a situation preferable to that of a field hand, as I was better fed, better clothed, and not obliged to rise at the ringing of the bell, but about half an hour after. I have often laid and heard the crack of the whip, and the screams of the slave. My mother was a field hand, and one morning was ten or fifteen minutes behind the others in getting into the field. As soon as she reached the spot where they were at work, the overseer commenced whipping her. She cried, "Oh! pray—Oh! pray—Oh! pray"— these are generally the words of slaves, when imploring mercy at the hands of their oppressors. I heard her voice, and knew it, and jumped out of my bunk, and went to the door. Though the field was some distance from the house, I could hear every crack of the whip, and every groan and cry of my poor mother. I remained at the door, not daring to venture any further. The cold chills ran over me, and I wept aloud. After giving her ten lashes, the sound of the whip ceased, and I returned to my bed, and found no consolation but in my tears. Experience has taught me that nothing can be more heart-rending than for one to see a dear and beloved mother or sister tortured, and to hear their cries, and not be able to render them assistance. But such is the position which an American slave occupies.

My master, being a politician, soon found those who were ready to put him into office, for the favors he could render them; and a few years after his arrival in Missouri he was elected to a seat in the legislature. In his absence from home everything was left in charge of Mr. Cook, the overseer, and he soon became more tyrannical and cruel. Among the slaves on the plantation was one by the name of Randall. He was a man about six feet high, and well-proportioned, and known as a man of great strength and power. He was considered the most valuable and able-bodied slave on the plantation; but no matter how good or useful a slave may be, he seldom escapes the lash. But it was not so with Randall. He had been on the plantation since my earliest recollection, and I had never known of his being flogged. No thanks were due to the master or overseer for this. I have often heard him declare that no white man should ever whip him—that he would die first.

Cook, from the time that he came upon the plantation, had frequently declared that he could and would flog any nigger that was put into the field to work under him. My master had repeatedly told him not to attempt to whip Randall, but he was determined to try it. As soon as he was left sole dictator, he thought the time had come to put his threats into execution. He soon began to find fault with Randall, and threatened to whip him if he did not do better. One day he gave him a very hard task—more than he could possibly do; and at night, the task not being performed, he told Randall that he should remember him the next morning. On the following morning, after the hands had taken breakfast, Cook called out to Randall, and told him that he intended to whip him, and ordered him to cross his hands and be tied. Randall asked why he wished to whip him. He answered, because he had not finished his task the day before. Randall said that the task was too great, or he should have done it. Cook said it made no difference—he should whip him. Randall stood silent for a moment, and then said, "Mr. Cook, I have always tried to please you since you have been on the plantation, and I find you are determined not to be satisfied with my work, let me do as well as I may. No man has laid hands on me, to whip me, for the last ten years, and I have long since come to the conclusion not to be whipped by any man living." Cook, finding by Randall's determined look and gestures, that he would resist, called three of the hands from their work, and commanded them to seize Randall, and tie him. The hands stood still;—they knew Randall—and they also knew him to be a powerful man, and were afraid to grapple with him. As soon as Cook had ordered the men to seize him, Randall turned to them, and said—"Boys, you all know me; you know that I can handle any three of you, and the man that lays hands on me shall die. This white man can't whip me himself, and therefore he has called you to help him." The overseer was unable to prevail upon them to seize and secure Randall, and finally ordered them all to go to their work together.

Nothing was said to Randall by the overseer for more than a week. One morning, however, while the hands were at work in the field, he came into it, accompanied by three friends of his, Thompson, Woodbridge and Jones. They came up to where Randall was at work, and Cook ordered him to leave his work, and go with them to the barn. He refused to go; whereupon he was attacked by the overseer and his companions, when he turned upon them, and laid them, one after another, prostrate on the ground. Woodbridge drew out his pistol, and fired at him, and brought him to the ground by a pistol ball. The others rushed upon him with their clubs, and beat him over the head and face, until they succeeded in tying him. He was then taken to the barn, and tied to a beam. Cook gave him over one hundred lashes with a heavy cowhide, had him washed with salt and water, and left him tied during the day. The next day he was untied, and taken to a blacksmith's shop, and had a ball and chain attached to his leg. He was compelled to labor in the field, and perform the same amount of work that the other hands did. When his master returned home, he was much pleased to find that Randall had been subdued in his absence.

CHAPTER II

Soon afterwards, my master removed to the city of St. Louis, and purchased a farm four miles from there, which he placed under the charge of an overseer by the name of Friend Haskell. He was a regular Yankee from New England. The Yankees are noted for making the most cruel overseers.

My mother was hired out in the city, and I was also hired out there to Major Freeland, who kept a public house. He was formerly from Virginia, and was a horse-racer, cock-fighter, gambler, and withal an inveterate drunkard. There were ten or twelve servants in the house, and when he was present, it was cut and slash—knock down and drag out. In his fits of anger, he would take up a chair, and throw it at a servant; and in his more rational moments, when he wished to chastise one, he would tie them up in the smoke-house, and whip them; after which, he would cause a fire to be made of tobacco stems, and smoke them. This he called *"Virginia play."*

I complained to my master of the treatment which I received from Major Freeland; but it made no difference. He cared nothing about it, so long as he received the money for my labor. After living with Major Freeland five or six months, I ran away, and went into the woods back of the city; and when night came on, I made my way to my master's farm, but was afraid to be seen, knowing that if Mr. Haskell, the overseer, should discover me, I should be again carried back to Major Freeland; so I kept in the woods. One day, while in the woods, I heard the barking and howling of dogs, and in a short time they came so near that I knew them to be the bloodhounds of Major Benjamin O'Fallon. He kept five or six, to hunt runaway slaves with.

As soon as I was convinced that it was them, I knew there was no chance of escape. I took refuge in the top of a tree, and the hounds were soon at its base, and there remained until the hunters came up in a half or three quarters of an hour afterwards. There were two men with the dogs, who, as soon as they came up, ordered me to descend. I came down, was tied, and taken to St. Louis jail. Major Freeland soon made his appearance, and took me out, and ordered me to follow him, which I did. After we returned home, I was tied up in the smoke-house, and was very severely whipped. After the major had flogged me to his satisfaction, he sent out his son Robert, a young man eighteen or twenty years of age, to see that I was well smoked. He made a fire of tobacco stems, which soon set me to coughing and sneezing. This, Robert told me, was the way his father used to do to his slaves in Virginia. After giving me what they conceived to be a decent smoking, I was untied and again set to work.

Robert Freeland was a "chip of the old block." Though quite young, it was not unfrequently that he came home in a state of intoxication. He is now, I believe, a popular commander of a steamboat on the Mississippi river. Major Freeland soon after failed in business, and I was put on board the steamboat *Missouri*, which plied between St. Louis and Galena. The commander of the boat was William B. Culver. I remained on her during the sailing season, which was the most pleasant time for me that I had ever experienced. At the close of navigation I was hired to Mr. John Colburn, keeper of the Missouri Hotel. He was from one of the free states; but a more inveterate hater of the negro I do not believe ever walked God's green earth. This hotel was at that time one of the largest in the city, and there were employed in it twenty or thirty servants, mostly slaves.

Mr. Colburn was very abusive, not only to the servants, but to his wife also, who was an excellent woman, and one from whom I never knew a servant to receive a harsh word; but never did I know a kind one to a servant from her husband. Among the slaves employed in the hotel was one by the name of Aaron, who belonged to Mr. John F. Darby, a lawyer. Aaron was the knife-cleaner. One day, one of the knives was put on the table, not as clean as it might have been. Mr. Colburn, for this offence, tied Aaron up in the wood-house, and gave him over fifty lashes on the bare back with a cow-hide, after which, he made me wash him down with rum. This seemed to put him into more agony than the whipping. After being untied he went home to his master, and complained of the treatment which he had received. Mr. Darby would give no heed to anything he had to say, but sent him directly back. Colburn, learning that he had been to his master with complaints, tied him up again, and gave him a more severe whipping than before. The poor fellow's back was literally cut to pieces; so much so, that he was not able to work for ten or twelve days.

There was, also, among the servants, a girl whose master resided in the country. Her name was Patsey. Mr. Colburn tied her up one evening, and whipped her until several of the boarders came out and begged him to desist. The reason for whipping her was this. She was engaged to be married to a man belonging to Major William Christy, who resided four or five miles north of the city. Mr. Colburn had forbid her to see John Christy. The reason of this was said to be the regard which he himself had for Patsey. She went to meeting that evening, and John returned home with her. Mr. Colburn had intended to flog John, if he came within the inclosure; but John knew too well the temper of his rival, and kept at a safe distance:— so he took vengeance on the poor girl. If all the slave-drivers had been called together, I do not think a more cruel man than John Colburn—and he too a northern man—could have been found among them.

While living at the Missouri hotel, a circumstance occurred which caused me great unhappiness. My master sold my mother, and all her children, except myself. They were sold to different persons in the city of St. Louis.

CHAPTER III

I WAS SOON AFTER taken from Mr. Colburn's, and hired to Elijah P. Lovejoy, who was at that time publisher and editor of the "St. Louis Times." My work, while with him, was mainly in the printing office, waiting on the hands, working the press, &c. Mr. Lovejoy was a very good man, and decidedly the best master that I had ever had. I am chiefly indebted to him, and to my employment in the printing office, for what little learning I obtained while in slavery.

Though slavery is thought, by some, to be mild in Missouri, when compared with the cotton, sugar and rice growing states, yet no part of our slaveholding country is more noted for the barbarity of its inhabitants than St. Louis. It was here that Col. Harney, a United States officer, whipped a slave woman to death. It was here that Francis McIntosh, a free colored man from Pittsburgh, was taken from the steamboat Flora and burned at the stake. During a residence of eight years in this city, numerous cases of extreme cruelty came under my own observation; to record them all would occupy more space than could possibly be allowed in this little volume. I shall, therefore, give but a few more in addition to what I have already related.

Capt. J. B. Brant, who resided near my master, had a slave named John. He was his body servant, carriage driver, &c. On one occasion, while driving his master through the city—the streets being very muddy, and the horses going at a rapid rate—some mud spattered upon a gentleman by the name of Robert More. More was determined to be revenged. Some three or four months after this occurrence, he purchased John, for the express purpose, as he said, "to tame the d— —d nigger." After the purchase he took him to a blacksmith's shop, and had a ball and chain fastened to his leg, and then put him to driving a yoke of oxen, and kept him at hard labor, until the iron around his leg was so worn into the flesh, that it was thought mortification would ensue. In addition to this, John told me that his master whipped him regularly three times a week for the first two months:—and all this to *"tame him."* A more noble looking man than he was not to be found in all St. Louis, before he fell into the hands of More; and a more degraded and spirit-crushed looking being was never seen on a southern plantation, after he had been subjected to this *"taming"* process for three months. The last time that I saw him, he had nearly lost the entire use of his limbs.

While living with Mr. Lovejoy, I was often sent on errands to the office of the "Missouri Republican," published by Mr. Edward Charles. Once, while returning to the office with type, I was attacked by several large boys, sons of slave-holders, who pelted me with snow-balls. Having the heavy form of type in my hands, I could not make my escape by running; so I laid down the type and gave them battle. They gathered around me, pelting me with stones and sticks, until they overpowered me, and would have captured me, if I had not resorted to my heels. Upon my retreat they took possession of the type; and what to do to regain it I could not devise. Knowing Mr. Lovejoy to be a very humane man, I went to the office and laid the case before him. He told me to remain in the office. He took one of the apprentices with him and went after the type, and soon returned with it; but on his return informed me that Samuel McKinney had told him he would whip me, because I had hurt his boy. Soon after, McKinney was seen making his way to the office by one of the printers, who informed me of the fact, and I made my escape through the back door.

McKinney not being able to find me on his arrival, left the office in a great rage, swearing that he would whip me to death. A few days after, as I was walking along Main street, he seized me by the collar, and struck me over the head five or six times with a large cane, which caused the blood to gush from my nose and ears in such a manner that my clothes were completely saturated with blood. After beating me to his satisfaction he let me go, and I returned to the office so weak from the loss of blood that Mr. Lovejoy sent me home to my master. It was five weeks before I was able to walk again. During this time it was necessary to have some one to supply my place at the office, and I lost the situation.

After my recovery, I was hired to Capt. Otis Reynolds, as a waiter on board the steamboat *Enterprise,* owned by Messrs. John and Edward Walsh, commission merchants at St. Louis. This boat was then running on the upper Mississippi. My employment on board was to wait on gentlemen, and the captain being a good man, the situation was a pleasant one to me;—but in passing from place to place, and seeing new faces every day, and knowing that they could go where they pleased, I soon became unhappy, and several times thought of leaving the boat at some landing-place, and trying to make my escape to Canada, which I had heard much about as a place where the slave might live, be free, and be protected.

But whenever such thoughts would come into my mind, my resolution would soon be shaken by the remembrance that my dear mother was a slave in St. Louis, and I could not bear the idea of leaving her in that condition. She had often taken me upon her knee, and told me how she had carried me upon her back to the field when I was an infant—how often she had been whipped for leaving her work to nurse me—and how happy I would appear when she would take me into her arms. When these thoughts came over me, I would resolve never to leave the land of slavery without my mother. I thought that to leave her in slavery, after she had undergone and suffered so much for me, would be proving recreant to the duty which I owed to her. Besides this, I had three brothers and a sister there—two of my brothers having died.

My mother, my brothers Joseph and Millford, and my sister Elizabeth, belonged to Mr. Isaac Mansfield, formerly from one of the free states, (Massachusetts, I believe.) He was a tinner by trade, and carried on a large manufacturing establishment. Of all my relatives, mother was first, and sister next. One evening, while visiting them, I made some allusion to a proposed journey to Canada, and sister took her seat by my side, and taking my hand in hers, said, with tears in her eyes—

"Brother, you are not going to leave mother and your dear sister here without a friend, are you?"

I looked into her face, as the tears coursed swiftly down her cheeks, and bursting into tears myself, said—

"No, I will never desert you and mother!"

She clasped my hand in hers, and said—

"Brother, you have often declared that you would not end your days in slavery. I see no possible way in which you can escape with us; and now, brother, you are on a steamboat where there is some chance for you to escape to a land of liberty. I beseech you not to let us hinder you. If we cannot get our liberty, we do not wish to be the means of keeping you from a land of freedom."

I could restrain my feelings no longer, and an outburst of my own feelings caused her to cease speaking upon that subject. In opposition to their wishes, I pledged myself not to leave them in the hand of the oppressor. I took leave of them, and returned to the boat, and laid down in my bunk; but "sleep departed from mine eyes, and slumber from mine eyelids."

A few weeks after, on our downward passage, the boat took on board, at Hannibal, a drove of slaves, bound for the New Orleans market. They numbered from fifty to sixty, consisting of men and women from eighteen to forty years of age. A drove of slaves on a southern steamboat, bound for the cotton or sugar regions, is an occurrence so common, that no one, not even the passengers, appear to notice it, though they clank their chains at every step. There was, however, one in this gang that attracted the attention of the passengers and crew. It was a beautiful girl, apparently about twenty years of age, perfectly white, with straight light hair and blue eyes. But it was not the whiteness of her skin that created such sensation among those who gazed upon her—it was her almost unparalleled beauty. She had been on the boat but a short time, before the attention of all the passengers, including the ladies, had been called to her, and the common topic of conversation was about the beautiful slave-girl. She was not in chains. The man who claimed this article of human merchandise was a Mr. Walker—a well known slave-trader, residing in St. Louis. There was a general anxiety among the passengers and crew to learn the history of the girl. Her master kept close by her side, and it would have been considered impudent for any of the passengers to have spoken to her, and the crew were not allowed to have any conversation with them. When we reached St. Louis, the slaves were removed to a boat bound for New Orleans, and the history of the beautiful slave-girl remained a mystery.

I remained on the boat during the season, and it was not an unfrequent occurrence to have on board gangs of slaves on their way to the cotton, sugar and rice plantations of the south.

Toward the latter part of the summer Captain Reynolds left the boat, and I was sent home. I was then placed on the farm, under

Mr. Haskell, the overseer. As I had been some time out of the field, and not accustomed to work in the burning sun, it was very hard; but I was compelled to keep up with the best of the hands.

I found a great difference between the work in the steamboat cabin and that in a corn-field.

My master, who was then living in the city, soon after removed to the farm, when I was taken out of the field to work in the house as a waiter. Though his wife was very peevish, and hard to please, I much preferred to be under her control than the overseer's. They brought with them Mr. Sloane, a Presbyterian minister; Miss Martha Tulley, a niece of theirs from Kentucky; and their nephew William. The latter had been in the family a number of years, but the others were all newcomers.

Mr. Sloane was a young minister, who had been at the south but a short time, and it seemed as if his whole aim was to please the slaveholders, especially my master and mistress. He was intending to make a visit during the winter, and he not only tried to please them, but I think he succeeded admirably. When they wanted singing, he sung; when they wanted praying, he prayed; when they wanted a story told, he told a story. Instead of his teaching my master theology, my master taught theology to him. While I was with Captain Reynolds my master "got religion," and new laws were made on the plantation. Formerly we had the privilege of hunting, fishing, making splint brooms, baskets, &c., on Sunday; but this was all stopped. Every Sunday we were all compelled to attend meeting. Master was so religious that he induced some others to join him in hiring a preacher to preach to the slaves.

CHAPTER IV

MY MASTER HAD FAMILY worship, night and morning. At night the slaves were called in to attend; but in the mornings they had to be at their work, and master did all the praying. My master and mistress were great lovers of mint julep, and every morning, a pitcher-full was made, of which they all partook freely, not excepting little master William. After drinking freely all round, they would have family worship, and then breakfast. I cannot say but I loved the julep as well as any of them, and during prayer was always careful to seat myself close to the table where it stood, so as to help myself when they were all busily engaged in their devotions. By the time prayer was over, I was about as happy as any of them. A sad accident happened one morning. In helping myself, and at the same time keeping an eye on my old mistress, I accidentally let the pitcher fall upon the floor, breaking it in pieces, and spilling the contents. This was a bad affair for me; for as soon as prayer was over, I was taken and severely chastised.

My master's family consisted of himself, his wife, and their nephew, William Moore.[1] He was taken into the family when only a few weeks of age. His name being that of my own, mine was changed for the purpose of giving precedence to his, though I was his senior by ten or twelve years. The plantation being four miles from the city, I had to drive the family to church. I always dreaded the approach of the Sabbath; for, during service, I was obliged to stand by the horses in the hot, broiling sun, or in the rain, just as it happened.

One Sabbath, as we were driving past the house of D. D. Page, a gentleman who owned a large baking establishment, as I was sitting upon the box of the carriage, which was very much elevated, I saw Mr. Page pursuing a slave around the yard with a long whip, cutting him at every jump. The man soon escaped from the yard, and was followed by Mr. Page. They came running past us, and the slave, perceiving that he would be overtaken, stopped suddenly, and Page stumbled over him, and falling on the stone pavement, fractured one of his legs, which crippled him for life. The same gentleman, but a short time previous, tied up a woman of his, by the name of Delphia, and whipped her nearly to death; yet he was a deacon in the Baptist church, in good and regular standing. Poor Delphia! I was well acquainted with her, and called to see her while upon her sick bed; and I shall never forget her appearance. She was a member of the same church with her master.

Soon after this, I was hired out to Mr. Walker, the same man whom I have mentioned as having carried a gang of slaves down the river on the steamboat Enterprise. Seeing me in the capacity of a steward on the boat, and thinking that I would make a good hand to take care of slaves, he determined to have me for that purpose; and finding that my master would not sell me, he hired me for the term of one year.

When I learned the fact of my having been hired to a negro speculator, or a "soul driver," as they are generally called among slaves, no one can tell my emotions. Mr. Walker had offered a high price for me, as I afterwards learned, but I suppose my master was restrained from selling me by the fact that I was a near relative of his. On entering the service of Mr. Walker, I found that my opportunity of getting to a land of liberty was gone, at least for the time being. He had a gang of slaves in readiness to start for New Orleans, and in a few days we were on our journey. I am at a loss for language to express my feelings on that occasion. Although my master had told me that he had not sold me, and Mr. Walker had told me that he had not purchased me, I did not believe them; and not until I had been to New Orleans, and was on my return, did I believe that I was not sold.

There was on the boat a large room on the lower deck, in which the slaves were kept, men and women, promiscuously—all chained two and two, and a strict watch kept that they did not get loose; for cases have occurred in which slaves have got off their chains, and made their escape at landing-places, while the boats were taking in wood;—and with all our care, we lost one woman who had been taken from her husband and children, and having no desire to live without them, in the agony of her soul jumped overboard, and drowned herself. She was not chained.

It was almost impossible to keep that part of the boat clean.

On landing at Natchez, the slaves were all carried to the slave-pen, and there kept one week, during which time several of them were sold. Mr. Walker fed his slaves well. We took on board at St. Louis several hundred pounds of bacon (smoked meat) and corn-meal, and his slaves were better fed than slaves generally were in Natchez, so far as my observation extended.

At the end of a week, we left for New Orleans, the place of our final destination, which we reached in two days. Here the slaves were placed in a negro-pen, where those who wished to purchase could call and examine them. The negro-pen is a small yard, sur-rounded by buildings, from fifteen to twenty feet wide, with the ex-ception of a large gate with iron bars. The slaves are kept in the building during the night, and turned out into the yard during the day. After the best of the stock was sold at private sale at the pen, the balance were taken to the Exchange Coffee-House Auction Rooms, kept by Isaac L. McCoy, and sold at public auction. After the sale of this lot of slaves, we left New Orleans for St. Louis.

CHAPTER V

On our arrival at St. Louis I went to Dr. Young, and told him that I did not wish to live with Mr. Walker any longer. I was heart-sick at seeing my fellow-creatures bought and sold. But Mr. Walker had hired me for the year, and stay I must. Mr. Walker again commenced purchasing another gang of slaves. He bought a man of Colonel John O'Fallon, who resided in the suburbs of the city. This man had a wife and three children. As soon as the purchase was made, he was put in jail for safe keeping, until we should be ready to start for New Orleans. His wife visited him while there, several times, and several times when she went for that purpose was refused admittance.

In the course of eight or nine weeks Mr. Walker had his cargo of human flesh made up. There was in this lot a number of old men and women, some of them with gray locks. We left St. Louis in the steamboat Carlton, Captain Swan, bound for New Orleans. On our way down, and before we reached Rodney, the place where we made our first stop, I had to prepare the old slaves for market. I was ordered to have the old men's whiskers shaved off, and the grey hairs plucked out where they were not too numerous, in which case he had a preparation of blacking to color it, and with a blacking brush we would put it on. This was new business to me, and was performed in a room where the passengers could not see us. These slaves were also taught how old they were by Mr. Walker, and after going through the blacking process they looked ten or fifteen years younger; and I am sure that some of those who purchased slaves of Mr. Walker were dreadfully cheated, especially in the ages of the slaves which they bought.

We landed at Rodney, and the slaves were driven to the pen in the back part of the village. Several were sold at this place, during our stay of four or five days, when we proceeded to Natchez. There we landed at night, and the gang were put in the warehouse until morning, when they were driven to the pen. As soon as the slaves are put in these pens, swarms of planters may be seen in and about them. They knew when Walker was expected, as he always had the time advertised beforehand when he would be in Rodney, Natchez, and New Orleans. These were the principal places where he offered his slaves for sale.

When at Natchez the second time, I saw a slave very cruelly whipped. He belonged to a Mr. Broadwell, a merchant who kept a store on the wharf. The slave's name was Lewis. I had known him several years, as he was formerly from St. Louis. We were expecting a steamboat down the river, in which we were to take passage for New Orleans. Mr. Walker sent me to the landing to watch for the boat, ordering me to inform him on its arrival. While there I went into the store to see Lewis. I saw a slave in the store, and asked him where Lewis was. Said he, "They have got Lewis hanging between the heavens and the earth." I asked him what he meant by that. He told me to go into the warehouse and see. I went in, and found Lewis there. He was tied up to a beam, with his toes just touching the floor. As there was no one in the warehouse but himself, I inquired the reason of his being in that situation. He said Mr. Broadwell had sold his wife to a planter six miles from the city, and that he had been to visit her—that he went in the night, expecting to return before daylight, and went without his master's permission. The patrol had taken him up before he reached his wife. He was put in jail, and his master had to pay for his catching and keeping, and that was what he was tied up for.

Just as he finished his story, Mr. Broadwell came in, and inquired what I was doing there. I knew not what to say, and while I was thinking what reply to make he struck me over the head with the cowhide, the end of which struck me over my right eye, sinking deep into the flesh, leaving a scar which I carry to this day. Before I visited Lewis he had received fifty lashes. Mr. Broadwell gave him fifty lashes more after I came out, as I was afterwards informed by Lewis himself.

The next day we proceeded to New Orleans, and put the gang in the same negro-pen which we occupied before. In a short time the planters came flocking to the pen to purchase slaves. Before the slaves were exhibited for sale, they were dressed and driven out into the yard. Some were set to dancing, some to jumping, some to singing, and some to playing cards. This was done to make them appear cheerful and happy. My business was to see that they were placed in those situations before the arrival of the purchasers, and I have often set them to dancing when their cheeks were wet with tears. As slaves were in good demand at that time, they were all soon disposed of, and we again set out for St. Louis.

On our arrival, Mr. Walker purchased a farm five or six miles from the city. He had no family, but made a housekeeper of one of his female slaves. Poor Cynthia! I knew her well. She was a quadroon, and one of the most beautiful women I ever saw. She was a native of St. Louis, and bore an irreproachable character for virtue and propriety of conduct. Mr. Walker bought her for the New Orleans market, and took her down with him on one of the trips that I made with him. Never shall I forget the circumstances of that voyage! On the first night that we were on board the steamboat, he directed me to put her into a state-room he had provided for her, apart from the other slaves. I had seen too much of the workings of slavery not to know what this meant. I accordingly watched him into the state-room, and listened to hear what passed between them. I heard him make his base offers, and her reject them. He told her that if she would accept his vile proposals, he would take her back with him to St. Louis, and establish her as his housekeeper on his farm. But if she persisted in rejecting them, he would sell her as a field hand on the worst plantation on the river. Neither threats nor bribes prevailed, however, and he retired, disappointed of his prey.

The next morning poor Cynthia told me what had passed, and bewailed her sad fate with floods of tears. I comforted and encouraged her all I could; but I foresaw but too well what the result must be. Without entering into any further particulars, suffice it to say that Walker performed his part of the contract at that time. He took her back to St. Louis, established her as his mistress and housekeeper at his farm, and before I left, he had two children by her. But, mark the end! Since I have been at the North, I have been credibly informed that Walker has been married, and, as a previous measure, sold poor Cynthia and her four children (she having had two more since I came away) into hopeless bondage!

He soon commenced purchasing to make up the third gang. We took steamboat, and went to Jefferson City, a town on the Missouri river. Here we landed, and took stage for the interior of the state. He bought a number of slaves as he passed the different farms and villages. After getting twenty-two or twenty-three men and women, we arrived at St. Charles, a village on the banks of the Missouri. Here he purchased a woman who had a child in her arms, appearing to be four or five weeks old.

We had been travelling by land for some days, and were in hopes to have found a boat at this place for St. Louis, but were disappointed. As no boat was expected for some days, we started for St. Louis by land. Mr. Walker had purchased two horses. He rode one, and I the other. The slaves were chained together, and we took up our line of march, Mr. Walker taking the lead, and I bringing up the rear. Though the distance was not more than twenty miles, we did not reach it the first day. The road was worse than any that I have ever travelled.

Soon after we left St. Charles the young child grew very cross, and kept up a noise during the greater part of the day. Mr. Walker complained of its crying several times, and told the mother to stop the child's d——d noise, or he would. The woman tried to keep the child from crying, but could not. We put up at night with an acquaintance of Mr. Walker, and in the morning, just as we were about to start, the child again commenced crying. Walker stepped up to her, and told her to give the child to him. The mother tremblingly obeyed. He took the child by one arm, as you would a cat by the leg, walked into the house, and said to the lady,

"Madam, I will make you a present of this little nigger; it keeps such a noise that I can't bear it."

"Thank you, sir," said the lady.

The mother, as soon as she saw that her child was to be left, ran up to Mr. Walker, and falling upon her knees, begged him to let her have her child; she clung around his legs, and cried, "Oh, my child! my child! master, do let me have my child! oh, do, do, do! I will stop its crying if you will only let me have it again." When I saw this

woman crying for her child so piteously, a shudder—a feeling akin
to horror—shot through my frame. I have often since in imagination heard her crying for her child:—

> "O, master, let me stay to catch
>   My baby's sobbing breath,
> His little glassy eye to watch,
>   And smooth his limbs in death,
>
> And cover him with grass and leaf,
>   Beneath the large oak tree:
> It is not sullenness, but grief—
>   O, master, pity me!
>
> The morn was chill—I spoke no word,
>   But feared my babe might die,
> And heard all day, or thought I heard,
>   My little baby cry.
>
> At noon, oh, how I ran and took
>   My baby to my breast!
> I lingered—and the long lash broke
>   My sleeping infant's rest.
>
> I worked till night—till darkest night,
>   In torture and disgrace;
> Went home and watched till morning light,
>   To see my baby's face.
>
> Then give me but one little hour—
>   O! do not lash me so!
> One little hour—one little hour—
>   And gratefully I'll go."[2]

Mr. Walker commanded her to return into the ranks with the
other slaves. Women who had children were not chained, but those
that had none were. As soon as her child was disposed of she was
chained in the gang.

The following song I have often heard the slaves sing, when about to be carried to the far south. It is said to have been composed by a slave.

"See these poor souls from Africa
Transported to America;
We are stolen, and sold to Georgia—
Will you go along with me?
We are stolen, and sold to Georgia—
Come sound the jubilee!

See wives and husbands sold apart,
Their children's screams will break my heart;—
There's a better day a coming—
Will you go along with me?
There's a better day a coming,
Go sound the jubilee!

O, gracious Lord! when shall it be,
That we poor souls shall all be free?
Lord, break them slavery powers—
Will you go along with me?
Lord, break them slavery powers,
Go sound the jubilee!

Dear Lord, dear Lord, when slavery'll cease,
Then we poor souls will have our peace;—
There's a better day a coming—
Will you go along with me?
There's a better day a coming,
Go sound the jubilee!"*

We finally arrived at Mr. Walker's farm. He had a house built during our absence to put slaves in. It was a kind of domestic jail. The slaves were put in the jail at night, and worked on the farm during

---

*"Sound the Jubilee" (author unknown); recorded by William Wells Brown.

the day. They were kept here until the gang was completed, when we again started for New Orleans, on board the steamboat North America, Capt. Alexander Scott. We had a large number of slaves in this gang. One, by the name of Joe, Mr. Walker was training up to take my place, as my time was nearly out, and glad was I. We made our first stop at Vicksburg, where we remained one week and sold several slaves.

Mr. Walker, though not a good master, had not flogged a slave since I had been with him, though he had threatened me. The slaves were kept in the pen, and he always put up at the best hotel, and kept his wines in his room, for the accommodation of those who called to negotiate with him for the purchase of slaves. One day, while we were at Vicksburg, several gentlemen came to see him for that purpose, and as usual the wine was called for. I took the tray and started around with it, and having accidentally filled some of the glasses too full, the gentlemen spilled the wine on their clothes as they went to drink. Mr. Walker apologized to them for my carelessness, but looked at me as though he would see me again on this subject.

After the gentlemen had left the room, he asked me what I meant by my carelessness, and said that he would attend to me. The next morning he gave me a note to carry to the jailer, and a dollar in money to give to him. I suspected that all was not right, so I went down near the landing, where I met with a sailor, and, walking up to him, asked him if he would be so kind as to read the note for me. He read it over, and then looked at me. I asked him to tell me what was in it. Said he,

"They are going to give you hell."

"Why?" said I.

He said, "This is a note to have you whipped, and says that you have a dollar to pay for it."

He handed me back the note, and off I started. I knew not what to do, but was determined not to be whipped. I went up to the jail—took a look at it, and walked off again. As Mr. Walker was acquainted with the jailer, I feared that I should be found out if I did not go, and be treated in consequence of it still worse.

While I was meditating on the subject, I saw a colored man about my size walk up, and the thought struck me in a moment to send him with my note. I walked up to him, and asked him who he belonged to. He said he was a free man, and had been in the city but a short time. I told him I had a note to go into the jail, and get a trunk to carry to one of the steamboats; but was so busily engaged that I could not do it, although I had a dollar to pay for it. He asked me if I would not give him the job. I handed him the note and the dollar, and off he started for the jail.

I watched to see that he went in, and as soon as I saw the door close behind him, I walked around the corner, and took my station, intending to see how my friend looked when he came out. I had been there but a short time, when a colored man came around the corner, and said to another colored man with whom he was acquainted—

"They are giving a nigger scissors in the jail."

"What for?" said the other. The man continued,

"A nigger came into the jail, and asked for the jailer. The jailer came out, and he handed him a note, and said he wanted to get a trunk. The jailer told him to go with him, and he would give him the trunk. So he took him into the room, and told the nigger to give up the dollar. He said a man had given him the dollar to pay for getting the trunk. But that lie would not answer. So they made him strip himself, and then they tied him down, and are now whipping him."

I stood by all the while listening to their talk, and soon found out that the person alluded to was my customer. I went into the street opposite the jail, and concealed myself in such a manner that I could not be seen by any one coming out. I had been there but a short time, when the young man made his appearance, and looked around for me. I, unobserved, came forth from my hiding place, behind a pile of brick, and he pretty soon saw me, and came up to me complaining bitterly, saying that I had played a trick upon him. I denied any knowledge of what the note contained, and asked him what they had done to him. He told me in substance what I heard the man tell who had come out of the jail.

"Yes," said he, "they whipped me and took my dollar, and gave me this note."

He showed me the note which the jailer had given him, telling him to give it to his master. I told him I would give him fifty cents for it—that being all the money I had. He gave it to me and took his money. He had received twenty lashes on his bare back, with the negro-whip.

I took the note and started for the hotel where I had left Mr. Walker. Upon reaching the hotel, I handed it to a stranger whom I had not seen before, and requested him to read it to me. As near as I can recollect, it was as follows:—

"Dear Sir: —By your direction, I have given your boy twenty lashes. He is a very saucy boy, and tried to make me believe that he did not belong to you, and I put it on to him well for lying to me.

"I remain
"Your obedient servant."

It is true that in most of the slave-holding cities, when a gentleman wishes his servants whipped, he can send him to the jail and have it done. Before I went in where Mr. Walker was, I wet my cheeks a little, as though I had been crying. He looked at me, and inquired what was the matter. I told him that I had never had such a whipping in my life, and handed him the note. He looked at it and laughed;—"And so you told him that you did not belong to me?" "Yes, sir," said I. "I did not know that there was any harm in that." He told me I must behave myself, if I did not want to be whipped again.

This incident shows how it is that slavery makes its victims lying and mean; for which vices it afterwards reproaches them, and uses them as arguments to prove that they deserve no better fate. Had I entertained the same views of right and wrong which I now do, I am sure I should never have practised the deception upon that poor fellow which I did. I know of no act committed by me while in slavery which I have regretted more than that; and I heartily desire that it may be at some time or other in my power to make him amends for his vicarious sufferings in my behalf.

CHAPTER VI

IN A FEW DAYS we reached New Orleans, and arriving there in the night, remained on board until morning. While at New Orleans this time, I saw a slave killed; an account of which has been published by Theodore D. Weld, in his book entitled "Slavery as it is." The circumstances were as follows. In the evening, between seven and eight o'clock, a slave came running down the levee, followed by several men and boys. The whites were crying out, "Stop that nigger! stop that nigger!" while the poor panting slave, in almost breathless accents, was repeating, "I did not steal the meat—I did not steal the meat." The poor man at last took refuge in the river. The whites who were in pursuit of him, run on board of one of the boats to see if they could discover him. They finally espied him under the bow of the steamboat Trenton. They got a pike-pole, and tried to drive him from his hiding place. When they would strike at him he would dive under the water. The water was so cold, that it soon became evident that he must come out or be drowned.

While they were trying to drive him from under the bow of the boat or drown him, he would in broken and imploring accents say, "I did not steal the meat; I did not steal the meat. My master lives up the river. I want to see my master. I did not steal the meat. Do let me go home to master." After punching him, and striking him over the head for some time, he at last sunk in the water, to rise no more alive.

On the end of the pike-pole with which they were striking him was a hook, which caught in his clothing, and they hauled him up on the bow of the boat. Some said he was dead; others said he was *"playing possum;"* while others kicked him to make him get up; but it was of no use—he was dead.

As soon as they became satisfied of this, they commenced leaving, one after another. One of the hands on the boat informed the captain that they had killed the man, and that the dead body was lying on the deck. The captain came on deck, and said to those who were remaining, "You have killed this nigger; now take him off of my boat." The captain's name was Hart. The dead body was dragged on shore and left there. I went on board of the boat where our gang of slaves were, and during the whole night my mind was occupied with what I had seen. Early in the morning I went on shore to see if the dead body remained there. I found it in the same position that it was left the night before. I watched to see what they would do with it. It was left there until between eight and nine o'clock, when a cart, which takes up the trash out of the streets, came along, and the body was thrown in, and in a few minutes more was covered over with dirt which they were removing from the streets. During the whole time, I did not see more than six or seven persons around it, who, from their manner, evidently regarded it as no uncommon occurrence.

During our stay in the city I met with a young white man with whom I was well acquainted in St. Louis. He had been sold into slavery, under the following circumstances. His father was a drunkard, and very poor, with a family of five or six children. The father died, and left the mother to take care of and provide for the children as best she might. The eldest was a boy, named Burrill, about thirteen years of age, who did chores in a store kept by Mr. Riley, to assist his mother in procuring a living for the family. After working with him two years, Mr. Riley took him to New Orleans to wait on him while in that city on a visit, and when he returned to St. Louis, he told the mother of the boy that he had died with the yellow fever. Nothing more was heard from him, no one supposing him to be alive. I was much astonished when Burrill told me his story. Though I sympathized with him I could not assist him. We were both slaves. He was poor, uneducated, and without friends; and, if living, is, I presume, still held as a slave.

After selling out his cargo of human flesh, we returned to St. Louis, and my time was up with Mr. Walker.[3] I had served him one year, and it was the longest year I ever lived.

CHAPTER VII

I WAS SENT HOME, and was glad enough to leave the service of one who was tearing the husband from the wife, the child from the mother, and the sister from the brother—but a trial more severe and heart-rending than any which I had yet met with awaited me. My dear sister had been sold to a man who was going to Natchez, and was lying in jail awaiting the hour of his departure. She had expressed her determination to die, rather than go to the far south, and she was put in jail for safekeeping. I went to the jail the same day that I arrived, but as the jailer was not in I could not see her.

I went home to my master, in the country, and the first day after my return he came where I was at work, and spoke to me very politely. I knew from his appearance that something was the matter. After talking to me about my several journeys to New Orleans with Mr. Walker, he told me that he was hard pressed for money, and as he had sold my mother and all her children except me, he thought it would be better to sell me than any other one, and that as I had been used to living in the city, he thought it probable that I would prefer it to country life. I raised up my head, and looked him full in the face. When my eyes caught his he immediately looked to the ground. After a short pause, I said,

"Master, mother has often told me that you are a near relative of mine, and I have often heard you admit the fact; and after you have hired me out, and received, as I once heard you say, nine hundred dollars for my services—after receiving this large sum, will you sell me to be carried to New Orleans or some other place?"

"No," said he, "I do not intend to sell you to a negro trader. If I had wished to have done that, I might have sold you to Mr. Walker for a large sum, but I would not sell you to a negro trader. You may go to the city, and find you a good master."

"But," said I, "I cannot find a good master in the whole city of St. Louis."

"Why?" said he.

"Because there are no good masters in the state."

"Do you not call me a good master?"

"If you were you would not sell me."

"Now I will give you one week to find a master in, and surely you can do it in that time."

The price set by my evangelical master upon my soul and body was the trifling sum of five hundred dollars. I tried to enter into some arrangement by which I might purchase my freedom; but he would enter into no such arrangement.

I set out for the city with the understanding that I was to return in a week with some one to become my new master. Soon after reaching the city, I went to the jail, to learn if I could once more see my sister; but could not gain admission. I then went to mother, and learned from her that the owner of my sister intended to start for Natchez in a few days.

I went to the jail again the next day, and Mr. Simonds, the keeper, allowed me to see my sister for the last time. I cannot give a just description of the scene at that parting interview. Never, never can be erased from my heart the occurrences of that day! When I entered the room where she was, she was seated in one corner, alone. There were four other women in the same room, belonging to the same man. He had purchased them, he said, for his own use. She was seated with her face towards the door where I entered, yet she did not look up until I walked up to her. As soon as she observed me she sprung up, threw her arms around my neck, leaned her head upon my breast, and, without uttering a word, burst into tears. As soon as she recovered herself sufficiently to speak, she advised me to take mother, and try to get out of slavery. She said there was no hope for herself—that she must live and die a slave. After giving her some advice, and taking from my finger a ring and placing it upon hers, I bade her farewell forever, and returned to my mother, and then and there made up my mind to leave for Canada as soon as possible.

I had been in the city nearly two days, and as I was to be absent only a week, I thought best to get on my journey as soon as possible. In conversing with mother, I found her unwilling to make the attempt to reach a land of liberty, but she counselled me to get my liberty if I could. She said, as all her children were in slavery, she did not wish to leave them. I could not bear the idea of leaving her among those pirates, when there was a prospect of being able to get away from them. After much persuasion I succeeded in inducing her to make the attempt to get away.

The time fixed for our departure was the next night. I had with me a little money that I had received, from time to time, from gentlemen for whom I had done errands. I took my scanty means and purchased some dried beef, crackers and cheese, which I carried to mother, who had provided herself with a bag to carry it in. I occasionally thought of my old master, and of my mission to the city to find a new one. I waited with the most intense anxiety for the appointed time to leave the land of slavery, in search of a land of liberty.

The time at length arrived, and we left the city just as the clock struck nine. We proceeded to the upper part of the city, where I had been two or three times during the day, and selected a skiff to carry us across the river. The boat was not mine, nor did I know to whom it did belong; neither did I care. The boat was fastened with a small pole, which, with the aid of a rail, I soon loosened from its moorings. After hunting round and finding a board to use as an oar, I turned to the city, and bidding it a long farewell, pushed off my boat. The current running very swift, we had not reached the middle of the stream before we were directly opposite the city.

We were soon upon the Illinois shore, and, leaping from the boat, turned it adrift, and the last I saw of it it was going down the river at good speed. We took the main road to Alton, and passed through just at daylight, when we made for the woods, where we remained during the day. Our reason for going into the woods was, that we expected that Mr. Mansfield (the man who owned my mother) would start in pursuit of her as soon as he discovered that she was missing. He also knew that I had been in the city looking for a new master, and we thought probably he would go out to my master's to see if he could find my mother, and in so doing, Dr. Young might be led to suspect that I had gone to Canada to find a purchaser.

We remained in the woods during the day, and as soon as darkness overshadowed the earth, we started again on our gloomy way, having no guide but the NORTH STAR. We continued to travel by night, and secrete ourselves in the woods by day; and every night, before emerging from our hidingplace, we would anxiously look for our friend and leader—the NORTH STAR. And in the language of Pierpont we might have exclaimed,

"Star of the North! while blazing day
Pours round me its full tide of light,
And hides thy pale but faithful ray,
I, too, lie hid, and long for night.
For night;—I dare not walk at noon,
Nor dare I trust the faithless moon,
Nor faithless man, whose burning lust
For gold hath riveted my chain;
No other leader can I trust
But thee, of even the starry train;
For, all the host around thee burning,
Like faithless man, keep turning, turning.

In the dark top of southern pines
I nestled, when the driver's horn
Called to the field, in lengthening lines,
My fellows, at the break of morn.
And there I lay, till thy sweet face
Looked in upon my 'hiding place,'
Star of the North!
Thy light, that no poor slave deceiveth,
Shall set me free."

CHAPTER VIII

As we travelled towards a land of liberty, my heart would at times leap for joy. At other times, being, as I was, almost constantly on my feet, I felt as though I could travel no further. But when I thought of slavery, with its democratic whips—its republican chains—its evangelical blood-hounds, and its religious slave-holders—when I thought of all this paraphernalia of American democracy and religion behind me, and the prospect of liberty before me, I was encouraged to press forward, my heart was strengthened, and I forgot that I was tired or hungry.

On the eighth day of our journey, we had a very heavy rain, and in a few hours after it commenced we had not a dry thread upon our bodies. This made our journey still more unpleasant. On the tenth day, we found ourselves entirely destitute of provisions, and how to obtain any we could not tell. We finally resolved to stop at some farmhouse, and try to get something to eat. We had no sooner determined to do this, than we went to a house, and asked them for some food. We were treated with great kindness, and they not only gave us something to eat, but gave us provisions to carry with us. They advised us to travel by day and lie by at night. Finding ourselves about one hundred and fifty miles from St. Louis, we concluded that it would be safe to travel by daylight, and did not leave the house until the next morning. We travelled on that day through a thickly settled country, and through one small village. Though we were fleeing from a land of oppression, our hearts were still there. My dear sister and two beloved brothers were behind us, and the idea of giving them up, and leaving them forever, made us feel sad. But with all this depression of heart, the thought that I should one day be free, and call my body my own, buoyed me up, and made my heart leap for joy. I had just been telling my mother how I should try to get employment as soon as we reached Canada, and how I intended to purchase us a little farm, and how I would earn money enough to buy sister and brothers, and how happy we would be in our own FREE HOME—when three men came up on horseback, and ordered us to stop.

I turned to the one who appeared to be the principal man, and asked him what he wanted. He said he had a warrant to take us up. The three immediately dismounted, and one took from his pocket a handbill, advertising us as runaways, and offering a reward of two hundred dollars for our apprehension and delivery in the city of St. Louis. The advertisement had been put out by Isaac Mansfield and John Young.

While they were reading the advertisement, mother looked me in the face, and burst into tears. A cold chill ran over me, and such a sensation I never experienced before, and I hope never to again. They took out a rope and tied me, and we were taken back about six miles, to the house of the individual who appeared to be the leader. We reached there about seven o'clock in the evening, had supper, and were separated for the night. Two men remained in the room during the night. Before the family retired to rest, they were all called together to attend prayers. The man who but a few hours before had bound my hands together with a strong cord, read a chapter from the Bible, and then offered up prayer, just as though God had sanctioned the act he had just committed upon a poor, panting, fugitive slave.

The next morning a blacksmith came in, and put a pair of handcuffs on me, and we started on our journey back to the land of whips, chains and Bibles. Mother was not tied, but was closely watched at night. We were carried back in a wagon, and after four days' travel, we came in sight of St. Louis. I cannot describe my feelings upon approaching the city.

As we were crossing the ferry, Mr. Wiggins, the owner of the ferry, came up to me, and inquired what I had been doing that I was in chains. He had not heard that I had run away. In a few minutes we were on the Missouri side, and were taken directly to the jail. On the way thither, I saw several of my friends, who gave me a nod of recognition as I passed them. After reaching the jail, we were locked up in different apartments.

CHAPTER IX

I HAD BEEN IN jail but a short time when I heard that my master was sick, and nothing brought more joy to my heart than that intelligence. I prayed fervently for him—not for his recovery, but for his death. I knew he would be exasperated at having to pay for my apprehension, and knowing his cruelty, I feared him. While in jail, I learned that my sister Elizabeth, who was in prison when we left the city, had been carried off four days before our arrival.

I had been in jail but a few hours when three negro-traders, learning that I was secured thus for running away, came to my prison-house and looked at me, expecting that I would be offered for sale. Mr. Mansfield, the man who owned mother, came into the jail as soon as Mr. Jones, the man who arrested us, informed him that he had brought her back. He told her that he would not whip her, but would sell her to a negro-trader, or take her to New Orleans himself. After being in jail about one week, master sent a man to take me out of jail, and send me home. I was taken out and carried home, and the old man was well enough to sit up. He had me brought into the room where he was, and as I entered, he asked me where I had been? I told him I had acted according to his orders. He had told me to look for a master, and I had been to look for one. He answered that he did not tell me to go to Canada to look for a master. I told him that as I had served him faithfully, and had been the means of putting a number of hundreds of dollars into his pocket, I thought I had a right to my liberty. He said he had promised my father that I should not be sold to supply the New Orleans market, or he would sell me to a negro-trader.

I was ordered to go into the field to work, and was closely watched by the overseer during the day, and locked up at night. The overseer gave me a severe whipping on the second day that I was in the field. I had been at home but a short time, when master was able to ride to the city; and on his return he informed me that he had sold me to Samuel Willi, a merchant tailor. I knew Mr. Willi. I had lived with him three or four months some years before, when he hired me of my master.

Mr. Willi was not considered by his servants as a very bad man, nor was he the best of masters. I went to my new home, and found my new mistress very glad to see me. Mr. Willi owned two servants before he purchased me—Robert and Charlotte. Robert was an excellent white-washer, and hired his time from his master, paying him one dollar per day, besides taking care of himself. He was known in the city by the name of Bob Music. Charlotte was an old woman, who attended to the cooking, washing, &c. Mr. Willi was not a wealthy man, and did not feel able to keep many servants around his house; so he soon decided to hire me out, and as I had been accustomed to service in steamboats, he gave me the privilege of finding such employment.

I soon secured a situation on board the steamer Otto, Capt. J. B. Hill, which sailed from St. Louis to Independence, Missouri. My former master, Dr. Young, did not let Mr. Willi know that I had run away, or he would not have permitted me to go on board a steamboat. The boat was not quite ready to commence running, and therefore I had to remain with Mr. Willi. But during this time, I had to undergo a trial for which I was entirely unprepared. My mother, who had been in jail since her return until the present time, was now about being carried to New Orleans, to die on a cotton, sugar, or rice plantation!

I had been several times to the jail, but could obtain no interview with her. I ascertained, however, the time the boat in which she was to embark would sail, and as I had not seen mother since her being thrown into prison, I felt anxious for the hour of sailing to come. At last, the day arrived when I was to see her for the first time after our painful separation, and, for aught that I knew, for the last time in this world!

At about ten o'clock in the morning I went on board of the boat, and found her there in company with fifty or sixty other slaves. She was chained to another woman. On seeing me, she immediately dropped her head upon her heaving bosom. She moved not, neither did she weep. Her emotions were too deep for tears. I approached, threw my arms around her neck, kissed her, and fell upon my knees, begging her forgiveness, for I thought myself to blame for her sad condition; for if I had not persuaded her to accompany me, she would not then have been in chains.

She finally raised her head, looked me in the face, (and such a look none but an angel can give!) and said, *"My dear son, you are not to blame for my being here. You have done nothing more nor less than your duty. Do not, I pray you, weep for me. I cannot last long upon a cotton plantation. I feel that my heavenly Master will soon call me home, and then I shall be out of the hands of the slave-holders!"*

I could bear no more—my heart struggled to free itself from the human form. In a moment she saw Mr. Mansfield coming toward that part of the boat, and she whispered into my ear, *"My child, we must soon part to meet no more this side of the grave. You have ever said that you would not die a slave; that you would be a freeman. Now try to get your liberty! You will soon have no one to look after but yourself!"* and just as she whispered the last sentence into my ear, Mansfield came up to me, and with an oath, said, "Leave here this instant; you have been the means of my losing one hundred dollars to get this wench back"—at the same time kicking me with a heavy pair of boots. As I left her, she gave one shriek, saying, "God be with you!" It was the last time that I saw her, and the last word I heard her utter.

I walked on shore. The bell was tolling. The boat was about to start. I stood with a heavy heart, waiting to see her leave the wharf. As I thought of my mother, I could but feel that I had lost

> "— — the glory of my life,
> My blessing and my pride!
> I half forgot the name of slave,
> When she was by my side."

The love of liberty that had been burning in my bosom had wellnigh gone out. I felt as though I was ready to die. The boat moved gently from the wharf, and while she glided down the river, I realized that my mother was indeed

> "Gone—gone—sold and gone,
> To the rice swamp, dank and lone!"

After the boat was out of sight I returned home; but my thoughts were so absorbed in what I had witnessed, that I knew not what I was about half of the time. Night came, but it brought no sleep to my eyes.

In a few days, the boat upon which I was to work being ready, I went on board to commence. This employment suited me better than living in the city, and I remained until the close of navigation; though it proved anything but pleasant. The captain was a drunken, profligate, hard-hearted creature, not knowing how to treat himself, or any other person.

The boat, on its second trip, brought down Mr. Walker, the man of whom I have spoken in a previous chapter, as hiring my time. He had between one and two hundred slaves, chained and manacled. Among them was a man that formerly belonged to my old master's brother, Aaron Young. His name was Solomon. He was a preacher, and belonged to the same church with his master. I was glad to see the old man. He wept like a child when he told me how he had been sold from his wife and children.

The boat carried down, while I remained on board, four or five gangs of slaves. Missouri, though a comparatively new state, is very much engaged in raising slaves to supply the southern market. In a former chapter, I have mentioned that I was once in the employ of a slave-trader, or driver, as he is called at the south. For fear that some may think that I have misrepresented a slave-driver, I will here give an extract from a paper published in a slave-holding state, Tennessee, called the "Millennial Trumpeter."

"Droves of negroes, chained together in dozens and scores, and hand-cuffed, have been driven through our country in numbers far surpassing any previous year, and these vile slave-drivers and dealers are swarming like buzzards around a carrion. Through this county, you cannot pass a few miles in the great roads without having every feeling of humanity insulted and lacerated by this spectacle, nor can you go into any county or any neighborhood, scarely, without seeing or hearing of some of these despicable creatures, called negro-drivers.

"Who is a negro-driver? One whose eyes dwell with delight on lacerated bodies of helpless men, women and children; whose soul feels diabolical raptures at the chains, and hand-cuffs, and cart-whips, for inflicting tortures on weeping mothers torn from helpless babes, and on husbands and wives torn asunder forever!"

Dark and revolting as is the picture here drawn, it is from the pen of one living in the midst of slavery. But though these men may cant about negro-drivers, and tell what despicable creatures they are, who is it, I ask, that supplies them with the human beings that they are tearing asunder? I answer, as far as I have any knowledge of the state where I came from, that those who raise slaves for the market are to be found among all classes, from Thomas H. Benton down to the lowest political demagogue who may be able to purchase a woman for the purpose of raising stock, and from the doctor of divinity down to the most humble lay member in the church.

It was not uncommon in St. Louis to pass by an auction-stand, and behold a woman upon the auction-block, and hear the seller crying out, *"How much is offered for this woman? She is a good cook, good washer, a good obedient servant. She has got religion!"* Why should this man tell the purchasers that she has religion? I answer, because in Missouri, and as far as I have any knowledge of slavery in the other states, the religious teaching consists in teaching the slave that he must never strike a white man; that God made him for a slave; and that, when whipped, he must not find fault—for the Bible says, "He that knoweth his master's will and doeth it not, shall be beaten with many stripes!" And slave-holders find such religion very profitable to them.

After leaving the steamer *Otto,* I resided at home, in Mr. Willi's family, and again began to lay my plans for making my escape from slavery. The anxiety to be a freeman would not let me rest day or night. I would think of the northern cities that I had heard so much about;—of Canada, where so many of my acquaintances had found a refuge. I would dream at night that I was in Canada, a freeman, and on waking in the morning, weep to find myself so sadly mistaken.

> "I would think of Victoria's domain,
>   And in a moment I seemed to be there!
> But the fear of being taken again,
>   Soon hurried me back to despair."

Mr. Willi treated me better than Dr. Young ever had; but instead of making me contented and happy, it only rendered me the more miserable, for it enabled me better to appreciate liberty. Mr. Willi was a man who loved money as most men do, and without looking for an opportunity to sell me, he found one in the offer of Captain Enoch Price, a steamboat owner and commission merchant, living in the city of St. Louis. Captain Price tendered seven hundred dollars, which was two hundred more than Mr. Willi had paid. He therefore thought best to accept the offer. I was wanted for a carriage driver, and Mrs. Price was very much pleased with the captain's bargain. His family consisted besides of one child. He had three servants besides myself—one man and two women.

Mrs. Price was very proud of her servants, always keeping them well dressed, and as soon as I had been purchased, she resolved to have a new carriage. And soon one was procured, and all preparations were made for a turn-out in grand style, I being the driver.

One of the female servants was a girl some eighteen or twenty years of age, named Maria. Mrs. Price was very soon determined to have us united, if she could so arrange matters. She would often urge upon me the necessity of having a wife, saying that it would be so pleasant for me to take one in the same family! But getting married, while in slavery, was the last of my thoughts; and had I been ever so inclined, I should not have married Maria, as my love had already gone in another quarter. Mrs. Price soon found out that her efforts at this match-making between Maria and myself would not prove successful. She also discovered (or thought she had) that I was rather partial to a girl named Eliza, who was owned by Dr. Mills. This induced her at once to endeavor the purchase of Eliza, so great was her desire to get me a wife!

Before making the attempt, however, she deemed it best to talk to me a little upon the subject of love, courtship, and marriage. Accordingly, one afternoon she called me into her room—telling me to take a chair and sit down. I did so, thinking it rather strange, for servants are not very often asked thus to sit down in the same room with the master or mistress. She said that she had found out that I did not care enough about Maria to marry her. I told her that was true. She then asked me if there was not a girl in the city that I loved. Well, now, this was coming into too close quarters with me! People, generally, don't like to tell their love stories to everybody that may think fit to ask about them, and it was so with me. But, after blushing a while and recovering myself, I told her that I did not want a wife. She then asked me if I did not think something of Eliza. I told her that I did. She then said that if I wished to marry Eliza, she would purchase her if she could.

I gave but little encouragement to this proposition, as I was determined to make another trial to get my liberty, and I knew that if I should have a wife, I should not be willing to leave her behind; and if I should attempt to bring her with me, the chances would be difficult for success. However, Eliza was purchased, and brought into the family.

CHAPTER X

BUT THE MORE I thought of the trap laid by Mrs. Price to make me satisfied with my new home, by getting me a wife, the more I determined never to marry any woman on earth until I should get my liberty. But this secret I was compelled to keep to myself, which placed me in a very critical position. I must keep upon good terms with Mrs. Price and Eliza. I therefore promised Mrs. Price that I would marry Eliza; but said that I was not then ready. And I had to keep upon good terms with Eliza, for fear that Mrs. Price would find out that I did not intend to get married.

I have here spoken of marriage, and it is very common among slaves themselves to talk of it. And it is common for slaves to be married; or at least to have the marriage ceremony performed. But there is no such thing as slaves being lawfully married. There has never yet a case occurred where a slave has been tried for bigamy. The man may have as many women as he wishes, and the women as many men; and the law takes no cognizance of such acts among slaves. And in fact some masters, when they have sold the husband from the wife, compel her to take another.

There lived opposite Captain Price's, Doctor Farrar, well known in St. Louis. He sold a man named Ben, to one of the traders. He also owned Ben's wife, and in a few days he compelled Sally (that was her name) to marry Peter, another man belonging to him. I asked Sally "why she married Peter so soon after Ben was sold." She said, "because master made her do it."

Mr. John Calvert, who resided near our place, had a woman named Lavinia. She was quite young, and a man to whom she was about to be married was sold, and carried into the country near St. Charles, about twenty miles from St. Louis. Mr. Calvert wanted her to get a husband; but she had resolved not to marry any other man, and she refused. Mr. Calvert whipped her in such a manner that it was thought she would die. Some of the citizens had him arrested, but it was soon hushed up. And that was the last of it. The woman did not die, but it would have been the same if she had.

Captain Price purchased me in the month of October, and I remained with him until December, when the family made a voyage to New Orleans, in a boat owned by himself, and named the *Chester*. I served on board as one of the stewards. On arriving at New Orleans, about the middle of the month, the boat took in freight for Cincinnati; and it was decided that the family should go up the river in her, and what was of more interest to me, I was to accompany them.

The long looked for opportunity to make my escape from slavery was near at hand.

Captain Price had some fears as to the propriety of taking me near a free state, or a place where it was likely I could run away, with a prospect of liberty. He asked me if I had ever been in a free state. "Oh yes," said I, "I have been in Ohio; my master carried me into that state once, but I never liked a free state."

It was soon decided that it would be safe to take me with them, and what made it more safe, Eliza was on the boat with us, and Mrs. Price, to try me, asked if I thought as much as ever of Eliza. I told her that Eliza was very dear to me indeed, and that nothing but death should part us. It was the same as if we were married. This had the desired effect. The boat left New Orleans, and proceeded up the river.

I had at different times obtained little sums of money, which I had reserved for a "rainy day." I procured some cotton cloth, and made me a bag to carry provisions in. The trials of the past were all lost in hopes for the future. The love of liberty, that had been burning in my bosom for years, and had been well-nigh extinguished, was now resuscitated. At night, when all around was peaceful, I would walk the decks, meditating upon my happy prospects.

I should have stated, that, before leaving St. Louis, I went to an old man named Frank, a slave, owned by a Mr. Sarpee. This old man was very distinguished (not only among the slave population, but also the whites) as a fortune-teller. He was about seventy years of age, something over six feet high, and very slender. Indeed, he was so small around his body, that it looked as though it was not strong enough to hold up his head.

Uncle Frank was a very great favorite with the young ladies, who would go to him in great numbers to get their fortunes told. And it was generally believed that he could really penetrate into the mysteries of futurity. Whether true or not, he had the *name*, and that is about half of what one needs in this gullible age. I found Uncle Frank seated in the chimney corner, about ten o'clock at night. As soon as I entered, the old man left his seat. I watched his movement as well as I could by the dim light of the fire. He soon lit a lamp, and coming up, looked me full in the face, saying, "Well, my son, you have come to get uncle to tell your fortune, have you?" "Yes," said I. But how the old man should know what I came for, I could not tell. However, I paid the fee of twenty-five cents, and he commenced by looking into a gourd, filled with water. Whether the old man was a prophet, or the son of a prophet, I cannot say; but there is one thing certain, many of his predictions were verified.

I am no believer in soothsaying; yet I am sometimes at a loss to know how Uncle Frank could tell so accurately what would occur in the future. Among the many things he told was one which was enough to pay me for all the trouble of hunting him up. It was that I *should be free!* He further said, that in trying to get my liberty I would meet with many severe trials. I thought to myself any fool could tell me that!

The first place in which we landed in a free state was Cairo, a small village at the mouth of the Ohio river. We remained here but a few hours, when we proceeded to Louisville. After unloading some of the cargo, the boat started on her upward trip. The next day was the first of January. I had looked forward to New Year's day as the commencement of a new era in the history of my life. I had decided upon leaving the peculiar institution that day.

During the last night that I served in slavery I did not close my eyes a single moment. When not thinking of the future, my mind dwelt on the past. The love of a dear mother, a dear sister, and three dear brothers, yet living, caused me to shed many tears. If I could only have been assured of their being dead, I should have felt satisfied; but I imagined I saw my dear mother in the cotton-field, followed by a merciless taskmaster, and no one to speak a consoling word to her! I beheld my dear sister in the hands of a slave-driver, and compelled to submit to his cruelty! None but one placed in such a situation can for a moment imagine the intense agony to which these reflections subjected me.

CHAPTER XI

AT LAST THE TIME for action arrived. The boat landed at a point
which appeared to me the place of all others to start from. I found
that it would be impossible to carry anything with me but what was
upon my person. I had some provisions, and a single suit of clothes,
about half worn. When the boat was discharging her cargo, and the
passengers engaged carrying their baggage on and off shore, I improved the opportunity to convey myself with my little effects on
land. Taking up a trunk, I went up the wharf, and was soon out of
the crowd. I made directly for the woods, where I remained until
night, knowing well that I could not travel, even in the state of
Ohio, during the day, without danger of being arrested.

I had long since made up my mind that I would not trust myself
in the hands of any man, white or colored. The slave is brought up
to look upon every white man as an enemy to him and his race; and
twenty-one years in slavery had taught me that there were traitors,
even among colored people. After dark, I emerged from the woods
into a narrow path, which led me into the main travelled road. But
I knew not which way to go. I did not know north from south, east
from west. I looked in vain for the North Star; a heavy cloud hid it
from my view. I walked up and down the road until near midnight,
when the clouds disappeared, and I welcomed the sight of my
friend—truly the slave's friend—the North Star!

As soon as I saw it, I knew my course, and before daylight I travelled twenty or twenty-five miles. It being in the winter, I suffered
intensely from the cold; being without an overcoat, and my other
clothes rather thin for the season. I was provided with a tinder-box,
so that I could make up a fire when necessary. And but for this, I
should certainly have frozen to death; for I was determined not to
go to any house for shelter. I knew of a man belonging to Gen.
Ashly, of St. Louis, who had run away near Cincinnati, on the way

to Washington, but had been caught and carried back into slavery; and I felt that a similar fate awaited me, should I be seen by any one. I travelled at night, and lay by during the day.

On the fourth day my provisions gave out, and then what to do I could not tell. Have something to eat I must; but how to get it was the question! On the first night after my food was gone, I went to a barn on the road-side and there found some ears of corn. I took ten or twelve of them, and kept on my journey. During the next day, while in the woods, I roasted my corn and feasted upon it, thanking God that I was so well provided for.

My escape to a land of freedom now appeared certain, and the prospects of the future occupied a great part of my thoughts. What should be my occupation, was a subject of much anxiety to me; and the next thing what should be my name? I have before stated that my old master, Dr. Young, had no children of his own, but had with him a nephew, the son of his brother, Benjamin Young. When this boy was brought to Dr. Young, his name being William, the same as mine, my mother was ordered to change mine to something else. This, at the time, I thought to be one of the most cruel acts that could be committed upon my rights; and I received several very severe whippings for telling people that my name was William, after orders were given to change it. Though young, I was old enough to place a high appreciation upon my name. It was decided, however, to call me "Sandford," and this name I was known by, not only upon my master's plantation, but up to the time that I made my escape. I was sold under the name of Sandford.

But as soon as the subject came to my mind, I resolved on adopting my old name of William, and let Sandford go by the board, for I always hated it. Not because there was anything peculiar in the name; but because it had been forced upon me. It is sometimes common, at the south, for slaves to take the name of their masters. Some have a legitimate right to do so. But I always detested the idea of being called by the name of either of my masters. And as for my father, I would rather have adopted the name of "Friday," and been known as the servant of some Robinson Crusoe,[4] than to have taken his name. So I was not only hunting for my liberty, but also hunting for a name; though I regarded the latter as of little consequence, if I could but gain the former. Travelling along the road, I would sometimes speak to myself, sounding my name over, by way of getting used to it, before I should arrive among civilized human beings. On the fifth or six day, it rained very fast, and froze about as fast as it fell, so that my clothes were one glare of ice. I travelled on at night until I became so chilled and benumbed—the wind blowing into my face—that I found it impossible to go any further, and accordingly took shelter in a barn, where I was obliged to walk about to keep from freezing.

I have ever looked upon that night as the most eventful part of my escape from slavery. Nothing but the providence of God, and that old barn, saved me from freezing to death. I received a very severe cold, which settled upon my lungs, and from time to time my feet had been frostbitten, so that it was with difficulty I could walk. In this situation I travelled two days, when I found that I must seek shelter somewhere, or die.

The thought of death was nothing frightful to me, compared with that of being caught, and again carried back into slavery. Nothing but the prospect of enjoying liberty could have induced me to undergo such trials, for

> "Behind I left the whips and chains,
> Before me were sweet Freedom's plains!"

This, and this alone, cheered me onward. But I at last resolved to seek protection from the inclemency of the weather, and therefore I secured myself behind some logs and brush, intending to wait there until some one should pass by; for I thought it probable that I might see some colored person, or, if not, some one who was not a slave-holder; for I had an idea that I should know a slave-holder as far as I could see him.

The first person that passed was a man in a buggy-wagon. He looked too genteel for me to hail him. Very soon another passed by on horseback. I attempted to speak to him, but fear made my voice fail me. As he passed, I left my hidingplace and was approaching the road, when I observed an old man walking towards me, leading a white horse. He had on a broad-brimmed hat and a very long coat, and was evidently walking for exercise. As soon as I saw him, and observed his dress, I thought to myself, "You are the man that I have been looking for!" Nor was I mistaken. He was the very man!

On approaching me, he asked me, "if I was not a slave." I looked at him some time, and then asked him "if he knew of any one who would help me, as I was sick." He answered that he would; but again asked, if I was not a slave. I told him I was. He then said that I was in a very pro-slavery neighborhood, and if I would wait until he went home, he would get a covered wagon for me. I promised to remain. He mounted his horse, and was soon out of sight.

After he was gone, I meditated whether to wait or not; being apprehensive that he had gone for some one to arrest me. But I finally concluded to remain until he should return; removing some few rods to watch his movements. After a suspense of an hour and a half or more, he returned with a two-horse covered wagon, such as are usually seen under the shed of a Quaker[5] meetinghouse on Sundays and Thursdays; for the old man proved to be a Quaker of the George Fox stamp.

He took me to his house, but it was some time before I could be induced to enter it; not until the old lady came out, did I venture into the house. I thought I saw something in the old lady's cap that told me I was not only safe, welcome, in her house. I was not, however, prepared to receive their hospitalities. The only fault I found with them was their being too kind. I had never had a white man treat me as an equal, and the idea of a white lady waiting on me at the table was still worse! Though the table was loaded with the good things of this life, I could not eat. I thought if I could only be allowed the privilege of eating in the kitchen I should be more than satisfied!

Finding that I could not eat, the old lady, who was a "Thompsonian," made me a cup of "composition," or "number six;" but it was so strong and hot, that I called it *"number seven!"* However, I soon found myself at home in this family. On different occasions, when telling these facts, I have been asked how I felt upon finding myself regarded as a man by a white family; especially just having run away from one. I cannot say that I have ever answered the question yet.

The fact that I was in all probability a freeman, sounded in my ears like a charm. I am satisfied that none but a slave could place such an appreciation upon liberty as I did at that time. I wanted to see mother and sister, that I might tell them "I was free!" I wanted to see my fellow-slaves in St. Louis, and let them know that the chains were no longer upon my limbs. I wanted to see Captain

Price, and let him learn from my own lips that I was no more a chattel, but a man! I was anxious, too, thus to inform Mrs. Price that she must get another coachman. And I wanted to see Eliza more than I did either Mr. or Mrs. Price!

The fact that I was a freeman—could walk, talk, eat and sleep, as a man, and no one to stand over me with the blood-clotted cowhide—all this made me feel that I was not myself.

The kind friend that had taken me in was named Wells Brown.[6] He was a devoted friend of the slave; but was very old, and not in the enjoyment of good health. After being by the fire awhile, I found that my feet had been very much frozen. I was seized with a fever, which threatened to confine me to my bed. But my Thompsonian friends soon raised me, treating me as kindly as if I had been one of their own children. I remained with them twelve or fifteen days, during which time they made me some clothing, and the old gentleman purchased me a pair of boots.

I found that I was about fifty or sixty miles from Dayton, in the State of Ohio, and between one and two hundred miles from Cleaveland, on Lake Erie, a place I was desirous of reaching on my way to Canada. This I know will sound strangely to the ears of people in foreign lands, but it is nevertheless true. An American citizen was fleeing from a democratic, republican, Christian government, to receive protection under the monarchy of Great Britain.* While the people of the United States boast of their freedom, they at the same time keep three millions of their own citizens in chains; and while I am seated here in sight of Bunker Hill Monument,[7] writing this narrative, I am a slave, and no law, not even in Massachusetts, can protect me from the hands of the slave-holder!

Before leaving this good Quaker friend, he inquired what my name was besides William. I told him that I had no other name. "Well," said he, "thee must have another name. Since thee has got out of slavery, thee has become a man, and men always have two names."

---

*In 1833 Great Britain passed the Abolition of Slavery Act, providing for the emancipation of slaves throughout the British Empire; it took effect in August 1834.

I told him that he was the first man to extend the hand of friendship to me, and I would give him the privilege of naming me.

"If I name thee," said he, "I shall call thee Wells Brown, after myself."

"But," said I, "I am not willing to lose my name of William. As it was taken from me once against my will, I am not willing to part with it again upon any terms.

"Then," said he, "I will call thee William Wells Brown."

"So be it," said I; and I have been known by that name ever since I left the house of my first white friend, Wells Brown.

After giving me some little change, I again started for Canada. In four days I reached a public house, and went in to warm myself. I there learned that some fugitive slaves had just passed through the place. The men in the bar-room were talking about it, and I thought that it must have been myself they referred to, and I was therefore afraid to start, fearing they would seize me; but I finally mustered courage enough, and took my leave. As soon as I was out of sight, I went into the woods, and remained there until night, when I again regained the road, and travelled on until next day.

Not having had any food for nearly two days, I was faint with hunger, and was in a dilemma what to do, as the little cash supplied me by my adopted father, and which had contributed to my comfort, was now all gone. I however concluded to go to a farmhouse, and ask for something to eat. On approaching the door of the first one presenting itself, I knocked, and was soon met by a man who asked me what I wanted. I told him that I would like something to eat. He asked me where I was from, and where I was going. I replied that I had come some way, and was going to Cleaveland.

After hesitating a moment or two, he told me that he could give me nothing to eat, adding, "that if I would work, I could get something to eat."

I felt bad, being thus refused something to sustain nature, but did not dare tell him that I was a slave.

Just as I was leaving the door, with a heavy heart, a woman, who proved to be the wife of this gentleman, came to the door, and asked her husband what I wanted. He did not seem inclined to inform her. She therefore asked me herself. I told her that I had asked for something to eat. After a few other questions, she told me to come in, and that she would give me something to eat.

I walked up to the door, but the husband remained in the passage, as if unwilling to let me enter.

She asked him two or three times to get out of the way, and let me in. But as he did not move, she pushed him on one side, bidding me walk in! I was never before so glad to see a woman push a man aside! Ever since that act, I have been in favor of "woman's rights!"

After giving me as much food as I could eat, she presented me with ten cents, all the money then at her disposal, accompanied with a note to a friend, a few miles further on the road. Thanking this angel of mercy from an overflowing heart, I pushed on my way, and in three days arrived at Cleaveland, Ohio.

Being an entire stranger in this place, it was difficult for me to find where to stop. I had no money, and the lake being frozen, I saw that I must remain until the opening of the navigation, or go to Canada by way of Buffalo. But believing myself to be somewhat out of danger, I secured an engagement at the Mansion House, as a table waiter, in payment for my board. The proprietor, however, whose name was E. M. Segur, in a short time, hired me for twelve dollars a month; on which terms I remained until spring, when I found good employment on board a lake steamboat.

I purchased some books, and at leisure moments perused them with considerable advantage to myself. While at Cleaveland, I saw, for the first time, an anti-slavery newspaper. It was the *"Genius of Universal Emancipation,"* published by Benjamin Lundy; and though I had no home, I subscribed for the paper. It was my great desire, being out of slavery myself, to do what I could for the emancipation of my brethren yet in chains, and while on Lake Erie, I found many opportunities of "helping their cause along."

It is well known that a great number of fugitives make their escape to Canada, by way of Cleaveland; and while on the lakes, I always made arrangement to carry them on the boat to Buffalo or Detroit, and thus effect their escape to the "promised land." The friends of the slave, knowing that I would transport them without charge, never failed to have a delegation when the boat arrived at Cleaveland. I have sometimes had four or five on board at one time.

In the year 1842, I conveyed, from the first of May to the first of December, sixty-nine fugitives over Lake Erie to Canada. In 1843, I visited Malden, in Upper Canada, and counted seventeen in that small village, whom I had assisted in reaching Canada. Soon after coming north I subscribed for the *Liberator*, edited by that champion of freedom, William Lloyd Garrison. I had heard nothing of the anti-slavery movement while in slavery, and as soon as I found that my enslaved countrymen had friends who were laboring for their liberation, I felt anxious to join them, and give what aid I could to the cause.

I early embraced the temperance cause, and found that a temperance reformation was needed among my colored brethren. In company with a few friends, I commenced a temperance reformation among the colored people in the city of Buffalo, and labored three years, in which time a society was built up, numbering over five hundred out of a population of less than seven hundred.

In the autumn, 1843, impressed with the importance of spreading anti-slavery truth, as a means to bring about the abolition of slavery, I commenced lecturing as an agent of the western New York Anti-Slavery Society, and have ever since devoted my time to the cause of my enslaved countrymen.

From the Liberty Bell of 1848

THE AMERICAN SLAVE-TRADE

BY WILLIAM WELLS BROWN

OF THE MANY FEATURES which American slavery presents, the most cruel is that of the slave-trade. A traffic in the bodies and souls of native-born Americans is carried on in the slave-holding states to an extent little dreamed of by the great mass of the people in the non-slave-holding states. The precise number of slaves carried from the slave-raising to the slave-consuming states we have no means of knowing. But it must be very great, as forty thousand were sold and carried out of the State of Virginia in one single year!

This heart-rending and cruel traffic is not confined to any particular class of persons. No person forfeits his or her character or standing in society by being engaged in raising and selling slaves to supply the cotton, sugar, and rice plantations of the south. Few persons who have visited the slave states have not, on their return, told of the gangs of slaves they had seen on their way to the southern market. This trade presents some of the most revolting and atrocious scenes which can be imagined. Slave-prisons, slave-auctions, handcuffs, whips, chains, bloodhounds, and other instruments of cruelty, are part of the furniture which belongs to the American slave-trade. It is enough to make humanity bleed at every pore, to see these implements of torture.

Known to God only is the amount of human agony and suffering which sends its cry from these slave-prisons, unheard or unheeded by man, up to His ear; mothers weeping for their children— breaking the night-silence with the shrieks of their breaking hearts. We wish no human being to experience emotions of needless pain, but we do wish that every man, woman, and child in New England, could visit a southern slave-prison and auction-stand.

I shall never forget a scene which took place in the city of St. Louis, while I was in slavery. A man and his wife, both slaves, were brought from the country to the city, for sale. They were taken to the rooms of Austin & Savage, auctioneers. Several slave-speculators, who are always to be found at auctions where slaves are to be sold, were present. The man was first put up, and sold to the highest bidder. The wife was next ordered to ascend the platform. I was present. She slowly obeyed the order. The auctioneer commenced, and soon several hundred dollars were bid. My eyes were intensely fixed on the face of the woman, whose cheeks were wet with tears. But a conversation between the slave and his new master attracted my attention. I drew near them to listen. The slave was begging his new master to purchase his wife. Said he, "Master, if you will only buy Fanny, I know you will get the worth of your money. She is a good cook, a good washer, and her last mistress liked her very much. If you will only buy her how happy I shall be." The new master replied that he did not want her, but if she sold cheap he would purchase her. I watched the countenance of the man while the different persons were bidding on his wife. When his new master bid on his wife you could see the smile upon his countenance, and the tears stop; but as soon as another would bid, you could see the countenance change and the tears start afresh. From this change of countenance one could see the workings of the inmost soul. But this suspense did not last long; the wife was struck off to the highest bidder, who proved not to be the owner of her husband. As soon as they became aware that they were to be separated, they both burst into tears; and as she descended from the auction-stand, the husband, walking up to her and taking her by the hand, said, "Well, Fanny, we are to part forever, on earth; you have been a good wife to me. I did all that I could to get my new master to buy you; but he did not want you, and all I have to say is, I hope you will try to meet me in heaven. I shall try to meet you there." The wife made no reply, but her sobs and cries told, too well, her own feelings. I saw the countenances of a number of whites who were present, and whose eyes were dim with tears at hearing the man bid his wife farewell.

Such are but common occurrences in the slave states. At these auction-stands, bones, muscles, sinews, blood and nerves, of human beings, are sold with as much indifference as a farmer in the north sells a horse or sheep. And this great American nation is, at the present time, engaged in the slave-trade. I have before me now the Washington "Union," the organ of the government, in which I find an advertisement of several slaves to be sold for the benefit of the government.[8] They will, in all human probability, find homes among the rice-swamps of Georgia, or the cane-brakes of Mississippi.

With every disposition on the part of those who are engaged in it to veil the truth, certain facts have, from time to time, transpired, sufficient to show, if not the full amount of the evil, at least that it is one of prodigious magnitude. And what is more to be wondered at, is the fact that the greatest slave-market is to be found at the capital of the country! The American slave-trader marches by the capitol with his "coffle-gang,"—the stars and stripes waving over their heads, and the constitution of the United States in his pocket!

The Alexandria Gazette, speaking of the slave-trade at the capital, says, "Here you may behold fathers and brothers leaving behind them the dearest objects of affection, and moving slowly along in the mute agony of despair; there, the young mother, sobbing over the infant whose innocent smile seems but to increase her misery. From some you will hear the burst of bitter lamentation, while from others, the loud hysteric laugh breaks forth, denoting still deeper agony. Such is but a faint picture of the American slave-trade."

BOSTON, MASSACHUSETTS.

THE BLIND SLAVE BOY

by Mrs. Bailey

Come back to me mother! why linger away
From thy poor little blind boy the long weary day!
I mark every footstep, I list to each tone,
And wonder my mother should leave me alone!
There are voices of sorrow, and voices of glee,
But there's no one to joy or to sorrow with me;

For each hath of pleasure and trouble his share,
And none for the poor little blind boy will care.

My mother, come back to me! close to thy breast
Once more let thy poor little blind boy be pressed;
Once more let me feel thy warm breath on my cheek,
And hear thee in accents of tenderness speak.
O mother! I've no one to love me—no heart
Can bear like thine own in my sorrows a part,
No hand is so gentle, no voice is so kind,
Oh! none like a mother can cherish the blind!

Poor blind one! No mother thy wailing can hear,
No mother can hasten to banish thy fear;
For the slave-owner drives her o'er mountain and wild,
And for one paltry dollar hath sold thee, poor child;
Ah, who can in language of mortals reveal
The anguish that none but a mother can feel.
When man in his vile lust of mammon hath trod
On her child, who is stricken or smitten of God!

Blind, helpless, forsaken, with strangers alone,
She hears in her anguish his piteous moan;
As he eagerly listens—but listens in vain—
To catch the loved tones of his mother again!
The curse of the broken in spirit shall fall
On the wretch who hath mingled this wormwood and gall,
And his gain like a mildew shall blight and destroy,
Who hath torn from his mother the little blind boy!

APPENDIX

IN GIVING A HISTORY of my own sufferings in slavery, as well as the sufferings of others with which I was acquainted, or which came under my immediate observation, I have spoken harshly of slaveholders, in church and state.

Nor am I inclined to apologize for anything which I have said. There are exceptions among slaveholders, as well as among other sinners; and the fact that a slaveholder feeds his slaves better, clothes them better, than another, does not alter the case; he is a slaveholder. I do not ask the slaveholder to feed, clothe, or to treat his victim better as a slave. I am not waging a warfare against the collateral evils, or what are sometimes called the abuses, of slavery. I wage a war against slavery itself, because it takes man down from the lofty position which God intended he should occupy, and places him upon a level with the beasts of the field. It decrees that the slave shall not worship God according to the dictates of his own conscience; it denies him the word of God; it makes him a chattel, and sells him in the market to the highest bidder; it decrees that he shall not protect the wife of his bosom; it takes from him every right which God gave him. Clothing and food are as nothing compared with liberty. What care I for clothing or food, while I am the slave of another? You may take me and put cloth upon my back, boots upon my feet, a hat upon my head, and cram a beef-steak down my throat, and all of this will not satisfy me as long as I know that you have the power to tear me from my dearest relatives. All I ask of the slaveholder is to give the slave his liberty. It is freedom I ask for the *slave*. And that the American slave will eventually get his freedom, no one can doubt. You cannot keep the human mind forever locked up in darkness. A ray of light, a spark from freedom's altar, the idea of inherent right, each, all, will become fixed in the soul; and that moment his "limbs swell beyond the measure of his chains," that moment he is free; then it is that the slave dies to become a freeman; then it is felt that one hour of virtuous liberty is worth an eternity of bondage; then it is, in the madness and fury of his blood, that the excited soul exclaims,

> "From life without freedom, oh! who would not fly;
> For one day of freedom, oh! who would not die?"

The rising of the slaves in Southampton, Virginia, in 1831,[9] has not been forgotten by the American people. Nat Turner, a slave for life,—a Baptist minister,—entertained the idea that he was another Moses, whose duty it was to lead his people out of bondage. His soul was fired with the love of liberty, and he declared to his fellow-slaves that the time had arrived, and that "They who would be free, themselves must strike the blow." He knew that it would be "liberty or death" with his little band of patriots, numbering less than three hundred. He commenced the struggle for liberty; he knew his cause was just, and he loved liberty more than he feared death. He did not wish to take the lives of the whites; he only demanded that himself and brethren might be free. The slaveholders found that men whose souls were burning for liberty, however small their numbers, could not be put down at their pleasure; that something more than water was wanted to extinguish the flame. They trembled at the idea of meeting men in open combat, whose backs they had lacerated, whose wives and daughters they had torn from their bosoms, whose hearts were bleeding from the wounds inflicted by them. They appealed to the United States government for assistance. A company of United States troops was sent into Virginia to put down men whose only offence was, that they wanted to be free. Yes! northern men, men born and brought up in the free states, at the demand of slavery, marched to its rescue. They succeeded in reducing the poor slave again to his chains; but they did not succeed in crushing his spirit.

Not the combined powers of the American Union, not the slaveholders, with all their northern allies, can extinguish that burning desire of freedom in the slave's soul! Northern men may stand by as the body-guard of slaveholders. They may succeed for the time being in keeping the slave in his chains; but unless the slaveholders liberate their victims, and that, too, speedily, some modern Hannibal will make his appearance in the southern states, who will trouble the slaveholders as the noble Carthaginian did the Romans. Abolitionists deprecate the shedding of blood; they have warned the slaveholders again and again. Yet they will not give heed, but still persist in robbing the slave of liberty.

"But for the fear of northern bayonets, pledged for the master's protection, the slaves would long since have wrung a peaceful emancipation from the fears of their oppressors, or sealed their own redemption in blood." To the shame of the northern people, the slaveholders confess that to them they are "indebted for a permanent safe-guard against insurrection;" that "a million of their slaves stand ready to strike for liberty at the first tap of the drum;" and but for the aid of the north they would be too weak to keep them in their chains. I ask in the language of the slave's poet,*

> "What! shall ye guard your neighbor still,
> While woman shrieks beneath his rod,
> And while he tramples down at will
> The image of a common God?
> Shall watch and ward be 'round him set,
> Of northern nerve and bayonet?"

The countenance of the people at the north has quieted the fears of the slaveholders, especially the countenance which they receive from northern churches. "But for the countenance of the northern church, the southern conscience would have long since awakened to its guilt: and the impious sight of a church made up of slaveholders, and called the church of Christ, been scouted from the world." So says a distinguished writer.

Slaveholders hide themselves behind the church. A more praying, preaching, psalm-singing people cannot be found than the slaveholders at the south. The religion of the south is referred to every day, to prove that slaveholders are good, pious men. But with

---

*John Greenleaf Whittier (1807–1892); the passage is from Whittier's "Stanzas for the Times," written in 1835 following a pro-slavery meeting at Boston's Faneuil Hall, where restrictions on free speech were advocated to thwart the abolitionists.

all their pretensions, and all the aid which they get from the northern church, they cannot succeed in deceiving the Christian portion of the world. Their child-robbing, man-stealing, woman-whipping, chain-forging, marriage-destroying, slave-manufacturing, man-slaying religion, will not be received as genuine; and the people of the free states cannot expect to live in union with slaveholders, without becoming contaminated with slavery. They are looked upon as one people; they *are* one people; the people in the free and slave states form the "American Union." Slavery is a national institution. The nation licenses men to traffic in the bodies and souls of men; it supplies them with public buildings at the capital of the country to keep their victims in. For a paltry sum it gives the auctioneer a license to sell American men, women, and children, upon the auction-stand. The American slave-trader, with the constitution in his hat and his license in his pocket, marches his gang of chained men and women under the very eaves of the nation's capitol. And this, too, in a country professing to be the freest nation in the world. They profess to be democrats, republicans, and to believe in the natural equality of men; that they are "all created with certain inalienable rights, among which are life, liberty, and the pursuit of happiness." They call themselves a Christian nation; they rob three millions of their countrymen of their liberties, and then talk of their piety, their democracy and their love of liberty; and in the language of Shakspeare, say,

> "And thus I clothe my naked villany,
> And seem a saint when most I play the devil."*

The people of the United States, with all their high professions, are forging chains for unborn millions, in their wars for slavery. With all their democracy, there is not a foot of land over which the "stars and stripes" fly, upon which the American slave can stand and claim protection. Whenever the United States constitution has jurisdiction, and the American flag is seen flying, they point out the

---

*Lines from Shakespeare's *Richard III* (act 1, scene 3): "And thus I clothe my naked villany / With odd old ends stol'n forth of holy writ / And seem a saint when most I play the devil."

slave as a chattel, a thing, a piece of property. But I thank God there is one spot in America upon which the slave can stand and be a man. No matter whether the claimant be a United States president, or a doctor of divinity; no matter with what solemnities some American court may have pronounced him a slave; the moment he makes his escape from under the "stars and stripes," and sets foot upon the soil of CANADA, "the altar and the god sink together in the dust; his soul walks abroad in his own majesty; his body swells beyond the measure of his chains, that burst from around him; and he stands redeemed, regenerated, and disenthralled, by the irresistible genius of universal emancipation."

But slavery must and will be banished from the United States soil:

> "Let tyrants scorn, while tyrants dare,
> The shrieks and writhings of despair;
> The end will come, it will not wait,
> Bonds, yokes, and scourges have their date;
> Slavery itself must pass away,
> And be a tale of yesterday."

But I will now stop, and let the slaveholders speak for themselves. I shall here present some evidences of the treatment which slaves receive from their masters; after which I will present a few of the slave-laws. And it has been said, and I believe truly, that no people were ever found to be better than their laws. And, as an American slave,—as one who is identified with the slaves of the south by the scars which I carry on my back,—as one identified with them by the tenderest ties of nature,—as one whose highest aspirations are to serve the cause of truth and freedom,—I beg of the reader not to lay this book down until he or she has read every page it contains. I ask it not for my own sake, but for the sake of three millions who cannot speak for themselves.

From the Livingston County (Alabama) Whig of Nov. 16, 1845

"Negro Dogs.—The undersigned having bought the entire pack of Negro Dogs, (of the Hays & Allen stock,) he now proposes to catch runaway Negroes. His charge will be three dollars per day for hunting, and fifteen dollars for catching a runaway. He resides three and a half miles north of Livingston, near the lower Jones' Bluff road.

"William Gambrel.

"Nov. 6, 1845."

The Wilmington [North Carolina] Advertiser of July 13, 1838, contains the following advertisement:

"Ranaway, my Negro man Richard. A reward of $25 will be paid for his apprehension, DEAD or ALIVE. Satisfactory proof will only be required of his being killed. He has with him, in all probability, his wife Eliza, who ran away from Col. Thompson, now a resident of Alabama, about the time he commenced his journey to that state.

"D.H. Rhodes."

The St. Louis Gazette says—

"A wealthy man here had a boy named Reuben, almost white, whom he caused to be branded in the face with the words 'A slave for life.' "

From the N. C. Standard, July 28, 1838.

"Twenty Dollars Reward.—Ranaway from the subscriber, a negro woman and two children; the woman is tall and black, and *a few days before she went off* I burnt her on the left side of her face: I tried to make the letter M, *and she kept a cloth over her head and face, and a fly bonnet over her head, so as to cover the burn;* her children are both boys, the oldest is in his seventh year; he is a *mulatto* and has blue eyes; the youngest is a black, and is in his fifth year.

"Micajah Ricks, Nash County."

"One of my neighbors sold to a speculator a negro boy, about 14 years old. It was more than his poor mother could bear. Her reason fled, and she became a perfect *maniac,* and had to be kept in close confinement. She would occasionally get out and run off to the neighbors. On one of these occasions she came to my house. With tears rolling down her cheeks, and her frame shaking with agony, she would cry out, *'Don't you hear him—they are whipping him now, and he is calling for me!'* This neighbor of mine, who tore the boy away from his poor mother, and thus broke her heart, was a *member of the Presbyterian church."—Rev. Francis Hawley, Baptist minister, Colebrook, Ct.*

A colored man in the city of St. Louis was taken by a mob, and burnt alive at the stake. A bystander gives the following account of the scene:—

"After the flames had surrounded their prey, and when his clothes were in a blaze all over him, his eyes burnt out of his head, and his mouth seemingly parched to a cinder, some one in the *crowd*, more compassionate then the rest, proposed to put an end to his misery by shooting him, when it was replied, that it would be of no use, since he was already out of his pain. 'No,' said the wretch, 'I am not, I am suffering as much as ever,—shoot me, shoot me.' 'No, no,' said one of the fiends, who was standing about the sacrifice they were roasting, 'he shall not be shot; I would sooner slacken the fire, if that would increase his misery;' and the man who said this was, we understand, an *officer of justice."—Alton Telegraph.*

"We have been informed that the slave William, who murdered his master (Huskey) some weeks since, was taken by a party a few days since from the sheriff of Hot Spring, and *burned alive!* yes, tied up to the limb of a tree and a fire built under him, and consumed in a slow lingering torture."—*Arkansas Gazette,* Oct. 29, 1836.

The Natchez Free Trader, 16th June, 1842, gives a horrible account of the execution of the negro Joseph on the 5th of that month for murder.

"The body," says the paper, "was taken and chained to a tree immediately on the bank of the Mississippi, on what is called Union Point. The torches were lighted and placed in the pile. He watched unmoved the curling flame as it grew, until it began to entwine itself around and feed upon his body; then he sent forth cries of agony painful to the ear, begging some one to blow his brains out; at the same time surging with almost superhuman strength, until the staple with which the chain was fastened to the tree, not being well secured, drew out, and he leaped from the burning pile. At that moment the sharp ring of several rifles was heard, and the body of the negro fell a corpse to the ground. He was picked up by two or three, and again thrown into the fire and consumed."

"Another Negro burned.—We learn from the clerk of the Highlander, that, while wooding a short distance below the mouth of Red river, they were *invited to stop a short time and see another negro burned.*"—*New Orleans Bulletin.*

"We can assure the Bostonians, one and all, who have embarked in the nefarious scheme of abolishing slavery at the south, that lashes will hereafter be spared the backs of their emissaries. Let them send out their men to Louisiana; they will never return to tell their sufferings, but they shall expiate the crime of interfering in our domestic institutions by being burned at the stake."—*New Orleans True American.*

"The cry of the whole south should be death, instant death, to the abolitionist, wherever he is caught."—*Augusta (Geo.) Chronicle.*

"Let us declare through the public journals of our country, that the question of slavery is not and shall not be open for discussion: that the system is too deep-rooted among us, and must remain forever; that the very moment any private individual attempts to lecture us upon its evils and immorality, and the necessity of putting means in operation to secure us from them, in the same moment his tongue shall be cut out and cast upon the dunghill."—*Columbia (S. C.) Telescope.*[10]

From the St. Louis Republican.

"On Friday last the coroner held an inquest at the house of Judge Dunica, a few miles south of the city, over the body of a negro girl, about 8 years of age, belonging to Mr. Cordell. The body exhibited evidence of the most cruel whipping and beating we have ever heard of. The flesh on the back and limbs were beaten to a jelly—one shoulder-bone was laid bare—there were several cuts, apparently from a club, on the head—and around the neck was the indentation of a cord, by which it is supposed she had been confined to a tree. She had been hired by a man by the name of Tanner, residing in the neighborhood, and was sent home in this condition. After coming home, her constant request, until her death, was for bread, by which it would seem that she had been starved as well as unmercifully whipped. The jury returned a verdict that she came to her death by the blows inflicted by some persons unknown whilst she was in the employ of Mr. Tanner. Mrs. Tanner has been tried and acquitted."

A correspondent of the *N.Y. Herald* writes from St. Louis, Oct. 19:

"I yesterday visited the cell of Cornelia, the slave charged with being the accomplice of Mrs. Ann Tanner (recently acquitted) in the murder of a little negro girl, by whipping and starvation. She admits her participancy, but says she was compelled to take the part she did in the affair. On one occasion she says the child was tied to a tree from Monday morning till Friday night, exposed by day to the scorching rays of the sun, and by night to the stinging of myriads of musquitoes; and that during all this time the child had nothing to eat, but was whipped daily. The child told the same story to Dr. McDowell."

From the Carroll County Mississippian, May 4th, 1844.

"Committed to jail in this place, on the 29th of April last, a runaway slave named Creesy, and says she belongs to William Barrow, of Carroll county, Mississippi. Said woman is stout built, five feet four inches high, and appears to be about twenty years of age; she has a band of iron on each ankle, and a trace chain around her neck, fastened with a common padlock.

"J. N. Spencer, Jailer.

"May 15, 1844."

The Savannah, Ga., Republican of the 13th of March, 1845, contains an advertisement, one item of which is as follows:—

"Also, at the same time and place, the following negro slaves, to wit: Charles, Peggy, Antonnett, Davy, September, Maria, Jenny, and Isaac—levied on as the property of Henry T. Hall, to satisfy a mortgage fi. fia. issued out of McIntosh Superior Court, in favor of the board of directors of the *Theological Seminary of the Synod of South Carolina and Georgia,* vs. said Henry T. Hall. Conditions, cash.

"C. O'Neal, Deputy Sheriff, M.C."

In the *"Macon (Georgia) Telegraph,"* May 28, is the following:

"About the first of March last, the negro man Ransom left me, without the least provocation whatever. I will give a reward of $20 dollars for said negro, if taken dead or alive,—and if killed in any attempt an advance of $5 will be paid.

"Bryant Johnson.
"Crawford Co., Ga."

From the Apalachicola Gazette, May 9.

"One Hundred and Fifty Dollars Reward.—Ranaway from my plantation on the 6th inst., three negro men, all of dark complexion.

"Bill is about five feet four inches high, aged about twenty-six, *a scar on his upper lip,* also *one on his shoulder,* and has been *badly cut on his arm;* speaks quick and broken, and a venomous look.

"Daniel is about the same height, chunky and well set, broad, flat mouth, with a pleasing countenance, rather inclined to show his teeth when talking, no particular marks recollected, aged about twenty-three.

"Noah is about six feet three or four inches high, twenty-eight years old, with rather a down, impudent look, insolent in his discourse, with a large mark on his breast, *a good many large scars,* caused by the whip, on his back—*has been shot in the back of his arm* with small shot. The above reward will be paid to any one who will kill the three, or fifty for each one, or twenty dollars apiece for them delivered to me at my plantation alive, on Chattahoochie, Early county.

"J. McDonald."

From the Alabama Beacon, June 14, 1845.

"Ranaway, on the 15th of May, from me, a negro woman named Fanny. Said woman is twenty years old; is rather tall, can read and write, and so forge passes for herself. Carried away with her a pair of ear-rings, a Bible with a red cover, is very pious. She prays a great deal, and was, as supposed, contented and happy. She is as white as most white women, with straight light hair, and blue eyes, and can pass herself for a white woman. I will give five hundred dollars for her apprehension and delivery to me. She is very intelligent.

"John Balch.
"Tuscaloosa, May, 29, 1845."

From the N. O. Commercial Bulletin, Sept. 30.

"Ten Dollars Reward.—Ranaway from the subscribers, on the 15th of last month, the negro man Charles, about 45 years of age, 5 feet 6 inches high; red complexion, has had the *upper lid of his right eye torn, and a scar on his forehead;* speaks English only, and stutters when spoken to; he had on when he left, *an iron collar, the prongs of which he broke off before absconding.* The above reward will be paid for the arrest of said slave.

"W. E. & R. Murphy,
"132 Old Raisin."

From the N. O. Bee, Oct. 5.

"Ranaway from the residence of Messrs. F. Duncom & Co., the negro Francois, aged from 25 to 30 years, about 5 feet 1 inch in height; the *upper front teeth are missing;* he had *chains on both of his legs,* dressed with a kind of blouse made of sackcloth. A proportionate reward will be given to whoever will bring him back to the bakery, No. 74, Bourbon street."

From the N. O. Picayune of Sunday, Dec. 17.

"Cock-Pit.—*Benefit of Fire Company No. 1, Lafayette.* —A cock-fight will take place on Sunday, the 17th inst., at the well-known house of the subscriber. As the entire proceeds are for the benefit of the fire company, a full attendance is respectfully solicited.
"*Corner of Josephine and Tchoupitolas streets, Lafayette.*"

From the N. O. Picayune.

"Turkey Shooting.—This day, Dec. 17, from 10 o'clock, A. M., until 6 o'clock, P. M., and the following Sundays at M'Donoughville, opposite the Second Municipality Ferry."

The next is an advertisement from the *New Orleans Bee,* an equally popular paper.

"A Bull Fight, between a ferocious bull and a number of dogs, will take place on Sunday next, at $4\frac{1}{4}$ o'clock, P. M., on the other side of the river, at Algiers, opposite Canal street. After the bull fight, a fight will take place between a bear and some dogs. The whole to conclude by a combat between an ass and several dogs.

"Amateurs bringing dogs to participate in the fight will be admitted gratis. Admittance—Boxes, 50 cts.; Pit, 30 cts. The spectacle will be repeated every Sunday, weather permitting.

"Pepe Llulla."

Extracts from the American Slave Code.

The following are mostly abridged selections from the statutes of the slave states and of the United States. They give but a faint view of the cruel oppression to which the slaves are subject, but a strong one enough, it is thought, to fill every honest heart with a deep abhorrence of the atrocious system. Most of the important provisions here cited, though placed under the name of only one state, prevail in nearly all the states, with slight variations in language, and some diversity in the penalties. The extracts have been made in part from Stroud's Sketch of the Slave Laws, but chiefly from authorized editions of the statute books referred to, found in the Philadelphia Law Library. As the compiler has not had access to many of the later enactments of the several states, nearly all he has cited are acts of an earlier date than that of the present anti-slavery movement, so that their severity cannot be ascribed to its influence.

The cardinal principal of slavery, that the slave is not to be ranked among *sentient beings,* but among things—is an article of property, a chattel personal—obtains as undoubted law in all the slave states.*—*Stroud's Sketch*, p. 22.

The dominion of the master is as unlimited as is that which is tolerated by the laws of any civilized country in relation to brute animals—to *quadrupeds;* to use the words of the civil law.— *Ib.* 24.

Slaves cannot even contract matrimony.[†]—*Ib.* 61.

LOUISIANA.—A slave is one who is in the power of his master, to whom he belongs. The master may sell him, dispose of his person, his industry and his labor; he can do nothing, possess nothing, nor acquire anything, but what must belong to his master.— *Civil Code*, Art. 35.

Slaves are incapable of inheriting or transmitting property.— *Civil Code*, Art. 945; also Art. 175, and *Code of Practice*, Art. 103.

Martin's Digest, Act of June 7, 1806.—Slaves shall always be reputed and considered real estate; shall be as such subject to be mortgaged, according to the rules prescribed by law, and they shall be seized and sold as real estate.—*Vol. I.*, p. 612.

Dig. Stat. Sec 13—No owner of slaves shall hire his slaves to themselves, under a penalty of twenty-five dollars for each offence.—*Vol. 1.*, p. 102.

Sec. 15.—No slave can possess anything in his own right, or dispose of the produce of his own industry, without the consent of his master.—p. 103.

Sec. 16.—No slave can be party in a civil suit, or witness in a civil or criminal matter, against any white person.—p. 103. *See also Civil Code*, Art. 117, p. 28.

Sec. 18.—A slave's subordination to his master is susceptible of no restriction, (except in what incites to crime,) and he owes to him and all his family, respect without bounds, and absolute obedience.—p. 103.

---

*In accordance with this doctrine, an act of Maryland, 1798, enumerates among articles of property, *"slaves, working beasts, animals of any kind, stock, furniture, plate, and so forth."*—*Ib* 23. [author's note]

†A slave is not admonished for incontinence, punished for adultery, nor prosecuted for bigamy.—*Attorney General of Maryland, Md. Rep. Vol I.* 561. [author's note]

Sec. 25.—Every slave found on horseback, without a written permission from his master, shall receive twenty-five lashes.—p. 105.

Sec. 32.—Any freeholder may seize and correct any slave found absent from his usual place of work or residence, without some white person, and if the slave resist or try to escape, he may use arms, and if the slave *assult** and strike him, he may *kill* the slave.— p. 109—p. 115.

Sec. 35.—It is lawful to fire upon runaway negroes who are armed, and upon those who, when pursued, refuse to surrender.—p. 109.

Sec. 38.—No slave may buy, sell, or exchange any kind of goods, or hold any boat, or bring up for his own use any horses or cattle, under a penalty of forfeiting the whole.—p. 110.

Sec. 7.—Slaves or free colored persons are punished with *death* for wilfully burning or destroying any stack of produce or any building.

Sec. 15.—The punishment of a slave for striking a white person, shall be for the first and second offences at the discretion of the court,[†] but not extending to life or limb, and for the third offence *death;* but for grievously wounding or mutilating a white person, *death* for the first offence; provided, if the blow or wound is given in defence of the person or *property of his master,* or the person having charge of him, he is entirely justified.

Act of Feb. 22, 1824, Sec. 2.—A slave for wilfully striking his master or mistress, or the child of either, or his white overseer, so as to cause a bruise or shedding of blood, *shall be punished with death.*—p. 125.

Act of March 6, 1819.—Any person cutting or breaking any iron chain or collar used to prevent the escape of slaves, shall be fined not less than two hundred dollars, nor more than one thousand dollars, and be imprisoned not more than two years nor less than six months.—p. 64 of the session.

Law of January 8, 1813, Sec. 71.—All slaves sentenced to death or perpetual imprisonment, in virtue of existing laws, shall be paid for out of the public treasury, provided the sum paid shall not exceed $300 for each slave.

---

*The legal meaning of assult is to *offer* to do personal violence. [author's note]
†A court for the trial of slaves consists of one justice of the peace, and three freeholders, and the justice and one freeholder, i.e., *one half the court, may convict, though the other two are for acquittal.—Martin's Dig.,* I. 646. [author's note]

Law of March 16, 1830, Sec. 93.—The state treasurer shall pay the owners the value of all slaves whose punishment has been commuted from that of death to that of imprisonment for life, &c.

If any slave shall *happen* to be slain for refusing to surrender him or herself, contrary to law, or in unlawfully resisting any officer or *other person,* who shall apprehend, or endeavor to apprehend, such slave or slaves, &c., such officer or *other person so killing such slave as aforesaid,* making resistance, shall be, and he is by this act, *indemnified,* from any prosecution for such killing aforesaid, &c.—*Maryland Laws, act of* 1751, *chap xiv.,* §9.

And by the negro act of 1740 of South Carolina,[11] it is declared:

If any slave who shall be out of the house or plantation where such slave shall live, or shall be usually employed, or without some white person in company with such slave, shall *refuse to submit* to undergo the examination of *any white* person, it shall be lawful for such white person to pursue, apprehend, and moderately correct such slave; and if such slave shall assault and strike such white person, such slave may be *lawfully killed!!*—2 *Brevard's Digest,* 231.

MISSISSIPPI. *Chapt.* 92, Sec. 110.—Penalty for any slave or free colored person exercising the functions of a minister of the gospel, thirty-nine lashes; but any master may permit his slave to preach on his own premises, no slaves but his own being permitted to assemble.—*Digest of Stat.,* p. 770.

Act of June 18, 1822, Sec. 21.—No negro or mulatto can be a witness in any case, except against negroes or mulattoes.—p. 749. *New Code,* 372.

Sec. 25.—Any master licensing his slave to go at large and trade as a freeman, shall forfeit fifty dollars to the state for the literary fund.

Penalty for teaching a slave to read, imprisonment one year. For using language having a *tendency* to promote discontent among free colored people, or insubordination among slaves, imprisonment at *hard labor,* not less than three, nor more than twenty-one years, or death, at the discretion of the court.—*L. M. Child's Appeal,* p. 70.

Sec. 26.—It is *lawful* for *any* person, and the duty of every sheriff, deputy-sheriff, coroner and constable to apprehend any slave going at large, or hired out by him, or herself, and take him or her before a justice of the peace, who shall impose a penalty of not less than twenty dollars, nor more than fifty dollars, on the owner, who has permitted such slave to do so.

Sec. 32.—Any negro or mulatto, for using abusive language, or lifting his hand in opposition to any white person, (except in self-defence against a wanton assault,) shall, on proof of the offence by oath of such person, receive such punishment as a justice of the peace may order, not exceeding thirty-nine lashes.

Sec. 41.—Forbids the holding of cattle, sheep or hogs by slaves, even with consent of the master, under penalty of forfeiture, half to the county, and half to the *informer*.

Sec. 42—Forbids a slave keeping a dog, under a penalty of twenty-five stripes; and requires any master who permits it to pay a fine of five dollars, and make good all damages done by such dog.

Sec. 43—Forbids slaves cultivating cotton for his own use, and imposes a fine of fifty dollars on the master or overseer who permits it.

Revised Code.—Every negro or mulatto found in the state, not able to show himself entitled to freedom, may be sold as a slave— p. 389. The owner of any plantation, on which a slave comes without written leave from his master, and not on lawful business, may inflict ten lashes for every such offence.—p. 371.

ALABAMA.—*Aiken's Digest.* Tit. *Slaves, &c.,* Sec. 31.—For *attempting* to teach any free colored person, or slave, to spell, read or write, a fine of not less than two hundred and fifty dollars, nor more than five hundred dollars!—p. 397.

Sec. 35 and 36.—Any free colored person found with slaves in a kitchen, outhouse or negro quarter, without a written permission from the master or overseer of said slaves, and any slave found without such permission with a free negro on his premises, shall receive fifteen lashes for the first offence, and thirty-nine for each subsequent offence; to be inflicted by master, overseer, or member of any patrol company.—p. 397.

Toulmin's Digest.—No slave can be emancipated but by a *special* act of the Legislature.—p. 623.

Act Jan. 1st, 1823—Authorizes an agent to be appointed by the governor of the state, *to sell for the benefit of the state* all persons of color brought into the United States and within the jurisdiction of Alabama, *contrary to the laws of congress prohibiting the slave trade.*— p. 643.

GEORGIA.—*Prince's Digest.* Act Dec. 19, 1818.—Penalty for any free person of color (except regularly articled seamen) coming into the state, a fine of one hundred dollars on failure of payment to be sold as a slave.—p. 465.

Penalty for permitting a slave to labor or do business for himself, except on his master's premises, thirty dollars per week.—p. 457.

No slave can be a party to any suit against a white man, except on claim of his freedom, *and every colored person is presumed to be a slave, unless he can prove himself free.*—p. 446.

Act Dec. 13, 1792—Forbids the assembling of negroes under pretence of divine worship, contrary to the act regulating patrols, p. 342. This act provides that any justice of the peace may disperse any assembly of slaves which *may* endanger the peace; and every slave found at such meeting shall receive, *without trial,* twenty-five stripes!—p. 447.

Any person who sees more than seven men slaves without any white person, in a high road, may whip each slave *twenty* lashes.—p. 454.

Any slave who harbors a runaway, may suffer punishment *to any extent,* not affecting life or limb.—p. 452.

SOUTH CAROLINA.—*Brevard's Digest.*—Slaves shall be deemed sold, taken, reputed, and adjudged in law to be *chattels personal* in the hands of their owners and possessors, and their executors, administrators, and assigns, *to all intents, constructions and purposes whatever.*—Vol. ii., p. 229.

Act of 1740, in the preamble, states that "*many* owners of slaves and others that have the management of them do confine them *so closely to hard labor,* that they have *not sufficient time for natural rest,*" and enacts that no slave shall be compelled to labor more than *fifteen* hours in the twenty-four from March 25th to Sept. 25th, or *fourteen* in the twenty-four for the rest of the year. Penalty from £5 to £20.—Vol. ii., p. 243.

[Yet, in several of the slave states, the time of work for *criminals* whose *punishment* is hard labor, is eight hours a day for three months, nine hours for two months, and ten for the rest of the year.]

A slave endeavoring to entice another slave to run away, if provision be prepared for the purpose of aiding or abetting such endeavor, shall suffer *death.*—pp. 233 and 244.

Penalty for cruelly scalding or burning a slave, cutting out his tongue, putting out his eye, or depriving him of any limb, a fine of £100. For beating with a *horse*-whip, cow-skin, switch or small stick, or putting irons on, or imprisoning a slave, *no penalty or prohibition.*—p. 241.

Any person who, not having lawful authority to do so, shall beat a slave, so as to disable him from *working*, shall pay fifteen shillings a day *to the owner*, for the slave's lost time, and the charge of his cure.—pp. 231 and 232.

A slave claiming his freedom may sue for it by some friend who will act as guardian, but if the action be judged groundless, said guardian shall pay *double* costs of suit, and such damages to the owner as the court may decide.—p. 260.

Any assembly of slaves or free colored persons, in a secret or confined place, for mental instruction, (even if white persons *are* present,) is an unlawful meeting, and magistrates must disperse it, breaking doors if necessary, and may inflict *twenty lashes* upon each slave or colored person present.—pp. 254 and 255.

Meetings for religious worship, before sunrise, or after 9 o'clock, P. M., unless a majority are white persons, are forbidden; and magistrates are required to disperse them.—p. 261.

A slave who lets loose any boat from the place where the owner has fastened it, for the first *offence shall receive thirty-nine lashes, and for the second shall have one ear cut off.*—p. 228.

James' Digest.—Penalty for *killing* a slave, on *sudden heat of passion*, or by *undue correction*, a fine of $500 and imprisonment not over six months.—p. 392.

NORTH CAROLINA.—*Haywood's Manual.*—Act of 1798, Sec. 3, enacts, that the killing of a slave shall be punished like that of a free man; *except* in the case of a slave *out-lawed*,* or a slave *offering to resist* his master, or a slave *dying under moderate correction.*—p. 530.

Act of 1799.—Any slave set free, except for meritorious services, to be adjudged of by the county court, may be seized by any freeholder, committed to jail, *and sold to the highest bidder.*[†]—p. 525.

---

*A slave may be out-lawed when he runs away, conceals himself, and, to sustain life, kills a hog, or any animal of the cattle kind.—*Haywood's Manual*, p. 521. [author's note]

[†]In South Carolina, *any* person may seize such freed man and keep him as his property. [author's note]

Patrols are not liable to the master for punishing his slave, unless their conduct clearly shows malice *against the master.*—*Hawk's Reps.,* vol. i., p. 418.

TENNESSEE.—*Stat. Law,* Chap. 57, Sec. 1.—Penalty on master for hiring to any slave his own time, a fine of not less than one dollar nor more than two dollars a day, *half* to the informer.— p. 679.

Chap. 2, Sec. 102.—No slave can be emancipated but on condition of immediately removing from the state, and the person emancipating shall give bond, in a sum equal to the slave's value, to have him removed.—p. 279.

Laws of 1813. Chap. 35.—In the trial of slaves, the sheriff chooses the court, which must consist of three justices and twelve *slaveholders* to serve as jurors.

ARKANSAS.—*Rev. Stat.,* Sec. 4, requires the patrol to visit all places suspected of unlawful assemblages of slaves; and sec. 5 provides that any slave found at such assembly, or strolling about without a pass, *shall receive* any number of *lashes,* at the discretion of the patrol, not exceeding twenty.—p. 604.

MISSOURI.—*Laws, I.*—Any master may commit to jail, there to remain, at *his pleasure,* any slave who refuses to obey him or his overseer.—p. 309.

Whether a slave claiming freedom may even commence a suit for it, may depend on the decision of a single judge.—*Stroud's Sketch,* p. 78, note which refers to Missouri laws, I., 404.

KENTUCKY.—*Dig. of Stat.,* Act Feb. 8, 1798, Sec. 5.—No colored person may *keep* or *carry* gun, powder, shot, *club* or *other weapon,* on penalty of *thirty-nine lashes,* and forfeiting the weapon, which any person is authorized to take.

VIRGINIA.—*Rev. Code.*—Any emancipated slave remaining in the state more than a year, may be sold by the overseers of the *poor,* for the benefit of the *literary fund!*—Vol. i., p. 436.

Any slave or free colored person found at any school for teaching reading or writing, by day or night, may be whipped, at the discretion of a justice, not exceeding twenty lashes.—p. 424.

Suppl. Rev. Code.—Any white person assembling with slaves, for the *purpose* of teaching them to read or write, shall be fined, not less than 10 dollars, nor more than 100 dollars; or with free colored persons, shall be fined not more than fifty dollars, and imprisoned not more than two months.—p. 245.

By the revised code, *seventy-one* offences are punished with *death* when commited by slaves, and by nothing more than imprisonment when by the whites.—*Stroud's Sketch*, p. 107.

Rev. Code.—In the trial of slaves, the court consists of five justices without juries, even in capital cases.—I., p. 420.

MARYLAND.—*Stat. Law*, Sec. 8.—Any slave, for rambling in the night, or riding horses by day without leave, or running away may be punished by whipping, cropping, or branding in the cheek, or otherwise, not rendering him unfit for labor.—p. 237.

Any slave convicted of petty treason, murder, or *wilful burning of dwelling houses*, may be sentenced *to have the right hand cut off, to be hanged in the usual manner, the head severed from the body, the body divided into four quarters, and the head and quarters set up in the most public place in the country where such fact was committed!!*—p. 190.

Act 1717, Chap. 13, Sec. 5—Provides that any free colored person marrying a slave, becomes a slave for life, except mulattoes born of white women.

DELAWARE.—*Laws.*—More than six men slaves, meeting together, not belonging to one master, unless on lawful business of their owners, may be whipped to the extent of twenty-one lashes each.—p. 104.

UNITED STATES.—*Constitution.*—The chief proslavery provisions of the constitution, as is generally known, are, 1st, that by virtue of which the slave states are represented in congress for three-fifths of their slaves;* 2nd, that requiring the giving up of any runaway slaves to their masters: 3rd, that pledging the physical force of the whole country to suppress insurrections, i.e., attempts to gain freedom by such means as the framers of the instrument themselves used.

Act of Feb. 12, 1793—Provides that any master or his agent may seize any person whom he claims as a "fugitive from service," and take him before a judge of the U.S. court, or magistrate of the city

---

*By the operation of this provision, twelve slaveholding states, whose white population only equals that of New York and Ohio, send to congress 24 senators and 102 representatives, while these two states only send 4 senators and 59 representatives. [author's note]

or county where he is taken, and the magistrate, on proof, in support of the claim, to his satisfaction, must give the claimant a certificate authorizing the removal of such fugitive to the state he fled from.*

DISTRICT OF COLUMBIA.—The act of congress incorporating Washington city, gives the corporation power to prescribe the terms and conditions on which free negroes and mulattoes may reside in the city. *City Laws*, 6 and 11. By this authority, the city in 1827 enacted that any free colored person coming there to reside, should give the mayor satisfactory evidence of his freedom, and enter into bond with two freehold sureties, in the sum of five hundred dollars, for his good conduct, to be renewed each year for three years; or failing to do so, must leave the city, or be committed to the workhouse, for not more than one year, and if he still refuse to go, may be again committed for the same period, and so on.—*Ib.* 198.

Colored persons residing in the city, who cannot prove their title to freedom, shall be imprisoned as absconding slaves.—*Ib.* 198.

Colored persons found without free papers may be arrested as runaway slaves, and after two months' notice, if no claimant appears, must be advertised ten days, and sold to pay their jail fees.†— *Stroud,* 85, note.

The city of Washington grants a license to *trade in slaves,* for profit, as agent, or otherwise, for four hundred dollars.—*City Laws,* p. 249.

Reader, you uphold these laws *while you do nothing for their repeal.* You *can do* much. You can take and read the antislavery journals. They will give you an impartial history of the cause, and arguments with which to convert its enemies. You can countenance and aid those who are laboring for its promotion. You can petition against

---

* Thus it may be seen that a *man* may be doomed to slavery by an authority not considered sufficient to settle a claim of *twenty dollars.* [author's note]

† The prisons of the district, built with the money of the nation, are used as storehouses of the slaveholder's human merchandise. "From the statement of the keeper of a jail at Washington, it appears that in five years, upwards of 450 colored persons were committed to the national prison in that city, for safekeeping, i.e., until they could be disposed of in the course of the *slave trade,* besides nearly 300 who had been taken up as runaways."—*Miner's Speech in H. Rep.,* 1829. [author's note]

slavery; you can refuse to vote for slaveholders or pro-slavery men, constitutions and compacts; can abstain from products of slave labor; and can use your social influence to spread right principles and awaken a right feeling. Be as earnest for freedom as its foes are for slavery, and you can diffuse an anti-slavery sentiment through your whole neighborhood, and merit "the blessing of them that are ready to perish."

*   *   *   *

The following is from the old colonial law of North Carolina:

Notice of the commitment of runaways—viz., 1741, c. 24, §29. "An act concerning servants and slaves."

Copy of notice containing a full description of such runaway and his clothing.—The sheriff is to "cause a copy of such notice to be sent to the clerk or reader of each church or chapel within his county, who are hereby required to make publication thereof by setting up the same in some open and convenient place, near the said church or chapel, on every Lord's day, during the space of two months from the date thereof."

1741, c. 24, §45.—"Which proclamation shall be published on a Sabbath day at the door of every church or chapel, or, for want of such, at the place where divine service shall be performed in the said county, by the parish clerk or reader, immediately after divine service; and if any slave or slaves, against whom proclamation hath been thus issued, stay out and do not immediately return home, it shall be lawful for any person or persons whatsoever to kill and destroy such slave or slaves by such way or means as he or she shall think fit, without accusation or impeachment of any crime for the same."

It is well known that slavery makes labor disreputable in the slave states. Laboring men of the north, hear how contemptibly slaveholders speak of you.

Mr. Robert Wickliffe of Kentucky, in a speech published in the Louisville Advertiser, in opposition to those who were averse to the importation of slaves from the states, thus discourseth:

"Gentlemen wanted to drive out the black population that they may obtain white negroes in their place. White negroes have this advantage over black negroes, they can be converted into voters; and the men who live upon the sweat of their brow, and pay them but a dependent and scanty subsistence, can, if able to keep then thousand of them in employment, come up to the polls and change the destiny of the country.

"How improved will be our condition when we have such white negroes as perform the servile labors of Europe, of old England, and he would add now of *New England,* when our body servants and our cart drivers, and our street sweepers, are *white negroes* instead of black. Where will be the independence, the proud spirit, and chivalry of the Kentuckians then?"

"We believe the servitude which prevails in the south far preferable to that of the *north,* or in Europe. Slavery will exist in all communities. There is a class which may be nominally free, but they will be virtually *slaves.*"—*Mississippian, July 6th, 1838.*

"Those who depend on their daily labor for their daily subsistence can never enter into political affairs, they never do, never will, never can."—*B. W. Leigh in Virginia Convention,* 1829.

"All society settles down into a classification of capitalists and laborers. The former will *own* the latter, either collectively through the government, or individually in a state of domestic servitude as exists in the southern states of this confederacy. If laborers ever obtain the political power of a country, it is in fact in a state of Revolution. The capitalists north of Mason and Dixon's line[12] have precisely the same interest in the labor of the country that the capitalists of England have in their labor. Hence it is, that they must have a strong federal government (!) *to control* the labor of the nation. But it is precisely the reverse with us. We have already not only a right to the proceeds of our laborers, but we own a *class of laborers* themselves. But let me say to gentlemen who represent the great class of capitalists in the north, beware that you do not drive us into a separate system, for if you do, as certain as the decrees of heaven, you will be compelled to *appeal to the sword to maintain yourselves at home.* It may not come in your day; but your children's children will be covered with the blood of domestic factions, and a *plundering mob contending for power and conquest.*"—*Mr. Pickens, of South Carolina, in Congress, 21st Jan.,* 1836.

"In the very nature of things there must be classes of persons to discharge all the different offices of society from the highest to the lowest. Some of these offices are regarded as *degraded,* although they must and will be performed. Hence those manifest forms of dependent servitude which produce a sense of superiority in the masters or employers, and of inferiority on the part of the servants. Where these offices are performed by *members of the political community,* a dangerous element is obviously introduced into the body politic. Hence the alarming tendency to violate the rights of property by agrarian legislation which is beginning to be manifest in the older states where universal suffrage *prevails without* domestic slavery.

"In a word, the institution of domestic slavery supersedes the *necessity* of An Order of Nobility and All the Other Appendages of a Hereditary System of Government."—*Gov. M'Duffie's Message to the South Carolina Legislature, 1836.*

"We of the south have cause now, and shall soon have greater, to congratulate ourselves on the existence of a population among us which excludes the populace which in effect rules some of our northern neighbors, and is rapidly gaining strength wherever slavery does not exist—a populace made up of the dregs of Europe, and the most worthless portion of the native population."—*Richmond Whig,* 1837.

"Would you do a benefit to the horse or the ox by giving him a cultivated understanding, a fine feeling! So far as the mere laborer has the pride, the knowledge or the aspiration of a freeman, he is unfitted for his situation. If there are sordid, servile, *laborious* offices to be performed, is it not better that there should be sordid, servile, laborious beings to perform them?

"Odium has been cast upon our legislation on account of its forbidding the elements of education being communicated to slaves. But in truth what injury is done them by this? *He who works during the day with his hands,* does not read in the intervals of leisure for his amusement or the improvement of his mind, or the exception is so very rare as scarcely to need the being provided for."—*Chancellor Harper,** *of South Carolina.—Southern Lit. Messenger.*

---

*Most likely a reference to Robert Goodloe Harper. See the Glossary of Names for more information.

"Our slave population is decidedly preferable, as an orderly and laboring class, to a northern laboring class, that have just learning enough to make them wondrous wise, and make them the most dangerous class to well regulated liberty under the sun." *Richmond (Virginia) Enquirer.*

NARRATIVE

OF

HENRY BOX BROWN,

WHO ESCAPED FROM SLAVERY ENCLOSED IN A BOX 3 FEET LONG AND 2 WIDE.

WRITTEN FROM A

STATEMENT OF FACTS MADE BY HIMSELF.

WITH REMARKS UPON THE REMEDY FOR SLAVERY.

BY CHARLES STEARNS.

[1849]

PREFACE

NOT FOR THE PURPOSE of administering to a prurient desire to "hear and see some new thing," nor to gratify any inclination on the part of the hero of the following story to be honored by man, is this simple and touching narrative of the perils of a seeker after the "boon of liberty," introduced to the public eye; but that the people of this country may be made acquainted with the horrid sufferings endured by one as, in a *portable prison*, shut out from the light of heaven, and nearly deprived of its balmy air, he pursued his fearful journey directly through the heart of a country making its boasts of liberty and freedom to all, and that thereby a chord of human sympathy may be touched in the hearts of those who listen to his plaintive tale, which may be the means of furthering the spread of those principles, which under God, shall yet prove "mighty to the pulling down of the strong-holds" of slavery.

O reader, as you peruse this heart-rending tale, let the tear of sympathy roll freely from your eyes, and let the deep fountains of human feeling, which God has implanted in the breast of every son and daughter of Adam, burst forth from their enclosure, until a stream shall flow therefrom on to the surrounding world, of so invigorating and purifying a nature, as to arouse from the "death of the sin" of slavery, and cleanse from the pollutions thereof, all with whom you may be connected. As Henry Box Brown's thrilling escape is portrayed before you, let it not be perused by you as an idle tale, while you go away "forgetting what manner of persons you are;" but let truth find an avenue through your sensibilities, by which it can reach the citadel of your soul, and there dwell in all its life-giving power, expelling the whole brotherhood of pro-slavery errors, which politicians, priests, and selfish avarice, have introduced to the acquaintance of your intellectual faculties. These faculties are oftener

blinded by selfishness, than are imbecile of themselves, as the powerful intellect of a Webster is led captive to the inclinations of a not
unselfish heart; so that that which should be the ruling power of
every man's nature, is held in degrading submission to the inferior
feelings of his heart. If man is blinded to the appreciation of the
good, by a mass of selfish sensibilities, may he not be induced to surrender his will to the influence of truth, by *benevolent* feelings being
caused to spring forth in his heart? That this may be the case with
all whose eyes gaze upon the picture here drawn of misery, and of
endurance, worthy of a Spartan, and such as a hero of olden times
might be proud of, and transmit to posterity, along with the armo-
rial emblazonry of his ancestors, is the ardent desire of all connected
with the publication of this work. A word in regard to the literary
character of the tale before you. The narrator is freshly from a land
where books and schools are forbidden under severe penalties, to all
in his former condition, and of course knoweth not letters, having
never learned them; but of his capabilities otherwise, no one can
doubt, when they recollect that if the records of all nations, from the
time when Adam and Eve first placed their free feet upon the soil
of Eden, until the conclusion of the scenes depicted by Hildreth and
Macaulay, should be diligently searched, a parallel instance of heroism, in behalf of personal liberty, could not be found. Instances of
fortitude for the defence of religious freedom, and in cases of a violation of conscience being required; and for the sake of offspring, of
friends and of one's country are not uncommon; but whose heroism
and ability to contrive, united, have equalled our friend's whose
story is now before you?*

A William and an Ellen Craft, indeed performed an almost
equally hazardous undertaking, and one which, as a devoted ad-
mirer of human daring has said, far exceeded any thing recorded
by Macaulay, and will yet be made the ground-work for a future
Scott to build a more intensely interesting tale upon than "the author of Waverly" ever put forth, but they had the benefit of their

---

*Hugo Grotius was, in the year 1620, sent from prison, confined in a small chest of
drawers, by the affectionate hands of a faithful wife, but he was taken by *friends* on
horseback and carried to the house of a friend, without undergoing much suffering
or running the terrible risk which our friend ran. [Charles Stearns's note]

eyes and ears—they were not entirely helpless; enclosed in a moving tomb, and as utterly destitute of power to control your movements as if death had fastened its icy arm upon you, and yet possessing all the full tide of gushing sensibilities, and a complete knowledge of your existence, as was the case with our friend. We read with horror of the burial of persons before life has entirely fled from them, but here is a man who voluntarily assumed a condition in which he well knew all the chances were against him, and when his head seemed well-nigh severed from his body, on account of the concussion occasioned by the rough handling to which he was subject, see the Spartan firmness of his soul. Not a groan escaped from his agonized heart, as the realities of his condition were so vividly presented before him. Death stared him in the face, but like Patrick Henry, only when the alternative was more a matter of fact than it was to that patriot, he exclaims, "Give me liberty or give me death;" and death seemed to say, as quickly as the lion seizes the kid cast into its den, "You are already mine," and was about to wrap its sable mantle around the form of our self-martyred hero—bound fast upon the altars of freedom, as the Hindoo widow is bound upon the altar of a husband's love;* when the bright angel of liberty, whose dazzling form he had so long and so anxiously watched, as he pored over the scheme hid in the recesses of his own fearless brain, while yet a slave, and whose shining eyes had bewitched his soul, until he had said in the language of one of old to Jesus, "I will follow thee whithersoever thou goest;" when this blessed goddess stood at his side, and, as Jesus said to one lying cold in death's embrace, "I say unto thee, arise," said to him, as she took him by the hand and lifted him from his travelling tomb, "thy warfare is over, thy work is accomplished, a free man art thou, my guidance has availed thee, arise and breathe the air of freedom."

---

*Stearns is most likely making reference to one of the many nineteenth-century works of art, such as the illustration "Burning a Hindoo Widow," included in James Peggs's travel book about India (1832). The image depicts the practice of suttee (or sati), a South Asian custom in which the dead man's widow immolates herself on the husband's funeral pyre.

Did Lazarus* astonish his weeping sisters, and the surrounding multitude, as he emerged from his house of clay, clad in the habiliments of the grave, and did joy unfeigned spread throughout that gazing throng? How much more astonishing seemed the birth of Mr. Brown, as he "came forth" from a box, clothed not in the habiliments of the grave, but in those of slavery, worse than the "silent house of death," as his acts had testified; and what greater joy thrilled through the wondering witnesses, as the lid was removed from the travelling carriage of our friend's electing, and straightway arose therefrom a living man, a being made in God's own image, a son of Jehovah, whom the piety and republicanism of this nation had doomed to pass through this terrible ordeal, before the wand of the goddess of liberty could complete his transformation from a slave to a free man! But we will desist from further comments. Here is the plain narrative of our friend, and is it asking too much of you, whose sympathies may be aroused by the recital which follows, to continue to peruse these pages until the cause of all his sufferings is depicted before you, and your duty under the circumstances is clearly pointed out?

Here are the identical words uttered by him as soon as he inhaled the fresh air of freedom, after the faintness occasioned by his sojourn in his temporary tomb had passed away.

HYMN OF THANKSGIVING,

Sung by Henry Box Brown,

After being released from his confinement in the Box, at Philadelphia.

I waited patiently, I waited patiently for the Lord, for the Lord,
And he inclined unto me, and heard my calling;
I waited patiently, I waited patiently for the Lord,
And he inclined unto me, and heard my calling;
And he hath put a new song in my mouth,
Ev'n a thanksgiving, Ev'n a thanksgiving, Ev'n a thanksgiving
  unto our God.

---

*Subject of the miracle recounted in the Bible (John 11: 41–44) in which Jesus raises Lazarus from the dead.

Blessed, Blessed, Blessed, Blessed is the man, Blessed is the man,
Blessed is the man that hath set his hope, his hope in the Lord;
O Lord my God, Great, Great, Great,
Great are the wondrous works which thou hast done,
Great are the wondrous works which thou hast done, which
    thou hast done,
Great are the wondrous works,
Great are the wondrous works,
Great are the wondrous works, which thou hast done.

If I should declare them and speak of them, they should
    be more, more, more than I am able to express.
I have not kept back thy loving kindness and truth from
    the great congregation,
I have not kept back thy loving kindness and truth from
    the great congregation.

Withdraw not thou thy mercy from me,
Withdraw not thou thy mercy from me, O Lord;
Let thy loving kindness and thy truth always preserve me,
Let all those that seek thee be joyful and glad,
Let all those that seek thee, be joyful and glad, be joyful, be glad,
    be joyful and glad, be joyful, be joyful, be joyful, be joyful,
    be joyful and glad, be glad in thee.

And let such as love thy salvation,
And let such as love thy salvation, say always,
The Lord be praised,
The Lord be praised:
Let all those that seek thee be joyful and glad,
And let such as love thy salvation, say always,
The Lord be praised,
The Lord be praised,
The Lord be praised.

BOSTON, SEPT. I, 1849.

NARRATIVE

I AM NOT ABOUT to harrow the feelings of my readers by a terrific representation of the untold horrors of that fearful system of oppression, which for thirty-three long years entwined its snaky folds about my soul, as the serpent of South America coils itself around the form of its unfortunate victim. It is not my purpose to descend deeply into the dark and noisome caverns of the hell of slavery; and drag from their frightful abode those lost spirits who haunt the souls of the poor slaves, daily and nightly with their frightful presence, and with the fearful sound of their terrific instruments of torture; for other pens far abler than mine have effectually performed that portion of the labor of an exposer of the enormities of slavery. Slavery, like the shield discovered by the knights of olden time, has two diverse sides to it; the one, on which is fearfully written in letters of blood, the character of the mass who carry on that dreadful system of unhallowed bondage; the other, touched with the pencil of a gentler delineator, and telling the looker on, a tale of comparative freedom, from the terrible deprivations so vividly portrayed on its opposite side.

My book will represent, if possible, the beautiful side of the picture of slavery; will entertain you with stories of partial kindness on the part of my master, and of comparative enjoyment on my own part, as I grew up under the benign influence of the blessed system so closely connected with our "republican institutions," as Southern politicians tell us.

From the time I first breathed the air of human existence, until the hour of my escape from bondage, I did not receive but one whipping. I never suffered from lack of food, or on account of too extreme labor; nor for want of sufficient clothing to cover my person. My tale is not, therefore, one of horrid inflictions of the lash upon my naked body; of cruel starvings and of insolent treatment; but is the very best representation of slavery which can be given; therefore, reader, allow me to inform you, as you, for aught I know, may be one of those degraded mortals who fancy that if no blows are inflicted upon the slave's body, and a plenty of "bread and bacon" is dealed out to him, he is therefore no sufferer, and slavery is not a cruel institution; allow me to inform you, that I did not escape from such deprivations. It was not for fear of the lash's dreaded infliction, that I endured that fearful imprisonment, which you are waiting to read concerning; nor because of destitution of the necessaries of life, did I enclose myself in my travelling prison, and traverse your boasted land of freedom, a portion of the time with my head in an inverted position, as if it were a terrible crime for me to endeavor to escape from slavery.

Far beyond, in terrible suffering, all outward cruelties of the foul system, are those inner pangs which rend the heart of fond affection, when the "bone of your bone, and the flesh of your flesh" is separated from your embrace, by the ruthless hand of the merciless tyrant, as he plucks from your heart of love, the one whom God hath given you for a "help-meet" through the journey of life; and more fearful by far than all the blows of the bloody lash, or the pangs of cruel hunger are those lashings of the *heart*, which the best of slaveholders inflict upon their happy and "well off " slaves, as they tear from their grasp the pledges of love, smiling at the side of devoted attachment. Tell me not of kind masters under slavery's hateful rule! There is no such thing as a person of that description; for, as you will see, my master, one of the most distinguished of this uncommon class of slaveholders, hesitated not to allow the wife of my love to be torn from my fond embrace, and the darling idols of my heart, my little children, to be snatched from my arms, and thus to doom them to a separation from me, more dreadful to all of us than a large number of lashes, inflicted on us daily. And yet to this fate I was continually subject, during a large portion of the time, when heaven *seemed* to smile propitiously above me; and no black clouds of fearful character lowered over my head. Heaven save me from kind masters, as well as from those called more cruel; for even their "tender mercies are cruel," and what no freeman could endure for a moment. My tale necessarily lacks that thrilling interest which is attached to the more than romantic, although perfectly true descriptions of a life in slavery, given by my numerous forerunners in the work of sketching a slave's personal experience; but I shall endeavor to intermingle with it other scenes which came under my own observation, which will serve to convince you, that if I was spared a worse fate than actually fell to my lot, yet my comrades around me were not so fortunate; but were the victims of the ungovernable rage of those men, of whose characters one cannot be informed, without experiencing within his soul, a rushing of overflowing emotions of pity, indignation and horror.

I first drew the breath of life in Louisa County, Va., forty-five miles from the city of Richmond, in the year 1816.* I was born a slave. Not because at the moment of my birth an angel stood by, and declared that such was the will of God concerning me; although in a country whose most honored writings declare that all men have a right to liberty, given them by their Creator, it seems strange that I, or any of my brethren, could have been born without this inalienable right, unless God had thus signified his departure from his usual rule, as described by our fathers. Not, I say, on account of God's willing it to be so, was I born a slave, but for the reason that nearly all the people of this country are united in legislating against heaven, and have contrived to vote down our heavenly father's rules, and to substitute for them, that cruel law which binds the chains of slavery upon one sixth part of the inhabitants of this land. I was born a slave! and wherefore? Tyrants, remorseless, destitute of religion and principle, stood by the couch of my mother, as heaven placed a pure soul, in the infantile form, there lying in her arms—a new being, never having breathed earth's atmosphere before; and fearlessly, with no compunctions of remorse, stretched forth their bloody arms and pressed the life of God from me, baptizing my soul and body as their own property; goods and chattels in their hands! Yes, they robbed me of myself, before I could know the nature of their wicked acts; and for ever afterwards, until I took possession of my own soul and body, did they retain their stolen property. This was why I was born a slave. Reader, can you understand the horrors

---

*Brown was born on the Hermitage plantation in Louisa County, Virginia, around 1815.

of that fearful name? Listen, and I will assist you in this difficult work. My father, and my *mother* of course, were slaves before me; but both of them are now enjoying the invaluable boon of liberty, having purchased themselves, in this land of freedom! At an early age, my mother would take me on her knee, and pointing to the forest trees adjacent, now being stripped of their thick foliage by autumnal winds, would say to me, "my son, as yonder leaves are stripped from off the trees of the forest, so are the children of slaves swept away from them by the hands of cruel tyrants;" and her voice would tremble, and she would seem almost choked with her deep emotions, while the big tears would find their way down her saddened cheeks, as she fondly pressed me to her heaving bosom, as if to save me from so dreaded a calamity. I was young then, but I well recollect the sadness of her countenance, and the mournfulness of her words, and they made a deep impression upon my youthful mind. Mothers of the North, as you gaze upon the free forms of your idolized little ones, as they playfully and confidently move around you, O if you knew that the lapse of a few years would infallibly remove them from your affectionate care, not to be laid in the silent grave, "where the wicked cease from troubling," but to be the sport of cruel men, and the victims of barbarous tyrants, who would snatch them from your side, as the robber seizes upon the bag of gold in the traveller's hand; O, would not your life then be rendered a miserable one indeed? Who can trace the workings of a slave mother's soul, as she counts over the hours, the departure of which, she almost knows, will rob her of her darling children, and consign them to a fate more horrible than death's cold embrace! O, who can hear of these cruel deprivations, and not be aroused to action in the slave's behalf?

My mother used to instruct me in the principles of morality, as much as she was able; but I was deplorably ignorant on religious subjects, for what ideas can a slave have of religion, when those who profess it around him, are demons in human shape oftentimes, as you will presently see was the case with my master's overseer? My mother used to tell me not to steal, and not to lie, and to behave myself properly in other respects. She took a great deal of pains with me and my brother; which resulted in our endeavors to conduct ourselves with propriety. As a specimen of the religious knowledge of the slaves, I will state here my ideas in regard to my master; assuring the reader that I am not joking, but stating what was the opinion of all the slave children on my master's plantation; and I have often talked it over with my early associates, and my mother, and enjoyed hearty laughs at the absurdity of our youthful ideas.

I really believed my old master was Almighty God,* and that his son, my young master, was Jesus Christ.† One reason I had for this belief was, that when it was about to thunder, my old master would approach us, if we were in the yard, and say, "All you children run into the house now, for it is going to thunder," and after the shower was over, we would go out again, and he would approach us smilingly, and say, "What a fine shower we have had," and bidding us look at the flowers in the garden, would say, "how pretty the flowers look now." We thought that *he* thundered, and caused the rain to fall; and not until I was eight years of age, did I get rid of this childish superstition. Our master was uncommonly kind, and as he moved about in his dignity, he seemed like a god to us, and probably he did not dislike our reverential feelings towards him. All the slaves called his son, our Saviour, and the way I was enlightened on this point was as follows. One day after returning from church, my mother told father of a woman who wished to join the church. She told the preacher she had been baptized by one of the slaves, who was called from his office, "John the Baptist;" and on being asked by the minister if she believed "that our Saviour came into the world, and had died for the sins of man," she replied, that she "knew he had come into the world," but she "had not heard he was dead, as she lived so far from the road, she did not learn much that was going on in the world." I then asked mother, if young master was dead. She said it was not him they were talking about; it was "our Saviour in heaven." I then asked her if there were two Saviours, when she told me that young master was not "our Saviour," which filled me with

---

*John Barret, master of Hermitage plantation, was elected mayor of Richmond for several terms in the 1790s.

†The reader may be disposed to doubt the truth of the above assertion, but I once asked a girl in Ky., whose mistress was a Methodist church member, if she could tell me "who Jesus Christ was?" "Yes," said she, "he is the bad man." C. S. [Charles Stearns's note]

astonishment, and I could not understand it at first. Not long after this, my sister became anxious to have her soul converted, and shaved the hair from her head, as many of the slaves thought they could not be converted without doing this. My mother reproved her, and began to tell her of God who dwelt in heaven, and that she must pray to him to convert her. This surprised me still more, and I asked her if old master was not God; to which she replied that he was not, and began to instruct me a little in reference to the God of heaven. After this, I believed there was a God who ruled the world, but I did not previously have the least idea of any such being. And why should not my childish fancy be correct, according to the blasphemous teachings of the heathen system of slavery? Does not every slaveholder assume exclusive control over all the actions of his unfortunate victims? Most assuredly he does, as this extract from the laws of a slaveholding State will show you. "A slave is one who is in the power of his master, to whom he belongs. A slave owes to his master and all his family, *respect without bounds and absolute obedience.*" How tallies this with the unalterable law of Jehovah, "Thou shalt have no other gods before me?" Does not the system of slavery effectually shut out from the slave's heart, all true knowledge of the eternal God, and doom him to grope his perilous way, amid the thick darkness of unenlightened heathenism, although he dwells in a land professing much religion, and an entire freedom from the superstitions of paganism?

Let me tell you my opinion of the slaveholding religion of this land. I believe in a hell, where the wicked will forever dwell, and knowing the character of slaveholders and slavery, it is my settled belief, as it was while I was a slave, even though I was treated kindly, that *every* slaveholder will infallibly go to that hell, unless he repents. I do not believe in the religion of the Southern churches, nor do I perceive any great difference between them, and those at the North, which uphold them.

While a young lad, my principal employment was waiting upon my master and mistress, and at intervals taking lessons in what is the destiny of most of the slaves, the cultivation of the plantation. O how often as the hot sun sent forth its scorching rays upon my tender head, did I look forward with dismay, to the time, when I, like my fellow slaves, should be driven by the task-master's cruel lash, to the performance of unrequited toil upon the plantation of my master. To this expectation is the slave trained. Like the criminal under sentence of death, he notches upon his wooden stick, as Sterne's captive* did, the days, after the lapse of which he must be introduced to his dreaded fate; in the case of the criminal, merely death—a cessation from the pains and toils of life; but in our cases, the commencement of a living death; a death never ending, second in horror only to the eternal torment of the wicked in a future state. Yea, even worse than that, for there, a God of love and mercy holds the rod of punishment in his own hand; but in our case, it is held by men from whom almost the last vestige of goodness has departed, and in whose hearts there dwells hardly a spark of humanity, certainly not enough to keep them from the practice of the most inhuman crimes. Imagine, reader, a fearful cloud, gathering blackness as it advances towards you, and increasing in size constantly; hovering in the deep blue vault of the firmament above you, which cloud seems loaded with the elements of destruction, and from the contents of which you are certain you cannot escape. You are sailing upon the now calm waters of the broad and placid deep, spreading its "unadorned bosom" before you, as far as your eye can reach,

> "Calm as a slumbering babe,
> Tremendous Ocean lays;"†

and on its "burnished waves," gracefully rides your little vessel, without fear or dismay troubling your heart. But this fearful cloud is pointed out to you, and as it gathers darkness, and rushes to the point of the firmament overhanging your fated vessel, O what terror then seizes upon your soul, as hourly you expect your little bark to be deluged by the contents of the cloud, and riven by the fierce lightnings enclosed in that mass of angry elements. So with the

---

*Most likely a reference to Laurence Sterne's book *A Sentimental Journey* (1768) and the painting inspired by it, *The Captive* (1775–1777), by John Staveley. Sterne's character, Parson Yorick, upon losing his passport, contemplates an image of a captive.

†Passage from *Queen Mab* (1813), by Percy Bysshe Shelley.

slave, only that he knows his chances of escape are exceedingly small, while you may very likely outlive the storm.

To this terrible apprehension we are all constantly subject. To-day, master may smile lovingly upon us, and the sound of the cracking whip may be hushed, but the dread uncertainty of our future fate still hangs over us, and to-morrow may witness a return of all the elements of fearful strife, as we emphatically "know not what a day may bring forth." The sweet songsters of the air, as it were, may warble their musical notes ever so melodiously, harmonizing with the soft-blowing of the western winds which invigorates our frames, and the genial warmth of the early sun may fill us with pleasurable emotions; but we know that ere long, this sweet singing must be silenced by the fierce cracking of the bloody lash, falling on our own shoulders, and that the cool breezes and the gentle heat of early morn, must be succeeded by the hot winds and fiery rays of Slavery's meridian day. The slave has *no certainty* of the enjoyment of *any privilege whatever!* All his fancied blessings, without a moment's warning being granted to him, may be swept forever from his trembling grasp. Who will then say that "disguise itself" as Slavery will, it is not "a bitter cup," the mixture whereof is gall and wormwood?

My brother and myself, were in the practice of carrying grain to mill, a few times a year, which was the means of furnishing us with some information respecting other slaves. We often went twenty miles, to a mill owned by a Col. Ambler,* in Yansinville county, and used to improve our opportunities for gaining information. Especially desirous were we, of learning the condition of slaves around us, for we knew not how long we should remain in as favorable hands as we were then. On one occasion, while waiting for our grain, we entered a house in the neighborhood, and while resting ourselves there, we saw a number of forlorn-looking beings pass the door, and as they passed, we noticed that they turned and gazed earnestly upon us. Afterwards, about fifty performed the same act, which excited our minds somewhat, as we overheard some of them say, "Look there, and see those two colored men with shoes, vests

_____

*Brown and one of his brothers were sent to do work at the mill of Colonel John Ambler, "the county's largest slave owner," according to Ruggles (p. 5; see For Further Reading).

and hats on," and we determined to obtain an interview with them. Accordingly, after receiving some bread and meat from our hosts, we followed these abject beings to their quarters;—and such a sight we had never witnessed before, as we had always lived on our master's plantation, and this was about the first of our journeys to the mill. They were dressed with shirts made of coarse bagging, such as coffee-sacks are made from, and some kind of light substance for pantaloons, and *no other clothing whatever.* They had on no shoes, hats, vests, or coats, and when my brother asked them why they spoke of our being dressed with those articles of clothing, they said they had "never seen negroes dressed in that way before." They looked very hungry, and we divided our bread and meat among them, which furnished them only a mouthful each. They never had any meat, they said, given them by their masters. My brother put various questions to them, such as, "if they had wives?" "did they go to church?" "had they any sisters?" &c. The one who gave us the information, said they had wives, but were obliged to marry on their own plantation. Master would not allow them to go away from home to marry, consequently he said they were all related to each other, and master made them marry, *whether related or not.* My brother asked this man to show him his sisters; he said he could not tell them from the rest, *they were all his sisters;* and here let me state, what is well known by many people, that no such thing as real marriage is allowed to exist among the slaves. Talk of marriage under such a system! Why, the owner of a Turkish harem, or the keeper of a house of ill-fame, might as well allow the inmates of their establishments to marry as for a Southern slaveholder to do the same. Marriage, as is well known, is the voluntary and perfect union of one man with one woman, without depending upon the will of a third party. This never can take place under slavery, for the moment a slave is allowed to form such a connection as he chooses, the spell of slavery is dissolved. The slave's wife is his, only at the will of her master, who may violate her chastity with impunity. It is my candid opinion that one of the strongest motives which operate upon the slaveholders, and induce them to retain their iron grasp upon the unfortunate slave, is because it gives them such unlimited control in this respect over the female slaves. The greater part of slaveholders are licentious men, and the most respectable and the kindest of masters, keep some of their slaves as mistresses. It is for their pecuniary interest to do so in several respects. Their progeny is so many dollars and cents in their pockets, instead of being a bill of expense to them, as would be the case if their slaves were free; and mulatto slaves command a higher price than dark colored ones; but it is too horrid a subject to describe. Suffice it to say, that no slave has the least certainty of being able to retain his wife or her husband a single hour; so that the slave is placed under strong inducements not to form a union of *love*, for he knows not how soon the chords wound around his heart would be snapped asunder, by the hand of the brutal slave-dealer. Northern people sustain slavery, knowing that it is a system of perfect licentiousness, and yet go to church and boast of their purity and holiness!

On this plantation, the slaves were never allowed to attend church, but managed their religious affairs in their own way. An old slave, whom they called Uncle John, decided upon their piety, and would baptize them during the silent watches of the night, while their master was "taking his rest in sleep." Thus is the slave under the necessity of even "saving his soul" in the hours when the eye of his master, who usurps the place of God over him, is turned from him. Think of it, ye who contend for the necessity of these rites, to constitute a man a Christian! By night must the poor slave steal away from his bed of straw, and leaving his miserable hovel, must drag his weary limbs to some adjacent stream of water, where a fellow slave, as ignorant as himself, proceeds to administer the ordinance of baptism; and as he plunges his comrades into the water, in imitation of the Baptist of old, how he trembles, lest the footsteps of his master should be heard, advancing to their Bethesda,— knowing that if such should be the case, the severe punishment that awaits them all. Baptists, are ye striking hands with Southern churches, which thus exclude so many slaves from the "waters of salvation?"

But we were obliged to cut short our conversation with these slaves, by beholding the approach of the overseer, who was directing his steps towards us, like a bear seeking its prey. We had only time to ask this man, "if they were often whipped?" to which he replied, "that not a day passed over their heads, without some of their number being brutally punished; and," said he, "we shall have to suffer for this talk with you." He then told us, that many of them had been severely whipped that very morning, for having been baptized the night before. After we left them, we looked back, and heard the screams of these poor creatures, suffering under the blows of the hard-hearted overseer, for the crime of talking with us;—which screams sounded in our ears for some time. We felt thankful that we were exempted from such terrible treatment; but still, we knew not how soon we should be subject to the same cruel fate. By this time we had returned to the mill, where we met a young man, (a relation of the owner of this plantation,) who for some time appeared to be eyeing us quite attentively. At length he asked me if I had "ever been whipped," and when I told him I had not, he replied, "Well, you will neither of you ever be of any value, then;" so true is it that whipping is considered a necessary part of slavery. Without this practice, it could not stand a single day. He expressed a good deal of surprise that we were allowed to wear hats and shoes,—supposing that a slave had no business to wear such clothing as his master wore. We had brought our fishing-lines with us, and requested the privilege to fish in his stream, which he roughly denied us, saying, "we do not allow niggers to fish." Nothing daunted, however, by this rebuff, my brother went to another place, and was quite successful in his undertaking, obtaining a plentiful supply of the finny tribe; but as soon as this youngster perceived his good luck, he ordered him to throw them back into the stream, which he was obliged to do, and we returned home without them.

We finally abandoned visiting this mill, and carried our grain to another, a Mr. Bullock's, only ten miles distant from our plantation. This man was very kind to us, took us into his house and put us to bed, took charge of our horses, and carried the grain himself into the mill, and in the morning furnished us with a good breakfast. I asked my brother why this man treated us so differently from our old miller. "Oh," said he, "this man is not a slaveholder!" Ah, that explained the difference; for there is nothing in the southern character averse to gentleness. On the contrary, if it were not for slavery's withering touch, the Southerners would be the kindest people in the land. Slavery possesses the power attributed to one of old, of changing the nature of all who drink of its vicious cup.

"— — — Which, as they taste,
Soon as the potion works, their *human* countenance,
The express resemblance of the gods, is changed
Into some brutish form of wolf, or bear,
Or ounce, or tiger, hog, or bearded goat;
And they, so perfect is their misery,
Not once perceive their foul disfigurement,
But boast themselves more comely than before."*

Under the influence of slavery's polluting power, the most gentle women become the fiercest viragos, and the most benevolent men are changed into inhuman monsters. It is true of the northern man who goes South also.

"*Whoever* tastes, loses his upright shape,
And downward falls, into a *grovelling swine*."

This non-slaveholder also allowed us to catch as many fish as we pleased, and even furnished us with fishing implements. While at this mill, we became acquainted with a colored man from another part of the country; and as our desire was strong to learn how our brethren fared in other places, we questioned him respecting his treatment. He complained much of his hard fate,—said he had a wife and one child, and begged for some of our fish to carry to his wife; which my brother gladly gave him. He said he was expecting to have some money in a few days, which would be *"the first he ever had in his life!"* He had sent a thousand hickory-nuts to market, for which he afterwards informed us he had received thirty-six cents, which he gave to his wife, to furnish her with some little article of comfort. This was the sum total of all the money he had ever been the possessor of! Ye northern pro-slavery men, do you regard this as robbery, or not? The whole of this man's earnings had been robbed from him during his entire life, except simply his coarse food and miserable clothing, the whole expense of which, for a plantation slave, does not exceed twenty dollars a year. This is one reason why

---

*Passage from John Milton's masque (allegorical drama) *Comus* (1634).

I think every slaveholder will go to hell; for my Bible teaches me that no *thief* shall enter heaven; and I know every slaveholder is a thief; and I rather think you would all be of my opinion if you had ever been a slave. But now, assisting these thieves, and being made rich by them, you say they are not robbers; just as wicked men generally shield their abettors.

On our return from this place, we met a colored man and woman, who were very cross to each other. We inquired as to the cause of their trouble, and the man told us, that "women had such tongues!" that some of them had stolen a sheep, and this woman, after eating of it, went and told their master, and they all had to receive a severe whipping. And here follows a specimen of slaveholding morality, which will show you how much many of the masters care for their slaves' stealing. This man enjoined upon his slaves never to steal from him again, but to *steal from his neighbors*, and he would keep them from punishment, if they would furnish him with a portion of the meat! And why not? For is it any worse for the slaveholders to steal from one another, than it is to steal from their helpless slaves? Not long after, these slaves availed themselves of their master's assistance, and stole an animal from a neighboring plantation, and according to agreement, furnished their master with his share. Soon the owner of the missing animal came rushing into the man's house, who had just eaten of the stolen food, and, in a very excited manner, demanded reparation from him, for the beast stolen, as he said, by this man's slaves. The villain, hardly able to stand after eating so bountifully of his neighbor's pork, exclaimed loudly, "my servants know no more about your hogs than I do!" which was strictly true; and the loser of the swine went away satisfied. This man told his slaves that it was a sin to steal from him, but none to steal from his neighbors! My brother told the slave we were conversing with, that it was as much of a sin in God's sight, for him to steal from one, as from the other. "Oh," said the slave, "master says *negroes have nothing to do with God!*" He further informed us that his master and mistress lived very unhappily together, on account of the maid who waited upon them. She had no husband, but had several yellow children. After we left them, they went to a fodder-stack, and took out a jug, and drank of its contents. My brother's curiosity was excited to learn the nature of their drink; and watching his opportunity, unobserved by them, he slipped up to the stack, and ascertained that the jug was nearly full of Irish whiskey. He carried it home with him, and the next time we visited the mill, he returned the jug to its former place, filled with molasses, purchased with his own money, instead of the fiery drink which it formerly contained. Some time after this, the master of this man discovered a great falling off in the supply of stolen meat furnished him by the slaves, and questioned this man in reference to the cause of such a lamentable diminution in the supply of hog-meat in particular. The slave told him the story of the jug, and that he had ceased drinking, which was sad news for the pork-loving gentleman.

I will now return to my master's affairs. My young master's brother was a very benevolent man, and soon became convinced that it was wrong to hold men in bondage; which belief he carried into practice by emancipating forty slaves at one time, and paying the expenses of their transportation to a free state. But old master, although naturally more kind-hearted than his neighbors, could not always remain as impervious to the assaults of the pro-slavery demon; and as stated previously, that all who drank of this hateful cup were transformed into some vile animal, so he became a perfect brute in his treatment of his slaves. I cannot account for this change, only on the supposition, that experience had convinced him that kind treatment was not as well adapted to the production of crops as a severer kind of discipline. Under the elating influence of freedom's inspiring sound men will labor much harder, than when forced to perform unpleasant tasks, the accomplishment of which will be of no value to themselves; but while the slave is held as such, it is difficult for him to feel as he would feel, if he was a free man, however light may be his tasks and however kind may be his master. The lash is still held above his head, and *may* fall upon him, even if its blows are for a long time withheld. This the slave realizes; and hence no kind treatment can destroy the depressing influence of a consciousness of his being a slave,—no matter how lightly the yoke of slavery may rest upon his shoulders. He knows the yoke is there; and that at any time its weight may be made heavier, and his form almost sink under its weary burden; but give him his liberty, and new life enters into him immediately. The iron yoke falls from his chafed shoulders; the collar, even if it was a silken one, is removed from his enslaved person; and the chains, although made of gold, fall from his bound limbs, and he walks forth with an elastic step, to enjoy the realities of his new existence. Now he is ready to perform irksome tasks; for the avails of his labor will be of value to himself, and with them he can administer comfort to those near and dear to him, and to the world at large, as well as provide for his own intellectual welfare; whereas before, however kind his treatment, all his earnings more than his expenses went to enrich his master. It is on this account, probably, that those who have undertaken to carry out some principles of humanity in their treatment of their slaves, have been generally frowned upon by their neighbors; and they have been forced either to emancipate their slaves, or to return to the cruel practices of those around them. My young master preferred the former alternative; my old master adopted the latter. We now began to taste a little of the horrors of slavery; so that many of the slaves ran away, which had not been the case before. My master employed an overseer also about this time, which he always refused to do previously, preferring to take charge of us himself; but the clamor of the neighbors was so great at his mild treatment of his slaves, that he at length yielded to the popular will around him, and went "with the multitude to do evil," and hired an overseer. This was an end of our favorable treatment; and there is no telling what would have been the result of this new method among slaves so unused to the whip as we were, if in the midst of this experiment, old master had not been called upon to pay "the debt of nature," and to "go the way of all the earth." As he was about to expire, he sent for me and my brother, to come to his bedside. We ran with beating hearts, and highly elated feelings, not doubting that he was about to confer upon us the boon of freedom, as we expected to be set free when he died; but imagine my deep disappointment, when the old man called me to his side and said to me, "Henry, you will make a good plough-boy, or a good gardener; now you must be an honest boy, and never tell an untruth. I have given you to my son William,[1] and you must obey him." Thus did this old gentleman deceive us by his former kind treatment, and raise expectations in our youthful minds, which were thus doomed to be fatally overthrown. Poor man! he has gone to a higher tribunal than man's, and doubtless ere this, earnestly laments that he did not give us all our liberty at this

favorable moment; but sad as was our disappointment, we were con-
strained to submit to it, as we best were able. One old negro openly
expressed his wish that master would die, because he had not released him from his bondage.

If there is any one thing which operates as an impetus to the slave
in his toilsome labors and buoys him up, under all the hardships of
his severe lot, it is this hope of future freedom, which lights up his
soul and cheers his desolate heart in the midst of all the fearful
agonies of the varied scenes of his slave life, as the soul of the
tempest-tossed mariner is stayed from complete despair, by the faint
glimmering of the far-distant light which the kindness of man has
placed in a light-house, so as to be perceived by him at a long distance. Old ocean's tempestuous waves beat and roar against his frail
bark, and the briny deep seems ready to enclose him in its wide open
mouth, but "ever and anon" he perceives the glimmering of this feeble light in the distance, which keeps alive the spark of hope in his
bosom, which kind heaven has placed within every man's breast. So
with the slave. Freedom's fires are dimly burning in the far distant
future, and ever and anon a fresh flame appears to arise in the direction of this sacred altar, until at times it seems to approach so
near, that he can feel its melting power dissolving his chains, and
causing him to emerge from his darkened prison, into the full light
of freedom's glorious liberty. O the fond anticipations of the slave in
this respect! I cannot correctly describe them to you, but I can recollect the thrills of exulting joy which the name of freedom caused
to flow through my soul.

> Freedom, the dear and joyful sound,
> 'Tis music in the sad slave's ear.

How often this hope is destined to fade away, as the early dew
before the rising sun! Not unseldom, does the slave labor intensely
to obtain the means to purchase his freedom, and after having paid
the required sum, is still held a slave, while the master retains the
money! This *very often* transpires under the slave system. A good
many slaves have in this way paid for themselves several times, and
not received their freedom then! And masters often hold out this in-
ducement to their slaves, to labor more than they otherwise would,

when they have no intention of fulfilling their promise. O the ineffable meanness of the slave system! Instead of our being set free, a far different fate awaited us; and here you behold, reader, the closing scene of the kindest treatment which a man can bestow upon his slaves.

It mattered not how benign might have been our master's conduct to us, it was to be succeeded by a harrowing scene, the inevitable consequence of our being left slaves. We must now be separated and divided into different lots, as we were inherited by the four sons of my master. It is no easy matter to amicably divide even the old furniture and worn-out implements of husbandry, and sometimes the very clothing of a deceased person, and oftentimes a scene of shame ensues at the opening of the will of a departed parent, which is enough to cause humanity to blush at the meanness of man. What then must be the sufferings of those persons, who are to be the objects of this division and strife? See the heirs of a departed slaveholder, disputing as to the rightful possession of human beings, many of them their old nurses, and their playmates in their younger days! The scene which took place at the division of my master's human property, baffles all description. I was then only thirteen years of age, but it is as fresh in my mind as if but yesterday's sun had shone upon the dreadful exhibition. My mother was separated from her youngest child, and not until she had begged and pleaded most piteously for its restoration to her, was it again placed in her hands. Turning her eyes fondly upon me, who was now to be carried from her presence, she said, "You now see, my son, the fulfilment of what I told you a great while ago, when I used to take you on my knee, and show you the leaves blown from the trees by the fearful winds." Yes, I now saw that one after another were the slave mother's children torn from her embrace, and John was given to one brother, Sarah to another, and Jane to a third, while Samuel fell into the hands of the fourth. It is a difficult matter to satisfactorily divide the slaves on a plantation, for no person wishes for *all* children, or for all old people; while both old, young, and middle aged ones are to be divided. There is no equitable way of dividing them, but by allowing each one to take his portion of both children, middle aged and old people; which necessarily causes heart-rending separations; but "slaves have no feelings," I am sometimes told. "You get used to these things; it would not do for us to experience them, but you are not constituted as we are;" to which I reply, that a slave's friends are *all* he possesses that is of value to him. He cannot read, he has no property, he cannot be a teacher of truth, or a politician; he cannot be very religious, and all that remains to him, aside from the hope of freedom, that ever present deity, forever inspiring him in his most terrible hours of despair, is the society of his friends. We love our friends more than white people love theirs, for we risk more to save them from suffering. Many of our number who have escaped from bondage ourselves, have jeopardized our own liberty, in order to release our friends, and sometimes we have been retaken and made slaves of again, while endeavoring to rescue our friends from slavery's iron jaws.

But does not the slave love his friends! What mean then those frantic screams, which every slave-auction witnesses, where the scalding tears rush in agonizing torrents down the sorrow-stricken cheeks of the bereaved slave mother; and where clubs are sometimes used to drive apart two fond friends who cling to each other, as the merciless slave-trader is to separate them forever. O, to talk of our not having feelings for our friends, is to mock that Being who has created us in his own image, and implanted deep in every human bosom, a gushing fount of tender sensibilities, which no life of sin can ever fully erase. Talk of our not having feelings, and then calmly look on the scene described as taking place when my master died! Have you any feeling? Does this recital arouse those sympathetic feelings in your bosom which you make your boast of? How can white people have hearts *of tenderness*, and allow such scenes to daily transpire at the South? All over the blackened and marred surface of the whole slave territory do these heart-rending transactions continually occur. Not a day inscribes its departing hours upon the dial of human existence, but it marks the overthrow of more than one family altar, and the sundering of numerous family ties; and yet the hot blood of Southern oppression is allowed to find its way into the hearts of the Northern people, who politically and religiously are doing their utmost to sustain the dreadful system; yea, competing with the South in their devotion to the evil genius of their country's choice. Slavery reigns and rules the councils of this nation, as Satan presides over Pandemonium, and the loud and clear cry of the anti-slavery host, calling upon the people of the land to cease their connection with the tyrannical system, is universally unheeded. It falls upon the closed ears of the people of this nation like the noise of the random shots of a vessel at sea, upon the ears of the captain of the opposing squadron, but to arouse them to action in *opposition* to the utterance of the voice of warning.

What though the plaintive cries of three millions of heartbroken and dejected captives, are wafted on every Southern gale to the ears of our Northern brethren, and the hot winds of the South reach our fastnesses amid the mountains and hills of our rugged land, loaded with the stifled cries and choking sobs of poor desolate women, as her babes are torn one by one from her embrace; yet no Northern voice is heard to sound loudly enough among our hills and dales, to startle from their sleep of indifference, those who have it in their power to break the chains of the suffering bondmen *to-day*, saying to all who hear its clear sounding voice, "Come out from all connection with this terrible system of cruelty and blood, and form a government and a union free from this hateful curse." The Northern people have it in their power to-day, to cause all this suffering of which I have been speaking to cease, and to cause one loud and triumphant anthem of praise to ascend from the millions of panting, bleeding slaves, now stretched upon the plains of Southern oppression; and yet they talk of our being destitute of feeling. "O shame, where is thy blush!"

My father and mother were left on the plantation, and I was taken to the city of Richmond, to work in a tobacco manufactory, owned by my master's son William, who now became my only master. Old master, although he did not give me my freedom, yet left an especial charge with his son to take good care of me, and not to whip me, which charge my master endeavored to act in accordance with. He told me if I would behave well he would take good care of me, and would give me money to spend, &c. He talked so kindly to me that I determined I would exert myself to the utmost to please him, and would endeavor to do just what he wished me to, in every respect. He furnished me with a new suit of clothes, and gave me money to buy things with, to send to my mother. One day I overheard him telling the overseer that his father had raised me, and that I was a smart boy, and he must never whip me. I tried extremely hard to perform what

I thought was my duty, and escaped the lash almost entirely; although the overseer would oftentimes have liked to have given me a severe whipping; but fear of both me and my master deterred him from so doing. It is true, my lot was still comparatively easy; but reader, imagine not that others were so fortunate as myself, as I will presently describe to you the character of our overseer; and you can judge what kind of treatment, persons wholly in his power might expect from such a man. But it was some time before I became reconciled to my fate, for after being so constantly with my mother, to be torn from her side, and she on a distant plantation, where I could not see or but seldom hear from her, was exceedingly trying to my youthful feelings, slave though I was. I missed her smiling look when her eye rested upon my form; and when I returned from my daily toil, weary and dejected, no fond mother's arms were extended to meet me, no one appeared to sympathize with me, and I felt I was indeed alone in the world. After the lapse of about a year and a half from the time I commenced living in Richmond, a strange series of events transpired. I did not then know precisely what was the cause of these scenes, for I could not get any very satisfactory information concerning the matter from my master, only that some of the slaves had undertaken to kill their owners; but I have since learned that it was the famous Nat Turner's insurrection* that caused all the excitement I witnessed. Slaves were whipped, hung, and cut down with swords in the streets, if found away from their quarters after dark. The whole city was in the utmost confusion and dismay; and a dark cloud of terrific blackness, seemed to hang over the heads of the whites. So true is it, that "the wicked flee when no man pursueth." Great numbers of the slaves were locked in the prison, and many were "half hung," as it was termed; that is, they were suspended to some limb of a tree, with a rope about their necks, so adjusted as not to quite strangle them, and then they were pelted by the men and boys with rotten eggs. This half-hanging is a refined species of cruelty, peculiar to slavery, I believe.

Among the cruelties occasioned by this insurrection, which was however some distance from Richmond, was the forbidding of as

---

*See endnote 9.

many as five slaves to meet together, except they were at work, and the silencing of all colored preachers. One of that class in our city, refused to obey the imperial mandate, and was severely whipped; but his religion was too deeply rooted to be thus driven from him, and no promise could be extorted from his resolute soul, that he would not proclaim what he considered the glad tidings of the gospel. (Query. How many white preachers would continue their employment, if they were served in the same way?) It is strange that more insurrections do not take place among the slaves; but their masters have impressed upon their minds so forcibly the fact, that the United States Government is pledged to put them down, in case they should attempt any such movement, that they have no heart to contend against such fearful odds; and yet the slaveholder lives in constant dread of such an event.*

The rustling of

> "— — — the lightest leaf,
>   That quivers to the passing breeze,"†

fills his timid soul with visions of flowing blood and burning dwellings; and as the loud thunder of heaven rolls over his head, and the vivid lightning flashes across his pale face, straightway his imagination conjures up terrible scenes of the loud roaring of an enemy's cannon, and the fierce yells of an infuriated slave population, rushing to vengeance.‡ There is no doubt but this would be the case, if it were not for the Northern people, who are ready, as I have been often told, to shoot us down, if we attempt to rise and obtain our freedom. I believe that if the slaves could do as they wish, they would throw off their heavy yoke immediately, by rising against

---

*In proof of this, I would state that during my residence at the South, a whole town was once thrown into an uproar by my entering a slave hut, about Christmas time, and talking and praying with the inmates about an hour. I was told that it would not be safe for me to remain in the town over night. C. S. [Charles Stearns's note]

†Passage from *Queen Mab* (1813), by Percy Bysshe Shelley.

‡While at the South, a gentleman came one day to a friend of mine, and in a very excited manner said to him, "Why, are you not afraid to have that man about you? Do you not fear that your house will be burned? I cannot sleep nights lest the slaves should rise and burn all before them." C. S. [Charles Stearns's note]

their masters; but ten millions of Northern people stand with their feet on their necks, and how can they arise? How was Nat Turner's insurrection suppressed, but by a company of United States troops, furnished the governor of Virginia at his request, according to your Constitution?

About this time, I began to grow alarmed respecting my future welfare, as a great eclipse of the sun had recently taken place; and the cholera reaching the country not long after, I thought that perhaps the day of judgment was not far distant, and I must prepare for that dreaded event. After praying for about three months, it pleased Almighty God, as I believe, to pardon my sins, and I was received into the Baptist Church, by a minister who thought it was wicked to hold slaves. I was obliged to obtain permission from my master, however, before I could join. He gave me a note to carry to the preacher, saying that I had *his permission* to join the church!

I shall now make you acquainted with the manner in which affairs were conducted in my master's tobacco manufactory, after which I shall introduce you to the heart-rending scenes which give the principal interest to my narrative.

My master carried on a large tobacco manufacturing establishment in Richmond, which was almost wholly under the supervision of one of those low, miserable, cruel, barbarous, and sometimes religious beings, known under the name of overseers, with which the South abounds. These men hardly deserve the name of men, for they are lost to all regard for decency, truth, justice and humanity, and are so far gone in human depravity, that before they can be saved, Jesus Christ, or some other Saviour, will have to die a second time. I pity them sincerely, but as my mind recurs to the wicked conduct I so often witnessed on the part of this one, I cannot prevent these indignant feelings from arising in my soul. O reader, if you had seen the perfect recklessness of conduct so often exhibited by this man, as I witnessed it, you would not blame me for expressing myself so strongly. I know that even this man is my brother, but he is a very wicked brother, whose soul I commend to Almighty God, hoping that his sovereign grace may find its way, if it is a possible thing, to his sin-hardened soul; *and yet he was a pious man.* His name was *John F. Allen,* and I suppose he still lives in Richmond. After reading about his character, I apprehend your judgment of him will coincide with mine. The other overseers, however, were very different men, for hell could hardly spare more than one such man, for one tobacco manufactory; as it is not overstocked with such vile reprobates.

But before proceeding to speak farther of him, I will inform you a little respecting our business—as not many of you have ever seen the inside of a tobacco manufactory. The building I worked in was about 300 feet in length, and three stories high, and afforded room for 200 people to work in, but only 150 persons were employed, 120 of whom were slaves, and the remainder free colored people. We were obliged to work *fourteen* hours a day, in the summer, and *sixteen* in the winter.

This work consisted in removing the stems from the leaves of tobacco, which was performed by women and boys, after which the tobacco was moistened with a liquor made from liquorice and sugar, which gives the tobacco that sweetish taste which renders it not perfectly abhorrent to those who chew it. After being thus moistened, the tobacco was taken by the men and twisted into hands, and pressed into lumps, when it was sent to the machine-house, and pressed into boxes and casks. After remaining in what was called the "sweat-house" about thirty days, it was shipped for the market.

Mr. Allen was a thorough going Yankee in his mode of doing business. He was by no means one of your indolent, do-nothing Southerners, so effeminate as to be hardly able to wield his hands to administer to his own necessities, but he was a savage-looking, dare-devil sort of a man, ready apparently for any emergency to which Beelzebub might call him, a real servant of the bottomless pit. He understood how to turn a penny as well as any Yankee pedlar who ever visited our city. Whether he derived his skill from associating with that class of individuals, or whether it was the natural production of his own cunning mind, I know not. He used often to boast, that by his shrewdness in managing the negroes, he made enough to support his family, which cost him $1000, without touching a farthing of his salary, which was $1500 per annum. Of the probability of this assertion, I can bear witness; for I know he was very skilful in another department of cunning and cheatery.

Like many other servants of the evil one, he was an early riser; not for the purpose of improving his health, or that he might enjoy sweet communion with his heavenly Father, at his morning prisons, but that "while the master slept" he might more easily transact his nefarious business. At whatever hour of the morning I might arrive at the factory, I seldom anticipated the seemingly industrious steps of Mr. Allen, who by his punctuality in this respect, obtained a good reputation as a faithful and devoted overseer. But mark the conduct of the pious gentleman, for he was a member of an Episcopalian church. One would have supposed from observing the transactions around him, that Mr. Allen took time by the forelock, emphatically, for long before the early rays of the rising sun had gilded the eastern horizon, was this man busily engaged in loading a wagon with coal, oil, sugar, wood, &c., &c., which always found a place of deposit at *his own door*, entirely unknown to my master. This practice Mr. Allen carried on during my stay there, and yet he was a very pious man.

This man enjoyed the unlimited confidence of my master, so that he would never listen to a word of complaint on the part of any of the workmen. No matter how cruel or how *unjust* might be the punishment inflicted upon any of the hands, master would never listen to their complaints; so that this barbarous man was our master in reality. At one time a colored man, who had been in the habit of singing religious songs quite often, was taken sick and did not make his appearance at the factory. For two or three days no notice whatever was taken of him, no medicine provided for him, and no physician sent to heal him. At the end of that time, Mr. Allen ordered three strong men to go to the man's house, and bring him to the factory. This order being obeyed, the man, pale and hardly able to stand, was stripped to his waist, his hands tied together, and the rope fastened to a large post. The overseer then questioned him about his singing, told him that it consumed too much time, and that he was going to give him some medicine which would cure him. The poor trembling man made no reply, when the pious Mr. Allen, for no crime except that of sickness, inflicted 200 lashes upon the quivering flesh of the invalid, and he would have continued his "apostolic blows," if the emaciated form of the languishing man, had not sunken under their heavy weight, and Mr. Allen was obliged to desist.* I witnessed this transaction with my own eyes; but what could I do, for I was a slave, and any interference on my part would only have brought the same punishment upon me. This man was sick a month afterwards, during which time the weekly allowance of seventy-five cents for the hands to board themselves with, was withheld from him, and his wife was obliged to support him by washing for others; and yet Northern people tell me that a slave is better off than a free man, because when he is sick his master provides for him! Master knew all the circumstances of this case, but never uttered one word of reproof to the overseer, that I could learn; at any rate, he did not interfere at all with this cruel treatment of him, as his motto was, "Mr. Allen is always right."

Mr. Allen, although a church member, was much addicted to the habit of *profane swearing,* a vice which church members there, indulged in as frequently as non-professors did. He used particularly to expend his swearing breath, in denunciation of the whole race of negroes, calling us "d——d hogs, dogs, pigs," &c. At one time, he was busily engaged in reading in *the Bible,* when a slave came in who had absented himself from work the enormous length of ten minutes! The overseer had been cheated out of ten minutes' precious time; and as he depended upon the punctuality of the slave to support his family in the manner mentioned previously, his desire perhaps not to violate that precept, "he that provideth not for his family is worse than an infidel," led him to indulge in quite an outbreak of boisterous anger. "What are you so late for, you black scamp?" said he to the delinquent. "I am only ten minutes behind the time, sir," quietly responded the slave, when Mr. Allen exclaimed, "You are a d——d liar," and remembering, for aught that I can say to the contrary, that "he that con-

---

*While in Kentucky I knew of a case where a preacher punished a female slave in this way, and his wife stood by, throwing cold water into the slave's face, to keep her from fainting. In endeavoring to escape afterwards, the poor creature became faint from loss of blood, and her body was found partly devoured by the buzzards. C. S. [Charles Stearns's note] verteth a *sinner* from the error of his ways, shall save a soul from death," he proceeded to try the effect of the Bible upon the body of the "liar," striking him a heavy blow in the face, with the sacred book. But that not answering his purpose, and the man remaining incorrigible, he caught up a stick and beat him with that. The slave complained to master, but he would take no notice of him, and directed him back to the overseer.

Mr. Allen, although a superintendent of the Sabbath school, and very fervid in his exhortations to the slave children, whom he endeavored to instruct in reference to their duties to their masters, that they must never disobey them, or lie, or steal, and if they did they would assuredly "go to hell," yet was not wholly destitute of "that fear which hath torment," for always when a heavy thunder storm came up, would he shut himself up in a little room where he supposed the lightning would not harm him; and I frequently overheard him praying earnestly to God to spare his life. He evidently had not that "perfect *love* which casteth out fear." The same day on which he had beaten the poor sick man, did such a scene transpire; but generally after the storm had abated he would laugh at his own conduct, and say he did not believe the Lord had any thing to do with the thunder and lightning.

As I have stated, Mr. A. was a devout attendant upon public worship, and prayed much with the pupils in the Sabbath school, and was indefatigable in teaching them to repeat the catechism after him, although he was very particular never to allow them to hold the book in their hands. But let not my readers suppose on this account, that he desired the salvation of these slaves. No, far from that; for very soon after thus exhorting them, he would tell his visiters, that it was "a d——d lie that colored people were ever converted," and that they could "not go to heaven," for they had no souls; but that it was his duty to talk to them as he did. The reader can learn from this account of how much value the religious teaching of the slaves is, when such men are its administerers; and also for what purpose this instruction is given them.

This man's liberality to white people, was coextensive with his denunciation of the colored race. A white man, he said, could not be lost, let him do what he pleased—rob the slaves, which he said was not wrong, lie, swear, or any thing else, provided he *read the Bible and joined the Church.**

One word concerning the religion of the South. I regard it as all delusion, and that there is not a particle of religion in their slaveholding churches. The great end to which religion is there made to minister, is to keep the slaves in a docile and submissive frame of mind, by instilling into them the idea that if they do not obey their masters, they will infallibly "go to hell;" and yet some of the miserable wretches who teach this doctrine, do not themselves believe it. Of course the slave prefers obedience to his master, to an abode in the "lake of fire and brimstone." It is true in more senses than one, that slavery rests upon hell! I once heard a minister declare in public, that he had preached six years before he was converted; and that he was then in the habit of taking a glass of "mint julep" directly after prayers, which wonderfully refreshed him, soul and body. This dram he would repeat three or four times during the day; but at length an old slave persuaded him to abstain a while from his potations, the following of which advice, resulted in his conversion. I believe his second conversion, was nearer a true one, than his first, because he said his conscience reproved him for having sold slaves; and he finally left that part of the country, on account of slavery, and went to the North.

But as time passed along, I began to think seriously of entering into the matrimonial state, as much as a person can, who can "make no contract whatever," and whose wife is not his, only so far as her master allows her to be. I formed an acquaintance with a young woman by the name of Nancy[2]—belonging to a Mr. Lee, a clerk in the bank, and a pious man; and our friendship having ripened into mutual love, we concluded to make application to the powers that ruled us, for *permission* to be married, as I had previously applied for permission to join the church. I went to Mr. Lee, and made known to him my wishes, when he told me, he never meant to sell Nancy, and if my master would agree never to sell me, then I might marry her. This man was a member of a Presbyterian church in Richmond,

---

*Will not this be considered a sufficient exhibition of that *charity*, which proslavery divines exhort abolitionists to practise? C. S. [Charles Stearns's note]

and pretended to me, to believe it wrong to separate families; but after I had been married to my wife one year, his conscientious scruples vanished, and she was sold to a saddler living in Richmond, who was one of Dr. Plummer's church members. Mr. Lee gave me a note to my master, and they afterwards discussed the matter over, and I was allowed to marry the chosen one of my heart. Mr. Lee, as I have said, soon sold my wife, contrary to his promise, and she fell into the hands of a very cruel mistress, the wife of the saddler above mentioned, by whom she was much abused. This woman used to wish for some great calamity to happen to my wife, because she stayed so long when she *went to nurse her child;* which calamity came very near happening afterwards to herself. My wife was finally sold, on account of the solicitations of this woman; but four months had hardly elapsed, before she insisted upon her being purchased back again.

During all this time, my mind was in a continual agitation, for I knew not one day, who would be the owner of my wife the next. O reader, have you no heart to sympathize with the injured slave, as he thus lives in a state of perpetual torment, the dread uncertainty of his wife's fate, continually hanging over his head, and poisoning all his joys, as the naked sword hung by a *hair*, over the head of an ancient king's guest, as he was seated at a table loaded with all the luxuries of an epicure's devising? This sword, unlike the one alluded to, did often pierce my breast, and when I had recovered from the wound, it was again hung up, to torture me. This is slavery, a natural and concomitant part of the accursed system!

The saddler who owned my wife, whose name I suppress for particular reasons, was at one time taken sick, but when *his minister*, the Rev. (so called) Dr. Plummer came to pray with him, he would not allow him to perform that rite, which strengthened me in the opinion I entertained of Dr. Plummer, that he was *as wicked a man* as this saddler, and you will presently see, how bad a man he was. The saddler sent for *his slaves to pray* for him, and afterwards for me, and when I repaired to his bed-side, he beseeched me to pray for him, saying that he would live a much better life than he had done, if the Lord would only spare him. I and the other slaves prayed *three nights* for him, after our work was over, and we needed rest in sleep; but the earnest desire of this man, induced us to forego our necessary rest; and yet one of the first things he did after his recovery, was to *sell my wife*. When he was reminded of my praying for his restoration to health, he angrily exclaimed, that it was "all d——d lies" about the Lord restoring him to health in consequence of the negroes praying for him,—and that if any of them mentioned that they had prayed for him, he "would *whip them for it*."

The last purchaser of my wife, was Mr. Samuel S. Cartrell, also a member of Dr. Plummer's church.* He induced me to pay him $5,000 in order to assist him in purchasing my companion, so as to prevent her being sold away from me.[3] I also paid him $50 a year, for her time, although she would have been of but little value to him, for she had young children and could not earn much for him,—and rented a house for which I paid $72, and she took in washing, which with the remainder of my earnings, after deducting master's "lion's share," supported our family. Our bliss, as far as the term bliss applies to a slave's situation, was now complete in this respect, for a season; for never had we been so pleasantly situated before; but, reader, behold its cruel termination. O the harrowing remembrance of those terrible, terrible scenes! May God spare you from ever enduring what I then endured.

It was on a pleasant morning, in the month of August, 1848, that I left my wife and three children safely at our little home, and proceeded to my allotted labor. The sun shone brightly as he commenced his daily task, and as I gazed upon his early rays, emitting their golden light upon the rich fields adjacent to the city, and glancing across the abode of my wife and family, and as I beheld the numerous companies of slaves, hieing their way to their daily labors, and reflected upon the difference between their lot and mine, I felt that, although I was a slave, there were many alleviations to my cup of sorrow. It was true, that the greater portion of my earnings was taken from me, by the unscrupulous hands of my dishonest master,—that I was entirely at his mercy, and might at any hour be snatched from what sources of joy were open to me—that he might, if he chose, extend his robber hand, and demand a still larger portion of my earnings,—and above all, that intellectual privileges were

---

*Reader, do you wonder at abolitionists calling such churches the brotherhood of thieves? C. S. [Charles Stearns's note]

entirely denied me; but as I imprinted a parting kiss upon the lips of my faithful wife, and pressed to my bosom the little darling cherubs, who followed me saying, in their childish accents, "Father, come back soon," I felt that life was not all a blank to me; that there were some pure joys yet my portion. O, how my heart would have been riven with unutterable anguish, if I had then realized the awful calamity which was about to burst upon my unprotected head! Reader, are you a husband, and can you listen to my sad story, without being moved to cease all your connection with that stern power, which stretched out its piratical arm, and basely robbed me of all dear to me on earth!

The sun had traced his way to mid-heaven, and the hour for the laborers to turn from their tasks, and to seek refreshment for their toil-worn frames,—and when I should take my prattling children on my knee,—was fast approaching; but there burst upon me a sound so dreadful, and so sudden, that the shock well nigh overwhelmed me. It was as if the heavens themselves had fallen upon me, and the everlasting hills of God's erecting, like an avalanche, had come rolling over my head! And what was it? "Your wife and smiling babes are gone; in prison they are locked, and to-morrow's sun will see them far away from you, on their way to the distant South!" Pardon the utterance of my feelings here, reader, for surely a man may feel, when all that he prizes on earth is, at one fell stroke, swept from his reach! O God, if there is a moment when vengeance from thy righteous throne should be hurled upon guilty man, and hot thunderbolts of wrath, should burst upon his wicked head, it surely is at such a time as this! And this is Slavery; its certain, necessary and constituent part. Without this terrific pillar to its demon walls, it falls to the ground, as a bridge sinks, when its buttresses are swept from under it by the rushing floods. This is Slavery. No kind master's indulgent care can guard his chosen slave, his petted chattel, however fond he may profess to be of such a piece of property, from so fearful a calamity. My master treated me as kindly as he could, and retain me in slavery; but did that keep me from experiencing this terrible deprivation? The sequel will show you even his care for me. What could I do? I had left my fond wife and prattling children, as happy as slaves could expect to be; as I was not anticipating their loss, for the pious man who bought them last, had, as you recollect, received a sum of money from me, under the promise of not selling them. My first impulse, of course, was to rush to the jail, and behold my family once more, before our final separation. I started for this infernal place, but had not proceeded a great distance, before I met a gentleman, who stopped me, and beholding my anguish of heart, as depicted on my countenance, inquired of me what the trouble was with me. I told him as I best could, when he advised me not to go to the jail, for the man who had sold my wife, had told my master some falsehoods about me, and had induced him to give orders to the jailor to seize me, and confine me in prison, if I should appear there. He said I would undoubtedly be sold separate from my wife, and he thought I had better not go there. I then persuaded a young man of my acquaintance to go to the prison, and sent by him, to my wife, some money and a message in reference to the cause of my failure to visit her. It seems that it would have been useless for me to have ventured there, for as soon as this young man arrived, and inquired for my wife, he was seized and put in prison,—the jailor mistaking him for me; but when he discovered his mistake, he was very angry, and vented his rage upon the innocent youth, by kicking him out of prison. I then repaired to my Christian master, and three times, during the ensuing twenty-four hours, did I beseech and entreat him to purchase my wife; but no tears of mine made the least impression upon his obdurate heart. I laid my case before him, and reminded him of the faithfulness with which I had served him, and of my utmost endeavors to please him, but this *kind* master—recollect reader—utterly refused to advance a small portion of the $5,000 I had paid him, in order to relieve my sufferings; and he was a member, in good and regular standing, of an Episcopal church in Richmond! His reply to me was worthy of the morality of Slavery, and shows just how much religion, the kindest and most pious of Southern slaveholders have. "*You can get another wife,*" said he; but I told him the Bible said, "What God has joined together, let not man put asunder," and that I did not want any other wife but my own lawful one, whom I loved so much. At the mention of this passage of Scripture, he drove me from his house, saying, he did not wish to hear that!

I now endeavored to persuade two gentlemen of my acquaintance, to buy my wife; but they told me they did not think it was right to hold slaves, or else they would gladly assist me, for they sincerely pitied me, and advised me to go to my master again; but I knew this would be useless. My agony was now complete. She with whom I had travelled the journey of life, for the space of twelve years, with three little pledges of domestic affection, must now be forever separated from me—I must remain alone and desolate. O God, shall my wife and children never more greet my sight, with their cheerful looks and happy smiles? Far, far away, in Carolina's swamps are they now, toiling beneath the scorching rays of the hot sun, with no husband's voice to soothe the hardships of my wife's lot, and no father's kind look to gladden the heart of my disconsolate little ones.*

I call upon you, Sons of the North, if your blood has not lost its bright color of liberty, and is not turned to the blackened gore which surrounds the slaveholder's polluted hearts, to arise in your might, and demand the liberation of the slaves. If you do not, at the day of final account, I shall bear witness against you, as well as against the slaveholders themselves, as the cause of my and my brethren's bereavement. Think you, at that dread hour, you can escape the scrutinizing look of the Judge of all the earth, as he "maketh inquisition for the blood of the innocents?" Oh, no; but equally with the Southern slaveholders, will your character be condemned by the Ruler of the universe.

The next day, I stationed myself by the side of the road, along which the slaves, amounting to three hundred and fifty, were to pass. The purchaser of my wife was a *Methodist* minister, who was starting for North Carolina. Pretty soon five waggonloads of little children passed, and looking at the foremost one, what should I see but a little child, pointing its tiny hand towards me, exclaiming, "There's my father; I knew he would come and bid me good-bye." It was my eldest child! Soon the gang approached in which my wife was chained. I looked, and beheld her familiar face; but O, reader, that glance of agony! may God spare me ever again enduring the excruciating horror of that moment! She passed, and came near to

---

*I would here state, that Mr. Brown is endeavoring to raise money to purchase his family. Twelve hundred dollars being the sum demanded for them. Any person wishing to assist him in this laudable purpose, can enclose donations to him, directing No. 21 Cornhill, Boston. [Charles Stearns's note]

where I stood. I seized hold of her hand, *intending* to bid her farewell; but words failed me; the gift of utterance had fled, and I remained speechless. I followed her for some distance, with her hand grasped in mine, as if to save her from her fate, but I could not speak, and I was obliged to turn away in silence.

This is not an imaginary scene, reader; it is not a fiction, but an every-day reality at the South; and all I can say more to you, in reference to it is, that if you will not, after being made acquainted with these facts, consecrate your all to the slaves' release from bondage, you are utterly unworthy the name of a man, and should go and hide yourself, in some impenetrable cave, where no eye can behold your demon form.

One more scene occurs in the tragic history of my life, before the curtain drops, and I retire from the stage of observation, as far as past events are concerned; not, however, to shrink from public gaze, as if ashamed of my perilous adventures, or to retire into private life, lest the bloodhounds of the South should scent my steps, and start in pursuit of their missing property. No, reader, for as long as three millions of my countrymen pine in cruel bondage, on Virginia's exhausted soil, and in Carolina's pestilential rice swamps; in the cane-breaks of Georgia, and on the cotton fields of Louisiana and Mississippi, and in the insalubrious climate of Texas; as well as suffer under the slave-driver's cruel lash, all over the almost God-forsaken South; I shall never refuse to advocate their claims to your sympathy, whenever a fitting occasion occurs to speak in their behalf.

But you are eager to learn the particulars of my journey from freedom to liberty. The first thing that occurred to me, after the cruel separation of my wife and children from me, and I had recovered my senses, so as to know how to act, was, thoughts of freeing myself from slavery's iron yoke. I had suffered enough under its heavy weight, and I determined I would endure it no longer; and those reasons which often deter the slave from attempting to escape, no longer existed in reference to me, for my family were gone, and slavery now had no mitigating circumstances, to lessen the bitterness of its cup of woe. It is true, as my master had told me, that I could "get another wife;" but no man, excepting a brute below the human species, would have proposed such a step to a person in my circumstances; and as I was not such a degraded being, I did not dream of so conducting. Marriage was not a thing of personal convenience with me, to be cast aside as a worthless garment, whenever the slaveholder's will required it; but it was a sacred institution binding upon me, as long as the God who had "joined us together," refrained from untying the nuptial knot. What! leave the wife of my bosom for another! and while my heart was leaping from its abode, to pour its strong affections upon the kindred soul of my devoted partner, could I receive a stranger, another person to my embrace, as if the ties of love existed only in the presence of the object loved! Then, indeed, should I have been a traitor to that God, who had linked our hearts together in fond affection, and cemented our union, by so many additional cords, twining around our hearts; as a tree and an arbor are held together by the clinging of the tendrils of the adhering vine, which winds itself about them so closely. Slavery, and slavery abettors, seize hold of these tender scions, and cut and prune them away from both tree and arbor, as remorselessly as a gardener cuts down the briars and thorns which disturb the growth of his fair plants; but all humane, and every virtuous man, must instinctively recoil from such transactions, as they would from soul murder, or from the commission of some enormous deed of villany.

Reader, in the light of these scenes you may behold, as in a glass, your true character. Refined and delicate you may pretend to be, and may pass yourself off as a pure and virtuous person; but if you refuse to exert yourself for the overthrow of a system, which thus tramples human affection under its bloody feet, and demands of its crushed victims, the sacrifice of all that is noble, virtuous and pure, upon its smoking altars; you may rest assured, that if the balances of *purity* were extended before you, He who "searcheth the hearts, and trieth the reins," would say to you, as your character underwent his searching scrutiny, "Thou art weighed in the balance and found wanting."

I went to Mr. Allen, and requested of him permission to refrain from labor for a short time, in consequence of a disabled finger; but he refused to grant me this permission, on the ground that my hand was not lame enough to justify him in so doing. Nothing daunted by this rebuff, I took some oil of vitriol, intending to pour a few drops upon my finger, to make it sufficiently sore, to disable me from work, which I succeeded in, beyond my wishes; for in my hurry, a larger quantity than it was my purpose to apply to my finger, found

its way there, and my finger was soon eaten through to the bone.
The overseer then was obliged to allow me to absent myself from
business, for it was impossible for me to work in that situation. But
I did not waste my precious furlough in idle mourning over my fate.
I armed myself with determined energy, for action, and in the words
of one of old, in the name of God, "I leaped over a wall, and run
through a troop" of difficulties. After searching for assistance for
some time, I at length was so fortunate as to find a friend,[4] who
promised to assist me, for one half the money I had about me, which
was one hundred and sixty-six dollars. I gave him eighty-six, and he
was to do his best in forwarding my scheme. Long did we remain
together, attempting to devise ways and means to carry me away
from the land of separation of families, of whips and thumbscrews,
and auction blocks; but as often as a plan was suggested by my
friend, there would appear some difficulty in the way of its accomplishment. Perhaps it may not be best to mention what these plans
were, as some unfortunate slaves may thereby be prevented from
availing themselves of these methods of escape.

At length, after praying earnestly to Him, who seeth afar off, for
assistance, in my difficulty, suddenly, as if from above, there darted
into my mind these words, "Go and get a box, and put yourself in
it." I pondered the words over in my mind. "Get a box?" thought I;
"what can this mean?" But I was "not disobedient unto the heavenly
vision," and I determined to put into practice this direction, as I
considered it, from my heavenly Father.* I went to the depot, and
there noticed the size of the largest boxes, which commonly were
sent by the cars, and returned with their dimensions. I then repaired
to a carpenter, and induced him to make me a box of such a description as I wished, informing him of the use I intended to make
of it. He assured me I could not live in it; but as it was dear liberty
I was in pursuit of, I thought it best to make the trial.

When the box was finished, I carried it, and placed it before my
friend, who had promised to assist me, who asked me if that was to

---

*Reader, smile not at the above idea, for if there is a God of love, we must believe
that he suggests steps to those who apply to him in times of trouble, by which they
can be delivered from their difficulty. I firmly believe this doctrine, and know it to
be true from frequent experience. C. S. [Charles Stearns's note]

"put my clothes in?" I replied that it was not, but to "*put Henry Brown in!*" He was astonished at my temerity; but I insisted upon his placing me in it, and nailing me up, and he finally consented.

After corresponding with a friend in Philadelphia,* arrangements were made for my departure, and I took my place in this narrow prison, with a mind full of uncertainty as to the result.[5] It was a critical period of my life, I can assure you, reader; but if you have never been deprived of your liberty, as I was, you cannot realize the power of that hope of freedom, which was to me indeed, "an anchor to the soul, both sure and steadfast."

I laid me down in my darkened home of three feet by two, and like one about to be guillotined, resigned myself to my fate. My friend was to accompany me, but he failed to do so; and contented himself with sending a telegraph message to his correspondent in Philadelphia, that such a box was on its way to his care.

I took with me a bladder filled with water to bathe my neck with, in case of too great heat; and with no access to the fresh air, excepting three small gimblet holes, I started on my perilous cruise. I was first carried to the express office, the box being placed on its end, so that I started with my head downwards, although the box was directed, "this side up with care." From the express office, I was carried to the depot, and from thence tumbled roughly into the baggage car, where I *happened* to fall "right side up," but no thanks to my transporters. But after a while the cars stopped, and I was put aboard a steamboat, *and placed on my head.* In this dreadful position, I remained the space of an hour and a half, it seemed to me, when I began to feel of my eyes and head, and found to my dismay, that my eyes were almost swollen out of their sockets, and the veins on my temple seemed ready to burst. I made no noise however, determining to obtain "*victory or death*," but endured the terrible pain, as well as I could, sustained under the whole by the thoughts of sweet liberty. About half an hour afterwards, I attempted again to lift my

---

*Reference to James Miller McKim, who responded to the initial inquiry from Brown co-conspirator Samuel Smith about receiving Box Brown by mail at the Pennsylvania Anti-Slavery Society offices. He was on hand for Brown's arrival to "witness the unboxing" and became an early benefactor to Brown in freedom. See the Glossary of Names for more information.

hands to my face, but I found I was not able to move them. A cold sweat now covered me from head to foot. Death seemed my inevitable fate, and every moment I expected to feel the blood flowing over me, which had burst from my veins. One half hour longer and my sufferings would have ended in that fate, which I preferred to slavery; but I lifted up my heart to God in prayer, believing that he would yet deliver me, when to my joy, I overheard two men say, "We have been here *two* hours and have travelled twenty miles, now let us sit down, and rest ourselves." They suited the action to the word, and turned the box over, containing my soul and body, thus delivering me from the power of the grim messenger of death, who a few moments previously, had aimed his fatal shaft at my head, and had placed his icy hands on my throbbing heart. One of these men inquired of the other, what he supposed that box contained, to which his comrade replied, that he guessed it was the mail. "Yes," thought I, "it is a *male*, indeed, although not the *mail* of the United States."

Soon after this fortunate event, we arrived at Washington, where I was thrown from the wagon, and again as my luck would have it, fell on my head. I was then rolled down a declivity, until I reached the platform from which the cars were to start. During this short but rapid journey, my neck came very near being dislocated, as I felt it crack, as if it had snapped asunder. Pretty soon, I heard some one say, "there is no room for this box, it will have to remain behind." I then again applied to the Lord, my help in all my difficulties, and in a few minutes I heard a gentleman direct the hands to place it aboard, as "it came with the mail and must go on with it." I was then tumbled into the car, my head downwards again, as I seemed to be destined to escape on my head; a sign probably, of the opinion of American people respecting such bold adventurers as myself; that our heads should be held downwards, whenever we attempt to benefit ourselves. Not the only instance of this propensity, on the part of the American people, towards the colored race. We had not proceeded far, however, before more baggage was placed in the car, at a stopping place, and I was again turned to my proper position. No farther difficulty occurred until my arrival at Philadelphia. I reached this place at three o'clock in the morning, and remained in the depot until six o'clock, A. M., at which time, a waggon drove up, and a person inquired for a box directed to such a place, "right side up." I was soon placed on this waggon, and carried to the house of my friend's correspondent, where quite a number of persons were waiting to receive me. They appeared to be some afraid to open the box at first, but at length one of them rapped upon it, and with a trembling voice, asked, "Is all right within?" to which I replied, "All right." The joy of these friends[6] was excessive, and like the ancient Jews, who repaired to the rebuilding of Jerusalem, each one seized hold of some tool, and commenced opening my grave. At length the cover was removed, and I arose, and shook myself from the lethargy into which I had fallen; but exhausted nature proved too much for my frame, and I swooned away.

After my recovery from this fainting fit, the first impulse of my soul, as I looked around, and beheld my friends, and was told that I was safe, was to break out in a song of deliverance, and praise to the most high God, whose arm had been so signally manifest in my escape. Great God, was I a freeman! Had I indeed succeeded in effecting my escape from the human wolves of Slavery? O what extastic joy thrilled through every nerve and fibre of my system! My labor was accomplished, my warfare was ended, and I stood erect before my equal fellow men;* no longer a crouching slave, forever at the look and nod of a whimsical and tyrannical slave-owner. Long had seemed my journey, and terribly hazardous had been my attempt to gain my birth-right; but it all seemed a comparatively light price to pay for the precious boon of *Liberty*. O ye, who know not the value of this "pearl of great price," by having been all your life shut out from its life-giving presence; learn of how much importance its possession is regarded, by the panting fugitive, as he traces his way through the labyrinths of snares, placed between him and the object of his fond desires! Sympathize with the three millions of crushed and mangled ones who this day pine in cruel bondage, and arouse yourself to action in their behalf! This you will do, if you are not traitors to your God and to humanity. Aid not in placing in high offices, *baby-stealers and women-whippers*; and if these wicked men, all covered with the clotted gore of their mangled victims, come among you, scorn the idea of bowing in homage to them, whatever

---

*For a corroboration of this part of Mr. Brown's narrative, the reader is referred to the close of this book. [Charles Stearns's note]

may be the character of their claims to your regard. No matter, if they are called presidents of your nation, still utterly refuse to honor them; which *you will most certainly do*, if you are true to the Slave!

After remaining a short time in Philadelphia, it was thought expedient that I should proceed to Massachusetts, and accordingly funds sufficient to carry me there, were raised by some anti-slavery friends, and I proceeded to Boston. After remaining a short time in that city, I concluded to go to New Bedford, in which place I remained a few weeks, under the care of Mr. Joseph Rickerston of that place, who treated me very kindly. At length hearing of a large anti-slavery meeting to be held in Boston, I left New Bedford, and found myself again in that city, so famous for its devotion to liberty in the days of the American revolution; and here, in the presence of several thousand people, did I first relate in public, the story of my sufferings, since which time I have repeated my simple tale in different parts of Massachusetts, and in the State of Maine.

I now stand before you as a free man, but since my arrival among you, I have been informed that your laws require that I should still be held as a slave; and that if my master should espy me in any nook or corner of the free states, according to the constitution of the United States, he could secure me and carry me back into Slavery;* so that I am confident I am not safe, even here, if what I have heard concerning your laws is true. I cannot imagine why you should uphold such strange laws. I have been told that every time a man goes to the polls and votes, he virtually swears to sustain them, frightful as they are. It seems to me to be a hard case, for a man to endure what I have endured in effecting my escape, and then to be continually exposed to be seized by my master, and carried back into that horrid pit from which I have escaped. I have been told, however, that the people here would not allow me to be thus returned, that they would break their own laws in my behalf, which seems quite curious to me; for why should you make laws, and swear to uphold them, and then break them? I do not understand much about laws, to be sure, as the law of my master is the one I have been subject to all my life,

---

*Allusion to possible fugitive slave legislation that was brewing as a topic of discussion in 1849.

but somehow, it looks a little singular to me, that wise people should be obliged to break their own laws, or else do a very wicked act. I have been told that there are twice as many voters at the North as there are at the South, and much more wealth, as well as other things of importance, which makes me study much, why the Northern people live under such laws. If I was one of them, and had any influence among them, it appears to me, I should advocate the overthrow of such laws, and the establishment of better ones in their room. Many people tell me besides, that if the slaves should rise up, and do as they did in Nat Turner's time, endeavor to fight their way to freedom, that the Northern people are pledged to shoot them down, and keep them in subjection to their masters. Now I cannot understand this, for almost all the people tell me, that they "are opposed to Slavery," and yet they swear to prevent the slaves from obtaining their liberty! If these things could be made clear to my mind, I should be glad; but a fog hangs over my eyes at present in reference to this matter.

I now wish to introduce to your hearing, a friend of mine, who will tell you more about these things than I can, until I have had more time to examine this curious subject. What he shall have to say to you, may not be as interesting as the account of my sufferings, but if you really wish to help my brethren in bondage, you will not be unwilling to hear what he may say to you, in reference to the way to abolish slavery, as you cannot be opposed to my sufferings, unless you are willing to exert yourselves for the overthrow of the cruel system which caused them.

Cure for the Evil of Slavery.*

Dear Friends,—

You have listened with eager ears, and with tearful eyes, to the recital of Mr. Brown. He has alluded to the laws which many of you uphold, when you go to the polls and vote, but he has not informed you of your duty at the present crisis. What I have to say at this time, will be mainly directed to the remedy for this terrible evil, so strikingly portrayed in his eventful life.

---

*Essay by Charles Stearns included in the 1849 edition of Brown's narrative.

As one of those who desire the abolition of Slavery, it is my earnest desire to be made acquainted with a true and proper remedy for this dreadful disease. I apprehend that no moral evil exists, for the cure of which there cannot be found some specific, the application of which, will effectually eradicate the disorder. I am not a politician, and cannot write as politicians do. Still I may be pardoned for entering a little into their sphere of action, for the purpose of plucking some choice fruit from the overhanging boughs of that fruitful arena. I am not afraid of politics, for I do not regard them as too sacred, or as too profane, for me to handle. I believe that the people of this country are not ready for a truly Christian government; therefore, although I cannot unite myself with any other, yet I should be rejoiced, at beholding the faintest resemblance to such an one, in opposition to our present pro-slavery government.

I would like to see all men perfect Christians, but as I do not expect to witness this sight very soon, I am gratified at their becoming anti-slavery, or even temperance men. Any advance from the old corruptions of the past, is hailed with delight by me.

The point I would now urge upon your attention is, the immediate formation of *a new government at the North*, at all events, and at all hazards! I do not say, "Down with this Union" merely, but I do say, up with an Anti-Slavery government, in the free States. Our object should be the establishment of a form of government, directly in opposition to the one we at present live under. The stars and stripes of our country's flag, should be trodden into the dust, and a white banner, with the words, "Emancipation to the Slaves" inscribed upon it, should be unfurled to the breeze, in the room of the old emblem of despotic servitude. Too long have we been dilatory upon this point; but the period I believe has now arrived, for us to strike for freedom, in earnest. Let us see first, what we have to accomplish; and then the means whereby we can bring about the desired end; our capabilities for such a work; and the reasons why we should adopt this plan; and what will be the consequences of such a course of action. First. What have we to accomplish! A great and an important end truly, which is nothing less, than the establishment of a new government, right in the midst of our present pro-slavery one.

A government, is a system of authority sustained by either the rulers, or the ruled, or by both conjointly. If it depends on the will of the rulers, then they can change it at pleasure; but if the people are connected with it, their consent must be gained, before its character can be altered. If, as is the case with our government, it is the *people* who "ordain and establish" laws, then it lies with them to change those laws, and to remodel that government. Let this fact be distinctly understood; for the majority of the people of this land, seem to labor under the delusion, that our government is sustained by some other power than their own; and are very much in the situation of those heathen nations, condemned by one of the ancient prophets, who manufactured their deities, and then fell down and worshipped the work of their own hands. The people make laws for their own guidance, and then offer as an excuse for their bad conduct, that the *laws* require them to do so! The government appears to be yet surrounded with a halo of glory, as it was in the days of kingly authority, when "the powers that be" were supposed to have been approvingly "ordained of God," and men fear to touch the sacred structure of their own erecting, as if God's throne would be endangered thereby. This is not the only manifestation of self-esteem connected with their movements.

The people also fancy, that what their fathers created is divine, when their fathers have departed, and left them to do as they elect, without any obligation resting upon them to follow in their steps; but so great is the self-esteem of the people, as manifested in their pride of ancestry, that they seem to suppose, that God would cast them off forever, if they should cease to be children, and become men, casting from them, the doctrines and political creeds of their fathers; and yet they boast of their spirit of progress! They fear to act for themselves, lest they should mar the reputation of their ancestors, and be deprived of their feeling of self-adulation, in consequence of the perfection of their worthy sires. But we must humble our pride, and cease worshipping, either our own, or our father's handiwork,—in reference to the laws, of which we are speaking. What we want is, a very simple thing. Our fathers proclaimed themselves free and independent of the British government, and proceeded to establish a new one, in its room. They threw off the British yoke! We can do the same, in reference to the United States government! We can put forth *our* "declaration of independence," and issue our manifesto of grievances; and as our fathers did, can pledge to one another, "our lives, our property and our sacred honor," in promoting the accomplishment of this end. We can *immediately organize* a new government, independent of the present one under which we live. We may be deemed traitors for so doing; but were not Samuel Adams and John Hancock traitors? and did not our forefathers inscribe on their banners, "resistance to tyrants is obedience to God?" Are we more faint-hearted than they were? Are not our and the slave's grievances more unendurable than were their wrongs? A new government is what we want; and the sound should go forth from all these free hills, echoing across the plains of the far distant West, that New England and the whole North, are ready to do battle with the myrmidons* of the slave power, not with the sword of steel, but with the spirit of patient submission to robbery and death, in defence of our principles. We are not obliged to muster our squadrons in "hot haste," to the "sound of the cannon's deafening roar," nor to arm ourselves for physical combat; for there is more power in suffering death, for truth's sake, than in fighting with swords of steel, and with cannon balls. A new government we must have; and now let us consider, Secondly, how we shall bring this end about, and some reasons why we should adopt this course.

Step by step, do we progress in all improvements designed for man's well being. At first the people in a semi-barbarous state, are satisfied with a rude code of laws, similar to that given by a military commander, to the rough bandits under his direction; but as science unfolds its truthful wings, and spreads over the minds of the race, a mantle of wisdom, which covers their rude imperfections, and shuts out from the eye of man, their inelegant barbarities, a regard for the good opinion of others more civilized than they, induces such a people to demand the overthrow of their savage code, which they have become ashamed of acknowledging. The ancient Jews were supposed to stand in need of laws of this character; which hung over their

---

*The name means "ant people." In ancient Greek mythology, the myrmidons were a race of people created by Zeus from ants, and were known for their unyielding loyalty to their leaders. The word "myrmidon" came to have the same connotations as the modern terms "robot" and, later, "hired ruffian."

heads, threatening the most severe punishments for the commission of, sometimes, very light crimes; as Sinai's burning mountain* flashed its fierce lightnings in their awe-stricken faces, and sent forth its terrible thunders, sounding in their superstitious ears, like the voice of Deity. This people had just emerged from the depths of Egyptian slavery, and might have stood in need of such severe and terrible laws, so Draconic in their nature; but the refined inhabitants of polished Greece and Rome, needed not such barbarous enactments. The advancing spirit of civilization had swept along in its effacing train, all the necessity for such brutal ferocity, by destroying the ferocious character of the people; as it opened to them more refined sources of enjoyment, in the erection of works of art, and in mental cultivation. The muses too, had purified and rendered delicate their tastes, so that outward barbarity seemed no longer attractive; although their ancestors had indulged in such scenes with great gusto. Our Druidical,† Saxon and Norman ancestry, might have needed as cruel laws as those we now live under. At least such laws would have been more appropriate to their semi-barbarous condition, than they are to our improved state; but surely, we of the nineteenth century, having outlived the errors of the past, and having reached a point, from which we can cast our eyes far back into the distant past, and behold with utter astonishment, the absurd practices of our cruel and ignorant ancestors; are not obliged, out of regard for the memory of those not so far removed from us, in point of time, as those whose memories we do not hesitate to execrate, to retain as objectionable laws as ever disgraced the statute book of England, in the days of the bloody Jeffreys, or when the unalterable "Star chamber"‡ decisions, were the law of the land. For a country to make its boast of civilization, and to call itself

---

*Mount Sinai, the place where, according to the Biblical Old Testament (Exodus 19–20), God gave the Ten Commandments to Moses.

†The word "druid" denotes the priestly class in the ancient Celtic culture of western Europe and the British Isles. Druids venerated the sun, the moon, the stars, and other natural elements.

‡English court of law (1487–1641) established to allow prosecution of powerful people that existing courts could not convict; because the Star Chamber held secret sessions with no jury or right of appeal, its name came to signify an irresponsible and oppressive judicial body.

a refined nation, while it tenaciously grasps the worst errors of its ancestors, and plunges into a fit of madness, at the least allusion to an
alteration of its cannibal laws, seems somewhat astonishing. It makes
one think of a man, who should propose joining a church, and when
asked to give up dram-drinking and gambling, should break forth in
a torrent of abuse, against those who made the proposition to him; for
those practices are no more contrary to the sweet spirit of heavenly religion, than is slaveholding in opposition to true civilization, and perfect refinement. It is a remnant of that spirit of barbarity, which
formerly induced men to fight for conquest and territory, in the
palmiest days of the ancient Eastern empires, when the fields of the
earth, fair mother of our existence, were made fertile by the rich
streams of blood, flowing from the mangled corpses, strewn upon
its surface, by the fiendish barbarity of a Sennacherib, a Cyrus, a
Xerxes, and an Alexander.*

An alteration of our present laws is demanded; but who will ag-
itate this subject, where it must be agitated, in order to accomplish
the end so ardently desired? It is well known, that a simple majority of votes in Congress, can never affect the alteration proposed,—
that three fourths of the States of this Union must be penetrated
with the spirit of repentance, in reference to slavery, and bring forth
the legitimate fruit thereof, by consenting to this alteration, before
it can be accomplished; and who will go to the South, that "valley
of the shadow of death," in regard to all subjects having reference to
man's improvement, and urge this course upon its darkened inhabitants? But this step must be taken, before the Constitution can be
altered, or its meaning rendered unequivocal, so as not to be misun-
derstood by the authorities of this nation; for it is not to be expected
that the South will ever repent of their own accord, and change the
laws of the Union, because we demand it, unless the alternative is
presented them, of such change, or disunion on our part.

But the time expended in converting the people of the *North* to
a willingness to alter the Constitution, would amply suffice to persuade them to organize a new government; for the Northern people
are as ready to go for a dissolution of the Union, as they are for an

---

*See the Glossary of Names.

alteration of the Constitution; for much advance has already been made in indoctrinating them in reference to the former idea, and thousands and tens of thousands are probably converts to this doctrine, while but little or nothing has been said in reference to the latter alternative. No party has yet proposed this step; but a large and increasing one, embodying a great portion of the talent of the nation, is now earnestly engaged in advocating the former. Which would be the easiest of accomplishment then, the conversion of the North to disunion principles, or to a willingness to alter the Constitution? Every one at all versed in political affairs, must be aware, that an alteration of the Constitution, without the consent of the South, would be a virtual dissolution of the Union, even if such a step were possible; so that converting the Northern people to the doctrine of an alteration of the Constitution, would be, in fact, only another phase of conversion to disunion; for, of course, the South will never consent to such an alteration, only as an alternative, in opposition to dissolution. To be sure, if the Northern people would act as a body, and boldly say to the South, "give us an alteration of the 'three-fifths representation' clause of the Constitution;[7] a change of that in reference to 'domestic insurrection;' and an entire destruction of the one requiring 'persons held to service, under the laws of a state,' to be given up to 'those to whom *such* service or labor may be due,' or we will break away from your polluting embrace;" there would probably be no need of our ever dissolving the Union, if the South believed the North was speaking truly; for, a petted and indulged child, rendered effeminate by parental fondness and neglect of all discipline, would be in no more danger of leaving forever its parent's abode, without a farthing in its pocket, or the ability to walk a single step alone, because of its parents' refusal to gratify its whims any longer; than would the "spoiled child" of the South, who has been fed on the richest viands our Northern pantry could supply, and drank of the costliest wines our free cellars could furnish, be in danger of leaving its well-supplied table of Northern spreading, and spring from the soft lap of Northern indulgence, to go forth to its own poverty-stricken lands, obliged to earn its coarse bread and clear water, by the hard toil of its own delicate hands.

But will the Northern people ever be ready to say this to the South? Not until years of patient toil in cultivating the pro-slavery soil of their hearts, have been expended by those whose office it seems to be to labor for the slaves' release; and even then, it is questionable whether, after having been supported by the North so long, and so patiently, the South would believe all our affirmations; and we after all might be obliged to withdraw from her. But if the plan we propose, should be adopted, it would save all this uncertainty, for the South would then know we meant what we said, and would be frightened at our movements; as a woman is filled with dismay, when her only protector, talks of leaving her and her helpless babes, to the cold charities of an unfeeling world.

It is certain the South never would consent to an alteration of the Constitution, unless she was driven to it by the North, which object has not yet been proposed by any Northern party; and before any great progress could be made in the reception of such a doctrine, a little knot of patriots, armed with the invincible resolution of him, whose narrative has been presented to you, or with that of our revolutionary fathers; could have erected the standard of revolt, and have formed the basis of a new and powerful government. It is not a reform in our government that we need, but *a revolution—an overthrow of the present one*, and the establishment of a new one. Supposing a few individuals should be hung as traitors, would not that create a sympathy for us among the governments of the old world? and would not the universal voice of all civilized nations cry out against our immolation? Let but as many individuals unite, as signed the famous manifesto of our fathers, and armed with their Spartan spirit, *pledge our lives and fortunes* to the accomplishment of this end! Let our *declaration of independence* be sent forth to all the world, and our grievances be stated in the hearing of mankind! Let a new Continental Congress meet,[8] at some favorable point, draft a new Constitution, and all who drink of the spirit of liberty, which flowed into the hearts of our fathers, be requested to annex their names to the document! Let it go forth to the whole land as *our* Constitution! Let immediate measures be taken for an active and efficient agitation of the whole subject; our orators to go forth, and in the streets and lanes of our cities and villages, proclaim the object we have in view; or, if a more silent way of proceeding shall be deemed the most expedient, let committees visit every house and shop in our land, and see who will gird on this armor, and resolve to perish in an attempt to rescue the bleeding slave, from the hands of his cruel master, by refusing all support to this government, even to the deprivation of the necessaries of life.

And now comes the period of our proposed bloodless revolution, which will try men's souls. Let us do as our fathers did, and *refuse to pay taxes to the general government.* "Millions for defence, but not one cent for tribute," cried our ancestors, in order to save their descendants from the oppressive spirit of England's grasping avarice. They at first were ridiculed, and it is stated that when John Warren,* one of the aristocracy of Boston, made an inflammatory speech, at a rebel meeting, that he was denounced by the leading citizens of this place, and a copy of a letter is still preserved, written by some of them in reference to the transaction, in which they state, that "one Dr. Warren, had indeed made a rebellious speech, but he was applauded only by *a few rowdies.*" Shall not we be as willing to sacrifice our property and lives, as were our ancestors? Did not John Hancock hand the keys of his stores and dwelling to the authorities of the city, saying to them, "this is all of my property, but if the good of Boston requires its destruction, I freely yield it to you?" To pay taxes is to support the government, under which we live, for without this support it could not exist. These taxes are not paid of course directly, but still we eat, drink, and wear those things, on which a duty is paid, which gives the general government all its power. For instance. The Mexican War[9] has left a large debt resting on our shoulders. The only way in which it will be paid probably is, by an increased tariff on particular articles of consumption. Now if an entire cessation of such consumption should take place, would not the government be left destitute of the means to pay this debt? Who pays the salaries of the officers of this government, but the consumer of the articles taxed by it? If the consumption of all such articles can be prevented, would not our government be obliged to cease operations, for want of oil to grease its machinery with? It moves only as money is furnished it. Our navy and army, the protectors of the South, can only be supported by large sums of money,

---

*Reference to John Warren or to John Collins Warren. See the Glossary of Names for information on both.

derived from the revenue of the nation, which revenue we help to create by our consumption of these things. If sugar pays a large duty, or tea and coffee, or silks and satins, broadcloths and cassimeres, by refusing to use those articles, and inducing others to do the same, would not the revenue of the nation be affected? and when the actual tax-gatherer in the shape of the merchant, holds out his seductive wares for our purchase, could we not exhibit to him our pledge to "totally abstain" from the use of such articles; as the temperance man shows his ticket, as a reason why he should not partake of the intoxicating cup?

Another step could also be taken. A president could be chosen by us, and other necessary officers, and we could go on with our government, just as if no other existed, "beating for recruits" all the while, and offering no physical resistance to those who molest us. *Have we not a right so to do?*

> "Children of the glorious dead!
> Who for freedom fought and bled,"

have you become bond slaves to a power fully as oppressive of you, as that of Britain's tyrannical king, against whom your ancestors lifted their stout arms in rebellion, and unfurled their banner of revolt, on which was gloriously inscribed, "victory or death?" Have you forever lost all that portion of your ancestral fire, which armed three millions of poor and feeble men to engage in deadly combat with the richest and most powerful nation in Christendom? Ah, has God forsaken you so entirely, that no pulse of gladness beats in your frame, as you listen to the stirring notes of the wild, clarion sound of freedom, coming over these hills, and echoing from the far-distant prairies of the wide West? Oh is there not, friends, any deep fountain of sorrow gushing up from the inmost depths of your secret souls, for the sufferings and woes of the three millions of your Southern brethren? Ah, is there not any remnant of the spark of divinity which our Father in heaven has placed in every human heart, left to warm up your frigid souls? Say, breathes there not a particle of indignant life in your moral nature, as you listen to the mad agonies of shrieking mothers, the victims of remorseless tyrants who now stand defacing God's image and stamping in the dust the lineaments of their Creator? Oh, is there none of manhood left in you, that the shrieks of trampled upon and bleeding innocence, should not move you to contend with Slavery's cruel power? But is not your own safety a reason why you should cease to doff your beavers to the South, and should refuse to pay homage to her any longer? Listen a moment while I exhibit to you some more personal and selfish arguments. At the last election, the Southern States were allowed one electoral vote for every 7,500 voters, while at the North, it took 12,000 voters to entitle us to *one* elector. The number of electors, of which we were thus deprived, was about 100, which was the same as excluding from the privilege of the elective franchise, 750,000 voters, about the number in all New England and Pennsylvania! Now are not these persons taxed equally with those who have the privilege of voting? Do not all the citizens of the North pay taxes? Yes, and much more than their true proportion, for by far the greater portion of duty-paying goods, are consumed at the North. Then, is not the principle which our fathers died to oppose, fully carried out by our government, *taxation without representation?* and yet we tamely submit to this plucking our substance from us, by the fierce beak of our country's eagle; while our fathers would not so much as listen to the slight growling of the English lion, as he shook his shaggy mane in their faces, and touched them with but the extremities of his bloody paw! Robbery, if committed by a bird of prey, the American eagle, is to be patiently submitted to, and indeed we call it but the tickling of an affectionate friend or child; but let the valiant lion of Old England take the value of a pin's point, or a few old pine trees and worthless rocks from us, and how the welkin* rings with the sound of our abhorrence of such depredations. We are like the slaveholder, spoken of in our friend's narrative, who told the slaves it was a crime to steal from him, but none to rob his neighbors, because he reaped the benefits of the theft. So with us. We are *rewarded* for our submission to this robbery, by the paltry trade of the South, and as long as a few of us can make more money than we lose otherwise by our connection with the South, we care not for our principles, although every fourth of July we laud our fathers for

---

*Sky, heaven, firmament.

fighting in behalf of them; or for the losses of the mass of the people. *Taxation without representation!* This practice deluged the fields of our country, with our ancestor's and Briton's son's blood; and caused our prosperity, as a nation, to be stricken to the ground, and we magnify our fathers for their boldness, in reference to it; yet we cherish the same principle, and press it to our bosoms as a part of our religion!

Great Britain *tried* our fathers, accused of crime, away from their homes, across the waters of the ocean, and we call it a great oppression; but let one of our sons be guilty of an act in violation of Southern law, or be even suspected of it, and there is *no* law by which he can be tried. All law is trampled under foot, and he is doomed to waste away his life, in a gloomy prison, or to be whipped almost to death. Which is the worst, being tried across the sea, by an impartial court, or being strung up by Lynch law between the heavens and the earth, and left dangling on the limb of a tree, or else doomed to wear out a miserable existence in some foul dungeon?

But to make the case still more parallel. Great Britain, our fathers complained, quartered soldiers upon them[10] in times of peace, who eat out their substance and corrupted the people. For what other earthly purpose is the army of the United States continued in existence, but to watch the bidding of the monster Slavery, and be ready to fly at a moment's warning to her assistance, in case the least attempt should be made by their victims to regain their freedom? That this is a true statement, may be seen from the fact, that all our wars for the last thirty-five years, have been waged in behalf of Slavery, and even our last war with Great Britain, is attributed by many persons to the demands of the slave power. It is certain, that no war will ever be allowed by the South, except in behalf of Slavery, for it would be detrimental to their interests; and it is well known that she rules over the destinies of this country, and guides its affairs of state, as effectually as Alexander or Napoleon ruled the countries they had conquered. Slavery rules this nation, did we say? It can hardly be called ruling, for we are so submissive to the faintest manifestation of her will, that she has but to glance her glowing eye towards our craven souls, and we will prostrate our abject forms lowly on the ground, with our faces hid in the dust, which we are truly unworthy to touch; as submissively and reverentially, as the devout Mussulman* kisses the ground when the hour of prayer arrives, crying, "God is great." Our God is emphatically Slavery. To him we address our early matins, and in his ear are uttered our evening orisons. More devoutly do we render homage to our god, Slavery, than the most pious of us adore the God of heaven, which proves that we are a very religious people, worshipping, not crocodiles, leeks and onions, snakes, and images of wood and stone, but a god, whose service is infinitely more disgusting than that of any heathen idol, but one who *pays* us well, for our obeisance, as we imagine.

In this matter of a standing army, we go beyond our fathers in suffering oppression. They were not obliged to fight for England, when the object of the war was to enslave themselves; but it is well known that the great object the South has in view, in all her wars, is the aggrandizement of herself and the subjection of the North to her complete dictation; and we are called upon to engage in these wars, and after they are fought, we are compelled to foot the heavy bills.

But when our fathers were oppressed, they could plead in their own behalf. If they placed their feet on England's shores, no harm could befall them, as long as they were guilty of no crime. They could defend their own cause; and the thunders of a Burke's eloquence, shook the walls of Parliament to their foundation, and made the tyrants of England tremble and quake with fear, as he poured forth the fervor of his vehement eloquence in strong condemnation of the oppression of the colonies. A William Pitt[†] too, could frighten the British minister from his unhallowed security, amid the multitude of fawning sycophants surrounding him, in the height of his political power, by the thunders of his voice, uttered in faithful rebuke of the war measures of the government. This noble Earl, was allowed to plead in behalf of American freedom, until his earnest spirit was claimed by the grim messenger death, as he arose in his place in the House of Lords, to speak in our behalf. But suffer what we may, is there any redress for us at the hands of our government? Our property

---

*Muslim.

†Probably a reference to William Pitt, 1st Earl of Chatham, a British Whig states-man. See the Glossary of Names for more information.

may be injured by spoliations on our commerce, such as imprisoning our seamen, as well as by the crime of seizing our free citizens and depriving them of their liberty; and can we obtain the least redress? O the ignominy of our puerile connection with the South!

It is well known that under the system of Slavery, the three great blessings of republicanism are denied to a large portion of our citizens. These are, freedom of the press, of speech and of locomotion. And will we allow ourselves to be deprived of what even Europe's despotic kings have been bestowing upon their subjects? Are we more base and abject in our submission to the South, than are the oppressed millions of the old world, in their subjection to their kingly oppressors? O what falsifiers of our own professions, and truants to our own dearly prized principles, we are! Can an abolitionist travel unexposed at the South? I have had some little experience in the matter, and know that such is not the case. Men have pursued me with relentless hate, and implements of death have been brought into requisition against me, for no crime, only for exposing Slavery, in its own dominions. Can we send to any part of the South those newspapers we may wish to send there? While at the South, I was advised by a friend to conceal a paper I had received, because of its being opposed to Slavery; and it is in only particular portions of that ill-fated country, that anti-slavery publications, can be introduced. It is not many years, since a man was publicly whipped, for having an anti-slavery newspaper wrapped around a bible, which he was offering for sale. As to liberty of speech, not half the freedom is allowed the opponents of Slavery on the floors of Congress, that the British Parliament allowed the opposers of the American War. In Boston, on the day which ushered the famous *stamp act* into existence, the bells were tolled, and a funeral procession passed through the streets, bearing a coffin, on which the word *Liberty* was inscribed. "During the movement of the procession, minute guns were fired, and an oration was pronounced in favor of the *deceased*. Similar expressions of grief and indignation occurred in many parts of the land;" but, friends, no funeral procession passed through our streets when Liberty died the second time—no muffled bells sounded their melancholy peals in the ears of a mourning people; no liberty-loving orator was found to pronounce a requiem for the departed goddess; and yet she was slain—and slain too, not by foreign hands, nor by the natural allies of human oppressors, but, shall I tell the sad and dismal tale? by those, who twenty-five years before, had shrouded their faces in mantles of mourning, and rent the air with their expressions of grief, at the destruction of one of liberty's little fingers, by the passage of the stamp act;[11] but when Liberty lay a full length corpse, on the floors of that Congress, which sold her to the South, as Judas betrayed the Son of God, and for almost as small a boon, viz.: "the carrying trade" of the South; not only were there *no* lamentations made over her complete departure, but she was taken by night and buried hastily; while.

"Not a drum was heard nor a funeral note,"

as her corse was deposited without a "winding sheet," or even "a soldier's cloak" to wrap around her bleeding form. Clandestinely was she hurried out of the sight of the men who murdered her; and instead of songs of sorrow, being heard throughout the land, pæans of praise ascended from its every corner, and honors were heaped on the heads of her murderers. But Liberty as truly died then, as if loud lamentations had been made in her behalf, and the descendants of those very men, who in 1765 followed the coffin of liberty to its place of deposit, because no business was deemed lawful unless the records of it were made on *stamped paper;* the descendants of these very mourners of liberty, now, do what is infinitely worse than to use the stamped paper of a British king; they swear to support that sacrifice of Liberty upon the altar of Southern slavery, whenever they arc admitted to any offices of trust and renown. Is not this oppressive, when we may not administer justice to our fellow men, or exercise the most common authority, without renewing the thrust at the departed spirit of liberty, as our fathers actually slew her fair form?

> O Liberty! didst thou draw thy keen sword
>> For those, whom av'rice sought to rob, and slay,
>> And sent its minions far, to seek its prey,
>> That glittering gold might its coffers fill;
>> While they their foes should crush, and seek to kill,
> That England's lords, their gold could steal, and hoard?

Goddess celestial, and divine, and pure,
>   Wert thou, the champion brave, the soldier true,
>   Who fought with youthful vigor, with the few,
>   Of Columbia's sons, who stood, a sturdy band,
>   And bade their country's foes to leave their land,
While they, to thee didst vow allegiance sure?

Insulted nymph! thy fair form shone so bright,
>   That kings, as thee they saw, could not reject
>   That face, alive with claims to their respect;
>   E'en they, besotted with the lust of power,
>   Could not refuse to yield to thee thy dower,
But ceased at thy command, their foes to fight.

But ah! the men who thee so loud did call,
>   The souls, whom thou hadst saved from bondage dread,
>   O fearful tale! *themselves on thee did tread;*
>   And thy fair robe was pierced with traitorous thrusts.
>   As Cæasar groaning fell and kissed the dust,
When ingrate Brutus' blows on him did fall.

On the 5th of March, 1775, the Boston Massacre occurred—the fearful tragedy of State Street![12] All Boston was aroused, murders dreadful had been committed by the British troops, and it was a difficult task to allay the excitement occasioned thereby. What was the amount of this terrible massacre? Why, three Boston citizens had been shot in the heat of an affray with the British soldiery! What horror seemed to seize upon the hearts of the people! Why, "our brothers are being shot down in the face of open day, and our turn may come next." Terrible was the indignation of our fathers! And yet we, their descendants, calmly allow the South to slay our citizens at their leisure. The blood of a murdered Lovejoy, still cries out from the ground for vengeance! A Baltimore prison, still contains the impress of a departed spirit's feet, which left an impression on its gloomy pavement, as he fled from an earthly prison-house to the mansions of the blest. A C. C. Torrey still calls for redress for his wrongs at the hands of Southern tyrants. The jail of our own capital if it could speak, would tell of him who pined away within its noisome walls, as he lay in that republican enclosure, a victim to Southern tyranny. Yes, Dr. Crandall's blood has not yet been atoned for, by the wicked South. Here are, at least three victims who have teen slain, at the cruel dictation of Slavery's dreadful power. But time would fail me, to tell of a Van Zandt, of a Fairbanks, and of numerous others, whose lives have been forfeited to the South. And yet we submit to her dictation. Our own citizens slain, imprisoned, and cruelly beaten, but yet we have no heart to break away from this degrading alliance with our Southern man-stealing brethren.

But, I must bring this expostulation to a close, and proceed to show the *consequences* of this event, the formation of a new government. Of these it may be said; they could not be more disastrous to the North than Slavery has been; for like the "horse-leech's two daughters," she continually cries "give, give," and never seems to have enough. Hardly through with the digestion of the tremendous morsel just administered to her gormandizing appetite, she commences to lick her lips, and daintily ask for a dessert, with which to finish the full meal which she has already made of California and New Mexico, and as her mother deems it her duty, never to deny any of her darling daughter's reasonable requests, probably the Island of Cuba, will soon be placed at her side,[13] for her to nibble upon at leisure.

Many persons deprecate our plan, for fear of a civil war; and terrific ideas of rivers of blood rolling across our fields, and piles of bones heaped on our shores, startle them in their slumbers, as the rustling of a leaf fills the slaveholder's heart with fear. In the first place, how very absurd is this idea of a civil war being the result of disunion. Can any one seriously urge it, as an objection to this movement? Look at the vast extent of territory open to the incursions of an enemy, if the North should withdraw from the South. There are the Islands of the West Indies, filled with emancipated slaves, ready, some of them to join in an effort to redeem the Southern slaves from bondage. Then there is the long line of seaboard, entirely unprotected, which even in the last war was devastated in part by the British army, and the capital of our country reduced to ashes. On the Northern frontier, runs that talismanic line, over which a slave has but to place his foot, and glorious liberty becomes his possession. Here stand, twelve millions of freemen, ready to fight in behalf of the panting fugitive, while nearly 20,000 sturdy hearts beat quick to the sound of the trumpet of freedom, and are ready to leave their homes in *Canada*, to assist their brethren. Then, there is ill-treated and insulted Mexico, burning under a sense of the wrongs inflicted upon her, and watching an opportunity to redress those wrongs. Last of all, are the numerous Indian tribes, smarting under a deep sense of the wrongs they have received at our hands. Now will any sensible person assert that five millions of Southerners, allowing all her white population to be in favor of Slavery, with an intestine foe, ready to spring upon her, as soon as the last chance of freedom presents itself, will be in danger of fighting twelve millions of free Northerners, who can call to their aid all these, and numerous other allies? Why, the idea is preposterous, and none but an insane man, can seriously entertain it. Who would fight the North, if war should be declared? At the first sound of the trumpet of war, every slave would be instantly free; for never could the Southerners leave their homes exposed to the fury of an insurgent population, as they would be obliged to, if an army should be organized to fight the North.

But who are those persons who cry out "civil war, and bloodshed?" Are they not mostly those who believe the revolutionary war to have been right? If Slavery is wrong, to be consistent, they ought to hail any movement which will hasten an insurrection among the Slaves. What is a civil war of a few years' continuance, in comparison to the seven years' war we waged with Great Britain? *Then* our resources were limited, our treasury light, and we were only three millions strong. But *now*, we abound in resources, have become plethoric on account of our riches, and are twelve millions strong, while our enemy is less than half that number. We coped with twenty millions of British subjects, when we numbered but three millions, can we not now with twelve millions cope with five? Then has our glory departed indeed, and we are the veriest slaves in existence. But would our trade be endangered? Ah, that is *the* question. Said a person to me not long since, "I acknowledge there would be benefits in a dissolution of the Union, but there are also disadvantages." And what are they? we inquired. "Why, our trade would be injured." Let it perish then! Every mother's son of us, had better pack up and on board our numerous vessels go on a begging expedition to England or France, or we had better "tie millstones about our necks, and drown ourselves in the depths of the sea;" or, we had better lay down in the streets and perish with hunger, than to allow Slavery to continue its existence.

The moment it is granted that a dissolution of the Union would abolish Slavery quicker than any other course, then I think our point is gained, and there is no necessity of proving that we shall not lose the sale of a few hats and boots, or *slave whips*. It seems almost an insult to the character of the Northern people to answer such an argument as this, and yet I fear that it is the "strong reason" why this question meets with so much opposition.

If slavery is abolished, no one can deny that our *trade*, so important to Northern men, and for which they are ready to barter the welfare of three millions of human beings, would be materially increased; but for one I care not, whether this will be the case or not. I cannot, I will not argue this question. It is a sin against the Holy Ghost, to dream of balancing the matter in this way. Northern men, you are too much actuated by this spirit of Avarice! You must be converted from this accursed love for gold; for it will sink you into the lowest degradation of a life afar from Deity. You cannot be the friends of God, while it reigns in your hearts! You must arise, and cast it from you! You must be converted from your selfishness, and then you will have no objections to offer against a dissolution of the Union! If your eyes can only be anointed with the eye-salve of humanity, and be washed in the waters of benevolence, you will see the folly of all your objections, and will be ready to sink all your ships with their rich cargoes, into the depths of the sea, and to burn your well-filled stores, rather than to cause Slavery to continue another day! O, men of the North, can ye not be aroused to action in the slave's behalf? Shall the purple streams of the slave's blood, flow ceaselessly and rapidly o'er our land, gushing forth from every hillside of the South, and coloring all the fair fields of Southern industry, on account of your sustaining power? O that I could utter some word in your ear, which would quicken your dormant sensibilities and arouse you to action in the slave's cause! Shall I tell you of God, of heaven, and of hell? There is a God, and as he descends from his abode among the stars, and essays to find an entrance into your soul, by which he may make you "a joint heir with Christ to an inheritance, incorruptible and undefiled and which fadeth not away," depend upon it, that he will be frustrated in his benevolent purpose, if the demon of pro-slavery, lies coiled up in your heart. Whatever may be said of religion, it is true that God can never approve of any person, in league with slaveholders; for a just God is forever opposed to all forms of robbery and oppression. If God's favor then is of any value, flee, I beseech thee, to the arms of liberty, and be encircled by her protecting power; so that all approach to Slavery may be dreaded by thee, as an angel dreads the polluting touch of sin.

EXTRACT of an Address of Sam. J. May, Unitarian Clergy-Clergyman, in Syracuse, N. Y., delivered in Faneuil Hall,

Never will the story be forgotten in our country, or throughout the world, of the man—whom I trust you will all be permitted to see—who, that he might escape from Southern oppression, consented to a living entombment. He entered the box with the determination to be free or die: and as he heard the nails driven in, his fear was that death was to be his portion; yet, said he, let death come in preference to slavery! I happened to be in the City of Philadelphia—I have told the story to the convention already, but I will tell it again—in the midst of an excitement that was caused by the arrival of a man in a box. I measured it myself; *three feet one inch long, two feet wide, and two feet six inches deep.* IN THAT BOX A MAN WAS ENTOMBED FOR TWENTY SEVEN HOURS.

The box was placed in the express car in Richmond, Va., and subjected to all the rough treatment ordinarily given to boxes of merchandise; for, notwithstanding the admonition of *"this side up with care,"* the box was tumbled over, so that he was sometimes on his head; yes, at one time, for nearly two hours, as it seemed to him, *on his head*, and momentarily expecting that life would become extinct, from the terrible pressure of blood that poured upon his brain. Twenty-seven hours was this man subjected to this imminent peril, that he might, for one moment, at least, breathe the air of liberty. Does not such a man deserve to be free? Is there a heart here, that does not bid him welcome? Is there a heart here, that can doubt that there must be in him not merely the heart and soul of a deteriorated man—a degraded, inferior man—but the heart and soul of a noble man? Not a *nobleman*, sir, but a NOBLE MAN? Who can doubt it?

Representation of the Box,

In which a fellow mortal travelled a long journey, in quest of those rights which the piety and republicanism of this country denied to him, the right to possess.

3 feet 1 inch long, 2 feet wide, 2 feet 6 inches high.

As long as the temples of humanity contain a single worshipper, whose heart beats in unison with that of the God of the universe; must a religion and a government which could inflict such misery upon a human being, be execrated and fled from, as a bright angel, abhors and flees from the touch of hideous sin.

NARRATIVE

OF THE

LIFE OF HENRY BOX BROWN[1]

WRITTEN BY HIMSELF

Forget not the unhappy,
Though sorrow may annoy,
There's something then for memory,
Hereafter to enjoy!
Oh! still from Fortune's garland,
Some flowers *for others strew;*
And forget not the unhappy,
For, ah! their friends are few.

FIRST ENGLISH EDITION.

[1851]

PREFACE

So much has already been written concerning the evils of slavery, and by men so much more able to portray its horrid form than I am, that I might well be excused if I were to remain altogether silent on the subject; but however much has been written, however much has been said, and however much has been done, I feel impelled by the voice of my own conscience, from the recent experience which I have had of the alarming extent to which the traffic in human beings is carried on, and the cruelties, both bodily and mental, to which men in the condition of slaves are continually subjected, and also from the hardening and blasting influences which this traffic produces on the character of those who thus treat as goods and chattels the bodies and souls of their fellows, to add yet one other testimony of, and protest against, the foul blot on the state of morals, of religion, and of cultivation in the American republic. For I feel convinced that enough has not been written, enough has not been said, enough has not been done, while nearly four millions of human beings, possessing immortal souls, are, in chains, dragging out their existence in the southern states. They are keenly alive to the heaven born voice of liberty, and require the illumination of the grace of Almighty God. Having, myself, been in that same position, but by the blessing of God having been enabled to snap my chains and escape to a land of liberty—I owe it as a sacred duty to the cause of humanity, that I should devote my life to the redemption of my fellow men.

The tale of my own sufferings is not one of great interest to those who delight to read of hair-breadth adventures, of tragic occurrences, and scenes of blood—my life, even in slavery, has been in many respects comparatively comfortable. I have experienced a continuance of such kindness, as slaveholders have to bestow; but though my body has escaped the lash of the whip, my mind has

groaned under tortures which I believe will never be related, because, language is inadequate to express them, but those know them
who have them to endure. The whip, the cowskin, the gallows, the
stocks, the paddle, the prison, the perversion of the stomach—
although bloody and barbarous in their nature—have no comparison with those internal pangs which are felt by the soul when the
hand of the merciless tyrant plucks from one's bosom the object of
one's ripened affections, and the darlings who in requiring parental
care, confer the sweet sensations of parental bliss. I freely admit I
have enjoyed my full share of all those blessings which fall to the lot
of a slave's existence. I have felt the sweet influence of friendships'
power, and the still more delightful glow of love; and had I never
heard the name of liberty or seen the tyrant lift his cruel hand to
smite my fellow and my friend, I might perhaps have dragged my
chains in quietude to the grave, and have found a tomb in a slavery-
polluted land; but thanks be to God I heard the glorious sound and
felt its inspiring influence on my heart, and having satisfied myself
of the value of freedom, I resolved to purchase it whatever should be
its price.

INTRODUCTION

WHILE AMERICA IS BOASTING of her freedom and making the world ring with her professions of equality, she holds millions of her inhabitants in bondage. This surely must be a wonder to all who seriously reflect on the subject of man holding property in man, in a land of republican institutions. That slavery, in all its phases, is demoralizing to every one concerned, none who may read the following narrative, can for a moment doubt. In my opinion unless the Americans purge themselves of this stain, they will have to undergo very severe, if not protracted suffering. It is not at all unlikely that the great unsettledness which of late has attached to the prices of cotton; the very unsatisfactory circumstance of that slaveholding continent being the principal field employed in the production of that vegetable, by the dealing in, and the manufacture of, which, such astonishing fortunes have been amassed—will lead to arrangements being entered into, through the operation of which the bondmen will be made free. The popular mind is, in every land becoming impatient of its chains; and soon the American captives will be made to taste of that freedom, which by right, belongs to man. The manner in which this mighty change will be accomplished, may *not* be at present understood, but with the Lord all things are possible. It may be, that the very means which are being used by those who wish to perpetuate slavery, and to recapture those who have by any plans not approved of by those dealers in human flesh, become free, will be amongst the instruments which God will employ to overturn the whole system.

Another means which, in addition to the above, we think, will contribute to the accomplishment of this desirable object—the destruction of slavery—is the simple, but natural narrations of those who have been long under the yoke themselves. It is a lamentable fact that some ministers of religion are contaminated with the foulness of slavery. Those men, in the southern states, who ascend the pulpit to proclaim the world's jubilee, are themselves, in fearful numbers, the holders of slaves! When we reflect on the bar which slavery constituted to the advancement of the objects at one time contemplated by the almost defunct "Evangelical Alliance";[2] when we consider that Great Being who beheld the Israelites in their captivity, and beholding, came down to deliver them is still the same; have we not reason to believe that he will in his Providence raise up another Moses, to guide the now enslaved sons of Ham[3] to the privileges which humanity, irrespective of colour or clime, is always at liberty to demand. While the British mind retains its antipathy to slavery in all its kinds, and sends forth its waves of audibly expressed opinion on the subject, that opinion, meeting with one nearly allied in character to itself in the Northern States; and while both unite in tending towards the South the reiterated demand for an honest acting, one those turgid profession of equality peculiar to all American proceedings—in every thing but slavery—the Southern states must yield to the pressure from without; even the slaves will feel themselves growing beyond the dimensions which their chains can enclose, and backed by the roar of the British Lion, and supported by Northern Americans in their just demand for emancipation, the long downtrodden and despised bondmen will arise, and by a united voice assert their title to freedom. It may be that the subject of the following narrative has a mission from God to the human family. Certainly the deliverance of Moses, from destruction on the Nile, was scarcely more marvellous than was the deliverance of Mr. Henry Box Brown from the horrors of slavery. For any lengthy observations, by which the reader will be detained from the subject of the following pages, there can be no necessity whatever.

Mr. Brown was conveyed from Richmond, Virginia, to Philadelphia in a box, three feet long, and two feet six inches deep. For twenty-seven hours he was enclosed in this box. The following copy of a letter which was written by the gentleman to whom it was directed, will explain this part of the subject:—

Copy of a Letter respecting Henry Box Brown's escape from Slavery—a verification of Patrick Henry's Speech in Virginia

Legislature, March, 1775, when he said, *"Give me Liberty or give me Death."*

Philadelphia, March 26th, 1849.

Dear—

*Here is a man who has been the hero of one of the most extraor-dinary achievements I ever heard of;—he came to me on Saturday Morning last, in a box tightly hooped, marked "*THIS SIDE UP*,"* by overland express, from the city of Richmond!! *Did you ever hear of any thing in all your life to beat that? Nothing that was done on the barricades of Paris* exceeded this cool and deliberate intrepidity. To appreciate fully the boldness and risk of the achievement, you ought to see the box and hear all the circumstances. The box is in the clear three feet one inch long, two feet six inches deep, and two feet wide. It was a regular old store box, such as you see in Pearl street;—it was grooved at the joints and braced at the ends, leaving but the very slightest crevice to admit the air. Nothing saved him from suffocation but the free use of the water—a quantity of which he took in with him in a beef's bladder, and with which he bathed his face—and the constant fanning of himself with his hat. He fanned himself unremittingly all the time. The "this side up" on the box was not regarded, and he was twice put with his head downward, rest-ing with his back against the end of the box, his feet braced against the other,—the first time he succeeded in shifting his po-sition; but the second time was on board of the steam boat, where people were sitting and standing about the box, and where any motions inside would have been overheard and have led to dis-covery; he was therefore obliged to keep his position for* twenty miles. *This nearly killed him. He says the veins in his temples were as thick as his finger. I had been expecting him for several days, and was in mortal fear all the time lest his arrival should*

---

*Between 1827 and 1849 the people erected barricades in the streets of Paris eight times, always in the city's eastern half; three times these barricades were a prelude to revolution.

*only be a signal for calling in the coroner. You can better imag-
ine than I can describe my sensations, when, in answer to my rap
on the box and question, "all right," the prompt response came
"all right, sir." The man weighs 200 pounds, and is about five
feet eight inches in height; and is, as you will see, a noble looking
fellow. He will tell you the whole story. Please send him on to
Mr. McGleveland, Boston, with this letter, to save me the time
it would take to write another. He was boxed up in Richmond,
at five, A.M. on Friday shipped at eight, and I opened him up at
six (about daylight) next morning. He has a sister in New
Bedford.*[4]

Yours, truly,
M. McRoy.

The report of Mr. Brown's escape spread far and wide, so that he
was introduced to the Anti-Slavery Society in Philadelphia, from
the office of which society a letter, of which the following is a copy,
was written.

*Anti-Slavery Office,
Philadelphia, April 8th, 1850.*

H. Box Brown,

*My Dear Sir,—I was pleased to learn, by your letter, that it was
your purpose to publish a narrative of the circumstances of your escape from slavery; such a publication, I should think, would not
only be highly interesting, but well adapted to help on the cause of
anti-slavery. Facts of this kind illustrate, without comment, the
cruelty of the slave system, the fitness of its victims for freedom,
and, at the same time, the guilt of the nation that tolerates its existence.*

*As one privy to many of the circumstances of your escape, I con-
sider it one of the most remarkable exploits on record. That a man
should come all the way from Richmond to Philadelphia, by the
overland route, packed up in a box three feet long, by two and an
half feet wide and deep, with scarcely a perceptible crevice for the*

admission of fresh air, and subject, at that time, to the rough handling and frequent shiftings of other freight, and that he should
reach his destination alive, is a tale scarcely to be believed on the
most irresistible testimony. I confess, if I had not myself been present at the opening of the box on its arrival, and had not witnessed
with my own eyes, your resurrection from your living tomb, I
should have been strongly disposed to question the truth of the
story. As it was, however, seeing was believing, and believing was
with me, at least, to be impressed with the diabolical character of
American Slavery, and the obligation that rests upon every one to
labour for its overthrow.

Trusting that this may be the impression produced by your narrative, wherever it is read, and that it may be read wherever the
evils of slavery are felt, I remain,

Your friend, truly,
J. McKim.*

Were Mr. Brown in quest of an apology for publishing the following Narrative, the letter of Mr. McKim would form that
apology. The Narrative was published in America, and an edition
of 8,000 copies sold in about two months, such was the interest
excited by the astounding revelations made by Mr. Brown as
to the real character of slavery, and the hypocrisy of those
professors of religion who have any connection with its infernal
proceedings.

Several ministers of religion took a great interest in Mr. Brown,
and did what they could to bring the subject of his escape properly
before the public. The Rev. Mr. Spauldin, of Dover, N. H. was at the
trouble to write to two of his brethren in the ministry, a letter, of
which the following is a copy. The testimonials subjoining

---

*James Miller McKim responded to the initial inquiry from Brown co-conspirator
Samuel Smith about receiving Box Brown by mail at the Pennsylvania Anti-Slavery
Society offices. He was on hand for Brown's arrival to "witness the unboxing" and
became an early benefactor to Brown in freedom. For more information, see the
Glossary of Names.

Mr. Spauldin's letter were given by persons who had witnessed the exhibition.

TO THE REV. MESSRS. PIKE AND BROOKS.
Dover, 12th July, 1850

Dear Brethren,

A coloured gentleman, Mr. H. B. Brown, purposes to visit your village for the purpose of exhibiting his splendid PANORAMA *or* Mirror of Slavery. *I have had the pleasure of seeing it, and am prepared to say, from what I have myself seen, and known in times past, of slavery and of the slave trade, in my opinion, it is almost, if not quite, a perfect fac simile of the workings of that horrible and fiendish system. The real* life-like *scenes presented in this* PANORAMA, *are admirably calculated to make an unfading impression upon the heart and memory, such as no lectures, books, or colloquial correspondence can produce, especially on the minds of children and young people, who should everywhere be brought before the altar of Hannibal, to swear eternal hate to slavery, and love of rational freedom. If you can spare the time to witness the exhibition, I am quite certain you will feel yourselves amply rewarded. I know very well, there are a great many impostors and cheats going about through the country deceiving and picking up the people's money, but* this *is of another class altogether.*

Yours, very truly,
JUSTIN SPAULDING.

I hereby certify that I have attended the exhibition of H. B. Brown's Panorama, in this village, with very deep interest; and most cordially subscribe my name, as an expression of my full concurrence with the sentiment of the recommendation above.

A. LATHAM.

I agree cordially in the above testimonials.

A. CAVERNO.

I am not an experienced judge in paintings of this kind, but am only surprised that this is so well done and so much of it true to the life.

OLIVER AYER PORRER,
Of Franklin-street, Baptist Minister.
Dover, N.H. July 15th, 1850.

Although the following letter, as to date, should have occupied a place before the others, as it was addressed to the public and not to any particular person, its present position will answer every purpose of its publication.

Syracuse, April 26th, 1850.

To the Public,

There are few facts, connected with the terrible history of American Slavery, that will be longer remembered, than that a man escaped from the house of bondage, by coming from Richmond, Virginia, to Philadelphia, in a box three feet, one inch long, two feet wide, and *two* feet six inches deep. *Twenty-seven hours he was closely packed within those small dimensions, and was tumbled along on drays, railroad cars, steam-boat, and horse carts, as any other box of merchandize would have been, sometimes on his feet, sometimes on his side, and once, for an hour or two, actually on his head.*

Such is the well attested fact, and this volume contains the biography of the remarkable man, Henry Box Brown, who thus attained his freedom. Is there a man in our country, who better deserves his liberty? And is there to be found in these northern states, an individual base to assist in returning him to slavery! or to stand quietly by and consent to his recapture?

The narrative of such a man cannot fail to be interesting, and I cordially commend it to all who love liberty and hate oppression.

SAMUEL J. MAY.

After Mr. Brown's arrival in the Free States and the recovery of his health, in addition to the publishing of his Narrative he began to prepare the Panorama, which has been exhibited with such success both in America and in England.

January, 1851.

We, the Teachers of St. John's Sunday School, Blackburn, having seen the exhibition in our School-room, called the "Panorama of American Slavery," feel it our duty to call upon all our Christian brethren, who may have an opportunity, to go and witness this great mirror of slavery for themselves, feeling assured ourselves that it is calculated to leave a lasting impression upon the mind, and particularly that of the young.

We recommend it more especially on account of the exhibitor, Mr. Henry Box Brown, being himself a fugitive slave, and there-fore able to give a true account of all the horrors of American Slavery, together with his own miraculous escape.

Signed,

JOHN FRANCIS,	JOHN ALSTON,
JOHN PARKINSON,	GEORGE FIELDING,
HENRY AINSWORTH,	THOMAS HIGHAM,
JOHN TOMLINSON,	DANIEL TOMLINSON,
HENRY WILKINSON,	BENJAMIN CLIFF,
JOHN HARTLEY,	JOHN HOWCUTT,
JAMES GREAVES,	JAMES HOLT,
JOHN ROBERTS,	MARK SHAW,
FRANCIS BROUGHTON,	CHRISTOPHER HIGHAM.

Mr. Brown continued to travel in the United States until the Fugitive Slave Bill[5]—which passed into law last year—rendered it necessary for him to seek an asylum on British ground. Such was the vigilance with which the search for victims was pursued, that Mr. Brown had to travel under an assumed name, and by the most secret means shift his panorama to prevent suspicion and capture.

THOMAS G. LEE,
Minister of New Windsor Chapel, Salford.
April 8, 1851.

CHAPTER I

I WAS BORN ABOUT forty-five miles from the city of Richmond, in Louisa County, in the year 1815. I entered the world a slave—in the midst of a country whose most honoured writings declare that all men have a right to liberty—but had imprinted upon my body no mark which could be made to signify that my destiny was to be that of a bondman. Neither was there any angel stood by, at the hour of my birth, to hand my body over, by the authority of heaven, to be the property of a fellow-man; no, but I was a slave because my countrymen had made it lawful, in utter contempt of the declared will of heaven, for the strong to lay hold of the weak and to buy and to sell them as marketable goods. Thus was I born a slave; tyrants— remorseless, destitute of religion and every principle of humanity— stood by the couch of my mother and as I entered into the world, before I had done anything to forfeit my right to liberty, and while my soul was yet undefiled by the commission of actual sin, stretched forth their bloody arms and branded me with the mark of bondage, and by such means I became their own property. Yes, they robbed me of myself before I could know the nature of their wicked arts, and ever afterwards—until I forcibly wrenched myself from their hands—did they retain their stolen property.

My father and mother of course, were then slaves, but both of them are now enjoying such a measure of liberty, as the law affords to those who have made recompense to the tyrant for the right of property he holds in his fellow-man. It was not my fortune to be long under my mother's care; but I still possess a vivid recollection of her affectionate oversight. Such lessons as the following she would frequently give me. She would take me upon her knee and, pointing to the forest trees which were then stripped of their foliage by the winds of autumn, would say to me, my son, as yonder leaves are stripped from off the trees of the forest, so are the children of the slaves swept away from them by the hands of cruel tyrants; and her voice would tremble and she would seem almost choked with her deep emotion, while the tears would find their way down her saddened cheeks. On those occasions she fondly pressed me to her heaving bosom, as if to save me from so dreaded a calamity, or to feast on the enjoyments of maternal feeling while she yet retained possession of her child. I was then young, but I well recollect the sadness of her countenance, and the mournful sacredness of her words as they impressed themselves upon my youthful mind—never to be forgotten.

Mothers of the North! as you gaze upon the fair forms of your idolised little ones, just pause for a moment; how would you feel if you knew that at any time the will of a tyrant—who neither could nor would sympathise with your domestic feelings—might separate them for ever from your embrace, not to be laid in the silent grave "where the wicked cease from troubling and where the weary are at rest," but to live under the dominion of tyrants and avaricious men, whose cold hearts cannot sympathise with your feelings, but who will mock at any manifestation of tenderness, and scourge them to satisfy the cruelty of their own disposition; yet such is the condition of hundreds of thousands of mothers in the southern states of America.

My mother used to instruct me in the principles of morality according to her own notion of what was good and pure; but I had no means of acquiring proper conception of religion in a state of slavery, where all those who professed to be followers of Jesus Christ evinced more of the disposition of demons than of men; and it is really a matter of wonder to me now, considering the character of my position that I did not imbibe a strong and lasting hatred of every thing pertaining to the religion of Christ. My lessons in morality were of the most simple kind. I was told not to steal, not to tell lies, and to behave myself in a becoming manner towards everybody. My mother, although a slave, took great delight in watching the result of her moral training in the character of my brother and myself, whilst—whether successful or unsuccessful in the formation of superior habits in us it is not for me to say—there were sown for her a blissful remembrance in the minds of her children, which will be cherished, both by the bond and the free, as long as life shall last.

As a specimen of the religious knowledge of the slave, I may here state what were my impressions in regard to my master;* assuring the reader that I am not joking but stating what were the opinions of all the slaves' children on my master's plantation, so that some judgment may be formed of the care which was taken of our religious instruction. I really believed my old master was Almighty God, and that the young master was Jesus Christ! The reason of this error seems to have been that we were taught to believe thunder to be the voice of God, and when it was about to thunder my old master would approach us, if we were in the yard, and say, all you children run into the house now, for it is going to thunder; and after the thunder storm was over he would approach us smilingly and say "what a fine shower we have had," and bidding us look at the flowers would observe how prettily they appeared; we children seeing this so frequently, could not avoid the idea that it was he that thundered and made the rain to fall, in order to make his flowers look beautiful, and I was nearly my eight years of age before I got rid of this childish superstition. Our master was uncommonly kind (for even a slaveholder may be kind) and as he moved about in his dignity he seemed like a god to us, but not withstanding his kindness although he knew very well what superstitious notions we formed of him, he never made the least attempt to correct our erroneous impression, but rather seemed pleased with the reverential feelings which we entertained towards him. All the young slaves called his son saviour and the manner in which I was undeceived was as follows.—One Sabbath after preaching time my mother told my father of a woman who wished to join the church. She had told the preacher that she had been baptised by one of the slaves at night— a practice which is quite common. After they went from their work to the minister he asked her if she believed that our Saviour came into the world and had died for the sins of men? And she said "yes." I was listening anxiously to the conversation, and when my mother had finished, I asked her if my young master was not the saviour whom the woman said was dead? She said he was not, but it was our

---

*John Barret, master of Hermitage plantation, was elected mayor of Richmond for several terms in the 1790s.

Saviour in heaven. I then asked her if there was a saviour there too; when she told me that young master was not our Saviour;—which astonished me very much. I then asked her if old master was not he? to which she replied he was not, and began to instruct me more fully in reference to the God of heaven. After this I believed there was a God who ruled the world, but I did not previously entertain the least idea of any such Being; and however dangerous my former notions were, they were not at all out of keeping with the blasphemous teachings of the hellish system of slavery.

One of my sisters became anxious to have her soul converted, and for this purpose had the hair cut from her head, because it is a notion which prevails amongst the slaves, that unless the hair be cut the soul cannot be converted. My mother reproved her for this and told her that she must pray to God who dwelled in heaven, and who only could convert her soul; and said if she wished to renounce the sins of the world she should recollect that it was not by outside show, such as the cutting of the hair, that God measured the worthior unworthiness of his servants. "Only ask of God," she said, "with an humble heart, forsaking your sins in obedience to his divine commandment, and whatever mercy is most fitting for your condition he will graciously bestow."

While quite a lad my principal employment was waiting upon my master and mistress, and at intervals taking lessons in the various kinds of work which was carried on on the plantation: and I have often, there—where the hot sun sent forth its scorching rays upon my tender head—looked forward with dismay to the time when I, like my fellow slaves, should be driven by the taskmaster's cruel lash, to separate myself from my parents and all my present associates, to toil without reward and to suffer cruelties, as yet unknown. The slave has always the harrowing idea before him—however kindly he may be treated for the time being—that the auctioneer may soon set him up for public sale and knock him down as the property of the person who, whether man or demon, would pay his master the greatest number of dollars for his body.

CHAPTER II

MY BROTHER AND MYSELF were in the habit of carrying grain to the mill a few times in the year, which was the means of furnishing us with some information respecting other slaves, otherwise we would have known nothing whatever of what was going on anywhere in the world, excepting on our master's plantation. The mill was situated at a distance of about twenty miles from our residence, and belonged to one Colonel Ambler,* in Yansinville county. On these occasions we used to acquire some little knowledge of what was going on around us, and we neglected no opportunity of making ourselves acquainted with the condition of other slaves.

On one occasion, while waiting for grain, we entered a house in the neighborhood, and while resting ourselves there, we saw a number of forlorn looking beings pass the door, and as they passed we noticed they gazed earnestly upon us; afterwards about fifty did the very same, and we heard some of them remarking that we had shoes, vests, and hats. We felt a desire to talk with them, and, accordingly after receiving some bread and meat from the mistress of the house we followed those abject beings to their quarters, and such a sight we had never witnessed before, as we had always lived on our master's plantation, and this was the first of our journeys to the mill. These Slaves were dressed in shirts made of coarse bagging such as coffee sacks are made from, and some kind of light substance for pantaloons, and this was all their clothing! They had no shoes, hats, vests, or coats, and when my brother spoke of their poor clothing they said they had never before seen colored persons dressed as we were; they looked very hungry, and we divided our

---

*Brown and one of his brothers were sent to do work at the mill of Colonel John Ambler, "the county's largest slave owner," according to Ruggles (p. 5).

bread and meat among them. They said they never had any meat given them by their master. My brother put various questions to them, such as if they had wives? did they go to church? &c., they said they had wives, but were obliged to marry persons who worked on the same plantation, as the master would not allow them to take wives from other plantations, consequently they were all related to each other, and the master obliged them to marry their relatives or to remain single. My brother asked one of them to show him his sister:—he said he could not distinguish them from the rest, as they were all his sisters. Although the slaves themselves entertain considerable respect for the law of marriage as a moral principle, and are exceedingly well pleased when they can obtain the services of a minister in the performance of the ceremony, yet the law recognizes no right in slaves to marry at all. The relation of husband and wife, parent and child, only exists by the toleration of their master, who may insult the slave's wife, or violate her person at any moment, and there is no law to punish him for what he has done. Now this not only may be as I have said, but it actually is the case to an alarming extent; and it is my candid opinion, that one of the strongest motives which operate upon the slave-holders in inducing them to maintain their iron grasp upon the unfortunate slaves, is because it gives them such unlimited control over the person of their female slaves. The greater part of slave-holders are licentious men, and the most respectable and kind masters keep some of these slaves as mistresses. It is for their pecuniary interest to do so, as their progeny is equal to so many dollars and cents in their pockets, instead of being a source of expense to them, as would be the case, if their slaves were free. It is a horrible idea, but it is no less true, that no slave husband has any certainty whatever of being able to retain his wife a single hour; neither has any wife any more certainty of her husband their fondest affection may be utterly disregarded, and their devoted attachment cruelly ignored at any moment a brutal slave-holder may think fit.

The slaves on Col. Ambler's plantation were never allowed to attend church, but were left to manage their religious affairs in their own way. An old slave whom they called John, decided on their religious profession and would baptize the approved parties during the silent watches of the night, while their master was asleep. We might have got information on many things from these slaves of

Col. Ambler, but, while we were thus engaged, we perceived the overseer directing his steps towards us like a bear for its prey: we had however, time to ask one of them if they were ever whipped? to which he replied that not a day passed over their heads without some of them being brutally punished; "and" said he "we shall have to suffer for this talk with you. It was but this morning," he continued, "that many of us were severely whipped for having been baptized the night before!" After we left them we heard the screams of these poor creatures while they were suffering under the blows of the hard treatment received from the overseers, for the crime, as we supposed, of talking with us. We felt thankful that we were exempted from such treatment, but we had no certainty that we should not, ere long be placed in a similar position.

On returning to the mill we met a young man, a relation of the owner of this plantation, who for some time had been eyeing us very attentively. He at length asked us if we had ever been whipped? and when I told him we had not, he replied, "well neither of you will ever be of any value." He expressed a good deal of surprise that we were allowed to wear hats and shoes, supposing that slaves had no business to wear such clothing as their master wore. We had carried our fishing lines with us and requested the privilege of fishing in his stream, which he roughly denied us, saying "we do not allow niggers to fish." Nothing daunted, however, by the rebuff, my brother went to another place, where, without asking permission of any one, he succeeded in obtaining a plentiful supply of fish and on returning, the young slave-holder seemed to be displeased at our success, but, knowing that we caught them in a stream which was not under his control, he said nothing. He knew that our master was a rich slave-holder and, probably, he guessed from our appearance that we were favorites of his, perhaps he was somewhat induced, from that consideration, to let us alone, at any rate he did not molest us any more.

We afterwards carried our corn to a mill belonging to a Mr. Bullock, only about ten miles distant from our plantation. This man was very kind to us; if we were late at night he would take us into his house, give us beds to sleep upon, and take charge of our horses. He would even carry our grain himself into the mill; and he always furnished us in the morning with a good breakfast. We were rather astonished, for some time, that this man was so kind to us—and, in this respect, so different from the other miller—until we learned that he was not a slave-holder. This miller allowed us to catch as many fishes as we chose, and even furnished us with fishing implements when we had money for only very imperfect ones, of our own.

While at this mill we became acquainted with a coloured man from a northern part of the country; and as our desire was strong to learn how our brethren fared in other places, we questioned him respecting his treatment. He complained much of his hard fate; he said he had a wife and one child, and begged for some of our fish to carry to his wife, which we gladly gave him. He told us he had just sent a few hickory nuts to market for which he had received thirty-six cents, and that he had given the money to his wife, to furnish her with some little articles of comfort.

On our return from their place, one time, we met with a coloured man and woman, who were very cross to each other. We inquired as to the cause of their disagreement and the man told us that the woman had such a tongue, and that some of them had taken a sheep because they did not get enough to eat, and this woman, after eating of it, went and told their master, and they had all received a severe whipping. This man enjoined upon his slaves never to steal from him again, but to steal as much as they chose from any other person: and if they took care to do it in such a manner, as the owner could not catch them in the act, nor be able to swear to the property after they had fetched it, he would shield them from punishment provided they would give him a share of the meat. Not long after this the slaves availing themselves of their master's protection, stole a pig from a neighbouring plantation, and, according to their agreement, furnished their master with his share. The owner of the missing animal, however, having heard something to make him suspect what had become of his property, came rushing into the house of the man who had just eaten of the stolen food, and in a very excited manner demanded reparation from him for the beast which his slaves had stolen; and the villain, rising from the table where he had just been eating of the stolen property, said, my servants know no more about your stolen hog than I do, which indeed was perfectly true, and the loser of the swine went away without saying any more; but although the master of this slave with whom we were talking, had told him that it was no sin to steal from others, my brother took good care to let him know, before we separated, that it was as much a sin in the sight of God to steal from the one as the other, "Oh," said the master, "niggers has nothing to do with God," and indeed the whole feature of slavery is so utterly inconsistent with the principles of religion, reason, and humanity, that it is no wonder that the very mention of the word God grates upon the ear as if it typefied the degeneracy of this hellish system.

> Turn! great Ruler of the skies!
> Turn from their sins thy searching eyes;
> Nor let the offences of their hand,
> Within thy book recorded stand.
>
> There's not a sparrow or a worm
> O'erlooked in thy decrees,
> Thou raisest monarchs to a throne—
> They sink with equal ease.
>
> May Christ's example, all divine,
> To us a model prove!
> Like his, O God! our hearts incline,
> Our enemies to love!

CHAPTER III

My Master's son Charles, at one time, became impressed with the evils of slavery, and put his notion into practical effect by emancipating about forty of his slaves, and paying their expenses to a free state. Our old master, about this time, being unable to attend to all his affairs himself, employed an overseer whose disposition was so cruel as to make many of the slaves run away. I fancy the neighbours began to clamour about our master's mild treatment to his slaves, for which reason he was induced to employ an overseer. The change in our treatment was so great, and so much for the worse, that we could not help lamenting that the master had adopted such a change. There is no telling what might have been the result of this new method amongst slaves, so unused to the lash as we were, if in the midst of the experiment our old master had not been called upon to go the way of all the earth. As he was about to expire he sent for my mother and me to come to his bedside; we ran with beating hearts and highly elated feelings, not doubting, in the least, but that he was about to confer upon us the boon of freedom—for we had both expected that we should be set free when master died—but imagine our deep disappointment when the old man called me to his side and said, Henry you will make a good Plough-boy, or a good gardener; now you must be an honest boy and never tell an untruth.

I have given you to my son William,[6] and you must obey him; thus the old gentleman deceived us by his former kind treatment and raised expectation in our youthful minds which were doomed to be overthrown. He went to stand before the great Jehovah to give an account of the deeds done in the body, and we, disappointed in our expectations, were left to mourn, not so much our master's death, as our galling bondage. If there is any thing which tends to buoy up the spirit of the slave, under the pressure of his severe toils,

more than another, it is the hope of future freedom: by this his heart
is cheered and his soul is lighted up in the midst of the fearful scenes
of agony and suffering which he has to endure. Occasionally, as
some event approaches from which lie can calculate on a relaxation
of his sufferings, his hope burns with a bright blaze; but most generally the mind of the slave is filled with gloomy apprehension of a
still harder fate. I have known many slaves to labour unusually hard
with the view of obtaining the price of their own redemption, and,
after they paid for themselves over and over again, were—by the
unprincipled tyranny and fiendish mockery of moral principle in
which their barbarous masters delight to indulge—still refused what
they had so fully paid for, and what they so ardently desired. Indeed
a great many masters hold out to their slaves the object of purchasing their own freedom—in order to induce them to labour more—
without at the same time, entertaining the slightest idea of ever
fulfilling their promise.

On the death of my old master, his property was inherited by
four sons, whose names were, Stronn, Charles, John, and William
Barret; so the human as well as every other kind of property, came
to be divided equally amongst these four sons, which division—as it
separated me from my father and mother, my sister and brother,
with whom I had hitherto been allowed to live—was the most severe trial to my feelings which I had ever endured. I was then only
fifteen years of age, but it is as present in my mind as if but yesterday's sun had shone upon the dreadful exhibition. My mother was
separated from her youngest child, and it was not till after she had
begged most pitiously for its restoration, that she was allowed to
give it one farewell embrace, before she had to let it go for ever. This
kind of torture is a thousand fold more cruel and barbarous than the
use of the lash which lacerates the back; the gashes which the whip,
or the cow skin makes may heal, and the place which was marked,
in a little while may cease to exhibit the signs of what it had endured, but the pangs which lacerate the soul in consequence of the
forcible disruption of parent and the dearest family ties, only grow
deeper and more piercing, as memory fetches from a greater distance the horrid acts by which they have been produced. And there
is no doubt but they under the weighty infirmities of declining life,
and the increasing force and vividness with which the mind retains

the memoranda of the agonies of former years—which form so great a part of memory's possessions in the minds of most slaves—hurry thousands annually from off the stage of life.

Mother, my sister Jane,[7] and myself, fell into the hands of William Barret. My sister Mary and her children went another way; Edward, another, and John and Lewis and my sister Robinnet another. William Barret took my sister Martha for his "keep Miss." It is a difficult thing to divide all the slaves on a plantation; for no person wishes for all children, or all old people; while both old, young, and middle aged have to be divided:—but the tyrant slave-holder regards not the social, or domestic feelings of the slave, and makes his division according to the *moneyed* value they possess, without giving the slightest consideration to the domestic or social ties by which the individuals are bound to each other; indeed their common expression is, that "niggers have no feelings."

My father and mother were left on the plantation; but I was taken to the city of Richmond, to work in a tobacco manufactory, owned by my old master's son William, who had received a special charge from his father to take good care of me, and which charge my new master endeavoured to perform. He told me if I would behave well he would take good care of me and give me money to spend; he talked so kindly to me that I determined I would exert myself to the utmost to please him, and do just as he wished me in every respect. He furnished me with a new suit of clothes, and gave me money to buy things to send to my mother. One day I overheard him telling the overseer that *his father had raised me*—that I was a smart boy and that he must never whip me. I tried exceedingly hard to perform what I thought was my duty, and escaped the lash almost entirely, although I often thought the overseer would have liked to have given me a whipping, but my master's orders, which he dared not altogether to set aside, were my defence; so under these circumstances my lot was comparatively easy.

Our overseer at that time was a coloured man, whose name was Wilson Gregory;[8] he was generally considered a shrewd and sensible man, especially to be a man of colour; and after the orders which my master gave him concerning me, he used to treat me very kindly indeed, and gave me board and lodgings in his own house. Gregory acted as book keeper also to my master, and was much in favour with the merchants of the city and all who knew him; he instructed me how to judge of the qualities of tobacco, and with the view of making me a more proficient judge of that article, he advised me to learn to chew and to smoke which I therefore did.

About eighteen months after I came to the city of Richmond, an extraordinary occurrence took place which caused great excitement all over the town. I did not then know precisely what was the cause of this excitement, for I could get no satisfactory information from my master, only he said that some of the slaves had plotted to kill their owners. I have since learned that it was the famous Nat Turner's insurrection. Many slaves were whipped, hung, and cut down with the swords in the streets; and some that were found away from their quarters after dark, were shot; the whole city was in the utmost excitement, and the whites seemed terrified beyond measure, so true it is that the "wicked flee when no man pursueth." Great numbers of slaves were loaded with irons; some were half hung as it was termed—that is they were suspended from some tree with a rope about their necks, so adjusted as not quite to srangle them—and then they were pelted by men and boys with rotten eggs. This half hanging is a refined species of punishment peculiar to slaves! This insurrection took place some distance from the city, and was the occasion of the enacting of that law by which more than five slaves were forbidden to meet together unless they were at work; and also of that, for the silencing all coloured preachers. One of that class in our city, refused to obey the impious mandate, and in consequence of his refusal, was severely whipped. His religion was, however, found to be too deeply rooted for him to be silenced by any mere power of man, and consequently, no efforts could avail to extort from his lips, a promise that he would cease to proclaim the glad tidings of the gospel to his enslaved and perishing fellow-men.

I had now been about two years in Richmond city and not having, during that time, seen, and very seldom heard from, my mother, my feelings were very much tried by the separation which I had thus to endure. I missed severely her welcome smile when I returned from my daily task; no one seemed at that time to sympathise with me, and I began to feel, indeed, that I really was alone in the world; and worse than all, I could console myself with no hope, not even the most distant, that I should ever see my beloved parents again.

About this time Wilson Gregory, who was our overseer, died, and his place was supplied by a man named Stephen Bennett, who had a wooden leg; and who used to creep up behind the slaves to hear what they had to talk about in his absence; but his wooden leg generally betrayed him by coming into contact with something which would make a noise, and that would call the attention of the slaves to what he was about. He was a very mean man in all his ways, and was very much disliked by the slaves. He used to whip them, often, in a shameful manner. On one occasion I saw him take a slave, whose name was Pinkney, and make him take off his shirt; he then tied his hands and gave him one hundred lashes on his bare back; and all this, because he lacked three pounds of his task, which was valued at six cents. I saw him do many other things which were equally cruel, but it would be useless to multiply instances here, as no rational being doubts that slavery, even in its mildest forms is a hard and cruel fate. Yet with all his barbarities and cruelties this man was generally reckoned a very sensible man on religious subjects, and he used to be frequently talking about things of that sort, but sometimes he spoke with very great levity indeed. He used to say that if he died and went to hell, he had enough of sense to fool the devil and get out. He did take his departure at last, to that bower, whence borne, no traveller returns, and whether well or ill prepared for the change, I will not say.

Bennett was followed as overseer, by one Henry Bedman, and he was the best that we had. He neither used the whip nor cheated the hands of what little they had to receive, and I am confident that he had more work done by equal numbers of hands, than had been done under any overseer either before or since his appointment to office. He possessed a much greater influence by his kindness than any overseer did by his lash. He was altogether a very good man; was very fond of sacred music, and used to ask me and some of the other slaves, who were working in the same room to sing for him—something "smart" as he used to say, which we were generally as well pleased to do, as he was to ask us: it was not our fate however to enjoy his kindness long, he too very soon died, and his death was looked upon as a misfortune by all who had been slaves under him.

CHAPTER IV

AFTER THE DEATH OF our lamented overseer we were placed under the care of one of the meanest and cruelest men that I ever knew; but before alluding particularly to his conduct, it may be interesting to describe the circumstances and condition of the slaves he had to superintend. The building in which I worked was about three hundred feet in length, and three stories high; affording room for two hundred people to work, but only one hundred and fifty were kept. One hundred and twenty of the persons employed were slaves, and the remainder free coloured people. We were obliged to work fourteen hours a day in the summer, and sixteen in the winter. One week consisted in separating the stems from the leaves of Tobacco; the leaves were then moistened with a fluid made from Liquorice and Sugar, which renders it not perfectly abhorrent to the taste of those who work it. These operations were performed by the women and boys, and after being thus moistened the leaves were then taken by the men and with the hands pressed into lumps and then twisted; it was then sent to what is called the machine house, and pressed into boxes and casks, whence it went to the sweat house and after lying about thirty days there, are taken out and shipped for the market.

The name of our overseer was John F. Allen; he was a thorough-going villain in all his modes of doing business; he was a savage looking sort of a man; always apparently ready for any work of barbarity or cruelty to which the most depraved despot might call him. He understood how to turn a penny for his own advantage as well as any man. No person could match him in making a bargain; but whether he had acquired his low cunning from associating with that clan, or had it originally as one of the inherent properties of his diabolical disposition, I could not discover, but he excelled all I had ever seen in low mean trickery and artifice. He used to boast that by his shrewdness in managing the slaves, he made enough to support himself and family—and he had a very large family which I am sure consumed not less than one hundred dollars per annum—without touching one farthing of his own salary, which was fifteen hundred dollars per annum.

Mr. Allen used to rise very early in the morning, not that he might enjoy sweet communion with his own thoughts, or with his God; nor that he might further the *legitimate* interest of his master, but in order to look after matters which principally concerned himself; that was to rob his master and the poor slaves that were under his control, by every means in his power. His early rising was looked upon by our master as a token of great devotedness to his business; and as he was with-all very pious and a member of the Episcopalian Church, my master seemed to place great confidence in him. It was therefore no use for any of the workmen to complain to the master of anything the overseer did, for he would not listen to a word they said, but gave his sanction to his barbarous conduct in the fullest extent, no matter how tyrannical or unjust that conduct, or how cruel the punishments which he inflicted; so that that demon of an overseer was in reality our master.

As a specimen of Allen's cruelty I will mention the revolting case of a coloured man, who was frequently in the habit of singing. This man was taken sick, and although he had not made his appearance at the factory for two or three days, no notice was taken of him; no medicine was provided nor was there any physician employed to heal him. At the end of that time Allen ordered three men to go to the house of the invalid and fetch him to the factory; and of course, in a little while the sick man appeared; so feeble was he however from disease, that he was scarcely able to stand. Allen, notwithstanding, desired him to be stripped and his hands tied behind him; he was then tied to a large post and questioned about his singing; Allen told him that his singing consumed too much time, and that it hurt him very much, but that he was going to give him some medicine that would cure him; the poor trembling man made no reply and immediately the pious overseer Allen for no other crime than sickness, inflicted two-hundred lashes upon his bare back; and even this might probably have been but a small part of his punishment, had a not the poor man fainted away: and it was only then the blood-thirsty fiend ceased to apply the lash! I witnessed this transaction myself, but I durst not venture to say that the tyrant was doing wrong, because I was a slave and any interferance on my part, would have led to a similar punishment upon myself. This poor man was sick for four weeks afterwards, during which time the weekly allowance, of seventy cents, for the hands to board themselves with, was withheld, and the poor man's wife had to support him in the best way she could, which in a land of slavery is no easy matter.

The advocates of slavery will sometimes tell us, that the slave is in better circumstances than he would be in a state of freedom, because he has a master to provide for him when he is sick; but even if this doctrine were true it would afford no argument whatever in favor of slavery; for no amount of kindness can be made the lawful price of any man's liberty, to infringe which is contrary to the laws of humanity and the decrees of God. But what is the real fact? In many instances the severe toils and exposures the slave has to endure at the will of his master, brings on his disease, and even then he is liable to the *lash for medicine*, and to live, or die by starvation as he may, without any support from his owner; for there is no law by which the master may be punished for his cruelty—by which he may be compelled to support his suffering slave.

My master knew all the circumstances of the case which I have just related, but he never interfered, nor even reproved the cruel overseer for what he had done; his motto was, Mr. Allen is always right, and so, right or wrong, whatever he did was law, and from his will there was no appeal.

I have before stated, that Mr. Allen was a very pious man—he was also a church member, but was much addicted to the habit of profane swearing—a vice which is, in slave countries, not at all uncommon in church members. He used particularly to expend his swearing breath in denunciation of the whole race of negroes—using more bad terms than I could here employ, without polluting the pen with which I write. Amongst the best epithets, were; "hogs," "dogs," "pigs," &c., &c.

At one time he was busily engaged in reading the Bible, when a slave came in who had been about ten minutes behind his time—precious time! Allen depended upon the punctuallity of his slaves, for the support of his family, in the manner previously noticed: his anxiety to provide for his household led him to indulge in a boisterous outbreak of anger; so that when the slave came in, he said, what are you so late for you black scamp? The poor man endeavoured to apologize for his lateness, but it was to no purpose. This professing Christian proceeded to try the effects of the Bible on the slave's body, and actually dealt him a heavy blow in the face with the sacred book! But that not answering his purpose, and the man standing silent, he caught up a stick, and beat him with that. The slave afterwards complained to the master of the overseer's conduct, but was told that Mr. Allen would not do anything wrong.

Amongst Mr. Allen's other religious offices, he held that of superintendant of the sunday school, where he used to give frequent exhortations to the slaves' children, in reference to their duty to their master. He told them they must never disobey their master, nor lie, nor steal, for if they did any of these, they would be sure to go to hell. But notwithstanding the deceitfulness of his character, and the fiendishness of his disposition, he was not, himself, perfectly proof, against the influence of fear. One day it came on a heavy thunderstorm; the clouds lowered heavily, and darkness usurped the dominion of day—it was so dark that the hands could not see to work, and I then began to converse with Mr. Allen about the storm. I asked him if it was not dangerous for the hands to work while the lightning flashed so terribly? He replied, he thought so, but he was placed there to keep them at their work, and he could not do otherwise. Just as we were speaking, a flash of lightning appeared to pass so close to us, that Mr. Allen jumped up from where he was sitting, and ran and locked himself up in a small room, where he supposed the lightning would not harm him. Some of the slaves said, they heard him praying that God would spare his life. That was a very severe storm, and a little while afterwards, we heard that a woman had been killed by the lightning. Although in the thunderstorm alluded to, Mr. Allen seemed to be alarmed; at other times he did not appear to think seriously about such things, for I have heard him say, that he did not think God had anything to do with thunder and lightning. This same official had much apparent zeal in the cause of the sunday school; he used to pray with, and for the children, and was indefatigable in teaching them the catechism after him; he was very particular, however, in not allowing them to hold the book in their own hands. His zeal did not appear to have any higher object than that of making the children more willing slaves; for he used frequently to tell his visitors that coloured people were never converted—that they had no souls, and could not go to heaven, but it was his duty to talk to them as he did! His liberality to the white people, was coextensive with his denunciation of the coloured race; he said a white man may do what he pleased, and he could not be lost; he might lie, and rob the slaves, and do anything else, provided he read the Bible and joined the church!

CHAPTER V

IT MAY NOW BE proper to say a little about the state of the churches in slave countries. There was a baptist minister in the city of Richmond, whose name was John Cave. I have heard this man declare in public, that he had preached six years before he was converted and the reason of his conversion was as follows. He was in the habit of taking his glass of mint julep directly after prayers, or after preaching, which he thought wonderfully refreshed his soul and body; he would repeat the dram three or four times during the day. But an old slave of his, who had observed his practice hinted to him something about alternately drinking and preaching to the people; and, after thinking seriously on what the slave told him, he began to repent, and was converted. And now, he says he is truly converted, because his conscience reproved him for having made human beings articles of traffic; but I believe his second conversion is just about as complete as his first, for although he owed the second change to one of his own slaves, and ever confessed that the first effect of his conversion, was, to open up to his conscience the evil of the traffic in human beings, instead of letting those at liberty which he had under his control—and which might have been at once expected, as a natural consequence of his conviction—he endeavoured to apologize for the want of conscience, by finding, what he called, a good master for them, and selling them all to him.

But the religion of the slave-holder is everywhere a system of mere delusion, got up expressly for the purpose of deceiving the poor slaves, for everywhere the leading doctrine in the slave-holders' religion is, that it is the duty of the slave to obey his master in all things.

When Mr. Carr left the city he was succeeded by a Mr. Jeter, who remained for many years; but at the time when he commenced his ministerial duties, many of the slaves were running away to free states; on the learning of which Mr. Jeter's first object was to devise some plan by which the masters could more effectively prevent their negroes from escaping; and the result of his ingenuity was as follows. He got the deacons and many more of the good Christians of his church, whether to believe or not I do not know, but to hold out that the place of meeting which they then occupied was not large enough for them; and he seemed not to relish being in the same church with the negroes, but, however that was, he managed, with the assistance of his church members, to get the negroes all around the district to believe that out of love for them, and from pure regard to their spiritual interests, it had been agreed that the old meeting house was to be given to the negroes for their own use, on their paying a small portion of the price at which it was estimated. The church was valued at 13,000 dollars, but they would only be required to pay 3,000 dollars in order to have it for themselves. The negroes were pleased with the idea of having a place of meeting for themselves, and so were induced to save every cent they could to buy the chapel. They were thus provided with a strong motive for remaining where they were, and also by means of this pious fraud, which it afterwards proved itself to be, they were deprived of such little sums of money as might occasionally drop into their hands, and with which they might have been assisted in effecting their escape. These resolutions were punctually carried into effect; a splendid new church was built for the whites; and it was made a rule of that church, that if any coloured person entered it, without special business, he was liable to be taken to the watch-house and to receive thirty-nine lashes! The negroes paid what was at first demanded of them for the old building, but when they wished to get it placed entirely in their hands, they were charged with a still further sum; and after they had paid that, they had still more to pay, and never, so long as I was there, got possession of the church, and probably never will. A minister was, however, appointed to preach for them beside the one that preached for the white people.

A man named Knopp who came from the north preached once in the church of the negroes. He took for his text, *"O! Jerusalem, Jerusalem which killest the prophets and stonest them that are sent unto thee, how often would I have gathered thee as a hen gathereth her chickens under her wings, and ye would not."* Mr. Jeter and the members of the whites' church were so offended at this man's sermon, that they went in a body to his lodgings and were about to mob him, if he had not been defended by a number of his own friends, but I believe if he had been left to the tender mercies of this professed servant of the Most High, and his Christian associates, he would never have escaped with his life.

The Rev. R. Ryland, who preached for the coloured people, was professor at the Baptist seminary near the city of Richmond,[9] and the coloured people had to pay him a salary of 700 dollars per annum, although they neither chose him nor had the least control over him. He did not consider himself bound to preach regularly, but only when he was not otherwise engaged, so he preached about forty sermons a year and was a zealous supporter of the slave-holders' cause; and, so far as I could judge, he had no notion whatever of the pure religion of Jesus Christ. He used to preach from such texts as that in the epistle to the Ephesians, where St. Paul says, "servants be obedient to them that are your masters and mistresses according to the flesh, and submit to them with fear and trembling"; he was not ashamed to invoke the authority of heaven in support of the slave degrading laws under which masters could with impunity abuse their fellow-creatures.

CHAPTER VI

I NOW BEGAN TO think of entering the matrimonial state; and with that view I had formed an acquaintance with a young woman named Nancy, who was a slave belonging to a Mr. Leigh a clerk in the Bank, and, like many more slave-holders, professing to be a very pious man. We had made it up to get married, but it was necessary in the first place, to obtain our masters' permission, as we could do nothing without their consent. I therefore went to Mr. Leigh, and made known to him my wishes, when he told me he never meant to sell Nancy, and if my master would agree never to sell me, I might marry her. He promised faithfully that he would not sell her, and pretended to entertain an extreme horror of separating families. He gave me a note to my master, and after they had discussed the matter over, I was allowed to marry the object of my choice. When she became my wife she was living with a Mr. Reevs, a minister of the gospel, who had not long come from the north, where he had the character of being an anti-slavery man; but he had not been long in the south when all his anti-slavery notions vanished and he became a staunch advocate of slave-holding doctrines, and even wrote articles in favour of slavery which were published in the *Richmond Republican*.

My wife was still the property of Mr. Leigh and, from the apparent sincerity of his promises to us, we felt confident that he would not separate us. We had not; however, been married above twelve months, when his conscientious scruples vanished, and he sold my wife to a Mr. Joseph H. Colquitt, a saddler, living in the city of Richmond, and a member of Dr. Plummer's church there. This Mr. Colquitt was an exceedingly cruel man, and he had a wife who was, if possible, still more cruel. She was very contrary and hard to be pleased; she used to abuse my wife very much, not because she did not do her duty, but because, it was said, her manners were too

refined for a slave. At this time my wife had a child and this vexed
Mrs. Colquitt very much; she could not bear to see her nursing her
baby and used to wish some great calamity to happen to my wife.
Eventually she was so much displeased with my wife that she induced Mr. Colquitt to sell her to one Philip M. Tabb, Junr. for the
sum of 450 dollars; but coming to see the value of her more clearly
after she tried to do without her, she could not rest till she got Mr.
Colquitt to repurchase her from Mr. Tabb, which he did in about
four months after he had sold her, for 500 dollars, being fifty more
than he had sold her for.

Shortly after this Mr. Colquitt was taken sick, and his minister,
the Rev. Dr. Plummer, was sent for to visit him; the doctor came
and prayed for him and so did other members of the church; but he
did not get any better so that they all thought he must soon die; the
doctors had given up all hopes of him, and his wife and children,
and friends, stood round his bedside in tears, expecting every
minute he would breathe his last. All the servants were in readiness
lest they should be called to go on some message. I had just then got
home from labouring for my master; my wife was waiting for me,
but she said she expected, every minute, that some person would be
calling to tell her that master was gone, when, to my surprise, Joseph
Colquitt sent to my wife to tell me to come and speak with him. I
immediately left my room and went to his bed-side; and as soon as
he saw me he caught hold of my hand and said;—"Henry will you
pray for me and ask the Lord to spare my life, and restore me to
health?" I felt it my duty to do the best I could in asking the Lord
to have mercy upon him, because, although he was a slave-holder,
and a very cruel man, and had used my wife very badly, yet I had no
right to judge between him and his God, so I knelt down by his
bed-side and prayed for him. After I got up he caught hold of my
arm again and said, "one more favour I have to ask of you—go and
tell all my slaves that belong to the church to come and pray for
me." I went, according to his request, and we prayed three nights
with him, after our work was done, and although we needed rest
ourselves, yet at the earnest desire of the apparently dying man we
were induced to forego our rest, and to spend our time in comfort-
ing him. At the end of this time he began to get a little better, and
in a few weeks he was able to sit at table, and to take his meals with

the family. I happened to be at his house one day, at our breakfast
hour, after he got quite well, and his wife appeared as if she wished
to joke her husband about the coloured people praying for him
when he was sick. Mr. Colquitt had been expelled from the baptist
church, and since that time she had disliked religion. She pretended
that she did not believe either in God or Devil, and went on at such
a rate, plaguing Mr. Colquitt, about the negroes praying for him,
that he grew angry at last and exclaimed with an oath that it was all
lies about the negroes praying for him; he denied asking any person
to pray for him, and he said if he did ask the negroes to pray for him
he must have been out of his senses, and did not, at the time he
spoke, remember anything about it; but his wife still persisting in
what she said, he went to the back door and calling his slaves one at
a time, asked them who it was that prayed for him, until he got the
names of all those who had been concerned in the affair, and when
he had done so, he whipped every one of them which said he had
prayed as Mrs. Colquitt had stated. He seemed wishful to whip me
also, but, as I did not belong to him, he was deprived of the pleasure
of paying me for my services in the manner, in which others had
been rewarded. Mr. Colquitt, however, determined that I should
suffer too, and for that purpose he proceeded to sell my wife to one
Samuel Cottrell, who wished to purchase her. Cottrell was a saddler
and had a shop in Richmond. This man came to me one day and
told me that Mr. Colquitt was going to sell my wife and stated that
he wanted a woman to wait upon his wife, and he thought my wife
would precisely suit her; but he said her master asked 650 dollars for
her and her children, and he had only 600 that he could conve-
niently spare but if I would let him have fifty, to make up the price,
he would prevent her from being sold away from me. I was, however, a little suspicious about being fooled out of my money, and I
asked him if I did advance the money what security I could have
that he would not sell my wife as the others had done; but he said
to me "do you think if you allow me to have that money, that I could
have the heart to sell your wife to any other person but yourself,
and particularly knowing that your wife is my sister and you my brother
in the Lord; while all of us are members of the church? *Oh! no*, I
never could have the heart to do such a deed as that." After he had
shown off his religion in this manner, and lavished it upon me,

I thought I would let him have the money, not that I had implicit faith in his promise, but that I knew he could purchase her if he wished whether I were to assist him or not, and I thought by thus bringing him under an obligation to me it might at least be somewhat to the advantage of my wife and to me; so I gave him the fifty dollars and he went off and bought my wife and children:—and that very same day he came to me and told me, that my wife and children were now his property, and that I must hire a house for them and he would allow them to live there if I would furnish them with everything they wanted, and pay him fifty dollars, a year; "if you don't do this," he said, "I will sell her as soon as I can get a buyer for her." I was struck with astonishment to think that this man, in one day, could exhibit himself in two such different characters. A few hours ago filled with expressions of love and kindness, and now a monster tyrant, making light of the most social ties and imposing such terms as he chose on those whom, but a little, before, he had begged to conform to his will. Now, being a slave, I had no power to hire a house, and what this might have resulted in I do not know, if I had not met with a friend in the time of need, in the person of James C. A. Smith, Jr. He was a free man and I went to him and told him my tale and asked him to go and hire a house for me, to put my wife and children into; which he immediately did. He hired one at seventy-two dollars per annum, and stood master of it for me; and, notwithstanding the fearful liabilities under which I lay, I now began to feel a little easier, and might, perhaps, have managed to live in a kind of a way if we had been let alone here. But Mr. S. Cottrell had not yet done with robbing us; he no sooner saw that we were thus comfortably situated, than he said my wife must do some of his washing. I still had to pay the house hire, and the hire of my wife; to find her and the children with everything they required, and she had to do his washing beside. Still we felt ourselves more comfortable than we had ever been before. In this way, we went on for some time: I paid him the hire of my wife regularly, whenever he called for it—whether it was due or not—but he seemed still bent on robbing me more thoroughly than he had the previous day; for one pleasant morning, in the month of August, 1848, when my wife and children, and myself, were sitting at table, about to eat our breakfast, Mr. Cottrel called, and said, he wanted some money to day, as he had a demand for a large amount. I said to him, you know I have no money to spare, because it takes nearly all that I make for myself, to pay my wife's hire, the rent of my house, my own ties to my master, and to keep ourselves in meat and clothes; and if at any time, I have made any thing more than that, I have paid it to you in advance, and what more can I do? Mr. Cottrell, however said, "I want money, and money I will have." I could make him no answer; he then went away. I then said to my wife "I wonder what Mr. Cottrell means by saying I want money and money I will have," my poor wife burst into tears and said perhaps he will sell one of our little children, and our hearts were so full that neither of us could eat any breakfast, and after mutually embracing each other, as it might be our last meeting, and fondly pressing our little darlings to our bosoms, I left the the house and went off to my daily labour followed by my little children who called after me to come back soon. I felt that life had joys worth living for if I could only be allowed to enjoy them, but my heart was filled with deep anguish from the awful calamity, which I was thus obliged to contemplate, as not only a possible but a highly probable occurrence. I now went away to my work and I could as I went see many other slaves hastening in the same direction. I began to consider their lot and mine, and although my heart was filled with sorrow I felt still disposed to look upon the bright side of the future. I could still see some alleviation to my case of sorrow; it was true that the greater portion of my earnings were stolen from me by the unscrupulous hand of my master; that I was entirely at his mercy; and might at any moment be snatched from those enjoyments as well as those I thought were open to me; that if he chose he might still further gratify his robbing propensities and demand a larger portion of my earnings; so that the pleasures of intellect would be completely closed to my mind, but I could enjoy myself with my family about me while I listened to the pleasing prattle of my children, and experience the kindness of a wife, which were privileges that every slave could not enjoy.

I had not been many hours at my work, when I was informed that my wife and children were taken from their home, sent to the auction mart and sold, and then lay in prison ready to start away the next day for North Carolina with the man who had purchased them. I cannot express, in language, what were my feelings on this occasion. My master treated me kindly but he still retained me in a state of slavery. His kindness however did not keep me from feeling the smart of this awful deprivation. I had left my wife and children at home in the morning as well situated as slaves could be; I was not anticipating their loss, not on account of the feigned piety of their owner, for I had long ago learned to look through such hollow pretences in those who held slaves, but because of the obligation to me for money I had advanced to him, *on the expressed condition that he should not sell her to any person but myself*; such, however was the case, and as soon as I could get away, I went and purchased some things to take to the jail to them I so much loved; and to have one farewell embrace before parting for ever. I had not proceeded far however when I met with a gentleman who perceiving my anguish of heart, as depicted in my countenance, inquired what was the matter with me. I had no sooner hinted at my circumstances, however, than he knew all about it, having heard it, before. He advised me not to go to the jail, "for" said he "the man that bought your wife and family has told your master some falsehoods and has ordered the jailor to seize you and put you in prison if you should make your appearance there; when you would most likely be sold separately from them, because the *Methodist Minister* that bought your wife, does not want any men," so being thus advised I thought it better not to go to the jail myself, but I procured a friend to go in my stead, and take some money and the things which I had purchased for my wife, and tell her how it was that I could not come myself. And it turned out in the end to be much better that I did not go, for as soon as the young man arrived at the jail he was seized and put in prison, the jailor mistaking him for me: but when he discovered his mistake he was very angry and vented his rage upon the innocent youth by kicking him out of the prison. He discovered his mistake by asking my wife if that were not her husband, she said he was not; but he was not satisfied with her answer for he asked the children also if he were not their father, and as they too said no he was convinced, and then proceeded to abuse the young man in the manner before mentioned.

After I had heard of these things, I went to my *Christian* master and informed him how I was served, but he shoved me away from him as if I was not human. I could not rest with this however, I went to him a second time and implored him to be kind enough to buy my wife and to save me from so much trouble of mind; still he was inexorable and only answered me by telling me to go to my work and not bother him any more. I went to him a *third* time, which would be about ten o'clock and told him how Cottrell had robbed me, as this scoundrel was not satisfied with selling my wife and children, but he had no sooner got them out of the town than he took everything which he could find in my house and carried it off to be sold; the things which he then took had cost me nearly three hundred dollars. I begged master to write Cottrell and make him give me up my things, but his answer was Mr. Cottrell is a gentleman I am afraid to meddle with his business. So having satisfied myself that the master would do nothing for me, I left him and went to two young gentlemen with whom I was acquainted to try if I could induce them to buy my wife; but when I had stated my case to them they gave me to understand that they did not deal in slaves so they could not do that, but they expressed their willingness to do anything else that I might desire of them; so finding myself unsuccessful here, I went sorrowfully back to my own deserted home and found that what I had heard was quite true; not only had my wife and children been taken away, but every article of furniture had also been removed to the auction mart to be sold. I then made inquiry as to where my things had been put; and having found this out went to the sheriff's office and informed him, that the things Mr. Cottrell had brought to be sold did not belong to him, but that they were mine, and I hoped he would return them to me. I was then told by the sheriff that Mr. Cottrell had left the things to be sold in order to pay himself a debt of seventeen dollars and twenty-one cents, which he said if I would pay he would let me take away the things. I then went to my good friend Doctor Smith who was always ready and willing to do what he could for me, and having got the money, I paid it to the sherriff and took away the things which I was obliged to do that night, as far as I was able, and what were left I removed in the morning. When I was taking home the last of my things I met Mr. Cottrell, and two of his Christian brethren, in the street. He stopped me and said he had heard I had been to the sherriff's office and got away my things. Yes I said I have been and got away *my things* but I could not get away *my wife and children* whom you have put beyond my power to redeem. He then began to give me a round of abuse, while his two Christian friends stood by and heard him, but they did not seem to be the least offended at the terrible barbarity which was there placed before them.

I now left Mr. Cottrell and his friends, and going home, endeavored to court a little rest by lying down in a position so as to induce sleep. I had borne too heavy a load of grief on my mind to admit of me even closing my eyes for an hour during the whole night. Many schemes for effecting the redemption of my family passed through my mind, but when the morning's sun arose I found myself on my way towards my master's house, to make another attempt to induce him to purchase my wife. But although I besought him, with tears in my eyes, I did not succeed in making the least impression on his obdurate heart, and he utterly refused to advance the smallest portion of the 5000 dollars I had paid him in order to relieve my sufferings, and yet he was a church member of considerable standing in Richmond. He even told me that I could get another wife and so I need not trouble myself about that one; but I told him those that God had joined together let no man put assunder, and that I did not want another wife, but my own whom I had loved so long. The mentioning of the passage of scripture seemed to give him much offence for he instantly drove me from his house saying he did not wish to hear that!

My agony was now complete, she with whom I had travelled the journey of life *in chains*, for the space of twelve years, and the dear little pledges God had given us I could see plainly must now be separated from me forever, and I must continue, desolate and alone, to drag my chains through the world. O dear, I thought, shall my wife and children no more greet my sight with their cheerful looks and happy smiles! for far away in the North Carolina swamps are they henceforth to toil beneath the scorching rays of a hot sun deprived of a husband's and a father's care! Can I endure such agony—shall I stay behind while they are thus driven with the tyrant's rod? I must stay, I am a slave, the law of men gives me no power to ameliorate my condition; it shuts up every avenue of hope; but, thanks be to God, there is a law of heaven which senates' laws cannot control!

While I was thus musing I received a message, that if I wished to see my wife and children, and bid them the last farewell, I could do so, by taking my stand on the street where they were all to pass on

their way for North Carolina. I quickly availed myself of this information, and placed myself by the side of a street, and soon had the
melancholy satisfaction of witnessing the approach of a gang of
slaves, amounting to three hundred and fifty in number, marching
under the direction of a Methodist minister, by whom they were
purchased, and amongst which slaves were my wife and children. I
stood in the midst of many who, like myself, were mourning the loss
of friends and relations and had come there to obtain one parting
look at those whose company they but a short time before had
imagined they should always enjoy, but who were, without any regard to their own wills, now driven by the tyrant's voice and the
smart of the whip on their way to another scene of toil, and, to
them, another land of sorrow in a far off southern country. These
beings were marched with ropes about their necks, and staples on
their arms, and, although in that respect the scene was no very novel
one to me, yet the peculiarity of my own circumstances made it assume the appearance of unusual horror. This train of beings was accompanied by a number of wagons loaded with little children of
many different families, which as they appeared rent the air with
their shrieks and cries and vain endeavours to resist the separation
which was thus forced upon them, and the cords with which they
were thus bound; but what should I now see in the very foremost
wagon but a little child looking towards me and pitifully calling, father! father! This was my eldest child, and I was obliged to look
upon it for the last time that I should, perhaps, ever see it again in
life; if it had been going to the grave and this gloomy procession had
been about to return its body to the dust from whence it sprang,
whence its soul had taken its departure for the land of spirits, my
grief would have been nothing in comparison to what I then felt; for
then I could have reflected that its sufferings were over and that it
would never again require nor look for a father's care; but now it
goes with all those tender feelings riven, by which it was endeared
to a father's love; it must still live subject to the deprivation of pa-
ternal care and to the chains and wrongs of slavery, and yet be dead
to the pleasure of a father from whose heart the impression of its
early innocence and love will never be effaced. Thus passed my child
from my presence—it was my own child—I loved it with all the
fondness of a father; but things were so ordered that I could only

say, farewell, and leave it to pass in its chains while I looked for the approach of another gang in which my wife was also loaded with chains. My eye soon caught her precious face, but, gracious heavens! that glance of agony may God spare me from ever again enduring! My wife, under the influence of her feelings, jumped aside; I seized hold of her hand while my mind felt unutterable things, and my tongue was only able to say, we shall meet in heaven! I went with her for about four miles hand in hand, but both our hearts were so overpowered with feeling that we could say nothing, and when at last we were obliged to part, the look of mutual love which we exchanged was all the token which we could give each other that we should yet meet in heaven.

CHAPTER VII

I HAD FOR A long while been a member of the choir in the Affeviar church in Richmond, but after the severe family affliction to which I have just alluded in the last chapter and the knowledge that these cruelties were perpetrated by ministers and church members, I began strongly to suspect the Christianity of the slave-holding church members and hesitated much about maintaining my connection with them. The suspicion of these slave-dealing Christians was the means of keeping me absent from all their churches from the time that my wife and children were torn from me, until Christmas day in the year 1848; and I would not have gone then but being a leading member of the choir, I yielded to the entreaties of my associates to assist at a concert of sacred music which was to be got up for the benefit of the church. My friend Dr. Smith, who was the conductor of the underground railway,[10] was also a member of the choir, and when I had consented to attend he assisted me in selecting twenty-four pieces to be sung on the occasion.

On the day appointed for our concert I went along with Dr. Smith, and the singing commenced at half-past three o'clock, P.M. When we had sung about ten pieces and were engaged in singing the following verse—

> Again the day returns of holy rest,
> Which, when he made the world, Jehovah blest;
> When, like his own, he bade our labours cease,
> And all be piety, and all be peace,*

---

*Verse from "Again Returns the Day of Holy Rest," a hymn by William Mason that appeared in the *Protestant Magazine* in May 1796.

the members were rather astonished at Dr. Smith, who stood on my right hand, suddenly closing his book, and sinking down upon his seat his eyes being at the same time filled with tears. Several of them began to inquire what was the matter with him, but he did not tell them. I guessed what it was and afterwards found out that I had judged of the circumstances correctly. Dr. Smith's feelings were overcome with a sense of doing wrongly in singing for the purpose of obtaining money to assist those who were buying and selling their fellow-men. He thought at that moment he felt reproved by Almighty God for lending his aid to the cause of slaveholding religion; and it was under this impression he closed his book and formed the resolution which he still acts upon, of never singing again or taking part in the services of a pro-slavery church. He is now in New England publicly advocating the cause of emancipation.

After we had sung several other pieces we commenced the anthem, which run thus—

> Vital spark of heavenly flame,
> Quit, O! quit the mortal frame,—*

these words awakened in me feelings in which the sting of former sufferings was still sticking fast, and stimulated by the example of Dr. Smith, whose feelings I read so correctly, I too made up my mind that I would be no longer guilty of assisting those bloody dealers in the bodies and souls of men; and ever since that time I have steadfastly kept my resolution.

I now began to get weary of my bonds; and earnestly panted after liberty. I felt convinced that I should be acting in accordance with the will of God, if I could snap in sunder those bonds by which I was held body and soul as the property of a fellow man. I looked forward to the good time which every day I more and more firmly believed would yet come, when I should walk the face of the earth in full possession of all that freedom which the finger of God had so clearly written on the constitutions of man, and which was common to the

---

*Passage from Alexander Pope's "The Dying Christian to His Soul" (1730).

human race; but of which, by the cruel hand of tyranny, I, and millions of my fellow-men, had been robbed.

I was well acquainted with a store-keeper[11] in the city of Richmond, from whom I used to purchase my provisions; and having formed a favourable opinion of his integrity, one day in the course of a little conversation with him, I said to him if I were free I would be able to do business such as he was doing; he then told me that my occupation (a tobacconist) was a money-making one, and if I were free I had no need to change for another. I then told him my circumstances in regard to my master, having to pay him twenty-five dollars per month, and yet that he refused to assist me in saving my wife from being sold and taken away to the South, where I should never see her again; and even refused to allow me to go and see her until my hours of labour were over. I told him this took place about five months ago, and I had been meditating my escape from slavery since, and asked him, as no person was near us, if he could give me any information about how I should proceed. I told him I had a little money and if he would assist me I would pay him for so doing. The man asked me if I was not afraid to speak that way to him; I said no, for I imagined he believed that every man had a right to liberty. He said I was quite right, and asked me how much money I would give him if he would assist me to get away. I told him that I had 166 dollars and that I would give him the half; so we ultimately agreed that I should have his service in the attempt for eighty-six. Now I only wanted to fix upon a plan. He told me of several plans by which others had managed to effect their escape, but none of them exactly suited my taste. I then left him to think over what would be best to be done, and, in the mean time, went to consult my friend Dr. Smith, on the subject. I mentioned the plans which the store-keeper had suggested, and as he did not approve either of them very much, I still looked for some plan which would be more certain and more safe, but I was determined that come what may, I should have my freedom or die in the attempt.

One day, while I was at work, and my thoughts were eagerly feasting upon the idea of freedom, I felt my soul called out to heaven to breathe a prayer to Almighty God. I prayed fervently that he who seeth in secret and knew the inmost desires of my heart, would lend me his aid in bursting my fetters asunder, and in restoring me to the possession of those rights, of which men had robbed me; when the idea suddenly flashed across my mind of shutting myself *up in a box*, and getting myself conveyed as dry goods to a free state.

Being now satisfied that this was the plan for me, I went to my friend Dr. Smith and, having acquainted him with it, we agreed to have it put at once into execution not however without calculating the chances of danger with which it was attended; but buoyed up by the prospect of freedom and increased hatred to slavery I was willing to dare even death itself rather than endure any longer the clanking of those galling chains. It being still necessary to have the assistance of the store-keeper, to see that the box was kept in its right position on its passage, I then went to let him know my intention, but he said although he was willing to serve me in any way he could, he did not think I could live in a box for so long a time as would be necessary to convey me to Philadelphia, but as I had already made up my mind, he consented to accompany me and keep the box right all the way.

My next object was to procure a box, and with the assistance of a carpenter that was very soon accomplished, and taken to the place where the packing was to be performed. In the mean time the store-keeper had written to a friend in Philadelphia, but as no answer had arrived, we resolved to carry out our purpose as best we could. It was deemed necessary that I should get permission to be absent from my work for a few days, in order to keep down suspicion until I had once fairly started on the road to liberty; and as I had then a gathered finger I thought that would form a very good excuse for obtaining leave of absence; but when I showed it to one overseer, Mr. Allen, he told me it was not so bad as to prevent me from working, so with a view of making it bad enough, I got Dr. Smith to procure for me some oil of vitriol in order to drop a little of this on it, but in my hurry I dropped rather much and made it worse than there was any occasion for, in fact it was very soon eaten in to the bone, and on presenting it again to Mr. Allen I obtained the permission required, with the advice that I should go home and get a poultice of flax-meal to it, and keep it well poulticed until it got better. I took him instantly at his word and went off directly to the store-keeper who had by this time received an answer from his friend in Philadelphia, and had obtained permission to address the box to him, this friend in that city, arranging to call for it as soon as it should arrive. There being no time to be lost, the store-keeper, Dr. Smith, and myself, agreed to meet next morning at four o'clock, in order to get the box ready for the express train. The box which I had procured was three feet one inch wide, two feet six inches high, and two feet wide: and on the morning of the 29th day of March, 1849,[12] I went into the box—having previously bored three gimlet holes opposite my face, for air, and provided myself with a bladder of water, both for the purpose of quenching my thirst and for wetting my face, should I feel getting faint. I took the gimlet also with me, in order that I might bore more holes if I found I had not sufficient air. Being thus equipped for the battle of liberty, my friends nailed down the lid and had me conveyed to the Express Office, which was about a mile distant from the place where I was packed. I had no sooner arrived at the office than I was turned heels up, while some person nailed something on the end of the box. I was then put upon a wagon and driven off to the depôt with my head down, and I had no sooner arrived at the depôt, than the man who drove the wagon tumbled me roughly into the baggage car, where, however, I happened to fall on my right side.

The next place we arrived at was Potomac Creek, where the baggage had to be removed from the cars, to be put on board the steamer; where I was again placed with my head down, and in this dreadful position had to remain nearly an hour and a half, which, from the sufferings I had thus to endure, seemed like an age to me, but I was forgetting the battle of liberty, and I was resolved to conquer or die. I felt my eyes swelling as if they would burst from their sockets; and the veins on my temples were dreadfully distended with pressure of blood upon my head. In this position I attempted to lift my hand to my face but I had no power to move it; I felt a cold sweat coming over me which seemed to be a warning that death was about to terminate my earthly miseries, but as I feared even that, less than slavery, I resolved to submit to the will of God, and, under the influence of that impression, I lifted up my soul in prayer to God, who alone, was able to deliver me. My cry was soon heard, for I could hear a man saying to another, that he had travelled a long way and had been standing there two hours, and he would like to get somewhat to sit down; so perceiving my box, standing on end, he threw it down and then two sat upon it. I was thus relieved from a state of agony which may be more easily imagined than described. I could now listen to the men talking, and heard one of them asking the other what he supposed *the box contained*; his companion replied he guessed it was "THE MAIL." I too thought it was a mail but not such a mail as he supposed it to be.

The next place at which we arrived was the city of Washington, where I was taken from the steam boat, and again placed upon a wagon and carried to the depôt right side up with care; but when the driver arrived at the depôt I heard him call for some person to help to take the box off the wagon, and someone answered him to the effect that he might throw it off; but, says the driver, it is marked "this side up with care"; so if I throw it off I might break something the other answered him that it did not matter if he broke all that was in it, the railway company were able enough to pay for it. No sooner were these words spoken than I began to tumble from the wagon, and falling on the end where my head was, I could hear my neck give a crack, as if it had been snapped asunder and I was knocked completely insensible. The first thing I heard, after that, was some person saying, "there is no room for the box, it will have to remain and be sent through to-morrow with the luggage train"; but the Lord had not quite forsaken me, for in answer to my earnest prayer. He so ordered affairs that I should not be left behind; and I now heard a man say that the box had come with the express, and it must be sent on. I was then tumbled into the car with my head downwards again, but the car had not proceeded far before, more luggage having to be taken in, my box got shifted about and so happened to turn upon its right side; and in this position I remained till I got to Philadelphia, of our arrival in which place I was informed by hearing some person say, "We are in port and at Philadelphia." My heart then leaped for joy, and I wondered if any person knew that such a box was there.

Here it may be proper to observe that the man who had promised to accompany my box[13] failed to do what he promised; but, to prevent it remaining long at the station after its arrival, he sent a telegraphic message to his friend, and I was only twenty-seven hours in the box, though travelling a distance of three hundred and fifty miles.

I was now placed in the depôt amongst the other luggage, where I lay till seven o'clock, P.M., at which time a wagon drove up, and

I heard a person inquire for such a box as that in which I was. I was then placed on a wagon and conveyed to the house where my friend in Richmond had arranged. I should be received. A number of persons soon collected round the box after it was taken in to the house,[14] but as I did not know what was going on I kept myself quiet. I heard a man say "let us rap upon the box and see if he is alive"; and immediately a rap ensued and a voice said, tremblingly, "Is all right within?" to which I replied—"all right." The joy of the friends was very great; when they heard that I was alive they soon managed to break open the box, and then came my resurrection from the grave of slavery. I rose a freeman, but I was too weak, by reason of long confinement in that box, to be able to stand, so I immediately swooned away. After my recovery from the swoon the first thing, which arrested my attention was the presence of a number of friends, every one seeming more anxious than another, to have an opportunity of rendering me their assistance, and of bidding me a hearty welcome to the possession of my natural rights, I had risen as it were from the dead; I felt much more than I could readily express; but as the kindness of Almighty God had been so conspicuously shown in my deliverance, I burst forth into the following hymn of thanksgiving,[15]

> I waited patiently, I waited patiently for the Lord,
>   for the Lord;
> And he inclined unto me, and heard my calling:
> I waited patiently, I waited patiently for the Lord,
> And he inclined unto me, and heard my calling:
> And he hath put a new song in my mouth,
> Even a thanksgiving, even a thanksgiving even a
>   thanksgiving unto our God.
> Blessed, Blessed, Blessed, Blessed is the man, Blessed
>   is the man,
> Blessed is the man that hath set his hope, his hope in
>   the Lord;
> O Lord my God, Great, Great, Great,
>
> Great are the wondrous works which thou hast done.
> Great are the wondrous works which thou hast done,
>   which thou hast done:

If I should declare them and speak of them, they would
    be more, more, more, than I am able to express.
I have not kept back thy loving kindness and truth from
    the great congregation.
I have not kept back thy loving kindness and truth from
    the great congregation.
Withdraw not thou thy mercy from me,
Withdraw not thou thy mercy from me, O Lord;
Let thy loving kindness and thy truth always preserve me,
Let all those that seek thee be joyful and glad,
Let all those that seek thee be joyful and glad, be joyful,
    and glad, be joyful, be joyful, be joyful, be joyful, be joyful
    and glad—be glad in thee.
And let such as love thy salvation,
And let such as love thy salvation, say, always,
The Lord be praised,
The Lord be praised.
Let all those that seek thee be joyful and glad,
And let such as love thy salvation, say always,
The Lord be praised,
The Lord be praised,
The Lord be praised.

I was then taken by the hand and welcomed to the houses of the following friends—Mr. J. Miller, Mr. McKin, Mr. and Mrs. Motte,* Mr. and Mrs. Davis,[16] and many others, by all of whom I was treated in the kindest manner possible. But it was thought proper that I should not remain long in Philadelphia, so arrangements were made for me to proceed to Massachusetts, where, by the assistance of a few Anti-slavery friends, I was enabled shortly after to arrive. I went to New York, where I became acquainted with Mr. II. Long, and Mr. Eli Smith, who were very kind to me the whole time I remained there. My next journey was to New Bedford, where I remained some weeks under the care of Mr. II.

---

*Lucretia Coffin Mott and James Mott hosted Box Brown at their home in Philadelphia in the days following his arrival. See the Glossary of Names for more information.

Ricketson, my finger being still bad from the effects of the oil of vitriol with which I dressed it before I left Richmond. While I was here I heard of a great anti-slavery meeting which was to take place in Boston, and being anxious to identify myself with that public movement, I proceeded there and had the pleasure of meeting the hearty sympathy of thousands to whom I related the story of my escape. I have since attended large meetings in different towns in the states of Maine, New Hampshire, Vermont, Connecticut, Rhode Island, Pennsylvania, and New York, in all of which places I have found many friends and have endeavored, according to the best of my abilities, to advocate the cause of the emancipation of the slave; with what success I will not pretend to say—but with a daily increasing confidence in the humanity and justice of my cause, and in the assurance of the approbation of Almighty God.

I have composed the following song in commemoration of my fete in the box:—

Air:—"UNCLE NED."[17]

I

Here you see a man by the name of Henry Brown,
Run away from the South to the North;
Which he would not have done but they stole all his rights,
But they'll never do the like again.

> *Chorus*—Brown laid down the shovel and the hoe,
>   Down in the box he did go;
>   No more Slave work for Henry Box Brown,
>   In the box *by Express* he did go

II

Then the orders they were given, and the cars did start
    away,
Roll along—roll along—roll along,
Down to the landing, where the steamboat lay,
To bear the baggage off to the north.

Chorus

III

When they packed the baggage on, they turned him on
  his head,
There poor Brown liked to have died;
There were passengers on board who wished to sit down,
And they turned the box down on its side.
Chorus

IV

When they got to the cars they threw the box off,
And down upon his head he did fall,
Then he heard his neck crack, and he thought it was broke,
But they never threw him off any more.
Chorus

V

When they got to Philadelphia they said he was in port,
And Brown then began to feel glad,
He was taken on the waggon to his final destination,
And left, "this side up with care."
Chorus

VI

The friends gathered round and asked if all was right,
As down on the box they did rap,
Brown answered them, saying, "yes all is right!"
He was then set free from his pain.
Chorus

APPENDIX*

The allusion in my song to the shovel and the hoe, is founded on the following story, which forms the share-holder's version of the creation of the human race.

THE SLAVE-HOLDERS SAY THAT originally, there were four persons created (instead of only two) and, perhaps, it is owing to the Christian account of the origin of man, in which account two persons only are mentioned, that it is one of the doctrines of slave-holders that slaves have no souls: however these four persons were two whites and two blacks; and the blacks were made to wait upon the whites. But in man's original state when he neither required to manufacture clothes to cover his nakedness, or to shelter him from storm; when he did not require to till the earth or to sow or to reap its fruits, for his support! but when everything sprung up spontaneously; when the shady bowers invited him to rest, and the loaded trees dropped their luscious burdens into his hands; in this state of things the white pair were plagued with the incessant attendance of the two coloured persons, and they prayed that God would find them something else to do; and immediately while they stood, a black cloud seemed to gather over their heads and to descend to the earth before them! While they gazed on these clouds, they saw them open and two bags of different size drop from them. They immediately ran to lay hold of the bags, and unfortunately for the black man—he being the strongest and swiftest—he arrived first at them, and laid hold of the bags, and the white man, coming up afterwards, got the smaller one. They then proceeded to untie their bags, when lo in the large one, there was a

---

*The 1851 appendix may have been culled from a variety of anti-slavery lectures that Box Brown had delivered in conjunction with the panorama.

shovel and a hoe; and in the small one, a pen, ink, and paper; to write the declaration of the intention of the Almighty; they each proceeded to employ the Instruments which God had sent them, and ever since the coloured race have had to labour with the shovel and the hoe, while the rich man works with the pen and ink!

I have no apology whatever to make for what I have said, in regard to the pretended Christianity under which I was trained, while a slave. I have felt it my duty to speak of it harshly; because I have felt its blasting influence, and seen it used as a cloak under which to conceal the most foul and wicked deeds. Indeed the only thing I think it necessary to say in this place is what seems to me, and what may really be matter of serious doubt to persons who have the privilege of living in a free country, under the influence of liberal institutions; that there actually does exist in that land where men, women, and children are bought and sold, a church, calling itself the church of Christ; yes, my friends, it is true that the buyer and seller of the bodies and souls of his fellows; he who to day, can separate the husband from the wife, the parent from the child, or cut asunder the strongest ties of friendship, in order to gain a few dollars, to avert a trifling loss, or to please a whim of fancy, can ascend a pulpit tomorrow and preach, what he calls the gospel of Christ! Yes, and in many cases, the house, which he calls the house of God, has been erected from the price of human beings; the very stones of which it is composed, have actually been dragged to their places by men with chains at their heels, and ropes about their neck! It is not for me to judge between those men and the God whom they pretend to serve, if their own consciences do not condemn them. I pray that God may give them light to see the error of their ways, and if they know that they are doing wrongly, that he may give them grace to renovate, their hearts!

A few specimens of the laws of a slave-holding people may not be out of place here; not that by such means, we can hope to convey a true idea of the actual condition of the people of these places, because those matters on which the happiness or misery of a people principally depend, and in general such matters as are entirely beyond the reach of law. Beside—the various circumstances, which, independent of the law, in civilised and free countries, constitute the principal sources of happiness or misery—in the slave-holding states of America, there is a strong current of public opinion which the law is altogether incompetent to control. In many cases there are ideas of criminality, which are not by statute law attached to the commission of certain acts, but which are frequently found to exist under the title of "Lynch law" either augmenting the punishment which the law requires, or awarding punishment to what the law does not recognize as crime—as the following will be sufficient to show.

"The letter of the law would have been sufficient for the protection of the lives of the miserable gamblers, in Vicksburg, and other places in Mississippi, from the rage of those whose money they had won; but gentlemen of property and standing, laughed the law to scorn, rushed to the gambler's houses, put ropes round their necks, dragged them through the streets, hanged them in the public square, and thus saved the money they had not yet paid. Thousands witnessed this wholesale murder, yet of the scores of legal officers present, not one raised a finger to prevent it. How many hundreds of them helped to commit the murder with their own hands, does not appear, but many of them has been indicted for it, and no one has made the least effort to bring them to trial. Now the laws of Mississippi were not in fault, when those men were murdered, nor were they in fault, that the murders were not punished; the law demanded it, but the people of Mississippi, the legal officers, the grand juries, and legislature of the state, with one consent determine that the law shall be a dead letter, and thus, the whole state assumes the guilt of these murders, and, in bravado, flourish their reeking hands in the face of the world; for the people of Vicksburg have actually erected a monument in honor of Dr. H. S. Bodley, who was the ringleader of the Lynchers in this case."—*American Slavery as it is.*[18]

It may be also worthy of remark, that in all cases in which we have strong manifestation of public opinion, in opposition to the law, it is always exhibited in the direction of cruelty; indeed, that such should be the case, no person intimately acquainted with the nature of the human mind, need be in the least surprised. Who can consider the influence which the relationship of master and slave— so extensively subsisting between the members of slave states—in stimulating the passion and in degrading the moral feelings, without being prepared to credit all that is said of slavery? The most perfect abstract of the laws which regulate the duties of slaves and slave-owners, must doubtless fail to convey any proper idea of the actual state of the slave; and the few laws which we here cite, are not given for that purpose, but as a sample of trash, which is called justice by slave-holders and quasi legal authorities.

"All negroes, mulattoes, or mertizoes,* who now are, or shall hereafter, be in this province, and all their offspring, are hereby declared to be, and shall remain for ever hereafter, absolute slaves, and shall follow the condition of the mother."—*Law of South Carolina*.

The criminal offence of assault and battery, cannot, at common law, be committed upon the person of a slave, for, notwithstanding for some purposes, a slave is regarded in law, as a person, yet generally he is a mere chattel personal, and *his right of personal protection belongs to his master*, who can maintain an action of trespass, for the battery of his slave. There can be, therefore, no offence against the state for a mere beating of a slave, unaccompanied by any circumstances of cruelty, or an attempt to kill and murder. The peace of the state, is not thereby broken, for a slave is not generally regarded as legally capable of being within the pale of the State,—HE IS NOT A CITIZEN, AND IS NOT IN THAT CHARACTER ENTITLED TO HER PROTECTION."

"Any person may lawfully kill a slave who has been outlawed for running away and lurking in swamps, &c,"—*Law of North Carolina*.

"A slave endevouring to entice another slave to run away, if provision be prepared for the purpose of aiding in such running away, shall be punished with *death*: and a slave who shall aid the slave so endeavouring to run away, shall also suffer *death*."—*Law of South Carolina*.

"If a slave, when absent from his plantation, refuse to be examined by any white person, no matter what the moral character of such white person, or for what purpose he wishes to make the examination, such white person may chastise him, and if, in resisting his chastisement, he should strike the white person, by whom he is being chastised, he may be KILLED."—*Law of South Carolina*.

"If any slave shall presume to strike any white person provided such striking be not done by the command and in defence of the

---

*Mestizos; persons of mixed racial ancestry, especially of mixed European and Native American ancestry.

property of the owner, such slave shall, upon trial and conviction, before the justice or justices, suffer such punishment, for the first offence, as they shall think fit, not extending to life or limb, and for the second offence, *death*."—*Law of Georgia.*

"If any person cut any chain or collar, which any master of slaves has put upon his slave, to prevent such slave from running away, such person will be liable to a penalty not exceeding one thousand dollars, and imprisonment not exceeding two years."—*Law of Louisiana.*

"If any person cut out the tongue, put out the eye, cruelly burn, or deprive any slave of a limb, he shall be liable to a penalty not exceeding five hundred dollars."

"If a slave be attacked by any person not having sufficient cause for so doing, and be maimed or disabled so that THE OWNER SUFFERS A LOSS FROM HIS INABILITY TO LABOUR, the person so doing, shall pay the master of such disabled slave, for the time such slave shall be off work, and for the medical attendance on the slave."—*Law of South Carolina.*

Miscellaneous

If more than seven slaves be found together in any road without a white person, they shall be liable to twenty lashes each.

If any slave visit a plantation, other than that of his master, without a written pass, he shall be liable to ten lashes.

If a slave let loose a boat from where it has been made fast, he shall for the first offence be liable to a penalty of thirty-nine lashes, and for the second, to have one ear cut from his head.—for being, on horseback, without a written permission from his master—twenty-five lashes; for riding or going abroad at night, without a written permission, a slave may be cropped or branded in the cheek, with the letter E, or otherwise punished, not extending to life, or so as to render him unfit for labour.

HENRY BOX BROWN.

RUNNING A THOUSAND MILES FOR FREEDOM;

OR, THE ESCAPE

OF

WILLIAM AND ELLEN CRAFT

FROM SLAVERY.

"Slaves cannot breathe in England; if their lungs
Receive our air, that moment they are free;
They touch our country, and their shackles fall."*

Cowper.

[1860]

---

*Excerpt from poet and hymnodist William Cowper's *The Task* (1785).

PREFACE

HAVING HEARD WHILE IN Slavery that "God made of one blood all nations of men," and also that the American Declaration of Independence says, that "We hold these truths to be self-evident, that all men are created equal; that they are endowed by their Creator with certain inalienable rights; that among these, are life, liberty, and the pursuit of happiness;" we could not understand by what right we were held as "chattels." Therefore, we felt perfectly justified in undertaking the dangerous and exciting task of "running a thousand miles" in order to obtain those rights which are so vividly set forth in the Declaration. I beg those who would know the particulars of our journey, to peruse these pages. This book is not intended as a full history of the life of my wife, nor of myself; but merely as an account of our escape; together with other matter which I hope may be the means of creating in some minds a deeper abhorrence of the sinful and abominable practice of enslaving and brutifying our fellow-creatures. Without stopping to write a long apology for offering this little volume to the public, I shall commence at once to pursue my simple story.

W. CRAFT
12, CAMBRIDGE ROAD,
HAMMERSMITH,
LONDON

PART I

"God gave us only over beast, fish, fowl,
Dominion absolute; that right we hold
By his donation. But man over man
He made not lord; such title to himself
Reserving, human left from human free."

Milton

MY WIFE AND MYSELF were born in different towns in the State of Georgia, which is one of the principal slave States. It is true, our condition as slaves was not by any means the worst; but the mere idea that we were held as chattels, and deprived of all legal rights— the thought that we had to give up our hard earnings to a tyrant, to enable him to live in idleness and luxury—the thought that we could not call the bones and sinews that God gave us our own: but above all, the fact that another man had the power to tear from our cradle the new-born babe and sell it in the shambles like a brute, and then scourge us if we dared to lift a finger to save it from such a fate, haunted us for years.

But in December, 1848, a plan suggested itself that proved quite successful, and in eight days after it was first thought of we were free from the horrible trammels of slavery, rejoicing and praising God in the glorious sunshine of liberty.

My wife's first master was her father, and her mother his slave, and the latter is still the slave of his widow.

Notwithstanding my wife being of African extraction on her mother's side, she is almost white—in fact, she is so nearly so that the tyrannical old lady to whom she first belonged became so annoyed, at finding her frequently mistaken for a child of the family, that she gave her when eleven years of age to a daughter, as a wedding present. This separated my wife from her mother, and also from several other dear

224

friends. But the incessant cruelty of her old mistress made the change of owners or treatment so desirable, that she did not grumble much at this cruel separation.

It may be remembered that slavery in America is not at all confined to persons of any particular complexion; there are a very large number of slaves as white as any one; but as the evidence of a slave is not admitted in court against a free white person, it is almost impossible for a white child, after having been kidnapped and sold into or reduced to slavery, in a part of the country where it is not known (as often is the case), ever to recover its freedom.

I have myself conversed with several slaves who told me that their parents were white and free; but that they were stolen away from them and sold when quite young. As they could not tell their address, and also as the parents did not know what had become of their lost and dear little ones, of course all traces of each other were gone.

The following facts are sufficient to prove, that he who has the power, and is inhuman enough to trample upon the sacred rights of the weak, cares nothing for race or colour:—

In March, 1818, three ships arrived at New Orleans, bringing several hundred German emigrants from the province of Alsace, on the lower Rhine. Among them were Daniel Muller and his two daughters, Dorothea and Salomé, whose mother had died on the passage. Soon after his arrival, Muller, taking with him his two daughters, both young children, went up the river to Attakapas parish, to work on the plantation of John F. Miller. A few weeks later, his relatives, who had remained at New Orleans, learned that he had died of the fever of the country. They immediately sent for the two girls; but they had disappeared, and the relatives, notwithstanding repeated and persevering inquiries and researches, could find no traces of them. They were at length given up for dead. Dorothea was never again heard of; nor was any thing known of Salomé from 1818 till 1843.

In the summer of that year, Madame Karl, a German woman who had come over in the same ship with the Mullers, was passing through a street in New Orleans, and accidentally saw Salomé in a wine-shop, belonging to Louis Belmonte, by whom she was held as a slave. Madame Karl recognised her at once, and carried her to the house of another German woman, Mrs. Schubert, who was Salomé's cousin and godmother, and who no sooner set eyes on her than, without having any intimation that the discovery had been previously made, she unhesitatingly exclaimed, "My God! here is the long-lost Salomé Muller."

The *Law Reporter*, in its account of this case, says:—

"As many of the German emigrants of 1818[1] as could be gathered together were brought to the house of Mrs. Schubert, and every one of the number who had any recollection of the little girl upon the passage, or any acquaintance with her father and mother, immediately identified the woman before them as the long-lost Salomé Muller. By all these witnesses, who appeared at the trial, the identity was fully established. The family resemblance in every feature was declared to be so remarkable, that some of the witnesses did not hesitate to say that they should know her among ten thousand; that they were as certain the plaintiff was Salomé Muller, the daughter of Daniel and Dorothea Muller, as of their own existence."

Among the witnesses who appeared in Court was the midwife who had assisted at the birth of Salomé. She testified to the existence of certain peculiar marks upon the body of the child, which were found, exactly as described, by the surgeons who were appointed by the Court to make an examination for the purpose.

There was no trace of African descent in any feature of Salomé Muller. She had long, straight, black hair, hazel eyes, thin lips, and a Roman nose. The complexion of her face and neck was as dark as that of the darkest brunette. It appears, however, that, during the twenty-five years of her servitude, she had been exposed to the sun's rays in the hot climate of Louisiana, with head and neck unsheltered, as is customary with the female slaves, while labouring in the cotton or the sugar field. Those parts of her person which had been shielded from the sun were comparatively white.

Belmonte, the pretended owner of the girl, had obtained possession of her by an act of sale from John F. Miller, the planter in whose service Salomé's father died. This Miller was a man of consideration and substance, owning large sugar estates, and bearing a high reputation for honour and honesty, and for indulgent treatment of his slaves. It was testified on the trial that he had said to Belmonte, a few weeks after the sale of Salomé, "that she was white, and had as much right to her freedom as any one, and was only to be retained in slavery by care and kind treatment." The broker who negotiated the sale from Miller to Belmonte, in 1838, testified in Court that he then thought, and still thought, that the girl was white!

The case was elaborately argued on both sides, but was at length decided in favour of the girl, by the Supreme Court declaring that "she was free and white, and therefore unlawfully held in bondage."

The Rev. George Bourne, of Virginia, in his *Picture of Slavery,* published in 1834, relates the case of a white boy who, at the age of seven, was stolen from his home in Ohio, tanned and stained in such a way that he could not be distinguished from a person of colour, and then sold as a slave in Virginia. At the age of twenty, he made his escape, by running away, and happily succeeded in rejoining his parents.

I have known worthless white people to sell their own free children into slavery; and, as there are good-for-nothing white as well as coloured persons everywhere, no one, perhaps, will wonder at such inhuman transactions: particularly in the Southern States of America, where I believe there is a greater want of humanity and high principle amongst the whites, than among any other civilized people in the world.

I know that those who are not familiar with the working of "the peculiar institution," can scarcely imagine any one so totally devoid of all natural affection as to sell his own offspring into returnless bondage. But Shakespeare, that great observer of human nature, says:—

> "With caution judge of probabilities.
> Things deemed unlikely, e'en impossible,
> Experience often shews us to be true."

My wife's new mistress was decidedly more humane than the majority of her class. My wife has always given her credit for not exposing her to many of the worst features of slavery. For instance, it is a common practice in the slave States for ladies, when angry with their maids, to send them to the calybuce sugar-house, or to some other place established for the purpose of punishing slaves, and have them severely flogged; and I am sorry it is a fact, that the villains to whom those defenceless creatures are sent, not only flog them as they are ordered, but frequently compel them to submit to the greatest indignity. Oh! if there is any one thing under the wide canopy of heaven, horrible enough to stir a man's soul, and to make his very blood boil, it is the thought of his dear wife, his unprotected sister, or his young and virtuous daughters, struggling to save themselves from falling a prey to such demons!

It always appears strange to me that any one who was not born a slaveholder, and steeped to the very core in the demoralizing atmosphere of the Southern States, can in any way palliate slavery. It is still more surprising to see virtuous ladies looking with patience upon, and remaining indifferent to, the existence of a system that exposes nearly two millions of their own sex in the manner I have mentioned, and that too in a professedly free and Christian country. There is, however, great consolation in knowing that God is just, and will not let the oppressor of the weak, and the spoiler of the virtuous, escape unpunished here and hereafter.

I believe a similar retribution to that which destroyed Sodom* is hanging over the slaveholders. My sincere prayer is that they may not provoke God, by persisting in a reckless course of wickedness, to pour out his consuming wrath upon them.

I must now return to our history.

My old master had the reputation of being a very humane and Christian man, but he thought nothing of selling my poor old father, and dear aged mother, at separate times, to different persons, to be dragged off never to behold each other again, till summoned to appear before the great tribunal of heaven. But, oh! what a happy meeting it will be on that great day for those faithful souls. I say a happy meeting, because I never saw persons more devoted to the service of God than they. But how will the case stand with those reckless traffickers in human flesh and blood, who plunged the poisonous dagger of separation into those loving hearts which God had for so many years closely joined together—nay, sealed as it were with his own hands for the eternal courts of heaven? It is not for me to say what will become of those heartless tyrants. I must leave them in the

---

*In the Bible (see, for example, Genesis 19), Sodom (in Hebrew, "burnt") and Gomorrah ("a ruined heap") were cities destroyed by God for their sins.

hands of an all-wise and just God, who will, in his own good time, and in his own way, avenge the wrongs of his oppressed people.

My old master also sold a dear brother and a sister, in the same manner as he did my father and mother. The reason he assigned for disposing of my parents, as well as of several other aged slaves, was, that "they were getting old, and would soon become valueless in the market, and therefore he intended to sell off all the old stock, and buy in a young lot." A most disgraceful conclusion for a man to come to, who made such great professions of religion!

This shameful conduct gave me a thorough hatred, not for true Christianity, but for slaveholding piety.

My old master, then, wishing to make the most of the rest of his slaves, apprenticed a brother and myself out to learn trades: he to a black-smith, and myself to a cabinet-maker. If a slave has a good trade, he will let or sell for more than a person without one, and many slaveholders have their slaves taught trades on this account. But before our time expired, my old master wanted money; so he sold my brother, and then mortgaged my sister, a dear girl about fourteen years of age, and myself, then about sixteen, to one of the banks, to get money to speculate in cotton. This we knew nothing of at the moment; but time rolled on, the money became due, my master was unable to meet his payments; so the bank had us placed upon the auction stand and sold to the highest bidder.

My poor sister was sold first: she was knocked down to a planter who resided at some distance in the country. Then I was called upon the stand. While the auctioneer was crying the bids, I saw the man that had purchased my sister getting her into a cart, to take her to his home. I at once asked a slave friend who was standing near the platform, to run and ask the gentleman if he would please to wait till I was sold, in order that I might have an opportunity of bidding her good-bye. He sent me word back that he had some distance to go, and could not wait.

I then turned to the auctioneer, fell upon my knees, and humbly prayed him to let me just step down and bid my last sister farewell. But, instead of granting me this request, he grasped me by the neck, and in a commanding tone of voice, and with a violent oath, exclaimed, "Get up! You can do the wench no good; therefore there is no use in your seeing her."

On rising, I saw the cart in which she sat moving slowly off; and, as she clasped her hands with a grasp that indicated despair, and looked pitifully round towards me, I also saw the large silent tears trickling down her cheeks. She made a farewell bow, and buried her face in her lap. This seemed more than I could bear. It appeared to swell my aching heart to its utmost. But before I could fairly recover, the poor girl was gone;—gone, and I have never had the good fortune to see her from that day to this! Perhaps I should have never heard of her again, had it not been for the untiring efforts of my good old mother, who became free a few years ago by purchase, and, after a great deal of difficulty, found my sister residing with a family in Mississippi. My mother at once wrote to me, informing me of the fact, and requesting me to do something to get her free; and I am happy to say that, partly by lecturing occasionally, and through the sale of an engraving of my wife in the disguise in which she escaped, together with the extreme kindness and generosity of Miss Burdett Coutts, Mr. George Richardson of Plymouth, and a few other friends, I have nearly accomplished this. It would be to me a great and ever-glorious achievement to restore my sister to our dear mother, from whom she was forcibly driven in early life.

I was knocked down to the cashier of the bank to which we were mortgaged, and ordered to return to the cabinet shop where I previously worked.

But the thought of the harsh auctioneer not allowing me to bid my dear sister farewell, sent red-hot indignation darting like lightning through every vein. It quenched my tears, and appeared to set my brain on fire, and made me crave for power to avenge our wrongs! But, alas! we were only slaves, and had no legal rights; consequently we were compelled to smother our wounded feelings, and crouch beneath the iron heel of despotism.

I must now give the account of our escape; but, before doing so, it may be well to quote a few passages from the fundamental laws of slavery; in order to give some idea of the legal as well as the social tyranny from which we fled.

According to the law of Louisiana, "A slave is one who is in the power of a master to whom he belongs. The master may sell him, dispose of his person, his industry, and his labour; he can do nothing, possess nothing, nor acquire anything but what must belong to his master."—*Civil Code, art.* 35.

In South Carolina it is expressed in the following language:— "Slaves shall be deemed, sold, taken, reputed and judged in law to be *chattels personal* in the hands of their owners and possessors, and their executors, administrators, and assigns, *to all intents, constructions, and purposes whatsoever.*"—2 *Brevard's Digest,* 229.

The Constitution of Georgia has the following (Art. 4, sec. 12):—"Any person who shall maliciously dismember or deprive a slave of life, shall suffer such punishment as would be inflicted in case the like offence had been committed on a free white person, and on the like proof, except in case of insurrection of such slave, and unless SUCH DEATH SHOULD HAPPEN BY ACCIDENT IN GIVING SUCH SLAVE MODERATE CORRECTION."—*Prince's Digest,* 559.

I have known slaves to be beaten to death, but as they died under "moderate correction," it was quite lawful; and of course the murderers were not interfered with.

"If any slave, who shall be out of the house or plantation where such slave shall live, or shall be usually employed, or without some white person in company with such slave, shall *refuse to submit* to undergo the examination of *any white* person, (let him be ever so drunk or crazy), it shall be lawful for such white person to pursue, apprehend, and moderately correct such slave; and if such slave shall assault and strike such white person, such slave may be *lawfully killed.*"—2 *Brevard's Digest,* 231.

"Provided always," says the law, "that such striking be not done by the command and in the defence of the person or property of the owner, or other person having the government of such slave; in which case the slave shall be wholly excused."

According to this law, if a slave, by the direction of his overseer, strike a white person who is beating said overseer's pig, "the slave shall be wholly excused." But, should the bondman, of his own accord, fight to defend his wife, or should his terrified daughter instinctively raise her hand and strike the wretch who attempts to violate her chastity, he or she shall, saith the model republican law, suffer death.

From having been myself a slave for nearly twenty-three years, I am quite prepared to say, that the practical working of slavery is worse than the odious laws by which it is governed.

At an early age we were taken by the persons who held us as property to Macon, the largest town in the interior of the State of Georgia, at which place we became acquainted with each other for several years before our marriage; in fact, our marriage was postponed for some time simply because one of the unjust and worse than Pagan laws under which we lived compelled all children of slave mothers to follow their condition. That is to say, the father of the slave may be the President of the Republic; but if the mother should be a slave at the infant's birth, the poor child is ever legally doomed to the same cruel fate.

It is a common practice for gentlemen (if I may call them such), moving in the highest circles of society, to be the fathers of children by their slaves, whom they can and do sell with the greatest impunity; and the more pious, beautiful, and virtuous the girls are, the greater the price they bring, and that too for the most infamous purposes.

Any man with money (let him be ever such a rough brute), can buy a beautiful and virtuous girl, and force her to live with him in a criminal connexion; and as the law says a slave shall have no higher appeal than the mere will of the master, she cannot escape, unless it be by flight or death.

In endeavouring to reconcile a girl to her fate, the master sometimes says that he would marry her if it was not unlawful.* However, he will always consider her to be his wife, and will treat her as such; and she, on the other hand, may regard him as her lawful husband; and if they have any children, they will be free and well educated.

I am in duty bound to add, that while a great majority of such men care nothing for the happiness of the women with whom they live, nor for the children of whom they are the fathers, there are those

---

*It is unlawful in the slave States for any one of purely European descent to intermarry with a person of African extraction; though a white man may live with as many coloured women as he pleases without materially damaging his reputation in Southern society. [Crafts' note]

to be found, even in that heterogeneous mass of licentious monsters, who are true to their pledges. But as the woman and her children are legally the property of the man, who stands in the anomalous relation to them of husband and father, as well as master, they are liable to be seized and sold for his debts, should he become involved.

There are several cases on record where such persons have been sold and separated for life. I know of some myself, but I have only space to glance at one.

I knew a very humane and wealthy gentleman, that bought a woman, with whom he lived as his wife. They brought up a family of children, among whom were three nearly white, well educated, and beautiful girls.

On the father being suddenly killed it was found that he had not left a will; but, as the family had always heard him say that he had no surviving relatives, they felt that their liberty and property were quite secured to them, and, knowing the insults to which they were exposed, now their protector was no more, they were making preparations to leave for a free State.

But, poor creatures, they were soon sadly undeceived. A villain residing at a distance, hearing of the circumstance, came forward and swore that he was a relative of the deceased; and as this man bore, or assumed, Mr. Slator's name, the case was brought before one of those horrible tribunals, presided over by a second Judge Jeffreys,* and calling itself a court of justice, but before whom no coloured person, nor an abolitionist, was ever known to get his full rights.

A verdict was given in favour of the plaintiff, whom the better portion of the community thought had wilfully conspired to cheat the family.

The heartless wretch not only took the ordinary property, but actually had the aged and friendless widow, and all her fatherless children, except Frank, a fine young man about twenty-two years of age, and Mary, a very nice girl, a little younger than her brother, brought to the auction stand and sold to the highest bidder. Mrs. Slator had cash enough, that her husband and master left, to purchase the liberty of herself and children; but on her attempting to

---

*Probably a reference to George Jeffreys. See the Glossary of Names.

do so, the pusillanimous scoundrel, who had robbed them of their freedom, claimed the money as his property; and, poor creature, she had to give it up. According to law, as will be seen hereafter, a slave cannot own anything. The old lady never recovered from her sad affliction.

At the sale she was brought up first, and after being vulgarly criticised, in the presence of all her distressed family, was sold to a cotton planter, who said he wanted the "proud old critter to go to his plantation, to look after the little woolly heads, while their mammies were working in the field."

When the sale was over, then came the separation, and

> "O, deep was the anguish of that slave mother's heart,
> When called from her darlings for ever to part;
> The poor mourning mother of reason bereft,
> Soon ended her sorrows, and sank cold in death."*

Antoinette, the flower of the family, a girl who was much beloved by all who knew her, for her Christ-like piety, dignity of manner, as well as her great talents and extreme beauty, was bought by an uneducated and drunken slave-dealer.

I cannot give a more correct description of the scene, when she was called from her brother to the stand, than will be found in the following lines—

> "Why stands she near the auction stand?
>   That girl so young and fair;
> What brings her to this dismal place?
>   Why stands she weeping there?
>
> Why does she raise that bitter cry?
>   Why hangs her head with shame,
> As now the auctioneer's rough voice
>   So rudely calls her name!

---

*Verse taken from the abolitionist hymn "The Bereaved Mother" (1848), by Kathleen O'More; it was included in William Wells Brown's anti-slavery song collection *The Anti-Slavery Harp* (see For Further Reading).

But see! she grasps a manly hand,
　　And in a voice so low,
As scarcely to be heard, she says,
　　'My brother, must I go?'

A moment's pause: then, midst a wail
　　Of agonizing woe,
His answer falls upon the ear,—
　　'Yes, sister, you must go!

No longer can my arm defend,
　　No longer can I save
My sister from the horrid fate
　　That waits her as a SLAVE!'

Blush, Christian, blush! for e'en the dark
　　Untutored heathen see
Thy inconsistency, and lo!
　　They scorn thy God, and thee!"[2]

The low trader said to a kind lady who wished to purchase Antoinette out of his hands, "I reckon I'll not sell the smart critter for ten thousand dollars; I always wanted her for my own use." The lady, wishing to remonstrate with him, commenced by saying, "You should remember, Sir, that there is a just God." Hoskens not understanding Mrs. Huston, interrupted her by saying, "I does, and guess its monstrous kind an' him to send such likely niggers for our convenience." Mrs. Huston finding that a long course of reckless wickedness, drunkenness, and vice, had destroyed in Hoskens every noble impulse, left him.

Antoinette, poor girl, also seeing that there was no help for her, became frantic. I can never forget her cries of despair, when Hoskens gave the order for her to be taken to his house, and locked in an upper room. On Hoskens entering the apartment, in a state of intoxication, a fearful struggle ensued. The brave Antoinette broke loose from him, pitched herself head foremost through the window, and fell upon the pavement below.

Her bruised but unpolluted body was soon picked up— restoratives brought—doctor called in; but, alas! it was too late: her pure and noble spirit had fled away to be at rest in those realms of endless bliss, "where the wicked cease from troubling, and the weary are at rest."

Antoinette like many other noble women who are deprived of liberty, still

> "Holds something sacred, something undefiled;
> Some pledge and keepsake of their higher nature.
> And, like the diamond in the dark, retains
> Some quenchless gleam of the celestial light."*

On Hoskens fully realizing the fact that his victim was no more, he exclaimed "By thunder I am a used-up man!" The sudden disappointment, and the loss of two thousand dollars, was more than he could endure: so he drank more than ever, and in a short time died, raving mad with *delirium tremens*.†

The villain Slator said to Mrs. Huston, the kind lady who endeavoured to purchase Antoinette from Hoskens, "Nobody needn't talk to me 'bout buying them ar likely niggers, for I'm not going to sell em." "But Mary is rather delicate," said Mrs. Huston, "and, being unaccustomed to hard work, cannot do you much service on a plantation." "I don't want her for the field," replied Slator, "but for another purpose." Mrs. Huston understood what this meant, and instantly exclaimed, "Oh, but she is your cousin!" "The devil she is!" said Slator; and added, "Do you mean to insult me, Madam, by saying that I am related to niggers?" "No," replied Mrs. Huston, "I do not wish to offend you, Sir. But wasn't Mr. Slator, Mary's father, your uncle?" "Yes, I calculate he was," said Slator; "but I want you and everybody to understand that I'm no kin to his niggers." "Oh, very well," said Mrs. Huston; adding, "Now what will you take for the poor girl?" "Nothin'," he replied; "for, as I said before, I'm not goin' to sell, so you needn't trouble yourself no more. If the critter behaves herself, I'll do as well by her as any man."

---

*Probably a passage from Henry Wadsworth Longfellow's play *The Spanish Student* (1843).
†Also known as "the horrors," "the shakes," or "rum fits"; a condition associated with withdrawal from alcohol after excessive habitual consumption.

Slator spoke up boldly, but his manner and sheepish look clearly indicated that

> "His heart within him was at strife
>   such accursed gains;
> For he knew whose passions gave her life,
>   Whose blood ran in her veins."

> "The monster led her from the door,
>   He led her by the hand,
> To be his slave and paramour
>   In a strange and distant land!"*

Poor Frank and his sister were handcuffed together, and confined in prison. Their dear little twin brother and sister were sold, and taken where they knew not. But it often happens that misfortune causes those whom we counted dearest to shrink away; while it makes friends of those whom we least expected to take any interest in our affairs. Among the latter class Frank found two comparatively new but faithful friends to watch the gloomy paths of the unhappy little twins.

In a day or two after the sale, Slator had two fast horses put to a large light van, and placed in it a good many small but valuable things belonging to the distressed family. He also took with him Frank and Mary, as well as all the money for the spoil; and after treating all his low friends and bystanders, and drinking deeply himself, he started in high glee for his home in South Carolina. But they had not proceeded many miles, before Frank and his sister discovered that Slator was too drunk to drive. But he, like most tipsy men, thought he was all right; and as he had with him some of the ruined family's best brandy and wine, such as he had not been accustomed to, and being a thirsty soul, he drank till the reins fell from his fingers, and in attempting to catch them he tumbled out of the vehicle, and was unable to get up. Frank and Mary there and then contrived a plan by which to escape. As they were still

---

*A passage from Henry Wadsworth Longfellow's "The Quadroon Girl," in *Poems on Slavery* (1842).

handcuffed by one wrist each, they alighted, took from the drunken assassin's pocket the key, undid the iron bracelets, and placed them upon Slator, who was better fitted to wear such ornaments. As the demon lay unconscious of what was taking place, Frank and Mary took from him the large sum of money that was realized at the sale, as well as that which Slator had so very meanly obtained from their poor mother. They then dragged him into the woods, tied him to a tree, and left the inebriated robber to shift for himself, while they made good their escape to Savannah. The fugitives being white, of course no one suspected that they were slaves.

Slator was not able to call any one to his rescue till late the next day; and as there were no railroads in that part of the country at that time, it was not until late the following day that Slator was able to get a party to join him for the chase. A person informed Slator that he had met a man and woman, in a trap, answering to the description of those whom he had lost, driving furiously towards Savannah. So Slator and several slavehunters on horseback started off in full tilt, with their bloodhounds, in pursuit of Frank and Mary.

On arriving at Savannah, the hunters found that the fugitives had sold the horses and trap, and embarked as free white persons, for New York. Slator's disappointment and rascality so preyed upon his base mind, that he, like Judas, went and hanged himself.

As soon as Frank and Mary were safe, they endeavoured to redeem their good mother. But, alas! she was gone; she had passed on to the realm of spirit life.

In due time Frank learned from his friends in Georgia where his little brother and sister dwelt. So he wrote at once to purchase them, but the persons with whom they lived would not sell them. After failing in several attempts to buy them, Frank cultivated large whiskers and moustachios, cut off his hair, put on a wig and glasses, and went down as a white man, and stopped in the neighbourhood where his sister was; and after seeing her and also his little brother, arrangements were made for them to meet at a particular place on a Sunday, which they did, and got safely off.

I saw Frank myself, when he came for the little twins. Though I was then quite a lad, I well remember being highly delighted by hearing him tell how nicely he and Mary had served Slator.

Frank had so completely disguised or changed his appearance that his little sister did not know him, and would not speak till he showed their mother's likeness; the sight of which melted her to tears,—for she knew the face. Frank might have said to her

> " 'O, Emma! O, my sister, speak to me!
> Dost thou not know me, that I am thy brother?
> Come to me, little Emma, thou shalt dwell
> With me henceforth, and know no care or want.'
> Emma was silent for a space, as if
> 'Twere hard to summon up a human voice."

Frank and Mary's mother was my wife's own dear aunt.

After this great diversion from our narrative, which I hope dear reader, you will excuse, I shall return at once to it.

My wife was torn from her mother's embrace in childhood, and taken to a distant part of the country. She had seen so many other children separated from their parents in this cruel manner, that the mere thought of her ever becoming the mother of a child, to linger out a miserable existence under the wretched system of American slavery, appeared to fill her very soul with horror; and as she had taken what I felt to be an important view of her condition, I did not, at first, press the marriage, but agreed to assist her in trying to devise some plan by which we might escape from our unhappy condition, and then be married.

We thought of plan after plan, but they all seemed crowded with insurmountable difficulties. We knew it was unlawful for any public conveyance to take us as passengers, without our master's consent. We were also perfectly aware of the startling fact, that had we left without this consent the professional slave-hunters would have soon had their ferocious bloodhounds baying on our track, and in a short time we should have been dragged back to slavery, not to fill the more favourable situations which we had just left, but to be separated for life, and put to the very meanest and most laborious drudgery; or else have been tortured to death as examples, in order to strike terror into the hearts of others, and thereby prevent them from even attempting to escape from their cruel taskmasters. It is a fact worthy of remark, that nothing seems to give the slaveholders so much pleasure as the catching and torturing of fugitives. They had much rather take the keen and poisonous lash, and with it cut their poor trembling victims to atoms, than allow one of them to escape to a free country, and expose the infamous system from which he fled.

The greatest excitement prevails at a slave-hunt. The slaveholders and their hired ruffians appear to take more pleasure in this inhuman pursuit than English sportsmen do in chasing a fox or a stag. Therefore, knowing what we should have been compelled to suffer, if caught and taken back, we were more than anxious to hit upon a plan that would lead us safely to a land of liberty.

But, after puzzling our brains for years, we were reluctantly driven to the sad conclusion, that it was almost impossible to escape from slavery in Georgia, and travel 1,000 miles across the slave States. We therefore resolved to get the consent of our owners, be married, settle down in slavery, and endeavour to make ourselves as comfortable as possible under that system; but at the same time ever to keep our dim eyes steadily fixed upon the glimmering hope of liberty, and earnestly pray God mercifully to assist us to escape from our unjust thraldom.

We were married, and prayed and toiled on till December, 1848, at which time (as I have stated) a plan suggested itself that proved quite successful, and in eight days after it was first thought of we were free from the horrible trammels of slavery, and glorifying God who had brought us safely out of a land of bondage.

Knowing that slaveholders have the privilege of taking their slaves to any part of the country they think proper, it occurred to me that, as my wife was nearly white, I might get her to disguise herself as an invalid gentleman, and assume to be my master, while I could attend as his slave, and that in this manner we might effect our escape. After I thought of the plan, I suggested it to my wife, but at first she shrank from the idea. She thought it was almost impossible for her to assume that disguise, and travel a distance of 1,000 miles across the slave States. However, on the other hand, she also thought of her condition. She saw that the laws under which we lived did not recognize her to be a woman, but a mere chattel, to be bought and sold, or otherwise dealt with as her owner might see fit. Therefore the more she contemplated her helpless condition, the more anxious she was to escape from it. So she said, "I think it is almost too much for us to undertake; however, I feel that God is on our side, and with his assistance, notwithstanding all the difficulties, we shall be able to succeed. Therefore, if you will purchase the disguise, I will try to carry out the plan."

But after I concluded to purchase the disguise, I was afraid to go to any one to ask him to sell me the articles. It is unlawful in Georgia for a white man to trade with slaves without the master's consent. But, notwithstanding this, many persons will sell a slave any article that he can get the money to buy. Not that they sympathize with the slave, but merely because his testimony is not admitted in court against a free white person.

Therefore, with little difficulty I went to different parts of the town, at odd times, and purchased things piece by piece, (except the trowsers which she found necessary to make,) and took them home to the house where my wife resided. She being a ladies' maid, and a favourite slave in the family, was allowed a little room to herself; and amongst other pieces of furniture which I had made in my overtime, was a chest of drawers; so when I took the articles home, she locked them up carefully in these drawers. No one about the premises knew that she had anything of the kind. So when we fancied we had everything ready, the time was fixed for the flight. But we knew it would not do to start off without first getting our master's consent to be away for a few days. Had we left without this, they would soon have had us back into slavery, and probably we should never have got another fair opportunity of even attempting to escape.

Some of the best slaveholders will sometimes give their favourite slaves a few days' holiday at Christmas time; so, after no little amount of perseverance on my wife's part, she obtained a pass from her mistress, allowing her to be away for a few days. The cabinetmaker with whom I worked gave me a similar paper, but said that he needed my services very much, and wished me to return as soon as the time granted was up. I thanked him kindly; but somehow I have not been able to make it convenient to return yet; and, as the free air of good old England agrees so well with my wife and our dear little ones, as well as with myself, it is not at all likely we shall return at present to the "peculiar institution" of chains and stripes.

On reaching my wife's cottage she handed me her pass, and I showed mine, but at that time neither of us were able to read them. It is not only unlawful for slaves to be taught to read, but in some of the States there are heavy penalties attached, such as fines and imprisonment, which will be vigorously enforced upon any one who is humane enough to violate the so-called law.

The following case will serve to show how persons are treated in the most enlightened slaveholding community.

"Indictment.
Commonwealth of Virginia, Norfolk County, ss."

In the Circuit Court. The Grand Jurors empannelled and sworn to inquire of offences committed in the body of the said County on their oath present, that Margaret Douglass, being an evil disposed person, not having the fear of God before her eyes, but moved and instigated by the devil, wickedly, maliciously, and feloniously, on the fourth day of July, in the year of our Lord one thousand eight hundred and fifty-four, at Norfolk, in said County, did teach a certain black girl named Kate to read in the Bible, to the great displeasure of Almighty God, to the pernicious example of others in like case offending, contrary to the form of the statute in such case made and provided, and against the peace and dignity of the Commonwealth of Virginia.

"Victor Vagabond, Prosecuting Attorney."

"On this indictment Mrs. Douglass was arraigned as a necessary matter of form, tried, found guilty of course; and Judge Scalawag, before whom she was tried, having consulted with Dr. Adams, ordered the sheriff to place Mrs. Douglass in the prisoner's box, when he addressed her as follows: 'Margaret Douglass, stand up. You are guilty of one of the vilest crimes that ever disgraced society; and the jury have found you so. You have taught a slave girl to read in the Bible. No enlightened society can exist where such offences go unpunished. The Court, in your case, do not feel for you one solitary ray of sympathy, and they will inflict on you the utmost penalty of the law. In any other civilized country you would have paid the forfeit of your crime with your life, and the Court have only to regret that such is not the law in this country. The sentence for your offence is, that you be imprisoned one month in the county jail, and that you pay the costs of this prosecution. Sheriff, remove the prisoner to jail.' On the publication of these proceedings, the Doctors of Divinity preached each a sermon on the necessity of obeying the laws; the *New York Observer* noticed with much pious gladness a revival of religion on Dr. Smith's plantation in Georgia, among his slaves; while the *Journal of Commerce* commended this political preaching of the Doctors of Divinity because it favoured slavery. Let us do nothing to offend our Southern brethren."

However, at first, we were highly delighted at the idea of having gained permission to be absent for a few days; but when the thought flashed across my wife's mind, that it was customary for travellers to register their names in the visitors' book at hotels, as well as in the clearance or Custom-house book at Charleston, South Carolina— it made our spirits droop within us.

So, while sitting in our little room upon the verge of despair, all at once my wife raised her head, and with a smile upon her face, which was a moment before bathed in tears, said, "I think I have it!" I asked what it was. She said, "I think I can make a poultice* and bind up my right hand in a sling, and with propriety ask the officers to register my name for me." I thought that would do.

It then occurred to her that the smoothness of her face might betray her; so she decided to make another poultice, and put it in a white handkerchief to be worn under the chin, up the cheeks, and to tie over the head. This nearly hid the expression of the countenance, as well as the beardless chin.

The poultice is left off in the engraving, because the likeness could not have been taken well with it on.

My wife, knowing that she would be thrown a good deal into the company of gentlemen, fancied that she could get on better if she had something to go over the eyes; so I went to a shop and bought a pair of green spectacles.

---

*A soft, moist mass, often heated and medicated, that is spread on cloth to be applied on the skin to treat an aching, inflamed, or painful part of the body.

This was in the evening. We sat up all night discussing the plan, and making preparations. Just before the time arrived, in the morning, for us to leave, I cut off my wife's hair square at the back of the head, and got her to dress in the disguise and stand out on the floor. I found that she made a most respectable looking gentleman.

My wife had no ambition whatever to assume this disguise, and would not have done so had it been possible to have obtained our liberty by more simple means; but we knew it was not customary in the South for ladies to travel with male servants; and therefore, notwithstanding my wife's fair complexion, it would have been a very difficult task for her to have come off as a free white lady, with me as her slave; in fact, her not being able to write would have made this quite impossible. We knew that no public conveyance would take us, or any other slave, as a passenger, without our master's consent. This consent could never be obtained to pass into a free State. My wife's being muffled in the poultices, &c., furnished a plausible excuse for avoiding general conversation, of which most Yankee travellers are passionately fond.

There are a large number of free negroes residing in the southern States; but in Georgia (and I believe in all the slave States,) every coloured person's complexion is *primâ facie* evidence of his being a slave; and the lowest villain in the country, should he be a white man, has the legal power to arrest, and question, in the most inquisitorial and insulting manner, any coloured person, male or female, that he may find at large, particularly at night and on Sundays, without a written pass, signed by the master or some one in authority; or stamped free papers, certifying that the person is the rightful owner of himself.

If the coloured person refuses to answer questions put to him, he may be beaten, and his defending himself against this attack makes him an outlaw, and if he be killed on the spot, the murderer will be exempted from all blame; but after the coloured person has answered the questions put to him, in a most humble and pointed manner, he may then be taken to prison; and should it turn out, after further examination, that he was caught where he had no permission or legal right to be, and that he has not given what they term a satisfactory account of himself, the master will have to pay a fine. On his refusing to do this, the poor slave may be legally and severely flogged by public officers. Should the prisoner prove to be a free man, he is most likely to be both whipped and fined.

The great majority of slaveholders hate this class of persons with a hatred that can only be equalled by the condemned spirits of the infernal regions. They have no mercy upon, nor sympathy for, any negro whom they cannot enslave. They say that God made the black man to be a slave for the white, and act as though they really believed that all free persons of colour are in open rebellion to a direct command from heaven, and that they (the whites) are God's chosen agents to pour out upon them unlimited vengeance. For instance, a Bill has been introduced in the Tennessee Legislature to prevent free negroes from travelling on the railroads in that State. It has passed the first reading. The bill provides that the President who shall permit a free negro to travel on any road within the jurisdiction of the State under his supervision shall pay a fine of 500 dollars; any conductor permitting a violation of the Act shall pay 250 dollars; provided such free negro is not under the control of a free white citizen of Tennessee, who will vouch for the character of said free negro in a penal bond of one thousand dollars. The State of Arkansas has passed a law to banish all free negroes from its bounds, and it came into effect on the 1st day of January, 1860. Every free negro found there after that date will be liable to be sold into slavery, the crime of freedom being unpardonable. The Missouri Senate has before it a bill providing that all free negroes above the age of eighteen years who shall be found in the State after September, 1860, shall be sold into slavery; and that all such negroes as shall enter the State after September, 1861, and remain there twenty-four hours, shall also be sold into slavery for ever. Mississippi, Kentucky, and Georgia, and in fact, I believe, all the slave States, are legislating in the same manner. Thus the slaveholders make it almost impossible for free persons of colour to get out of the slave States, in order that they may sell them into slavery if they don't go. If no white persons travelled upon railroads except those who could get some one to vouch for their character in a penal bond of one thousand dollars, the railroad companies would soon go to the "wall." Such mean legislation is too low for comment; therefore I leave the villainous acts to speak for themselves.

But the Dred Scott decision[3] is the crowning act of infamous Yankee legislation. The Supreme Court, the highest tribunal of the Republic, composed of nine Judge Jeffries's, chosen both from the free and slave States, has decided that no coloured person, or persons of African extraction, can ever become a citizen of the United States, or have any rights which white men are bound to respect. That is to say, in the opinion of this Court, robbery, rape, and murder are not crimes when committed by a white upon a coloured person.

Judges who will sneak from their high and honourable position down into the lowest depths of human depravity, and scrape up a decision like this, are wholly unworthy the confidence of any people. I believe such men would, if they had the power, and were it to their temporal interest, sell their country's independence, and barter away every man's birthright for a mess of pottage. Well may Thomas Campbell say—

> "United States, your banner wears,
> Two emblems,—one of fame;
> Alas, the other that it bears
> Reminds us of your shame!
> The white man's liberty in types
> Stands blazoned by your stars;
> But what's the meaning of your stripes?
> They mean your Negro-scars."*

When the time had arrived for us to start, we blew out the lights, knelt down, and prayed to our Heavenly Father mercifully to assist us, as he did his people of old, to escape from cruel bondage; and we shall ever feel that God heard and answered our prayer. Had we not been sustained by a kind, and I sometimes think special, providence, we could never have overcome the mountainous difficulties which I am now about to describe.

After this we rose and stood for a few moments in breathless silence,—we were afraid that some one might have been about the

---

*Quote from Thomas Campbell (1777–1844), Scottish poet, taken from "To the United States of North America."

cottage listening and watching our movements. So I took my wife by the hand, stepped softly to the door, raised the latch, drew it open, and peeped out. Though there were trees all around the house, yet the foliage scarcely moved; in fact, everything appeared to be as still as death. I then whispered to my wife, "Come, my dear, let us make a desperate leap for liberty!" But poor thing, she shrank back, in a state of trepidation. I turned and asked what was the matter; she made no reply, but burst into violent sobs, and threw her head upon my breast. This appeared to touch my very heart, it caused me to enter into her feelings more fully than ever. We both saw the many mountainous difficulties that rose one after the other before our view, and knew far too well what our sad fate would have been, were we caught and forced back into our slavish den. Therefore on my wife's fully realizing the solemn fact that we had to take our lives, as it were, in our hands, and contest every inch of the thousand miles of slave territory over which we had to pass, it made her heart almost sink within her, and, had I known them at that time, I would have repeated the following encouraging lines, which may not be out of place here—

"The hill, though high, I covet to ascend,
The *difficulty will not me offend;*
For I perceive the way to life lies here:
Come, pluck up heart, let's neither faint nor fear;
Better, though difficult, the right way to go,—
Than wrong, though easy, where the end is woe."[4]

However, the sobbing was soon over, and after a few moments of silent prayer she recovered her self-possession, and said, "Come, William, it is getting late, so now let us venture upon our perilous journey."

We then opened the door, and stepped as softly out as "moonlight upon the water." I locked the door with my own key, which I now have before me, and tiptoed across the yard into the street. I say tiptoed, because we were like persons near a tottering avalanche, afraid to move, or even breathe freely, for fear the sleeping tyrants should be aroused, and come down upon us with double vengeance, for daring to attempt to escape in the manner which we contemplated.

We shook hands, said farewell, and started in different directions for the railway station. I took the nearest possible way to the train, for fear I should be recognized by some one, and got into the negro car in which I knew I should have to ride; but my *master* (as I will now call my wife) took a longer way round, and only arrived there with the bulk of the passengers. He obtained a ticket for himself and one for his slave to Savannah, the first port, which was about two hundred miles off. My master then had the luggage stowed away, and stepped into one of the best carriages.

But just before the train moved off I peeped through the window, and, to my great astonishment, I saw the cabinet-maker with whom I had worked so long, on the platform. He stepped up to the ticket-seller, and asked some question, and then commenced looking rapidly through the passengers, and into the carriages. Fully believing that we were caught, I shrank into a corner, turned my face from the door, and expected in a moment to be dragged out. The cabinet-maker looked into my master's carriage, but did not know him in his new attire, and, as God would have it, before he reached mine the bell rang, and the train moved off.

I have heard since that the cabinet-maker had a presentiment that we were about to "make tracks for parts unknown;" but, not seeing me, his suspicions vanished, until he received the startling intelligence that we had arrived safely in a free State.

As soon as the train had left the platform, my master looked round in the carriage, and was terror-stricken to find a Mr. Cray—an old friend of my wife's master, who dined with the family the day before, and knew my wife from childhood—sitting on the same seat.

The doors of the American railway carriages are at the ends. The passengers walk up the aisle, and take seats on either side; and as my master was engaged in looking out of the window, he did not see who came in.

My master's first impression, after seeing Mr. Cray, was, that he was there for the purpose of securing him. However, my master thought it was not wise to give any information respecting himself, and for fear that Mr. Cray might draw him into conversation and recognise his voice, my master resolved to feign deafness as the only means of self-defence.

After a little while, Mr. Cray said to my master, "It is a very fine morning, sir." The latter took no notice, but kept looking out of the window. Mr. Cray soon repeated this remark, in a little louder tone, but my master remained as before. This indifference attracted the attention of the passengers near, one of whom laughed out. This, I suppose, annoyed the old gentleman; so he said, "I will make him hear;" and in a loud tone of voice repeated, "It is a very fine morning, sir."

My master turned his head, and with a polite bow said, "Yes," and commenced looking out of the window again.

One of the gentlemen remarked that it was a very great deprivation to be deaf. "Yes," replied Mr. Cray, "and I shall not trouble that fellow any more." This enabled my master to breathe a little easier, and to feel that Mr. Cray was not his pursuer after all.

The gentlemen then turned the conversation upon the three great topics of discussion in first-class circles in Georgia, namely, Niggers, Cotton, and the Abolitionists.

My master had often heard of abolitionists, but in such a connection as to cause him to think that they were a fearful kind of wild animal. But he was highly delighted to learn, from the gentlemen's conversation, that the abolitionists were persons who were opposed to oppression; and therefore, in his opinion, not the lowest, but the very highest, of God's creatures.

Without the slightest objection on my master's part, the gentlemen left the carriage at Gordon, for Milledgeville (the capital of the State).

We arrived at Savannah early in the evening, and got into an omnibus, which stopped at the hotel for the passengers to take tea. I stepped into the house and brought my master something on a tray to the omnibus, which took us in due time to the steamer, which was bound for Charleston, South Carolina.

Soon after going on board, my master turned in; and as the captain and some of the passengers seemed to think this strange, and also questioned me respecting him, my master thought I had better get out the flannels and opodeldoc which we had prepared for the rheumatism, warm them quickly by the stove in the gentleman's saloon, and bring them to his berth. We did this as an excuse for my master's retiring to bed so early.

While at the stove one of the passengers said to me, "Buck, what have you got there?" "Opodeldoc,[5] sir," I replied. "I should think it's opo-*devil*," said a lanky swell, who was leaning back in a chair with his heels upon the back of another, and chewing tobacco as if for a wager; "it stinks enough to kill or cure twenty men. Away with it, or I reckon I will throw it overboard!"

It was by this time warm enough, so I took it to my master's berth, remained there a little while, and then went on deck and asked the steward where I was to sleep. He said there was no place provided for coloured passengers, whether slave or free. So I paced the deck till a late hour, then mounted some cotton bags, in a warm place near the funnel, sat there till morning, and then went and assisted my master to get ready for breakfast.

He was seated at the right hand of the captain, who, together with all the passengers, inquired very kindly after his health. As my master had one hand in a sling, it was my duty to carve his food. But when I went out the captain said, "You have a very attentive boy, sir; but you had better watch him like a hawk when you get on to the North. He seems all very well here, but he may act quite differently there. I know several gentlemen who have lost their valuable niggers among them d——d cut-throat abolitionists."

Before my master could speak, a rough slave-dealer, who was sitting opposite, with both elbows on the table, and with a large piece of broiled fowl in his fingers, shook his head with emphasis, and in a deep Yankee tone, forced through his crowded mouth the words, "Sound doctrine, captain, very sound." He then dropped the chicken into the plate, leant back, placed his thumbs in the armholes of his fancy waistcoat, and continued, "I would not take a nigger to the North under no consideration. I have had a deal to do with niggers in my time, but I never saw one who ever had his heel upon free soil that was worth a d——n." "Now stranger," addressing my master, "if you have made up your mind to sell that ere nigger, I am your man; just mention your price, and if it isn't out of the way, I will pay for him on this board with hard silver dollars." This hard-featured, bristly-bearded, wire-headed, red-eyed monster, staring at my master as the serpent did at Eve, said, "What do you say, stranger?" He replied, "I don't wish to sell, sir; I cannot get on well without him."

"You will have to get on without him if you take him to the North," continued this man; "for I can tell ye, stranger, as a friend, I am an older cove than you, I have seen lots of this ere world, and I reckon I have had more dealings with niggers than any man living or dead. I was once employed by General Wade Hampton,* for ten years, in doing nothing but breaking 'em in; and everybody knows that the General would not have a man that didn't understand his business. So I tell ye, stranger, again, you had better sell, and let me take him down to Orleans. He will do you no good if you take him across Mason's and Dixon's line; he is a keen nigger, and I can see from the cut of his eye that he is certain to run away." My master said, "I think not, sir; I have great confidence in his fidelity." "Fi-*devil*," indignantly said the dealer, as his fist came down upon the edge of the saucer and upset a cup of hot coffee in a gentleman's lap. (As the scalded man jumped up the trader quietly said, "Don't disturb yourself, neighbour; accidents will happen in the best of families.") "It always makes me mad to hear a man talking about fidelity in niggers. There isn't a d——d one on 'em who wouldn't cut sticks, if he had half a chance."

By this time we were near Charleston; my master thanked the captain for his advice, and they all withdrew and went on deck, where the trader fancied he became quite eloquent. He drew a crowd around him, and with emphasis said, "Cap'en, if I was the President of this mighty United States of America, the greatest and freest country under the whole universe, I would never let no man, I don't care who he is, take a nigger into the North and bring him back here, filled to the brim, as he is sure to be, with d——d abolition vices, to taint all quiet niggers with the hellish spirit of running away. These air, cap'en, my flat-footed, every day, right up and down sentiments, and as this is a free country, cap'en, I don't care who hears 'em; for I am a Southern man, every inch on me to the backbone." "Good!" said an insignificant-looking individual of the slave-dealer stamp. "Three cheers for John C. Calhoun and the whole fair sunny South!" added the trader. So off went their hats, and out burst a terrific roar of irregular but continued cheering. My master took

---

*Probably a reference to a senior brigadier in Stuart's cavalry division. See the Glossary of Names for more.

no more notice of the dealer. He merely said to the captain that the air on deck was too keen for him, and he would therefore return to the cabin.

While the trader was in the zenith of his eloquence, he might as well have said, as one of his kit did, at a great Filibustering meeting, that "When the great American Eagle gets one of his mighty claws upon Canada and the other into South America, and his glorious and starry wings of liberty extending from the Atlantic to the Pacific, oh! then, where will England be, ye gentlemen? I tell ye, she will only serve as a pocket-handkerchief for Jonathan to wipe his nose with."[6]

On my master entering the cabin he found at the breakfast-table a young southern military officer, with whom he had travelled some distance the previous day.

After passing the usual compliments the conversation turned upon the old subject,—niggers.

The officer, who was also travelling with a man-servant, said to my master, "You will excuse me, Sir, for saying I think you are very likely to spoil your boy by saying 'thank you' to him. I assure you, sir, nothing spoils a slave so soon as saying, 'thank you' and 'if you please' to him. The only way to make a nigger toe the mark, and to keep him in his place, is to storm at him like thunder, and keep him trembling like a leaf. Don't you see, when I speak to my Ned, he darts like lightning; and if he didn't I'd skin him."

Just then the poor dejected slave came in, and the officer swore at him fearfully, merely to teach my master what he called the proper way to treat me.

After he had gone out to get his master's luggage ready, the officer said, "That is the way to speak to them. If every nigger was drilled in this manner, they would be as humble as dogs, and never dare to run away."

The gentleman urged my master not to go to the North for the restoration of his health, but to visit the Warm Springs in Arkansas.

My master said, he thought the air of Philadelphia would suit his complaint best; and, not only so, he thought he could get better advice there.

The boat had now reached the wharf. The officer wished my master a safe and pleasant journey, and left the saloon.

There were a large number of persons on the quay waiting the arrival of the steamer: but we were afraid to venture out for fear that some one might recognise me; or that they had heard that we were gone, and had telegraphed to have us stopped. However, after remaining in the cabin till all the other passengers were gone, we had our luggage placed on a fly, and I took my master by the arm, and with a little difficulty he hobbled on shore, got in and drove off to the best hotel, which John C. Calhoun, and all the other great southern fire-eating statesmen, made their head-quarters while in Charleston.

On arriving at the house the landlord ran out and opened the door: but judging, from the poultices and green glasses, that my master was an invalid, he took him very tenderly by one arm and ordered his man to take the other.

My master then eased himself out, and with their assistance found no trouble in getting up the steps into the hotel. The proprietor made me stand on one side, while he paid my master the attention and homage he thought a gentleman of his high position merited.

My master asked for a bed-room. The servant was ordered to show a good one, into which we helped him. The servant returned. My master then handed me the bandages, I took them downstairs in great haste, and told the landlord my master wanted two hot poultices as quickly as possible. He rang the bell, the servant came in, to whom he said, "Run to the kitchen and tell the cook to make two hot poultices right off, for there is a gentleman upstairs very badly off indeed!"

In a few minutes the smoking poultices were brought in. I placed them in white handkerchiefs, and hurried upstairs, went into my master's apartment, shut the door, and laid them on the mantel-piece. As he was alone for a little while, he thought he could rest a great deal better with the poultices off. However, it was necessary to have them to complete the remainder of the journey. I then ordered dinner, and took my master's boots out to polish them. While doing so I entered into conversation with one of the slaves. I may state here, that on the sea-coast of South Carolina and Georgia the slaves speak worse English than in any other part of the country. This is owing to the frequent importation, or smuggling in, of Africans,[7] who mingle with the natives. Consequently the language cannot properly be called English or African, but a corruption of the two.

The shrewd son of African parents to whom I referred said to me, "Say, brudder, way you come from, and which side you goin day wid dat ar little don up buckra" (white man)?

I replied, "To Philadelphia."

"What!" he exclaimed, with astonishment, "to Philumadelphy?"

"Yes," I said.

"By squash! I wish I was going wid you! I hears um say dat dare's no slaves way over in dem parts; is um so?"

I quietly said, "I have heard the same thing."

"Well," continued he, as he threw down the boot and brush, and, placing his hands in his pockets, strutted across the floor with an air of independence—"Gorra Mighty, dem is de parts for Pompey; and I hope when you get dare you will stay, and nebber follow dat buckra back to dis hot quarter no more, let him be eber so good."

I thanked him; and just as I took the boots up and started off, he caught my hand between his two, and gave it a hearty shake, and, with tears streaming down his cheeks, said:—

"God bless you, broder, and may de Lord be wid you. When you gets de freedom, and sitin under your own wine and fig-tree, don't forget to pray for poor Pompey."

I was afraid to say much to him, but I shall never forget his earnest request, nor fail to do what little I can to release the millions of unhappy bondmen, of whom he was one.

At the proper time my master had the poultices placed on, came down, and seated himself at a table in a very brilliant dining-room, to have his dinner. I had to have something at the same time, in order to be ready for the boat; so they gave me my dinner in an old broken plate, with a rusty knife and fork, and said, "Here, boy, you go in the kitchen." I took it and went out, but did not stay more than a few minutes, because I was in a great hurry to get back to see how the invalid was getting on. On arriving I found two or three servants waiting on him; but as he did not feel able to make a very hearty dinner, he soon finished, paid the bill, and gave the servants each a trifle, which caused one of them to say to me, "Your massa is a big bug"—meaning a gentleman of distinction—"he is the greatest gentleman dat has been dis way for dis six months." I said, "Yes, he is some pumpkins," meaning the same as "big bug."

When we left Macon, it was our intention to take a steamer at Charleston through to Philadelphia; but on arriving there we found that the vessels did not run during the winter, and I have no doubt it was well for us they did not; for on the very last voyage the steamer made that we intended to go by, a fugitive was discovered secreted on board, and sent back to slavery. However, as we had also heard of the Overland Mail Route,[8] we were all right. So I ordered a fly to the door, had the luggage placed on; we got in, and drove down to the Custom-house Office, which was near the wharf where we had to obtain tickets, to take a steamer for Wilmington, North Carolina. When we reached the building, I helped my master into the office, which was crowded with passengers. He asked for a ticket for himself and one for his slave to Philadelphia. This caused the principal officer—a very mean-looking, cheese-coloured fellow, who was sitting there—to look up at us very suspiciously, and in a fierce tone of voice he said to me, "Boy, do you belong to that gentleman?" I quickly replied, "Yes, sir" (which was quite correct). The tickets were handed out, and as my master was paying for them the chief man said to him, "I wish you to register your name here, sir, and also the name of your nigger, and pay a dollar duty on him."

My master paid the dollar, and pointing to the hand that was in the poultice, requested the officer to register his name for him. This seemed to offend the "high-bred" South Carolinian. He jumped up, shaking his head; and, cramming his hands almost through the bottom of his trousers pockets, with a slave-bullying air, said, "I shan't do it."

This attracted the attention of all the passengers. Just then the young military officer with whom my master travelled and conversed on the steamer from Savannah stepped in, somewhat the worse for brandy; he shook hands with my master, and pretended to know all about him. He said, "I know his kin (friends) like a book;" and as the officer was known in Charleston, and was going to stop there with friends, the recognition was very much in my master's favor.

The captain of the steamer, a good-looking, jovial fellow, seeing that the gentleman appeared to know my master, and perhaps not wishing to lose us as passengers, said in an off-hand sailor-like manner, "I will register the gentleman's name, and take the responsibility upon myself." He asked my master's name. He said, "William Johnson." The names were put down, I think, "Mr. Johnson and slave." The captain said, "It's all right now, Mr. Johnson." He thanked him kindly, and the young officer begged my master to go with him, and have something to drink and a cigar; but as he had not acquired these accomplishments, he excused himself, and we went on board and came off to Wilmington, North Carolina. When the gentleman finds out his mistake, he will, I have no doubt, be careful in future not to pretend to have an intimate acquaintance with an entire stranger. During the voyage the captain said, "It was rather sharp shooting this morning, Mr. Johnson. It was not out of any disrespect to you, sir; but they make it a rule to be very strict at Charleston. I have known families to be detained there with their slaves till reliable information could be received respecting them. If they were not very careful, any d——d abolitionist might take off a lot of valuable niggers."

My master said, "I suppose so," and thanked him again for helping him over the difficulty.

We reached Wilmington the next morning, and took the train for Richmond, Virginia. I have stated that the American railway carriages (or cars, as they are called), are constructed differently to those in England. At one end of some of them, in the South, there is a little apartment with a couch on both sides for the convenience of families and invalids; and as they thought my master was very poorly, he was allowed to enter one of these apartments at Petersburg, Virginia, where an old gentleman and two handsome young ladies, his daughters, also got in, and took seats in the same carriage. But before the train started, the gentleman stepped into my car, and questioned me respecting my master. He wished to know what was the matter with him, where he was from, and where he was going. I told him where he came from, and said that he was suffering from a complication of complaints, and was going to Philadelphia, where he thought he could get more suitable advice than in Georgia.

The gentleman said my master could obtain the very best advice in Philadelphia. Which turned out to be quite correct, though he did not receive it from physicians, but from kind abolitionists who understood his case much better. The gentleman also said, "I reckon your master's father hasn't any more such faithful and smart boys as

you." "O, yes, sir, he has," I replied, "lots on 'em." Which was literally true. This seemed all he wished to know. He thanked me, gave
me a ten-cent piece, and requested me to be attentive to my good
master. I promised that I would do so, and have ever since endeavoured to keep my pledge. During the gentleman's absence, the ladies
and my master had a little cosy chat. But on his return, he said, "You
seem to be very much afflicted, sir." "Yes, sir," replied the gentleman
in the poultices. "What seems to be the matter with you, sir; may
I be allowed to ask?" "Inflammatory rheumatism, sir." "Oh! that is
very bad, sir," said the kind gentleman: "I can sympathise with you;
for I know from bitter experience what the rheumatism is." If he
did, he knew a good deal more than Mr. Johnson.

The gentleman thought my master would feel better if he would
lie down and rest himself; and as he was anxious to avoid conversation, he at once acted upon this suggestion. The ladies politely rose,
took their extra shawls, and made a nice pillow for the invalid's
head. My master wore a fashionable cloth cloak, which they took
and covered him comfortably on the couch. After he had been lying
a little while the ladies, I suppose, thought he was asleep; so one of
them gave a long sigh, and said, in a quiet fascinating tone, "Papa,
he seems to be a very nice young gentleman." But before papa could
speak, the other lady quickly said, "Oh! dear me, I never felt so
much for a gentleman in my life!" To use an American expression,
"they fell in love with the wrong chap."

After my master had been lying a little while he got up, the gentleman assisted him in getting on his cloak, the ladies took their
shawls, and soon all were seated. They then insisted upon Mr.
Johnson taking some of their refreshments, which of course he did,
out of courtesy to the ladies. All went on enjoying themselves until
they reached Richmond, where the ladies and their father left the
train. But, before doing so, the good old Virginian gentleman, who
appeared to be much pleased with my master, presented him with
a recipe, which he said was a perfect cure for the inflammatory
rheumatism. But the invalid not being able to read it, and fearing he
should hold it upside down in pretending to do so, thanked the
donor kindly, and placed it in his waistcoat pocket. My master's new
friend also gave him his card, and requested him the next time he
travelled that way to do him the kindness to call; adding, "I shall be

pleased to see you, and so will my daughters." Mr. Johnson expressed his gratitude for the proffered hospitality, and said he should feel glad to call on his return. I have not the slightest doubt that he will fulfil the promise whenever that return takes place. After changing trains we went on a little beyond Fredericksburg, and took a steamer to Washington.

At Richmond, a stout elderly lady, whose whole demeanour indicated that she belonged (as Mrs. Stowe's Aunt Chloe* expresses it) to one of the "firstest families," stepped into the carriage, and took a seat near my master. Seeing me passing quickly along the platform, she sprang up as if taken by a fit, and exclaimed, "Bless my soul! there goes my nigger, Ned!"

My master said, "No; that is my boy."

The lady paid no attention to this; she poked her head out of the window, and bawled to me, "You Ned, come to me, sir, you runaway rascal!"

On my looking round she drew her head in, and said to my master, "I beg your pardon, sir, I was sure it was my nigger; I never in my life saw two black pigs more alike than your boy and my Ned."

After the disappointed lady had resumed her seat, and the train had moved off, she closed her eyes, slightly raising her hands, and in a sanctified tone said to my master, "Oh! I hope, sir, your boy will not turn out to be so worthless as my Ned has. Oh! I was as kind to him as if he had been my own son. Oh! sir, it grieves me very much to think that after all I did for him he should go off without having any cause whatever."

"When did he leave you?" asked Mr. Johnson.

"About eighteen months ago, and I have never seen hair or hide of him since."

"Did he have a wife?" enquired a very respectable-looking young gentleman, who was sitting near my master and opposite to the lady.

"No, sir; not when he left, though he did have one a little before that. She was very unlike him; she was as good and as faithful a

---

*Reference to the character Chloe, a house slave in Harriet Beecher Stowe's *Uncle Tom's Cabin* (1852). See the Glossary of Names for more information on Stowe.

nigger as any one need wish to have. But, poor thing! she became so ill, that she was unable to do much work; so I thought it would be best to sell her, to go to New Orleans, where the climate is nice and warm."

"I suppose she was very glad to go South for the restoration of her health?" said the gentleman.

"No; she was not," replied the lady, "for niggers never know what is best for them. She took on a great deal about leaving Ned and the little nigger; but, as she was so weakly, I let her go."

"Was she good-looking?" asked the young passenger, who was evidently not of the same opinion as the talkative lady, and therefore wished her to tell all she knew.

"Yes; she was very handsome, and much whiter than I am; and therefore will have no trouble in getting another husband. I am sure I wish her well. I asked the speculator who bought her to sell her to a good master. Poor thing! she has my prayers, and I know she prays for me. She was a good Christian, and always used to pray for my soul. It was through her earliest prayers," continued the lady, "that I was first led to seek forgiveness of my sins, before I was converted at the great camp-meeting."

This caused the lady to snuffle and to draw from her pocket a richly embroidered handkerchief, and apply it to the corner of her eyes. But my master could not see that it was at all soiled.

The silence which prevailed for a few moments was broken by the gentleman's saying, "As your 'July' was such a very good girl, and had served you so faithfully before she lost her health, don't you think it would have been better to have emancipated her?"

"No, indeed I do not!" scornfully exclaimed the lady, as she impatiently crammed the fine handkerchief into a little work-bag. "I have no patience with people who set niggers at liberty. It is the very worst thing you can do for them. My dear husband just before he died willed all his niggers free. But I and all our friends knew very well that he was too good a man to have ever thought of doing such an unkind and foolish thing, had he been in his right mind, and, therefore we had the will altered as it should have been in the first place."

"Did you mean, madam," asked my master, "that willing the slaves free was unjust to yourself, or unkind to them?"

"I mean that it was decidedly unkind to the servants themselves. It always seems to me such a cruel thing to turn niggers loose to shift for themselves, when there are so many good masters to take care of them. As for myself," continued the considerate lady, "I thank the Lord my dear husband left me and my son well provided for. Therefore I care nothing for the niggers, on my own account, for they are a great deal more trouble than they are worth, I sometimes wish that there was not one of them in the world; for the ungrateful wretches are always running away. I have lost no less than ten since my poor husband died. It's ruinous, sir!"

"But as you are well provided for, I suppose you do not feel the loss very much," said the passenger.

"I don't feel it at all," haughtily continued the good soul; "but that is no reason why property should be squandered. If my son and myself had the money for those valuable niggers, just see what a great deal of good we could do for the poor, and in sending missionaries abroad to the poor heathen, who have never heard the name of our blessed Redeemer. My dear son who is a good Christian minister has advised me not to worry and send my soul to hell for the sake of niggers; but to sell every blessed one of them for what they will fetch, and go and live in peace with him in New York. This I have concluded to do. I have just been to Richmond and made arrangements with my agent to make clean work of the forty that are left."

"Your son being a good Christian minister," said the gentleman, "It's strange he did not advise you to let the poor negroes have their liberty and go North."

"It's not at all strange, sir; it's not at all strange. My son knows what's best for the niggers; he has always told me that they were much better off than the free niggers in the North. In fact, I don't believe there are any white labouring people in the world who are as well off as the slaves."

"You are quite mistaken, madam," said the young man. "For instance, my own widowed mother, before she died, emancipated all her slaves, and sent them to Ohio, where they are getting along well. I saw several of them last summer myself."

"Well," replied the lady, "freedom may do for your ma's niggers, but it will never do for mine; and, plague them, they shall never have it; that is the word, with the bark on it."

"If freedom will not do for your slaves," replied the passenger, "I have no doubt your Ned and the other nine negroes will find out their mistake, and return to their old home."

"Blast them!" exclaimed the old lady, with great emphasis, "if I ever get them, I will cook their infernal hash, and tan their accursed black hides well for them! God forgive me," added the old soul, "the niggers will make me lose all my religion!"

By this time the lady had reached her destination. The gentleman got out at the next station beyond. As soon as she was gone, the young Southerner said to my master, "What a d——d shame it is for that old whining hypocritical humbug to cheat the poor negroes out of their liberty! If she has religion, may the devil prevent me from ever being converted!"

For the purpose of somewhat disguising myself, I bought and wore a very good second-hand white beaver, an article which I had never indulged in before. So just before we arrived at Washington, an uncouth planter, who had been watching me very closely, said to my master, "I reckon, stranger, you are '*spiling*' that ere nigger of yourn, by letting him wear such a devilish fine hat. Just look at the quality on it; the President couldn't wear a better. I should just like to go and kick it overboard." His friend touched him, and said, "Don't speak so to a gentleman." "Why not?" exclaimed the fellow. He grated his short teeth, which appeared to be nearly worn away by the incessant chewing of tobacco, and said, "It always makes me itch all over, from head to toe, to get hold of every d——d nigger I see dressed like a white man. Washington is run away with *spiled* and free niggers. If I had my way I would sell every d——d rascal of 'em way down South, where the devil would be whipped out on 'em."

This man's fierce manner made my master feel rather nervous, and therefore he thought the less he said the better; so he walked off without making any reply. In a few minutes we were landed at Washington, where we took a conveyance and hurried off to the train for Baltimore.

We left our cottage on Wednesday morning, the 21st of December, 1848, and arrived at Baltimore, Saturday evening, the 24th (Christmas Eve). Baltimore was the last slave port of any note at which we stopped.

On arriving there we felt more anxious than ever, because we knew not what that last dark night would bring forth. It is true we were near the goal, but our poor hearts were still as if tossed at sea; and, as there was another great and dangerous bar to pass, we were afraid our liberties would be wrecked, and, like the ill-fated *Royal Charter,*[9] go down for ever just off the place we longed to reach.

They are particularly watchful at Baltimore to prevent slaves from escaping into Pennsylvania, which is a free State. After I had seen my master into one of the best carriages, and was just about to step into mine, an officer, a full-blooded Yankee of the lower order, saw me. He came quickly up, and, tapping me on the shoulder, said in his unmistakable native twang, together with no little display of his authority, "Where are you going, boy?" "To Philadelphia, sir," I humbly replied. "Well, what are you going there for?" "I am travelling with my master, who is in the next carriage, sir." "Well, I calculate you had better get him out; and be mighty quick about it, because the train will soon be starting. It is against my rules to let any man take a slave past here, unless he can satisfy them in the office that he has a right to take him along."

The officer then passed on and left me standing upon the platform, with my anxious heart apparently palpitating in the throat. At first I scarcely knew which way to turn. But it soon occurred to me that the good God, who had been with us thus far, would not forsake us at the eleventh hour. So with renewed hope I stepped into my master's carriage, to inform him of the difficulty. I found him sitting at the farther end, quite alone. As soon as he looked up and saw me, he smiled. I also tried to wear a cheerful countenance, in order to break the shock of the sad news. I knew what made him smile. He was aware that if we were fortunate we should reach our destination at five o'clock the next morning, and this made it the more painful to communicate what the officer had said; but, as there was no time to lose, I went up to him and asked him how he felt. He said "Much better," and that he thanked God we were getting on so nicely. I then said we were not getting on quite so well as we had anticipated. He anxiously and quickly asked what was the matter. I told him. He started as if struck by lightning, and exclaimed, "Good Heavens! William, is it possible that we are, after all, doomed to hopeless bondage?" I could say nothing, my heart was too full to speak, for at first I did not know what to do. However we knew it would never do to turn back to the "City of Destruction,"* like Bunyan's Mistrust and Timorous,[10] because they saw lions in the narrow way after ascending the hill Difficulty; but press on, like noble Christian and Hopeful, to the great city in which dwelt a few "shining ones." So, after a few moments, I did all I could to encourage my companion, and we stepped out and made for the office; but how or where my master obtained sufficient courage to face the tyrants who had power to blast all we held dear, heaven only knows! Queen Elizabeth could not have been more terror-stricken, on being forced to land at the traitors' gate leading to the Tower,[11] than we were on entering that office. We felt that our very existence was at stake, and that we must either sink or swim. But, as God was our present and mighty helper in this as well as in all former trials, we were able to keep our heads up and press forwards.

On entering the room we found the principal man, to whom my master said, "Do you wish to see me, sir?" "Yes," said this eagle-eyed officer; and he added, "It is against our rules, sir, to allow any person to take a slave out of Baltimore into Philadelphia, unless he can satisfy us that he has a right to take him along." "Why is that?" asked my master, with more firmness than could be expected. "Because, sir," continued he, in a voice and manner that almost chilled our blood, "if we should suffer any gentleman to take a slave past here into Philadelphia; and should the gentleman with whom the slave might be travelling turn out not to be his rightful owner; and should the proper master come and prove that his slave escaped on our road, we shall have him to pay for; and, therefore, we cannot let any slave pass here without receiving security to show, and to satisfy us, that it is all right."

This conversation attracted the attention of the large number of bustling passengers. After the officer had finished, a few of them said, "Chit, chit, chit;" not because they thought we were slaves endeavouring to escape, but merely because they thought my master was a slaveholder and invalid gentleman, and therefore it was wrong

---

*Reference to John Bunyan's *The Pilgrim's Progress from This World to That Which Is to Come* (1678), an allegorical novel in which Christian, an everyman character, makes his way from the City of Destruction to the Celestial City of Zion.

to detain him. The officer, observing that the passengers sympathised with my master, asked him if he was not acquainted with some gentleman in Baltimore that he could get to endorse for him, to show that I was his property, and that he had a right to take me off. He said, "No;" and added, "I bought tickets in Charleston to pass us through to Philadelphia, and therefore you have no right to detain us here." "Well, sir," said the man, indignantly, "right or no right, we shan't let you go." These sharp words fell upon our anxious hearts like the crack of doom, and made us feel that hope only smiles to deceive.

For a few moments perfect silence prevailed. My master looked at me, and I at him, but neither of us dared to speak a word, for fear of making some blunder that would tend to our detection. We knew that the officers had power to throw us into prison, and if they had done so we must have been detected and driven back, like the vilest felons, to a life of slavery, which we dreaded far more than sudden death.

We felt as though we had come into deep waters and were about being overwhelmed, and that the slightest mistake would clip asunder the last brittle thread of hope by which we were suspended, and let us down for ever into the dark and horrible pit of misery and degradation from which we were straining every nerve to escape. While our hearts were crying lustily unto Him who is ever ready and able to save, the conductor of the train that we had just left stepped in. The officer asked if we came by the train with him from Washington; he said we did, and left the room. Just then the bell rang for the train to leave; and had it been the sudden shock of an earthquake it could not have given us a greater thrill. The sound of the bell caused every eye to flash with apparent interest, and to be more steadily fixed upon us than before. But, as God would have it, the officer all at once thrust his fingers through his hair, and in a state of great agitation said, "I really don't know what to do; I calculate it is all right." He then told the clerk to run and tell the conductor to "let this gentleman and slave pass;" adding, "As he is not well, it is a pity to stop him here. We will let him go." My master thanked him, and stepped out and hobbled across the platform as quickly as possible. I tumbled him unceremoniously into one of the best carriages, and leaped into mine just as the train was gliding off towards our happy destination.

We thought of this plan about four days before we left Macon; and as we had our daily employment to attend to, we only saw each other at night. So we sat up the four long nights talking over the plan and making preparations.

We had also been four days on the journey; and as we travelled night and day, we got but very limited opportunities for sleeping. I believe nothing in the world could have kept us awake so long but the intense excitement, produced by the fear of being retaken on the one hand, and the bright anticipation of liberty on the other.

We left Baltimore about eight o'clock in the evening; and not being aware of a stopping-place of any consequence between there and Philadelphia, and also knowing that if we were fortunate we should be in the latter place early the next morning, I thought I might indulge in a few minutes' sleep in the car; but I, like Bunyan's Christian in the arbour, went to sleep at the wrong time, and took too long a nap. So, when the train reached Havre de Grace, all the first-class passengers had to get out of the carriages and into a ferry-boat, to be ferried across the Susquehanna river, and take the train on the opposite side.

The road was constructed so as to be raised or lowered to suit the tide. So they rolled the luggage-vans on to the boat, and off on the other side; and as I was in one of the apartments adjoining a baggage-car, they considered it unnecessary to awaken me, and tumbled me over with the luggage. But when my master was asked to leave his seat, he found it very dark, and cold, and raining. He missed me for the first time on the journey. On all previous occasions, as soon as the train stopped, I was at hand to assist him. This caused many slaveholders to praise me very much: they said they had never before seen a slave so attentive to his master: and therefore my absence filled him with terror and confusion; the children of Israel could not have felt more troubled on arriving at the Red Sea. So he asked the conductor if he had seen anything of his slave. The man being somewhat of an abolitionist, and believing that my master was really a slaveholder, thought he would tease him a little respecting me. So he said, "No, sir; I haven't seen anything of him for some time: I have no doubt he has run away, and is in Philadelphia, free, long before now." My master knew that there was nothing in this; so he asked the conductor if he would please to see if he could find me. The man indignantly replied, "I am no slave-hunter; and as far as I am concerned everybody must look after their own niggers." He went off and left the confused invalid to fancy whatever he felt inclined. My master at first thought I must have been kidnapped into slavery by some one, or left, or perhaps killed on the train. He also thought of stopping to see if he could hear anything of me, but he soon remembered that he had no money. That night all the money we had was consigned to my own pocket, because we thought, in case there were any pickpockets about, a slave's pocket would be the last one they would look for. However, hoping to meet me some day in a land of liberty, and as he had the tickets, he thought it best upon the whole to enter the boat and come off to Philadelphia, and endeavour to make his way alone in this cold and hollow world as best he could. The time was now up, so he went on board and came across with feelings that can be better imagined than described.

After the train had got fairly on the way to Philadelphia, the guard came into my car and gave me a violent shake, and bawled out at the same time, "Boy, wake up!" I started, almost frightened out of my wits. He said, "Your master is scared half to death about you." That frightened me still more—I thought they had found him out; so I anxiously inquired what was the matter. The guard said, "He thinks you have run away from him." This made me feel quite at ease. I said, "No, sir; I am satisfied my good master doesn't think that." So off I started to see him. He had been fearfully nervous, but on seeing me he at once felt much better. He merely wished to know what had become of me.

On returning to my seat, I found the conductor and two or three other persons amusing themselves very much respecting my running away. So the guard said, "Boy, what did your master want?"* I replied, "He merely wished to know what had become of me." "No," said the man, "that was not it; he thought you had taken French leave, for parts unknown. I never saw a fellow so badly scared about

---

*I may state here that every man slave is called boy till he is very old, then the more respectable slaveholders call him uncle. The women are all girls till they are aged, then they are called aunts. This is the reason why Mrs. Stowe calls her characters Uncle Tom, Aunt Chloe, Uncle Tiff, &c. [Crafts' note]

losing his slave in my life. "Now," continued the guard, "let me give
you a little friendly advice. When you get to Philadelphia, run away
and leave that cripple, and have your liberty." "No, sir," I indiffer-
ently replied, "I can't promise to do that." "Why not?" said the conductor, evidently much surprised; "don't you want your liberty?"
"Yes, sir," I replied; "but I shall never run away from such a good
master as I have at present."

One of the men said to the guard, "Let him alone; I guess he will
open his eyes when he gets to Philadelphia, and see things in another light." After giving me a good deal of information, which I afterwards found to be very useful, they left me alone.

I also met with a coloured gentleman on this train, who recommended me to a boarding-house that was kept by an abolitionist,
where he thought I would be quite safe, if I wished to run away from
my master. I thanked him kindly, but of course did not let him know
who we were. Late at night, or rather early in the morning, I heard
a fearful whistling of the steam-engine; so I opened the window and
looked out, and saw a large number of flickering lights in the distance, and heard a passenger in the next carriage—who also had his
head out of the window—say to his companion, "Wake up, old horse,
we are at Philadelphia!"

The sight of those lights and that announcement made me feel
almost as happy as Bunyan's Christian must have felt when he first
caught sight of the cross. I, like him, felt that the straps that bound
the heavy burden to my back began to pop, and the load to roll off.
I also looked, and looked again, for it appeared very wonderful to
me how the mere sight of our first city of refuge should have all at
once made my hitherto sad and heavy heart become so light and
happy. As the train speeded on, I rejoiced and thanked God with all
my heart and soul for his great kindness and tender mercy, in watching over us, and bringing us safely through.

As soon as the train had reached the platform, before it had fairly
stopped, I hurried out of my carriage to my master, whom I got at
once into a cab, placed the luggage on, jumped in myself, and we
drove off to the boarding-house which was so kindly recommended
to me. On leaving the station, my master—or rather my wife, as I
may now say—who had from the commencement of the journey
borne up in a manner that much surprised us both, grasped me by

the hand, and said, "Thank God, William, we are safe!" and then burst into tears, leant upon me, and wept like a child. The reaction was fearful. So when we reached the house, she was in reality so weak and faint that she could scarcely stand alone. However, I got her into the apartments that were pointed out, and there we knelt down, on this Sabbath, and Christmas-day,—a day that will ever be memorable to us,—and poured out our heartfelt gratitude to God, for his goodness in enabling us to overcome so many perilous difficulties, in escaping out of the jaws of the wicked.

PART II

AFTER MY WIFE HAD a little recovered herself, she threw off the disguise and assumed her own apparel. We then stepped into the sitting-room, and asked to see the landlord. The man came in, but he seemed thunderstruck on finding a fugitive slave and his wife, instead of a "young cotton planter and his nigger." As his eyes travelled round the room, he said to me, "Where is your master?" I pointed him out. The man gravely replied, "I am not joking, I really wish to see your master." I pointed him out again, but at first he could not believe his eyes; he said "he knew that was not the gentleman that came with me."

But, after some conversation, we satisfied him that we were fugitive slaves, and had just escaped in the manner I have described. We asked him if he thought it would be safe for us to stop in Philadelphia. He said he thought not, but he would call in some persons who knew more about the laws than himself. He then went out, and kindly brought in several of the leading abolitionists of the city, who gave us a most hearty and friendly welcome amongst them. As it was in December, and also as we had just left a very warm climate, they advised us not to go to Canada as we had intended, but to settle at Boston in the United States. It is true that the constitution of the Republic has always guaranteed the slaveholders the right to come into any of the so-called free States, and take their fugitives back to southern Egypt. But through the untiring, uncompromising, and manly efforts of Mr. Garrison, Wendell Phillips, Theodore Parker, and a host of other noble abolitionists of Boston and the neighbourhood, public opinion in Massachusetts had become so much opposed to slavery and to kidnapping, that it was almost impossible for any one to take a fugitive slave out of that State.

So we took the advice of our good Philadelphia friends, and settled at Boston. I shall have something to say about our sojourn there
presently.

Among other friends we met with at Philadelphia, was Robert
Purves, Esq., a well educated and wealthy coloured gentleman, who
introduced us to Mr. Barkley Ivens, a member of the Society of
Friends, and a noble and generous-hearted farmer, who lived at
some distance in the country.

This good Samaritan at once invited us to go and stop quietly
with his family, till my wife could somewhat recover from the fearful reaction of the past journey. We most gratefully accepted the invitation, and at the time appointed we took a steamer to a place up
the Delaware river, where our new and dear friend met us with his
snug little cart, and took us to his happy home. This was the first act
of great and disinterested kindness we had ever received from a
white person.

The gentleman was not of the fairest complexion, and therefore,
as my wife was not in the room when I received the information respecting him and his anti-slavery character, she thought of course
he was a quadroon like herself. But on arriving at the house, and
finding out her mistake, she became more nervous and timid than
ever.

As the cart came into the yard, the dear good old lady, and her
three charming and affectionate daughters, all came to the door to
meet us. We got out, and the gentleman said, "Go in, and make
yourselves at home; I will see after the baggage." But my wife was
afraid to approach them. She stopped in the yard, and said to me,
"William, I thought we were coming among coloured people?" I
replied, "It is all right; these are the same." "No," she said, "it is not
all right, and I am not going to stop here; I have no confidence
whatever in white people, they are only trying to get us back to slavery." She turned round and said, "I am going right off." The old lady
then came out, with her sweet, soft, and winning smile, shook her
heartily by the hand, and kindly said, "How art thou, my dear? We
are all very glad to see thee and thy husband. Come in, to the fire; I
dare say thou art cold and hungry after thy journey."

We went in, and the young ladies asked if she would like to go
upstairs and "fix" herself before tea. My wife said, "No, I thank you;

I shall only stop a little while." "But where art thou going this cold night?" said Mr. Ivens, who had just stepped in. "I don't know," was the reply. "Well, then," he continued, "I think thou hadst better take off thy things and sit near the fire; tea will soon be ready." "Yes, come, Ellen," said Mrs. Ivens, "let me assist thee;" (as she commenced undoing my wife's bonnet-strings;) "don't be frightened, Ellen, I shall not hurt a single hair of thy head. We have heard with much pleasure of the marvellous escape of thee and thy husband, and deeply sympathise with thee in all that thou hast undergone. I don't wonder at thee, poor thing, being timid; but thou needs not fear us; we would as soon send one of our own daughters into slavery as thee; so thou mayest make thyself quite at ease!" These soft and soothing words fell like balm upon my wife's unstrung nerves, and melted her to tears; her fears and prejudices vanished, and from that day she has firmly believed that there are good and bad persons of every shade of complexion.

After seeing Sally Ann and Jacob, two coloured domestics, my wife felt quite at home. After partaking of what Mrs. Stowe's Mose and Pete[12] called a "busting supper," the ladies wished to know whether we could read. On learning we could not, they said if we liked they would teach us. To this kind offer, of course, there was no objection. But we looked rather knowingly at each other, as much as to say that they would have rather a hard task to cram anything into our thick and matured skulls.

However, all hands set to and quickly cleared away the tea-things, and the ladies and their good brother brought out the spelling and copy books and slates, &c., and commenced with their new and green pupils. We had, by stratagem, learned the alphabet while in slavery, but not the written characters; and, as we had been such a time learning so little, we at first felt that it was a waste of time for any one at our ages to undertake to learn to read and write. But, as the ladies were so anxious that we should learn, and so willing to teach us, we concluded to give our whole minds to the work, and see what could be done. By so doing, at the end of the three weeks we remained with the good family we could spell and write our names quite legibly. They all begged us to stop longer; but, as we were not safe in the State of Pennsylvania, and also as we wished to commence doing something for a livelihood, we did not remain.

When the time arrived for us to leave for Boston, it was like parting with our relatives. We have since met with many very kind and hospitable friends, both in America and England; but we have never been under a roof where we were made to feel more at home, or where the inmates took a deeper interest in our well-being, than Mr. Barkley Ivens and his dear family. May God ever bless them, and preserve each one from every reverse of fortune!

We finally, as I have stated, settled at Boston, where we remained nearly two years, I employed as cabinet-maker and furniture broker, and my wife at her needle; and, as our little earnings in slavery were not all spent on the journey, we were getting on very well, and would have made money, if we had not been compelled by the General Government, at the bidding of the slaveholders, to break up business, and fly from under the Stars and Stripes to save our liberties and our lives.

In 1850, Congress passed the Fugitive Slave Bill,[13] an enactment too infamous to have been thought of or tolerated by any people in the world, except the unprincipled and tyrannical Yankees. The following are a few of the leading features of the above law; which requires, under heavy penalties, that the inhabitants of the *free* States should not only refuse food and shelter to a starving, hunted human being, but also should assist, if called upon by the authorities, to seize the unhappy fugitive and send him back to slavery.

In no case is a person's evidence admitted in Court, in defence of his liberty, when arrested under this law.

If the judge decides that the prisoner is a slave, he gets ten dollars; but if he sets him at liberty, he only receives five.

After the prisoner has been sentenced to slavery, he is handed over to the United States Marshal, who has the power, at the expense of the General Government, to summon a sufficient force to take the poor creature back to slavery, and to the lash, from which he fled.

Our old masters sent agents to Boston after us. They took out warrants, and placed them in the hands of the United States Marshal to execute. But the following letter from our highly esteemed and faithful friend, the Rev. Samuel May, of Boston, to our equally dear and much lamented friend, Dr. Estlin of Bristol, will show why we were not taken into custody.

"21, Cornhill, Boston,
"November 6th, 1850.

"My dear Mr. Estlin,

"I trust that in God's good providence this letter will be handed to you in safety by our good friends, William and Ellen Craft. They have lived amongst us about two years, and have proved themselves worthy, in all respects, of our confidence and regard. The laws of this republican and Christian land (tell it not in Moscow, nor in Constantinople) regard them only as slaves—chattels—personal property. But they nobly vindicated their title and right to freedom, two years since, by winning their way to it; at least, so they thought. But now, the slave power, with the aid of Daniel Webster and a band of lesser traitors, has enacted a law, which puts their dearly-bought liberties in the most imminent peril; holds out a strong temptation to every mercenary and unprincipled ruffian to become their kidnapper; and has stimulated the slaveholders generally to such desperate acts for the recovery of their fugitive property, as have never before been enacted in the history of this government.

"Within a fortnight, two fellows from Macon, Georgia, have been in Boston for the purpose of arresting our friends William and Ellen. A writ was served against them from the United States District Court; but it was not served by the United States Marshal; why not, is not certainly known: perhaps through fear, for a general feeling of indignation, and a cool determination not to allow this young couple to be taken from Boston into slavery, was aroused, and pervaded the city. It is understood that one of the judges told the Marshal that he would not be authorised in breaking the door of Craft's house. Craft kept himself close within the house, armed himself, and awaited with remarkable composure the event. Ellen, in the meantime, had been taken to a retired place out of the city. The Vigilance Committee[14] (appointed at a late meeting in Fanueil Hall) enlarged their numbers, held an almost permanent session, and appointed various subcommittees to act in different ways. One of these committees called repeatedly on Messrs. Hughes and Knight, the slave-catchers, and requested and advised them to leave the city. At first they peremptorily refused to do so,

'till they got hold of the niggers.' On complaint of different persons, these two fellows were several times arrested, carried before one of our county courts, and held to bail on charges of 'conspiracy to kidnap,' and of 'defamation,' in calling William and Ellen 'slaves.' At length, they became so alarmed, that they left the city by an indirect route, evading the vigilance of many persons who were on the look-out for them. Hughes, at one time, was near losing his life at the hands of an infuriated coloured man. While these men remained in the city, a prominent whig gentleman sent word to William Craft, that if he would submit peaceably to an arrest, he and his wife should be bought from their owners, cost what it might. Craft replied, in effect, that he was in a measure the representative of all the other fugitives in Boston, some 200 or 300 in number; that, if he gave up, they would all be at the mercy of the slave-catchers, and must fly from the city at any sacrifice; and that, if his freedom could be bought for two cents, he would not consent to compromise the matter in such a way. This event has stirred up the slave spirit of the country, south and north; the United States government is determined to try its hand in enforcing the Fugitive Slave law; and William and Ellen Craft would be prominent objects of the slaveholders' vengeance. Under these circumstances, it is the almost unanimous opinion of their best friends, that they should quit America as speedily as possible, and seek an asylum in England! Oh! shame, shame upon us, that Americans, whose fathers fought against Great Britain, in order to be FREE, should have to acknowledge this disgraceful fact! God gave us a fair and goodly heritage in this land, but man has cursed it with his devices and crimes against human souls and human rights. Is America the 'land of the free, and the home of the brave?' God knows it is not; and we know it too. A brave young man and a virtuous young woman must fly the American shores, and seek, under the shadow of the British throne, the enjoyment of 'life, liberty, and the pursuit of happiness.'

"But I must pursue my plain, sad story. All day long, I have been busy planning a safe way for William and Ellen to leave Boston. We dare not allow them to go on board a vessel, even in the port of Boston; for the writ is yet in the Marshal's hands, and he may be waiting an opportunity to serve it; so I am expecting to accompany *them to-morrow to Portland, Maine, which is beyond the reach of the Marshal's authority; and there I hope to see them on board a British steamer.*

"This letter is written to introduce them to you. I know your in-firm health; but I am sure, if you were stretched on your bed in your last illness, and could lift your hand at all, you would extend it to welcome these poor hunted fellow-creatures. Henceforth, England is their nation and their home. It is with real regret for our personal loss in their departure, as well as burning shame for the land that is not worthy of them, that we send them away, or rather allow them to go. But, with all the resolute courage they have shown in a most trying hour, they themselves see it is the part of a foolhardy rashness to attempt to stay here longer.

"I must close; and with many renewed thanks for all your kind words and deeds towards us,

"I am, very respectfully yours,
"Samuel May, Jun."

Our old masters, having heard how their agents were treated at Boston, wrote to Mr. Filmore, who was then President of the States, to know what he could do to have us sent back to slavery. Mr. Filmore said that we should be returned.* He gave instructions for military force to be sent to Boston to assist the officers in making the arrest. Therefore we, as well as our friends (among whom was George Thompson, Esq., late M.P. for the Tower Hamlets—the slave's long-tried, self-sacrificing friend, and eloquent advocate) thought it best, at any sacrifice, to leave the mock-free Republic, and come to a country where we and our dear little ones can be truly free.—"No one daring to molest or make us afraid." But, as the of-ficers were watching every vessel that left the port to prevent us from escaping, we had to take the expensive and tedious overland route to Halifax.

---

*Filmore "expressed his determination to fulfill both the letter and the spirit of the [Fugitive Slave] law by placing troops at the disposal of state and local authorities wherever necessary." See R. J. M. Blackett, "The Odyssey of William and Ellen Craft," pp. 94–95 (see For Further Reading).

We shall always cherish the deepest feelings of gratitude to the Vigilance Committee of Boston (upon which were many of the leading abolitionists), and also to our numerous friends, for the very kind and noble manner in which they assisted us to preserve our liberties and to escape from Boston, as it were like Lot from Sodom,[15] to a place of refuge, and finally to this truly free and glorious country; where no tyrant, let his power be ever so absolute over his poor trembling victims at home, dare come and lay violent hands upon us or upon our dear little boys (who had the good fortune to be born upon British soil), and reduce us to the legal level of the beast that perisheth. Oh! may God bless the thousands of unflinching, disinterested abolitionists of America, who are labouring through evil as well as through good report, to cleanse their country's escutcheon from the foul and destructive blot of slavery, and to restore to every bondman his God-given rights; and may God ever smile upon England and upon England's good, much-beloved, and deservedly-honoured Queen, for the generous protection that is given to unfortunate refugees of every rank, and of every colour and clime.

On the passing of the Fugitive Slave Bill, the following learned doctors, as well as a host of lesser traitors, came out strongly in its defence.

The Rev. Dr. Gardiner Spring, an eminent Presbyterian Clergyman of New York, well known in this country by his religious publications, declared from the pulpit that, "if by one prayer he could liberate every slave in the world he would not dare to offer it."

The Rev. Dr. Joel Parker, of Philadelphia, in the course of a discussion on the nature of Slavery, says, "What, then, are the evils inseparable from slavery? There is not one that is not equally inseparable from depraved human nature in other lawful relations."

The Rev. Moses Stuart, D.D., (late Professor in the Theological College of Andover), in his vindication of this Bill, reminds his readers that "many Southern slaveholders are true *Christians*." That "sending back a fugitive to them is not like restoring one to an idolatrous people." That "though we may *pity* the fugitive, yet the Mosaic Law[16] does not authorize the rejection of the claims of the slaveholders to their stolen or strayed *property*."

The Rev. Dr. Spencer, of Brooklyn, New York, has come forward in support of the "Fugitive Slave Bill," by publishing a sermon entitled the "Religious Duty of Obedience to the Laws," which has elicited the highest encomiums from Dr. Samuel H. Cox, the Presbyterian minister of Brooklyn (notorious both in this country and America for his sympathy with the slaveholder).

The Rev. W. M. Rogers, an orthodox minister of Boston, delivered a sermon in which he says, "When the slave asks me to stand between him and his master, what does he ask? He asks me to murder a nation's life; and I will not do it, because I have a conscience,—because there is a God." He proceeds to affirm that if resistance to the carrying out of the "Fugitive Slave Law" should lead the magistracy to call the citizens to arms, their duty was to obey and "if ordered to take human life, in the name of God to take it;" and he concludes by admonishing the fugitives to "hearken to the Word of God, and to count their own masters worthy of all honour."

The Rev. William Crowell, of Waterfield, State of Maine, printed a Thanksgiving Sermon of the same kind, in which he calls upon his hearers not to allow "excessive sympathies for a few hundred fugitives to blind them so as that they may risk increased suffering to the millions already in chains."

The Rev. Dr. Taylor, an Episcopal Clergyman of New Haven, Connecticut, made a speech at a Union Meeting, in which he deprecates the agitation on the law, and urges obedience to it; asking,—"Is that article in the Constitution contrary to the law of Nature, of nations, or to the will of God? Is it so? Is there a shadow of reason for saying it? I have not been able to discover it. Have I not shown you it is lawful to deliver up, in compliance with the laws, fugitive slaves, for the high, the great, the momentous interests of those [Southern] States?"

The Right Rev. Bishop Hopkins, of Vermont, in a Lecture at Lockport, says, "It was warranted by the Old Testament;" and inquires, "What effect had the Gospel in doing away with slavery? None whatever." Therefore he argues, as it is expressly permitted by the Bible, it does not in itself involve any sin; but that every Christian is authorised by the Divine Law to own slaves, provided they were not treated with unnecessary cruelty.

The Rev. Orville Dewey, D.D., of the Unitarian connexion, maintained in his lectures that the safety of the Union is not to be hazarded for the sake of the African race. He declares that, for his

part, he would send his own brother or child into slavery, if needed
to preserve the Union between the free and the slaveholding States;
and, counselling the slave to similar magnanimity, thus exhorts
him:—"*Your right to be free is not absolute, unqualified, irrespective of
all consequences.* If my espousal of your claim is likely to involve your
race and mine together in disasters infinitely greater than your personal servitude, then you ought not to be free. In such a case personal rights ought to be sacrificed to the general good. You yourself
ought to see this, and be willing to suffer for a while—one for
many."

If the Doctor is prepared, he is quite at liberty to sacrifice his
"personal rights to the general good." But, as I have suffered a long
time in slavery, it is hardly fair for the Doctor to advise me to go
back. According to his showing, he ought rather to take my place.
That would be practically carrying out his logic, as respects "suffering awhile—one for many."

In fact, so eager were they to prostrate themselves before the
great idol of slavery, and, like Balaam,[17] to curse instead of blessing
the people whom God had brought out of bondage, that they in
bringing up obsolete passages from the Old Testament to justify
their downward course, overlooked, or would not see, the following
verses, which show very clearly, according to the Doctor's own text-
book, that the slaves have a right to run away, and that it is un-
scriptural for any one to send them back.

In the 23rd chapter of Deuteronomy, 15th and 16th verses, it is
thus written:—"Thou shalt not deliver unto his master the servant
which is escaped from his master unto thee. He shall dwell with
thee, even among you, in that place which he shall choose in one of
thy gates, where it liketh him best: thou shalt not oppress him."

"Hide the outcast. Betray not him that wandereth. Let mine out-
casts dwell with thee. Be thou a covert to them from the face of the
spoiler."—(Isa. xvi. 3, 4.)

The great majority of the American ministers are not content
with uttering sentences similar to the above, or remaining wholly
indifferent to the cries of the poor bondman; but they do all they can
to blast the reputation, and to muzzle the mouths, of the few good
men who dare to beseech the God of mercy "to loose the bonds of
wickedness, to undo the heavy burdens, and let the oppressed go

free." These reverend gentlemen pour a terrible cannonade upon "Jonah," for refusing to carry God's message against Nineveh,[18] and tell us about the whale in which he was entombed; while they utterly overlook the existence of the whales which trouble their republican waters, and know not that they themselves are the "Jonahs" who threaten to sink their ship of state, by steering in an unrighteous direction. We are told that the whale vomited up the runaway prophet. This would not have seemed so strange, had it been one of the above lukewarm Doctors of Divinity whom he had swallowed; for even a whale might find such a morsel difficult of digestion.

> "I venerate the man whose heart is warm,
> Whose hands are pure; whose doctrines and whose life
> Coincident, exhibit lucid proof
> That he is honest in the sacred cause."

> "But grace abused brings forth the foulest deeds,
> As richest soil the most luxuriant weeds."*

I must now leave the reverend gentlemen in the hands of Him who knows best how to deal with a recreant ministry.

I do not wish it to be understood that all the ministers of the States are of the Balaam stamp. There are those who are as uncompromising with slaveholders as Moses was with Pharaoh, and, like Daniel, will never bow down before the great false God that has been set up.

On arriving at Portland, we found that the steamer we intended to take had run into a schooner the previous night, and was lying up for repairs; so we had to wait there, in fearful suspense, for two or three days. During this time, we had the honour of being the guest of the late and much lamented Daniel Oliver, Esq.,† one of the best and most hospitable men in the State. By simply fulfilling the Scripture

---

*From "Preaching," by English poet William Cowper (1731–1800).
†Perhaps a reference to Daniel Oliver, Esq. who, in the mid-1770s was disarmed by a mob and took refuge in Boston; as a result, he completely lost his business.

injunction, to take in the stranger, &c., he ran the risk of incurring a penalty of 2,000 dollars, and twelve months' imprisonment.

But neither the Fugitive Slave Law, nor any other Satanic enactment, can ever drive the spirit of liberty and humanity out of such noble and generous-hearted men.

May God ever bless his dear widow, and eventually unite them in His courts above!

We finally got off to St. John's, New Brunswick, where we had to wait two days for the steamer that conveyed us to Windsor, Nova Scotia.

On going into a hotel at St. John's, we met the butler in the hall, to whom I said, "We wish to stop here to-night." He turned round, scratching his head, evidently much put about. But thinking that my wife was white, he replied, "We have plenty of room for the lady, but I don't know about yourself; we never take in coloured folks." "Oh, don't trouble about me," I said; "if you have room for the lady, that will do; so please have the luggage taken to a bed-room." Which was immediately done, and my wife went upstairs into the apartment.

After taking a little walk in the town, I returned, and asked to see the "lady." On being conducted to the little sitting-room, where she then was, I entered without knocking, much to the surprise of the whole house. The "lady" then rang the bell, and ordered dinner for two. "Dinner for two, mum!" exclaimed the waiter, as he backed out of the door. "Yes, for two," said my wife. In a little while the stout, red-nosed butler, whom we first met, knocked at the door. I called out, "Come in." On entering, he rolled his whisky eyes at me, and then at my wife, and said, in a very solemn tone, "Did you order dinner for two, mum?" "Yes, for two," my wife again replied. This confused the chubby butler more than ever; and, as the landlord was not in the house, he seemed at a loss what to do.

When dinner was ready, the maid came in and said, "Please, mum, the Missis wishes to know whether you will have dinner up now, or wait till your friend arrives?" "I will have it up at once, if you please." "Thank you, mum," continued the maid, and out she glided.

After a good deal of giggling in the passage, some one said, "You are in for it, butler, after all; so you had better make the best of a bad job." But before dinner was sent up, the landlord returned, and having heard from the steward of the steamer by which we came that we were bound for England, the proprietor's native country, he treated us in the most respectful manner.

At the above house, the boots (whose name I forget) was a fugitive slave, a very intelligent and active man, about forty-five years of age. Soon after his marriage, while in slavery, his bride was sold away from him, and he could never learn where the poor creature dwelt. So after remaining single for many years, both before and after his escape, and never expecting to see again, nor even to hear from, his long-lost partner, he finally married a woman at St. John's. But, poor fellow, as he was passing down the street one day, he met a woman; at the first glance they nearly recognized each other; they both turned round and stared, and unconsciously advanced, till she screamed and flew into his arms. Her first words were, "Dear, are you married?" On his answering in the affirmative, she shrank from his embrace, hung her head, and wept. A person who witnessed this meeting told me it was most affecting.

This couple knew nothing of each other's escape or whereabouts. The woman had escaped a few years before to the free States, by secreting herself in the hold of a vessel; but as they tried to get her back to bondage, she fled to New Brunswick for that protection which her native country was too mean to afford.

The man at once took his old wife to see his new one, who was also a fugitive slave, and as they all knew the workings of the infamous system of slavery, they could (as no one else can,) sympathise with each other's misfortune.

According to the rules of slavery, the man and his first wife were already divorced, but not morally; and therefore it was arranged between the three that he should live only with the lastly married wife, and allow the other one so much a week, as long as she requested his assistance.

After staying at St. John's two days, the steamer arrived, which took us to Windsor, where we found a coach bound for Halifax. Prejudice against colour forced me on the top in the rain. On arriving within about seven miles of the town, the coach broke down and was upset. I fell upon the big crotchety driver, whose head stuck in the mud; and as he "always objected to niggers riding inside with white folks," I was not particularly sorry to see him deeper in the mire than myself. All of us were scratched and bruised more or less. After the passengers had crawled out as best they could, we all set off, and paddled through the deep mud and cold and rain, to Halifax.

On leaving Boston, it was our intention to reach Halifax at least two or three days before the steamer from Boston touched there, *en route* for Liverpool; but, having been detained so long at Portland and St. John's, we had the misfortune to arrive at Halifax at dark, just two hours after the steamer had gone; consequently we had to wait there a fortnight, for the *Cambria*.

The coach was patched up, and reached Halifax with the luggage, soon after the passengers arrived. The only respectable hotel that was then in the town had suspended business, and was closed; so we went to the inn, opposite the market, where the coach stopped: a most miserable, dirty hole it was.

Knowing that we were still under the influence of the low Yankee prejudice, I sent my wife in with the other passengers, to engage a bed for herself and husband. I stopped outside in the rain till the coach came up. If I had gone in and asked for a bed they would have been quite full. But as they thought my wife was white, she had no difficulty in securing apartments, into which the luggage was afterwards carried. The landlady, observing that I took an interest in the baggage, became somewhat uneasy, and went into my wife's room, and said to her, "Do you know the dark man downstairs?" "Yes, he is my husband." "Oh! I mean the black man—the *nigger?*" "I quite understand you; he is my husband." "My God!" exclaimed the woman as she flounced out and banged to the door. On going upstairs, I heard what had taken place: but, as we were there, and did not mean to leave that night, we did not disturb ourselves. On our ordering tea, the landlady sent word back to say that we must take it in the kitchen, or in our bed-room, as she had no other room for "niggers." We replied that we were not particular, and that they could send it up to our room,—which they did.

After the pro-slavery persons who were staying there heard that we were in, the whole house became agitated, and all sorts of oaths and fearful threats were heaped upon the "d——d niggers, for coming among white folks." Some of them said they would not stop there a minute if there was another house to go to.

The mistress came up the next morning to know how long we wished to stop. We said a fortnight. "Oh! dear me, it is impossible for us to accommodate you, and I think you had better go: you must understand, I have no prejudice myself; I think a good deal of the coloured people, and have always been their friend; but if you stop here we shall lose all our customers, which we can't do nohow." We said we were glad to hear that she had "no prejudice," and was such a staunch friend to the coloured people. We also informed her that we would be sorry for her "customers" to leave on our account; and as it was not our intention to interfere with anyone, it was foolish for them to be frightened away. However, if she would get us a comfortable place, we would be glad to leave. The landlady said she would go out and try. After spending the whole morning in canvassing the town, she came to our room and said, "I have been from one end of the place to the other, but everybody is full." Having a little foretaste of the vulgar prejudice of the town, we did not wonder at this result. However, the landlady gave me the address of some respectable coloured families, whom she thought, "under the circumstances," might be induced to take us. And, as we were not at all comfortable—being compelled to sit, eat and sleep, in the same small room—we were quite willing to change our quarters.

I called upon the Rev. Mr. Cannady, a truly goodhearted Christian man, who received us at a word; and both he and his kind lady treated us handsomely, and for a nominal charge.

My wife and myself were both unwell when we left Boston, and, having taken fresh cold on the journey to Halifax, we were laid up there under the doctor's care, nearly the whole fortnight. I had much worry about getting tickets, for they baffled us shamefully at the Cunard office.[19] They at first said that they did not book till the steamer came; which was not the fact. When I called again, they said they knew the steamer would come full from Boston, and therefore we had "better try to get to Liverpool by other means." Other mean Yankee excuses were made; and it was not till an influential gentleman, to whom Mr. Francis Jackson, of Boston, kindly gave us a letter, went and rebuked them, that we were able to secure our tickets. So when we went on board my wife was very poorly, and was also so ill on the voyage that I did not believe she could live to see Liverpool.

However, I am thankful to say she arrived; and, after laying up at Liverpool very ill for two or three weeks, gradually recovered.

It was not until we stepped upon the shore at Liverpool that we were free from every slavish fear.

We raised our thankful hearts to Heaven, and could have knelt down, like the Neapolitan exiles,* and kissed the soil; for we felt that from slavery

> "Heaven sure had kept this spot of earth uncurs'd,
> To show how all things were created first."

In a few days after we landed, the Rev. Francis Bishop and his lady came and invited us to be their guests; to whose unlimited kindness and watchful care my wife owes, in a great degree, her restoration to health.

We enclosed our letter from the Rev. Mr. May to Mr. Estlin, who at once wrote to invite us to his house at Bristol. On arriving there, both Mr. and Miss Estlin received us as cordially as did our first good Quaker friends in Pennsylvania. It grieves me much to have to mention that he is no more. Everyone who knew him can truthfully say—

> "Peace to the memory of a man of worth,
> A man of letters, and of manners too!
> Of manners sweet as Virtue always wears
> When gay Good-nature dresses her in smiles."†

It was principally through the extreme kindness of Mr. Estlin, the Right Hon. Lady Noel Byron, Miss Harriet Martineau, Mrs. Reid, Miss Sturch, and a few other good friends, that my wife and myself were able to spend a short time at a school in this country, to acquire a little of that education which we were so shamefully deprived of while in the house of bondage. The school is under the supervision of the Misses Lushington, D.C.L. During our stay at the school we received the greatest attention from every one; and I am

---

*Perhaps a reference to the 1859 arrival of Neapolitan exiles at Paddington Station in London.

†Passage taken from William Cowper's *The Task* (1785).

particularly indebted to Thomas Wilson, Esq., of Bradmore House, Chiswick, (who was then the master,) for the deep interest he took in trying to get me on in my studies. We shall ever fondly and gratefully cherish the memory of our endeared and departed friend, Mr. Estlin. We, as well as the Anti-Slavery cause, lost a good friend in him. However, if departed spirits in Heaven are conscious of the wickedness of this world, and are allowed to speak, he will never fail to plead in the presence of the angelic host, and before the great and just Judge, for downtrodden and outraged humanity.

"Therefore I cannot think thee wholly gone;
    The better part of thee is with us still;
Thy soul its hampering clay aside hath thrown,
    And only freer wrestles with the ill.

"Thou livest in the life of all good things;
    What words thou spak'st for Freedom shall not die;
Thou sleepest not, for now thy Love hath wings
    To soar where hence thy hope could hardly fly.

"And often, from that other world, on this
    Some gleams from great souls gone before may shine,
To shed on struggling hearts a clearer bliss,
    And clothe the Right with lustre more divine.

"Farewell! good man, good angel now! this hand
    Soon, like thine own, shall lose its cunning, too;
Soon shall this soul, like thine, bewildered stand,
    Then leap to thread the free unfathomed blue."

JAMES RUSSELL LOWELL*

* * * *

In the preceding pages I have not dwelt upon the great barbarities which are practised upon the slaves; because I wish to present the

---

*Lines from "To Lamartine" (1848), by American Romantic poet, critic, satirist, writer, diplomat, and abolitionist James Russell Lowell (1819–1891).

system in its mildest form, and to show that the "tender mercies of the wicked are cruel." But I do now, however, most solemnly declare, that a very large majority of the American slaves are overworked, under-fed, and frequently unmercifully flogged.

I have often seen slaves tortured in every conceivable manner. I have seen them hunted down and torn by bloodhounds. I have seen them shamefully beaten, and branded with hot irons. I have seen them hunted, and even burned alive at the stake, frequently for offences that would be applauded if committed by white persons for similar purposes.

In short, it is well known in England, if not all over the world, that the Americans, as a people, are notoriously mean and cruel towards all coloured persons, whether they are bond or free.

> "Oh, tyrant, thou who sleepest
> On a volcano, from whose pent-up wrath,
> Already some red flashes bursting up,
> Beware!"

GLOSSARY OF NAMES

Adams, Samuel (1722–1803). Revolutionary leader and powerful political agitator. Served as Boston's tax collector; elected to state legislature 1764–1774. Helped instigate the Stamp Act Riots in Boston; signer of the Declaration of Independence and member of the First and Second Continental Congresses; governor of Massachusetts (1793–1797).

Allen, John F. (dates unknown). Overseer for Henry Box Brown's master William Barret in the 1840s. According to historian Jeffrey Ruggles, John F. Allen was an Irish immigrant who moved to Richmond, Virginia, around 1819; he was described by Box Brown in his 1849 narrative as particularly cruel and abusive.

Alexander the Great (356–323 B.C.). Alexander III, king of Macedon; one of the most successful military commanders in history; conquered most of the known world before his death.

Benton, Thomas H. (1782–1858). Served in War of 1812; newspaper editor (*Missouri Inquirer*); elected to U.S. Senate in 1820 (served until 1850); ardent expansionist, Democrat, and hard-money advocate; nicknamed "Old Bullion" for his financial policies and advocacy. Opposed the annexation of Texas; maintained a growing opposition to slavery (including opposition to Compromise of 1850, which subsequently led to his election defeat); then elected to House of Representatives (opposed Kansas–Nebraska bill, which led to another election defeat); author of political autobiography *Thirty Years' View* (1856).

Bourne, George (Reverend) (1780–1845). Abolitionist and editor sometimes credited as the first person to publicly proclaim "immediate emancipation without compensation" of American slaves; published *Picture of Slavery in the United States* around 1812.

Brown, John (1800–1859). Abolitionist who led violent raids and revolts in order to free slaves in the south and overthrow slavery; hanged on

December 2, 1859, after being captured in a famous raid on the federal armory at Harpers Ferry, Virginia (modern-day West Virginia); remembered today both as a martyr for the abolitionist cause and as a modern terrorist.

Burke, Edmund (1729–1797). Anglo-Irish statesman, author, orator, and political philosopher. Served for many years in the British House of Commons as a member of the Whig party; supported the American colonies in the struggle against King George III that led to the American Revolution; strongly opposed the French Revolution.

Calhoun, John C. (1782–1850). Public official, political leader, and champion of southern sectional interests. Elected to South Carolina state legislature, then to U.S. House of Representatives; became secretary of war for James Monroe; elected as U.S. vice president in 1824 and 1828; resigned to enter U.S. Senate; secretary of state 1844–1845; later returned to the Senate.

Cyrus (c.590–529 B.C.). Also known as Cyrus II of Persia and Cyrus the Great; founder of the Persian Empire under the Achaemenid dynasty and creator of the Cyrus Cylinder, sometimes considered to be the first declaration of human rights.

Dewey, Orville (1794–1882). American Unitarian minister. Graduated from Williams College in 1814 and studied theology at Andover; became anti-slavery activist Dr. William Ellery Channing's assistant; from 1858 was pastor of the South Church in Boston.

Douglass, Frederick (1818–1895). Social reformer, journalist, and public official. Born into slavery; escaped in 1838; subsequently became a public speaker, author, and political organizer.

Elizabeth I (1533–1603). Queen of England from November 17, 1558, until her death; sometimes referred to as the Virgin Queen (she never married), Glorianna, or Good Queen Bess; last monarch of the Tudor dynasty. Various historians have questioned the extent of Elizabeth's involvement in encouraging the Atlantic slave trade; she was said to have sponsored lucrative slave-trading voyages led by seaman Sir John Hawkins to sub-Saharan Africa and the West Indies.

Fillmore, Millard (1800–1874). Thirteenth president of the United States (1850–1853). Appointed Daniel Webster as secretary of state;

supported and signed into law the Compromise of 1850: five pieces of legislation that admitted California to the Union as a free state, settled the Texas boundary, made New Mexico a U.S. territory, abolished the slave trade in the District of Columbia, and established the Fugitive Slave Act.

Fox, George (1624–1691). English religious dissenter and a major early figure in the Religious Society of Friends, commonly known as the Quakers; often considered the founder of the Society because he was one of its most vocal and visible early proponents.

Garrison, William Lloyd (1805–1879). Journalist and reformer; in 1831 founded the abolitionist newspaper *The Liberator*, which he published for thirty-five years, and in which he began a battle for complete and immediate emancipation; was a pacifist, advocate for women's rights, and president of the American Anti-Slavery Society (1841–1865); after passage of the Thirteenth Amendment, stopped publishing *The Liberator* and pressed for prohibition, women's suffrage, civil rights for Native Americans, and other social reforms.

Hampton, Wade (1752–1835). One of the wealthiest men in the South; when he died he was the richest planter in the United States, with 3,000 slaves. His grandson was General Wade Hampton (1818–1902), a planter and Confederate general who served South Carolina as a U.S. senator and governor; he was an opponent of Reconstruction.

Hancock, John (1737–1793). Merchant and public official. Elected as chairman of the Boston Town Committee in the wake of the Boston Massacre; president of Second Continental Congress; first to sign the Declaration of Independence; governor of Massachusetts (1780–1785); elected to Congress (1785); again became governor (1787) and served a total of nine terms.

Harper, Robert Goodloe (1765–1825). Revolutionary War soldier; state legislator in South Carolina; later elected to House of Representatives; left Congress in 1801; served in War of 1812; elected to Senate (though quickly resigned); was founding member of the American Colonization Society in 1817; helped choose Africa as the site for Liberia.

Hathaway, J. C. (dates unknown). Quaker abolitionist from Farmington, New York. Attended convention in August 1850 in

Cazenovia, New York, to protest the Fugitive Slave Act; remained active in the abolitionist movement.

Hauser, Caspar (or Kaspar) (1812–1833). When he was found in Nuremburg, Germany, in 1828, Hauser appeared to have never seen everyday things like fire; after learning to speak, he told of having been raised all his life in a dark cell; was put in the care of a schoolteacher who treated him with homeopathy and encouraged him to write a diary; on December 14, 1833, endured a mysterious attack and three days later died of his wounds; his headstone read: "Here lies Kaspar Hauser, riddle of his time. His birth was unknown, his death mysterious."

Henry, Patrick (1736–1799). Political leader and public official. Entered House of Burgesses (lower house of the colony of Virginia) in 1765 as leader of the party opposed to the dominant aristocrats; delegate to both Continental Congresses; popular orator, known for his assertion in 1775: "Give me liberty or give me death"; commander of the Virginia militia; elected governor; later served in state legislature.

Jeffreys, George (1645–1689). Also known as 1st Baron Jeffreys; sought royal favor with strict enforcement of the law that earned him the appellation "the hanging judge"; became notorious during the reign of King James II and rose to position of lord chancellor.

Lovejoy, Elijah P. (1802–1837). Minister, reformer, and editor. Edited *St. Louis Observer*; supported temperance and gradual emancipation; increasingly supported abolitionism; moved to Alton, Illinois, where his press (and his firm abolitionist stance) repeatedly came under attack; died in a confrontation in 1837 and quickly became a martyr for the abolitionist movement.

Lundy, Benjamin (1789–1839). Abolitionist and author. Born a Quaker in New Jersey; went to Virginia, where he developed distaste for slavery; advocated a central organization to oversee the efforts of the many anti-slavery groups; founded abolitionist paper *The Genius of Universal Emancipation* (William Lloyd Garrison served as associate editor for a short time).

Macaulay, Thomas Babington (1800–1859). Also known as 1st Baron Macaulay. British poet, historian, essayist, and Whig politician. The son of former African colonial governor and anti-slavery philanthropist Zachary Macaulay, Thomas Macaulay spent four years in India reforming

the criminal code of the colony and working to reform its educational system. In addition to writing major works on the history of England, Macaulay was elected to Parliament in 1839.

Martineau, Harriet (1802–1876). English writer, philosopher, supporter of American abolitionism.

May, Samuel J. (1797–1871). Unitarian minister, abolitionist, social reformer. Born in Boston; graduated from Harvard; became an ordained minister in 1822. A humanitarian and a pacifist, May organized the Windham County Peace Society, championed equal rights for women, and supported educational reform. As an abolitionist, he served as a general agent and secretary of the Massachusetts Anti-Slavery Society and utilized his house as a station on the Underground Railroad connecting Boston, Syracuse, and Canada. On May 31, 1849, he delivered a speech at the Massachusetts Anti-Slavery Society Convention in which he described Box Brown's escape at length in a program that also featured Frederick Douglass. (The meeting is documented in "Great Meeting in Faneuil Hall," *The Liberator*, June 8, 1849.)

McDuffie, George (1790–1851). Southern advocate of states rights and popular orator. State legislator in South Carolina; elected to U.S. House of Representatives; prominent advocate of nullification and secession; governor of South Carolina (1834–1836); elected to U.S. Senate in 1843.

McKim, James Miller (1810–1874). Presbyterian minister and leading abolitionist in Philadelphia. Left the pulpit to devote himself to the cause of emancipation; worked for Pennsylvania Antislavery Society as a lecturer, organizer, and corresponding secretary; served occasionally as editor of the *Pennsylvania Freeman*.

Milton, John (1608–1674). English poet best known for his epic poem *Paradise Lost* (1667).

Mott, James (1788–1868). Husband of Lucretia Coffin Mott. Engaged in cotton and wool trade; later focused only on wool trading as a protest against the slavery-dependent cotton industry in the South.

Mott, Lucretia Coffin (1793–1880). American Quaker, abolitionist, and social reformer. Beginning her work in the early 1800s, Lucretia Mott became one of the first women's rights activists in the United

States. Also a fierce abolitionist, she spoke at the International Anti-Slavery Convention in London in June 1840, where she was one of only six female delegates to attend. In 1850 Mott published *Discourse on Woman*, a study of socio-political restrictions faced by women in the United States. She married James Mott in 1811.

Parker, Joel (1816–1888). Presbyterian minister. Strong advocate for active evangelism; held pastorates in New York City, New Orleans, Newark (New Jersey), and Philadelphia; served as president of the Union Theological Seminary. A footnote with a controversial quote in chapter 12 of Harriet Beecher Stowe's *Uncle Tom's Cabin* (1852) was attributed to Parker; Stowe and Parker settled the dispute and future editions of the novel did not include the quote. In 1862 Parker ran for governor of New Jersey as a "war Democrat." He was fiercely opposed to the Lincoln administration and what he perceived as the President's attempts to curtail civil liberties in the name of war.

Parker, Theodore (1810–1860). Unitarian Church minister and social reformer. Born in Massachusetts; became a leader in movements for education, prison reform, temperance, and abolition; prominent opponent of the Fugitive Slave Law; strong supporter of John Brown; saw Civil War as inevitable.

Phillips, Wendell (1811–1884). Social reformer and popular orator. Born into a wealthy Boston family; briefly practiced law; prominent orator for the abolitionist cause and other social reform movements; allied with William Lloyd Garrison; contributed to *The Liberator*; was president of the American Anti-Slavery society for several years.

Pitt, William (1708–1778). Also known as the 1st Earl of Chatham. British Whig statesman who achieved his greatest fame as secretary of state during the Seven Years' War (1754 and 1756–1763); later prime minister (1766–1768); known as William Pitt the Elder to distinguish him from his son: William Pitt the Younger (1759–1806), who also served as prime minister (1783–1801, 1804–1806); on April 7, 1778, the son was present when his father collapsed while making a speech in the House of Lords and helped to carry his dying father from the chamber.

Quincy, Edmund (1808–1877). Abolitionist. Son of Josiah Quincy, a Boston Federalist leader and president of Harvard University; joined abolitionists in reaction to murder of Elijah Lovejoy in 1837; was a close associate of William Lloyd Garrison, contributed frequently to Garrison's

The Liberator, and often edited the paper during Garrison's absences; was corresponding secretary of the Massachusetts Anti-Slavery Society (1844–1853); served on a number of other abolitionist committees.

Ricketson, Joseph (dates unknown). Abolitionist located in New Bedford, Massachusetts. Briefly housed radical abolitionist John Brown in the spring of 1849.

Sennacherib (ruled 705–681 B.C.). King of Assyria. In response to an Egyptian-backed rebellion in 701 B.C., Sennacherib plundered several cities in Judah and attacked Jerusalem, though he was unsuccessful in conquering it. In addition to Sennacherib himself, Herodotus and several biblical writers wrote about the events of his life.

Smith, James Caesar, Jr. (dates unknown). Abolitionist who conspired with Henry Box Brown on his escape in a box. In *Narrative of Henry Box Brown* (1849), Brown describes his meeting with J. C. A. Smith, a free black man, dentist, and merchant who would subsequently follow Brown to Boston and assist him in touring with his panorama in Great Britain. Smith and Brown would later part there over what some speculate was a financial dispute.

Spring, Gardiner (1785–1873). Theologian. Born in Newburyport, Massachusetts. Taught in Bermuda; pastor of Brick Presbyterian church in New York City (1810–1856).

Stearns, Charles (1818–?). Boston printer and local activist aligned with radical abolitionists; hired to receive dictation for Henry Box Brown's 1849 narrative. Stearns was raised in Greenfield, Massachusetts, by Sarah Ripley Stearns, a reformist, humanitarian, and devout Christian. His uncle, two aunts, and sister were members of the original Brook Farm Transcendentalist community near Boston. A radical and an eccentric pacifist as well as an anti-slavery activist, Stearns studied the millennialist philosophies of William Miller, who prophesied the second coming of Christ in 1843. Stearns published a number of anti-slavery and historical pamphlets in the 1840s. He is widely believed to have written large portions of the 1849 Box Brown narrative; his involvement in the 1851 text remains uncorroborated.

Stowe, Harriet Beecher (1811–1896). Author and social reformer. Served as a teacher and wrote stories for periodicals; in June 1851 the first installment of her novel *Uncle Tom's Cabin* appeared in the anti-slavery journal *National Era*; became a leading lecturer in the United States and Britain.

Stuart, Moses (1780–1852). Theologian. Published an anti-slavery pamphlet entitled *Conscience and the Constitution* (1850).

Thompson, George (1804–1878). English reformer. Agitated against slavery in the British colonies and helped contribute to abolishing it; at the request of William Lloyd Garrison and others, came to the United States in 1834 to speak in favor of abolition; his work led to the formation of 150 anti-slavery societies.

Warren, John (1753–1815). Physician and educator. Born in Massachusetts; took part in the Boston Tea Party; served in medical department of the Continental Army; one of the first professors at Harvard Medical School (helped design the program); lecturer on surgery and anatomy. His son John Collins Warren (1778–1856) was a professor of anatomy and surgery at Harvard; co-founded Massachusetts General Hospital; leading American surgeon of his day; devoted himself to reform movements, experimental farming, and geology.

Webster, Daniel (1782–1852). Lawyer and statesman. Served in U.S. House of Representatives and U.S. Senate, and as secretary of state in the Harrison, Tyler, and Polk administrations. Considered one of the great American orators, Webster was more concerned with the evil of disunion than with the evil of slavery.

Weld, Theodore D. (1803–1895). Social reformer and evangelical abolitionist. Has been called the "greatest abolitionist"; wrote two books for which he is remembered: *American Slavery As It Is* and *The Bible Against Slavery*; preached at revivals and supported temperance; joined the anti-slavery movement in 1830 through the influence of English reformer Charles Stuart and organized anti-slavery debates at Lane Seminary, a school he helped found; was married to abolitionist and suffragist Angelina Grimké (with whom he collaborated as an author); did political organizing in the Whig Party; helped defeat the "gag rule" (see endnote 10 to *Narrative of William Wells Brown*).

Xerxes (c.519–465 B.C.). King of Persia (485–465 B.C.); during the Persian Wars against the Greeks, in 480 B.C. he led the Persian army in a massive invasion that resulted in an initial defeat of Athens. Xerxes eventually proclaimed an end to slavery within Persian lands.

ENDNOTES

Narrative of William W. Brown, A Fugitive Slave (1848)

1. (p. 23) *their nephew, William Moore:* In all probability this was Benjamin and Nancy (Moore) Young's son William, and it is also probable that Dr. and Mrs. Young had taken him because of the recent death of his mother (Farrison, *William Wells Brown: Author & Reformer*, p. 13; see For Further Reading).

2. (p. 30) *". . . And gratefully I'll go":* Mrs. Gamaliel Bailey, wife of the editor of the *National Era*, an anti-slavery newspaper in Washington, D.C., based her poem "The Blind Slave Boy" (see pp. 65–66) on this incident described in Wells Brown's *Narrative*.

3. (p. 36) *my time was up with Mr. Walker:* Wells Brown biographer William Farrison (p. 34) notes: "Brown accounted in his Narrative for only three trips with Walker to the Mississippi delta, but late in the 1850's he said that he had made not fewer than four. This discrepancy most probably resulted from confusion in his memory. . . . The account of his fourth trip belongs to the record of his servitude to [Enoch] Price during the last three months of 1833."

4. (p. 55) *Robinson Crusoe:* Daniel Defoe's *Robinson Crusoe* (1719), one of the earliest novels in English, is about a castaway who spends twenty-eight years on a remote island and encounters natives of the island, captives, and mutineers before being rescued.

5. (p. 57) *Quaker:* Quakers are members of a religious movement, the Society of Friends, that began in England in the seventeenth century. In the United States, many Quakers were social reformers; in the nineteenth century, they played prominent roles in the abolitionist movement, supported equal rights for women, and sought an end to warfare. They have also played key reformist roles in education and the humane treatment of prisoners and the mentally ill.

6. (p. 58) *Wells Brown:* Little is known about Wells Brown other than what is supplied by the author here. According to Farrison (p. 57), "The Wells Browns' home might have been anywhere in the rectangular area bounded by Washington Court House, Marysville, Delaware, and Circleville." Farrison speculates that they probably lived on the northern half of this grid since that was the more frequently traveled road that existed in 1834.

7. (p. 58) *Bunker Hill Monument:* The monument, 221 feet high, is located at the site of the first major battle of the American Revolution—the Battle of Bunker Hill (it actually took place on adjacent Breed's Hill)—on June 17, 1775, as part of the British siege of Boston. Though the British ultimately took the hill, they sustained heavy losses (more than 1,000 men), and the battle provided an encouraging indication of the ability of colonial militia to combat the regulars of the British army.

8. (p. 65) *Washington "Union," . . . several slaves to be sold for the benefit of the government:* The issue of slavery in the District of Columbia had particular importance in the antebellum era. Because the U.S. Congress was the sole authority in the District, the doctrine of states' rights could not apply. Because the policies of the District were under direct congressional control and essentially received congressional sanction, the persistence of slavery in the capital became an especially contentious issue.

9. (p. 68) *The rising of the slaves in Southampton, Virginia, in 1831:* At the peak of this slave revolt on August 21 and 22, 1831, in Southampton County, led by Nat Turner, close to sixty slaves came together after killing several whites and began to march toward the county seat in Jerusalem. Turner was captured two months later, and was tried and executed shortly thereafter. The insurrection had wide-ranging consequences, including violent reprisals against blacks, general conditions of panic in many southern regions, and the strengthening of laws restricting slaves' religious practices (Turner often preached at slave revivals).

10. (p. 74) *"Let us declare . . . cast upon the dunghill":* The *Columbia Telescope* here restates the policy that for eight years (1836–1844) was in place in the U.S. House of Representatives. The "gag rule" or "gag resolution" required that all petitions related to the issue of slavery be immediately tabled and not be open for debate. The rule eventually helped mobilize support for the anti-slavery movement in the North by increasing sectional concerns about the power that slaveholding states ostensibly maintained over the congressional agenda. While the Senate failed to officially adopt a gag rule, they followed an unofficial policy of denying each petition dealing with slavery as it appeared before them.

11. (p. 81) *the negro act of 1740 of South Carolina:* In 1740 South Carolina passed a new slave code that was commonly known as the "Negro Act." Passed in response to the Stono slave rebellion, which occurred 20 miles south of Charleston in 1739, the code remained largely unaltered until the Thirteenth Amendment, officially establishing emancipation, was ratified in 1865. The code stripped the enslaved of any kind of protection under the law. For instance, punishment for the murder of an enslaved person by a white was reduced to a mere misdemeanor punishable by a fine. Slaves could never physically attack a white person except in defense of the slaveholder who owned them.

12. (p. 89) *Mason and Dixon's line:* In response to a dispute over territory claimed by the British colonies Pennsylvania and Delaware, on one side, and Maryland, on the other, Charles Mason and Jeremiah Dixon began in 1763 and completed in 1767 a survey that established the official borders of those states and Virginia (now West Virginia). The line, extended westward in 1784, became the accepted boundary between free and slave soil.

Narrative of Henry Box Brown (1849)

1. (p. 114) *"I have given you to my son William":* John Barret gave Brown to his son, William, shortly before his death. William Barret owned a tobacco business in Richmond and had served in the War of 1812. (Historian Jeffrey Ruggles's *The Unboxing of Henry Brown*—see "For Further Reading"—is the key source for background on Henry Box Brown's life.)

2. (p. 126) *a young woman by the name of Nancy:* Nancy was enslaved to Hancock Lee, a teller at the Farmer's Bank of Virginia. Brown seeks permission to marry Nancy around 1836, as he nears twenty-one years of age. The two would have four children together in slavery.

3. (p. 128) *The last purchaser of my wife . . . to prevent her being sold away from me:* In *The Unboxing of Henry Brown* (pp. 14–15), Ruggles maintains that one of Nancy Brown's later slaveholders, Joseph Colquitt, offered to sell Nancy to Samuel Cottrell. Cottrell appealed to Brown for money to purchase Nancy from Colquitt. Brown concurred in order to keep her from being sold away from him. Fellow church choir member and future escape collaborator J. C. A. Smith assisted Brown in securing a house for Nancy and his family. Despite Brown's efforts, Cottrell eventually sold Brown's family in August 1848.

4. (p. 134) *to find a friend:* Box Brown received assistance from two key figures in executing his boxing escape. Freeman J. C. A. Smith, a fellow choir member, assisted Brown with the details leading up to his boxing and introduced him to eccentric Massachusetts transplant Samuel Smith, a white shoemaker in Richmond, who agreed to assist Brown in exchange for what was probably $40 (Ruggles, p. 25). According to Ruggles, Box Brown probably broached the subject of escaping with Samuel Smith in January 1849. Both J. C. A. Smith and Samuel Smith faced conviction in the wake of Brown's well-publicized escape. J. C. A. Smith was found not guilty of conspiracy to aid a fugitive, but Samuel Smith was sent to jail and served a short term. For more on their anti-slavery efforts and their encounters with the law in the wake of Box Brown's escape, see Ruggles (pp. 42–46).

5. (p. 135) *I took my place in this narrow prison, with a mind full of uncertainty as to the result:* Ruggles (p. 28) speculates that Henry Brown "likely slipped by dark back ways to the clandestine rendezvous" on Friday, March 23, 1849. He departed Richmond at 8 A.M., arrived at Washington at 4:30 P.M., at Baltimore at 7 P.M., and at Philadelphia, the first "free city," in the course of the night, arriving there by mail on Saturday, March 24, 1849; by 5 A.M. that day Brown had been in the box for twenty-four hours.

6. (p. 137) *The joy of these friends:* According to James Miller McKim, he was joined at the Anti-Slavery Office on the morning of Box Brown's arrival by black abolitionist William Still, as well as Lewis Thompson and Charles Dexter (Ruggles, p. 35).

7. (p. 145) *"give us an alteration of the 'three-fifths representation' clause of the Constitution":* This is most likely an allusion to the "three-fifths compromise," a compromise between southern and northern states reached during the 1787 United States Constitutional Convention that resulted in Article 1, which stated that three-fifths of the population of slaves would be counted (through a census) for enumeration purposes regarding both the distribution of taxes and the apportionment of the members of the U.S. House of Representatives and the U.S. Electoral College. The three-fifths compromise was rendered void in 1868 by ratification of the Fourteenth Amendment to the Constitution, which provided a broad definition of national citizenship and equal protection under the law to all persons, and apportionment of representatives based on the whole number of persons in each state.

8. (p. 146) *Let a new Continental Congress meet:* It was in fact the Constitutional Convention that adopted the U.S. Constitution in 1787. The First Continental Congress was held in 1774 to develop a common colonial response to coercive acts passed by the British Parliament; it served in an advisory capacity rather than as a legislative body. The Second Continental Congress (1775–1781) assumed responsibility for coordinating the rebellion, raised the Continental army, and eventually adopted the Declaration of Independence in 1776; it served as a central governing body (with relatively limited powers) during the Revolution.

9. (p. 147) *Mexican War:* Between 1846 and 1848, the United States and Mexico were at war over the admission to the Union of Texas, which Mexico claimed as its territory. By the terms of the concluding treaty of Guadalupe Hidalgo, Mexico acknowledged the loss of Texas and ceded to the United States a region that includes present-day California, Nevada, Utah, and parts of Colorado, Arizona, New Mexico, and Wyoming; the United States gave Mexico $15 million. Pressing concerns were raised regarding the expansion of slavery into the new American territories. Thus the Mexican War exacerbated the political tensions between pro- and anti-slavery advocates.

10. (p. 150) *Great Britain, our fathers complained, quartered soldiers upon them:* The British parliamentary legislation known as the Quartering Acts (1765, 1774) required that the American colonies supply barracks, bedding, and other essentials to British troops, and later required lodging them in inns, alehouses, and unoccupied homes. Both Continental Congresses addressed the Quartering Acts as grievances.

11. (p. 153) *Stamp Act:* The Stamp Act (1765) was a British parliamentary act requiring that tax stamps for various public documents (such as legal papers, licenses, custom papers, and newspapers) raise money to support British troops on the American continent. Protests to the Stamp Act were widespread, and public resistance led to its repeal in 1766.

12. (p. 154) *Boston massacre:* On March 5, 1770 (Box Brown's text is in error), a squad of British soldiers, stationed in part to protect British customs officials, killed five colonists in a confrontation. Their actions led to widespread public outrage and the withdrawal of troops from the city to a small island in the harbor.

13. (p. 155) *probably the Island of Cuba, will soon be placed at her side:* In the midst of American expansionist efforts, Cuba emerged as an attractive new territory to acquire. In particular, southerners encouraged the targeting of Cuba, a slave-holding island held by Spain and located in the Caribbean some 90 miles from Florida. In 1854 President Franklin Pierce made a bid to purchase the island from Spain. Pierre Soule, his minister to Spain, failed to execute a deal and, in the process, made threats that infuriated the Spanish government. Pierce then called a conference in Ostend, Belgium, that resulted in a document outlining a plan for the United States to seize Cuba if Spain would not sell it. The manifesto led to a national debate on the South's intentions to extend slavery and its efforts to conflate expansionism with slaveholding interests. Partly as a result of northern outrage, the U.S. government officially ended its efforts to annex Cuba.

Narrative of the Life of Henry Box Brown (1851)

1. (p. 163) *"of Henry Box Brown":* There is speculation that Box Brown may not have been the author of this second narrative. Ruggles (p. 132) maintains that the "writer of the 1851 Narrative remains unidentified."

2. (p. 166) *Evangelical Alliance:* One of the earliest efforts to create cooperation among various Protestant denominations, the Evangelical Alliance was founded in London in 1846. An American branch was established in 1867, with the help of Philip Schaff and Samuel S. Schmucker.

3. (p. 166) *Sons of Ham:* In the Old Testament, the sons of Ham include peoples who were traditionally enemies of the Jews, most notably the Egyptians and the Canaanites. Of Ham's four sons, Canaan fathered the Canaanites; Mizraim the Egyptians; Cush the Cushites; and Phut the Libyans. The Canaanites competed with the Israelites for the same territory. Ham's sons were said to have fathered the peoples of Africa.

4. (p. 168) *New Bedford:* Between 1790 and the Civil War, New Bedford, Massachusetts, became known not only as the whaling capital of the world but also as one of the greatest asylums for fugitive slaves. For more on New Bedford's abolitionist history, see Kathryn Grover's *The Fugitive's Gibralter*.

5. (p. 172) *Fugitive Slave Bill:* Part of the Compromise of 1850, this legislation required that federal commissioners be appointed to issue warrants, gather posses, and deputize/force citizens to aid in the capture of runaway slaves. Once captured, fugitive slaves (without the benefit of a jury trial or the ability to testify on their own behalf) could be sent back to slavery with only minimal evidence (that is, a sworn affidavit from their "owner"). The federal commissioners received compensation for each case, but received double the amount if they sent the accused back to the South. The law mobilized a great deal of resistance in the North both because of its obvious unfairness and because it could potentially force any northern citizen into the role of a slave-catcher. Some states circumvented the law by passing "personal liberty laws," while in other cases mobs physically prevented the capture or return of fugitives by the commissioners. (Source: *The Reader's Companion to American History*, edited by Eric Foner and John A. Garraty, Boston: Houghton Mifflin, 1991.)

 6. (p. 182) *William:* John Barret gave Brown to his son, William, shortly before his death. William Barret owned a tobacco business in Richmond and had served in the War of 1812.

 7. (p. 184) *Mother, my sister:* Box Brown "was one of the middle children in a family that included his mother and father; sisters Jane, Martha, Mary, and Robinnet; and brothers Edward, John, and Lewis" (Ruggles, p. 3).

 8. (p. 184) *Wilson Gregory:* At Barret's tobacco factory, Brown's first overseer was Wilson Gregory, a black man; it is not known whether he was enslaved or free (Ruggles, p. 6). Brown lives with Wilson Gregory when he first gets to Richmond.

 9. (p. 194) *Baptist seminary near the city of Richmond:* Having gained permission from his master to join Richmond's First Baptist Church in 1831, Brown became an active member of what would eventually become the First African Baptist Church. The church was governed by an all-white board but featured black assistants who led prayer and led the choir as well. During his time as a member, Box Brown remained an active participant in the church choir, along with J. C. A. Smith (Ruggles, p. 13–14).

 10. (p. 205) *underground railway:* The term "Underground Railway" was coined during the 1840s as a reference to the multiple networks of escape routes and secret sites of refuge utilized by runaway slaves as they made their way from southern slaveholding territories to free states in the North. The Underground Railway (or Railroad) evolved into the practical arm of a sophisticated social movement in the first half of the nineteenth century as various activist constituencies built coalitions with one another. Abolitionists and republican groups began to combine their political, spiritual and grassroot reform efforts. Through the "Railway" system, these groups put into practice their aggressive interest in subverting the slave system, and they created a practical means to assist women and men in their flights to freedom. With increasing numbers of fugitives able to testify to slavery's evils as a result of utilizing the "railway" to the North, the abolitionist movement was able to acquire increasing numbers of anti-slavery testimonials. Thus the Underground Railway served as a key

source of information during the congressional debates of 1850 which led to the Fugitive Slave Act of 1850. (Source: *Dictionary of American History*, third edition, 10 vols., edited by Stanley I. Kutler, New York: Charles Scribner's Sons, New York, 2003.)

11. (p. 207) *I was well acquainted with a store-keeper:* The store-keeper is Samuel Smith. J. C. A. Smith most likely introduced Box Brown to the other Smith, an eccentric, white transplant from Massachusetts, who emerged as a gambler and a shoemaker in Richmond. Samuel Smith agreed to assist Brown in exchange for what was probably $40 (Ruggles, p. 25). Box Brown probably broached the subject of escaping with Samuel Smith in January 1849.

12. (p. 209) *on the morning of the 29th day of March, 1849:* Ruggles (p. 28) speculates that Henry Brown "likely slipped by dark back ways to the clandestine rendezvous" on Friday, March 23, 1849. He departed Richmond at 8 A.M., arrived at Washington at 4:30 P.M., at Baltimore at 7 P.M., and at Philadelphia, the first "free city," in the course of the night, arriving there by mail in Philadelphia on Saturday, March 24, 1849; by 5 A.M. that day Brown had been in the box for twenty-four hours.

13. (p. 210) *the man who had promised to accompany my box:* Box Brown "later stated that Samuel Smith had 'consented' to accompany the box on the train," but "Smith did not go" (Ruggles, p. 33). It is not clear whether Box Brown knew when he left Richmond that Samuel Smith would not be coming with him on the trip.

14. (p. 211) *A number of persons soon collected round the box after it was taken in to the house:* According to James Miller McKim, he was joined at the Anti-Slavery Office on the morning of Box Brown's arrival by black abolitionist William Still, as well as Lewis Thompson and Charles Dexter (Ruggles, p. 35).

15. (p. 211) *hymn of Thanksgiving:* The English edition of the *Narrative* resituates Box Brown's "Hymn of Thanksgiving" in its originating context—his emergence from the box in Philadelphia. Previously situated at the very end of Stearns's 1849 preface, the hymn, as Marcus Wood argues, emerges in the 1851 text within "its proper context," where Brown is able to "replac[e] the earlier linguistically sanitized account of his experience with his own language and cultural form." See Marcus Wood, "All Right!", p. 81; also Brooks, *Bodies in Dissent*, pp. 112–130.

16. (p. 212) *Mr. and Mrs. Davis:* Edward M. Davis, son-in-law of Quaker activists Lucretia and James Mott, "agreed to help out McKim" and "arranged for Dan, an Irishman, one of Adam's Express drivers" . . . to "go to the depot after the box" (Ruggles, p. 31).

17. (p. 213) *Uncle Ned:* Brown's "Uncle Ned" revises an original 1848 Stephen Foster tune that was a staple of many minstrel revues of the period. While Foster's chorus laments the passing of "Old Ned," who works himself to death in slavery, Brown resituates himself in his own version of the song as having "laid down the shovel and the hoe . . . In the box *by Express* he did go."

18. (p. 217) American Slavery as it is: This is the title of a text by social reformer Theodore Weld (1803–1895). See the Glossary of Names for more information on him.

Running a Thousand Miles for Freedom (1860)

1. (p. 226) *German emigrants of 1818:* In a celebrated mid-1840s New Orleans court case, a German woman named Salome Muller successfully testified that she was not a slave by birth and that she had been wrongfully put to work as a slave for twenty-five years (McCaskill, p. xx).

2. (pp. 234–235) *"Why stands she near the auction stand? . . . They scorn thy God, and thee!":* The anonymously written poem "The Slave Auction—A Fact," was included in William Wells Brown's anti-slavery song collection *The Anti-Slavery Harp* (1848). Wells Brown also used the opening lines of this hymn as the epigraph to chapter 1 of the English edition of his novel *Clotel*, a text that includes references to the Craft narrative.

3. (p. 246) *the Dred Scott decision:* Dred Scott, a slave, sued his master's widow for freedom, and the case ultimately made its way to the Supreme Court. In 1857, in a 7–2 decision, the court ruled that Congress "had no authority to ban slavery in any of the territories" and that Congress's Missouri Compromise of 1820 was unconstitutional. The majority went further by declaring that "African Americans, free or slave, had no rights under the Constitution and could not be citizens." (Source: *The American Heritage Encyclopedia of American History*, edited by John Mack Faragher, New York: Henry Holt, 1998.)

4. (p. 247) *"The hill, though high, I covet to ascend . . . where the end is woe":* This is a passage from John Bunyan's *Pilgrim's Progress* (1678), an allegorical novel written while Bunyan was imprisoned for conducting unauthorized religious services outside of the Church of England.

5. (p. 250) *Opodeldoc:* The physician and alchemist Paracelsus (1493–1541) invented or perhaps simply named this liniment—a mixture of soap in alcohol, plus camphor, herbs, and wormwood.

6. (p. 252) *"When the great American Eagle . . . to wipe his nose with":* The discussion here is perhaps a reference to "manifest destiny," a phrase that expressed the belief that the United States had a mission to expand, spreading its form of democracy and freedom.

7. (p. 253) *the frequent importation, or smuggling in, of Africans:* This is perhaps a reference to the illegality of the international slave trade. In 1807 Great Britain outlawed the slave trade altogether. From 1815 to 1865, the British Royal Navy undertook anti-slavery patrols off the coast of West Africa, seizing hundreds of vessels. Illegal trading flourished until the 1860s.

8. (p. 255) *Overland Mail Route:* In 1857 Congress voted to subsidize a semiweekly overland mail service. From 1858 through 1861, the Butterfield Overland

Express Company carried the mail from St. Louis, following a southerly route through Texas and Arizona and then up the California coastline to San Francisco. From April 1860 to November 1861, the Pony Express took mail between St. Louis and Sacramento via a shorter, more central route.

9. (p. 262) *Royal Charter:* The steam clipper *Royal Charter* was wrecked off the east coast of Anglesey, Wales, with a loss of more than 450 lives, during what became known as the Royal Charter Storm, on October 25 and 26, 1859. Some 200 other ships were also destroyed during the storm.

10. (p. 263) *Bunyan's Mistrust and Timorous:* In the allegorical *Pilgrim's Progress*, by John Bunyan, "everyman" protagonist Christian encounters Mistrust and Timorous running down the Hill of Difficulty, toward the plain beyond the wicket gate, while Christian continues upon the way toward the Celestial City.

11. (p. 263) *Queen Elizabeth could not have been more terror-stricken . . . the Tower:* The Tower of London was begun in 1078 by William the Conqueror and completed in 1285 by Edward I. In 1554 Elizabeth Tudor, who would become queen as Elizabeth I, was imprisoned for two months in the Tower for her alleged involvement in Wyatt's Rebellion, an uprising intended to prevent "Bloody Mary," queen from 1553 to 1558, from returning England to Roman Catholicism.

12. (p. 271) *Mrs. Stowe's Mose and Pete:* Mose and Pete are the toddler sons of Uncle Tom & Chloe and "belong" to the slaveholding Shelby family in Harriet Beecher Stowe's *Uncle Tom's Cabin* (1852).

13. (p. 272) *Fugitive Slave Bill:* Part of the Compromise of 1850, this legislation required that federal commissioners be appointed to issue warrants, gather posses, and deputize/force citizens to aid in the capture of runaway slaves. Once captured, fugitive slaves (without the benefit of a jury trial or the ability to testify on their own behalf) could be sent back to slavery with only minimal evidence (that is, a sworn affidavit from their "owner"). The federal commissioners received compensation for each case, but received double the amount if they sent the accused back to the South. The law mobilized a great deal of resistance in the North both because of its obvious unfairness and because it could potentially force any northern citizen into the role of a slave-catcher. Some states circumvented the law by passing "personal liberty laws," while in other cases mobs physically prevented the capture or return of fugitives by the commissioners. (Source: *The Reader's Companion to American History*, edited by Eric Foner and John A. Garraty, Boston: Houghton Mifflin, Boston, 1991.)

14. (p. 273) *Vigilance Committee:* In the nineteenth century, vigilance committees were well-organized groups of private citizens established in areas where law enforcement and local government were deemed ineffective; the groups' aims and goals revolved around self-protection.

15. (p. 276) *Lot from Sodom:* In the Bible (for example, Genesis 19), Sodom (in Hebrew, "burnt") and Gomorrah ("a ruined heap") were cities destroyed by

God for their sins. The nephew of the patriarch Abraham, Lot was forewarned by two angels about God's intent to destroy Sodom. The angels led Lot, his wife, and his two daughters out of their house and urged them to "save yourselves with all haste" and "look not behind you." Lot's wife failed to heed this warning and, looking back on Sodom, was turned into a pillar of salt.

16. (p. 276) *Mosaic Law:* That is, the law that, according to the Old Testament, God gave to the Israelites through Moses. The Mosaic law begins with the Ten Commandments and includes the many rules of religious observance given in the first five books of the Old Testament. In Judaism, these books are called the Torah, or "the Law."

17. (p. 278) *Balaam:* Balaam, a prophet, appears in the biblical Book of Numbers. In Numbers 23–24, Balak, king of Moab, calls upon Balaam to curse his enemies, but Balaam instead blesses them, much to Balak's ire. Balaam maintains (Numbers 24:13), "I cannot go beyond the commandment of the Lord, to do either good or bad of mine own mind; but what the Lord saith, that will I speak" (King James Version).

18. (p. 279) *"Jonah," for refusing to carry God's message against Nineveh:* In the Old Testament, Jonah failed to obey the Lord's instruction to inform the inhabitants of Nineveh about the city's impending destruction because of their wickedness. Instead, Jonah fled by ship. When it was assailed by a great storm, the sailors saw it as a sign of God's anger at Jonah's disobedience and, with his consent, put him overboard. God rescued Jonah by providing him with refuge in the belly of a whale and eventually ordered the fish to vomit Jonah on dry land (Jonah 1–2).

19. (p. 283) *Cunard office:* The Cunard Line was an important participant in the history of trade. The first steamship of the Cunard line, the *Britannia*, was a pioneer in the transatlantic transportation of passengers.

INSPIRED BY *THE GREAT ESCAPES*

The popularity of the narratives in *The Great Escapes* and other stories of flight from slavery in the nineteenth century launched African-American writers into the mainstream of publishing—a remarkable accomplishment in light of the fact that many people refused to believe that a black slave could write a book unassisted or tell a story without exaggerating, particularly when it came to accusations of cruelty. Issues of credibility and authentication underlie all writing, but the burden was far greater on slave-narrative authors at a time when many Americans considered them to be nothing more than property. Yet each new tale of escape, however fantastic, made such accounts more difficult to doubt, particularly when a white person vouched for the integrity of the writer. Reader demand grew, and the success of these narratives encouraged African-Americans to publish works on a diversity of subjects in a variety of media.

Henry Box Brown's narratives shed light on the role of white validation in bringing stories of slavery and flight to the public eye. As the introduction in this volume describes, Brown wrote two versions of his wildly implausible story of escape that were published in 1849 and 1851. The title page of his first published account featured the name of his white collaborator, Charles Stearns, which helped authenticate the work. The success of the first narrative set the stage for Henry Box Brown to write and publish a second, revised version independently. Whether or not the second book was written entirely without outside assistance, Henry Box Brown by this point had the credibility to issue an account of his escape under his own name.

Meanwhile, increasing numbers of Americans and Europeans were accepting the accounts of African-American slaves as factual and accepting the authors as credible, and publishing opportunities increased as African-Americans came to be seen not as property but as human beings worthy of sympathy, respect, and admiration. Just as the celebrity of Henry Box Brown created an audience for a second, expanded narrative of his life, the popularity of William Wells Brown, who in 1847 had published *Narrative of William Wells Brown, A Fugitive Slave, Written by Himself*, increased the demand for information about him. No person felt this pressure more acutely than Brown's daughter, Josephine. As a fourteen-year-old in boarding school in Paris, she received a deluge of requests about her famous father from curious schoolmates. She obliged them by writing her own version of Brown's life, which she circulated privately and then expanded and published in 1855, soon after she returned to America and discovered that her father's *Narrative* was out of print. Her father's story opened the way for Josephine Brown, never a slave herself, to receive an education he was denied and to become one of history's youngest published biographers.

Josephine Brown's *Biography of an American Bondman* goes beyond the time frame of her father's autobiography to describe his ascent to celebrity. She details the European tour he embarked on two years after publishing his *Narrative*, detailing his reception in England and France and extensively quoting from European commentary on the man and his writings. The language used by Josephine Brown and the European commentators plainly demonstrates that, at the time, authentication by whites could bestow individuality and, in the case of some readers, even humanity upon African-Americans (see the Appendix to this volume for excerpts from Josephine Brown's work).

William Wells Brown went on to write *Clotel*, the first novel by an African-American and an early source of information about the sexual relationship between Thomas Jefferson and his slave Sally Hemmings. Brown continued publishing well into the 1880s, producing volumes of art criticism, collections of songs, travel narratives, plays, lectures, and histories, and establishing himself as a multifaceted commentator on American history and sociology. His success set a precedent for the influence of blacks in American cultural life that continued, to cite a few well-known examples, with the coordinated activism, publishing, and commentary of former slave Frederick Douglass, through the writings of historian and sociologist W. E. B. Du Bois and playwright and activist James Weldon Johnson, down to the present day and the work of John Harold Johnson, founder of a publishing empire that includes *Ebony* and *Jet* magazines, and multimedia powerhouse Oprah Winfrey, who, through her book club, has become one of America's most trusted literary authenticators.

Josephine Brown's *Biography of an American Bondman* **(1856)**

Josephine Brown's biography of her father, William Wells Brown, is a unique work in the history of African-American letters. The following excerpts provide the reader with a distinctive perspective on the issue of slavery and on the life of a great American. (See "Inspired by The Great Escapes" *for more on Josephine Brown's work.)*

CHAPTER XVI.

> "For 't is the mind that makes the body rich,
> And as the sun breaks through the darkest clouds,
> So honor peereth in the meanest habit."

The subject of our memoir no sooner felt himself safe from the pursuit of Southern bloodhounds, than he began to seek for that which the system of slavery had denied him, while one of its victims. During the first five years of his freedom, his chief companion was a book,—either an arithmetic, a spelling-book, a grammar, or a history. Though he never went through any systematic course of study, he nevertheless has mastered more, in useful education, than many who have had better privileges.

After lecturing in the Anti-Slavery cause for more than five years, Mr. Brown was invited to visit Great Britain. He at first declined; but being urged by many friends of the slave in the Old World, he at last, in the summer of 1849, resolved to go. As soon as it was understood that the fugitive slave was going abroad, the American Peace Society elected him as a delegate to represent them at the Peace Congress at Paris. Without any solicitation, the Executive Committee of the American Anti-Slavery Society strongly recommended Mr. Brown to the friends of freedom in Great Britain. The President of the above Society gave him private letters to some of the leading men and women in Europe. In addition to these, the colored citizens of Boston held a meeting the evening previous to his departure, and gave Mr. Brown a public *farewell*, and passed resolutions commending him to the confidence and hospitality of all lovers of liberty in the motherland.

Such were the auspices under which this self-educated man sailed for England on the 18th of July, 1849. Without being a salaried agent, or any promise of remuneration from persons either in Europe or America, the subject of our narrative arrived at Liverpool, after a passage of a few hours less than ten days.

CHAPTER XVII.

> "Erin, my country! o'er the swelling wave,
> Join the cry, ask freedom for the slave!"

> "Natives of a land of glory,
>   Daughters of the good and brave,
> Hear the injured negro's story,
>   Hear, and help the kneeling slave!"

From Liverpool, Mr. Brown went to Dublin, where he was warmly greeted by the Webbs, Haughtons, Allens, and others of the slave's friends in Ireland. Her Brittanic Majesty visiting her Irish subjects at the time, the fugitive had an opportunity of witnessing Royalty in all its magnificence and regal splendor. The land of Burke, Sheridan and O'Connell would not permit the American to leave without giving him an enthusiastic welcome. A large and enthusiastic meeting held in the Rotunda, and presided over by JAMES HAUGHTON, Esq., gave Mr. Brown the first reception which he had in the Old World.

After a sojourn of twenty days in the Emerald Isle, the fugitive started for the Peace Congress which was to assemble at Paris. The Peace Congress, and especially the French who were in attendance at the great meeting, most of whom had never seen a colored person, were somewhat taken by surprise on the last day, when Mr. Brown made a speech. "His reception," said *La Presse*, "was most flattering. He admirably sustained his reputation as a public speaker. His address produced a profound sensation. At its conclusion, the speaker was warmly greeted by Victor Hugo, President of the Congress, Richard Cobden, Esq., and other distinguished men on the platform. At the soirée given by M. de Tocqueville, the Minister for Foreign Affairs, the American slave was received with marked attention." More than thirty of the English delegates at the Congress gave Mr. Brown invitations to visit their towns on his return to England, and lecture on American Slavery.

Having spent a fortnight in Paris and vicinity, viewing the sights, he returned to London. GEORGE THOMPSON, Esq., was among the first to meet the fugitive on his arrival at the English metropolis. A few days after, a very large meeting, held in the spacious Music Hall, Bedford Square, and presided over by Sir Francis Knowles, Bart., welcomed Mr. Brown to England. Many of Britain's distinguished public speakers spoke on the occasion. George Thompson made one of his most brilliant efforts.

This flattering reception gained for the fugitive pressing invitations from nearly all parts of the United Kingdom. At the city of Worcester, His Honor the Mayor presided over the meeting, and introduced Mr. Brown as "the honorable gentleman from America." In the city of Norwich, the meeting was held in St. Andrew's Hall, one of the oldest and most venerated buildings in the Kingdom, and the Chairman on the occasion was John Henry Gurney, Esq., the distinguished banker, and son of the late Joseph John Gurney. At Newcastle-on-Tyne, two meetings were held. His Honor the Mayor presided over one, and Sir John Fife over the other. Here the friends of freedom gave Mr. Brown a public soirée, at which eight hundred sat down to tea. After tea was over, the Mayor arose, and, on behalf of the meeting, presented to Mr. Brown a purse containing twenty sovereigns, accompanied with the following Address:—"This purse, containing twenty sovereigns, is presented to WM. WELLS BROWN by the following ladies and some other friends of the slave in Newcastle, as a token of their high esteem for his character and admiration of his zeal in advocating the claims of three millions of his brethren and sisters in bonds in the Southern States of America. They also express their sincere wish that his life may be long spared to pursue his valuable labors—that success may soon crown his efforts and those of his fellow Abolitionists on both sides of the Atlantic, and his heart be gladdened by the arrival of the happy period when the *last shackle* shall be broken which binds the limbs of the *last slave.*"

At Glasgow, four thousand persons attended the meeting at the City Hall, which was presided over by Alexander Hastie, Esq., M.P. Meetings given to welcome Mr. Brown were also held at Edinburgh, Perth, Dundee, Aberdeeen, and nearly every city or town in the Kingdom. At Sheffield, James Montgomery, the poet, attended the meeting, and invited the fugitive to visit him at his residence. The following day, Mr. Brown went, by invitation, to visit the silver electro-plate manufactory of Messrs. Broadhead and Atkins. While going through the premises, a subscription was set on foot by the workmen, and on the fugitive's entering the counting-room, the purse was presented to him by the designer, who said that the donors gave it as a token of their esteem for Mr. Brown.

At Bolton, a splendid soirée was given to him, and the following Address presented:—

"Dear Friend and Brother,—

We cannot permit you to depart us without giving expression to the feelings which we entertain towards yourself personally, and to the sympathy which you have awakened in our breasts for the three millions of our sisters and brothers who still suffer and groan in the prison-house of American bondage. You came among us an entire stranger; we received you for the sake of your mission; and having heard the story of your personal wrongs, and gazed with horror on the atrocities of slavery, as seen through the medium of your touching descriptions, we are resolved henceforward, in reliance on divine assistance, to render what aid we can to the cause which you have so eloquently pleaded in our presence. We have no words to express our detestation of the crimes which, in the name of Liberty, are committed in the country which gave you birth. Language fails to tell our deep abhorrence of the impiety of those who, in the still more sacred name of Religion, rob immortal beings, not only of an earthly citizenship, but do much to prevent them from obtaining a heavenly one: and as mothers and daughters, we embrace this opportunity of giving utterance to our utmost indignation at the cruelties perpetrated upon our sex by a people professedly acknowledging the equality of all mankind. Carry with you, on your return to the land of your nativity, this solemn protest against the wicked institution which, like a dark and baleful cloud, hangs over it; and ask the unfeeling enslavers, as best you can, to open the prison-doors to them that are bound, and let the oppressed go free. Allow us to assure you, that your brief sojourn in our town has been to ourselves, and to vast multitudes, of a character long to be remembered; and when you are far removed from us, and toiling, as we hope you may long be spared to do, in this righteous enterprise, it may be some solace to your mind to know that your name is cherished with affectionate regard, and that the blessing of the Most High is earnestly supplicated in behalf of yourself and your family, and the cause to which you have consecrated your distinguished talents." [Signed by 200 ladies.]

In the spring of 1850, Mr. Brown was publicly welcomed at a large meeting held in the Broadmead Rooms, at Bristol, and presided over by the late JOHN B. ESTLIN, Esq., one of the most liberal-minded and philanthropic men of any country; a man who never appeared better satisfied than when doing good for others, and whose loss has been so universally lamented by the genuine friends of freedom in both hemispheres. But should we undertake to give a detailed account of the various meetings called to receive the American fugitive slave, it would occupy more space than we can think of giving in this volume. . . .

CHAPTER XIX.

"Take the spade of perseverance,
 Dig the field of progress wide,
Every bar to true instruction
 Carry out, and cast aside."

It was the intention of Mr. Brown, when he went to England, not to remain there more than one year at the furthest. But he was, by the laws of the United States, the *property* of another, and the passage of the Fugitive Slave Bill laid him liable to be arrested whenever he should return to his native land. WENDELL PHILLIPS, Esq., advised the fugitive, for his own safety, not to return. Mr. Brown therefore resolved to remove his two daughters to England, so that he could see to their education. In July, 1851, the girls arrived in Liverpool, in the Royal British Mail Steamer "America," under the charge of the Rev. CHARLES SPEAR, the distinguished and philanthropic friend of the prisoner. Even here, the fugitive was not without persecution in the person of his children, for Mr. Lewis, the Company's agent in Boston, would not receive them unless they were entered on the passenger's list as servants. The only reason assigned for this was their being colored! Thus the vile institution which had driven Mr. Brown into exile, followed his children on board a steamer over which the British flag waved.

Soon after the arrival of his daughters, Mr. Brown placed them in one of the best seminaries in France, where they encountered no difficulty on account of their complexion. The entire absence of prejudice against color in Europe is one of the clearest proofs that the hatred here to the colored person is solely owing to the overpowering influence of slavery. Mr. Brown's daughters, after remaining in France one year, were removed to the Home and Colonial School in London, the finest female educational college in Great Britain. Here, as well was in the French school, the girls saw nothing to indicate that the slightest feeling of ill-will existed on the part of the students toward them, because of their color. . . .

CHAPTER XXI.

——————"Yet press on!
For it shall make you mighty among men;
And from the eyrie of your eagle thought,
You shall look down on monarchs!"

In 1852, Mr. Brown found, from the shortness of the lecturing season, which in England lasts only from November to May, and is furnishing a precarious means of living, that he must adopt some other mode of providing support for himself and his daughters, and therefore, through the solicitation of some of his literary friends, commenced writing for the English press. Not having received a classical education, he had often to re-write his articles. His contributions were mainly on American questions. For instance, his articles on the death of Henry Clay, Daniel Webster, the return of Anthony Burns, were gladly received by the London press, and the fugitive was liberally paid for his labors. The writer of this has known Mr. Brown to be engaged all night, after the arrival of an American mail, in writing for a morning newspaper. In the autumn of 1852, he published his "Three Years in Europe," which paid him well. The criticisms on this work brought the fugitive prominently before the public, and gave him a position among literary men never before enjoyed by any colored American. The London *Morning Advertiser*, in its review, said:—"This remarkable book of a remarkable man cannot fail to add to the practical protests already entered in Britain against the absolute bondage of three millions of our fellow-creatures. The impressions of a self-educated son of slavery, here set forth, must hasten the period when the senseless and impious denial of common claims to a common humanity, on the score of color, shall be scouted with scorn in every civilized and Christian country. And when this shall be attained, among the means of destruction of the hideous abomination, his compatriots will remember with respect and gratitude the doings and saying of William Wells Brown. The volume consists of a sufficient variety of scenes, persons, arguments, inferences, speculations and opinions, to satisfy and amuse the most *exigeant* of those who read *pour se desennuyer*; while those who look deeper into things, and view with anxious hope the progress of nations and of mankind, will feel that the good cause of humanity and freedom, of Christianity, enlightenment and brotherhood, cannot fail to be served by such a book as this."

The London *Literary Gazette*, in speaking of the book, remarked:—"The appearance of this book is too remarkable a literary event to pass without a notice. At the moment when attention in this country is directed to the state of colored people in America, the book appears with additional advantage; if nothing else were attained by its publication, it is well to have another proof of the capability of the negro intellect. Altogether, Mr. Brown has written a

pleasing and amusing volume, and we are glad to bear this testimony to the literary merit of a work by a negro author."

"That a man," said the *Morning Chronicle*, "who was a slave for
the first twenty years of his life, and who has never had a day's
schooling, should produce such a book as this, cannot but astonish
those who speak disparagingly of the African race."

The *London Critic* pronounced it a "pleasingly and well written
book." "It is," said the *Athenæum*, "racy and amusing." The *Eclectic
Review*, in its long criticism, has the following:—"The extraordinary excitement produced by 'Uncle Tom's Cabin' will, we hope,
prepare the public of Great Britain and America for this lively book
of travels by a real fugitive slave. Though he never had a day's
schooling in his life, he has produced a literary work not unworthy
of a highly-educated gentleman. Our readers will find in these letters much instruction, not a little entertainment, and the beating of
a manly heart on behalf of a down-trodden race, with which they
will not fail to sympathise."

The *British Banner*, edited by Dr. Campbell, said:—"We have
read this book with an unusual measure of interest. Seldom, indeed,
have we met with any thing more captivating. It somehow happens
that all these fugitive slaves are persons of superior talents. The pith
of the volume consists in narratives of voyages and journeys made
by the author in England, Scotland, Ireland and France; and we can
assure our readers that Mr. Brown has travelled to some purpose.
The number of white men is not great who could have made more
of the many things that came before them. There is in the work a
vast amount of quotable matter, which, but for want of space, we
should be glad to extract. As the volume, however, is published with
a view to promote the benefit of the interesting fugitive, we deem it
better to give a general opinion, by which curiosity may be whetted,
than to gratify it by large citation. A book more worth the money
has not, for a considerable time, come into our hands."

The Provincial papers and the London press united in their
praise of this, the first literary production of travels by a fugitive
slave. The *Glasgow Citizen*, in its review, remarked:—"W. Wells
Brown is no ordinary man, or he could not have so remarkably sur-
mounted the many difficulties and impediments of his training as
a slave. By dint of resolution, self-culture and force of character, he

has rendered himself a popular lecturer to a British audience, and vigorous expositor of the evils and atrocities of that system whose chains he has shaken off so triumphantly and for ever. We may safely pronounce William Wells Brown a remarkable man, and a full refutation of the doctrine of the inferiority of the negro."

The *Glasgow Examiner* said:—"This is a thrilling book, independent of adventitious circumstances, which will enhance its popularity. The author of it is not a man in America, but a chattel,—a thing to be bought, and sold, and whipped; but in Europe, he is an author, and a successful one, too. He gives in this book an interesting and graphic description of a three years' residence in Europe. The book will no doubt obtain, as it well deserves, a rapid and wide popularity."

The *Caledonian Mercury* concludes an article of more than two columns of criticism and extracts as follows:—"The profound anti-slavery feeling produced by 'Uncle Tom's Cabin' needed only such a book as this, which shows so forcibly the powers and capacity of the negro intellect, to deepen the impression."

Mr. Brown's criticism on Thomas Carlyle brought about his ears a whirlwind of remarks from the friends of the distinguished Scotchman, while a portion of the press sided with the fugitive, and pronounced the article ably written and most just in its criticism. The following is the offensive part of the essay, and refers to his meeting Mr. Carlyle in an omnibus:—

"I had scarcely taken my seat, when my friend, who was seated opposite me, with looks and gestures informed me that we were in the presence of some distinguished individual. I eyed the countenances of the different persons, but in vain, to see if I could find any who, by his appearance, showed signs of superiority over his fellow-passengers. I had given up the hope of selecting the person of note, when another look from my friend directed my attention to a gentleman seated in the corner of the omnibus. He was a tall man, with strongly marked features, dark hair and coarse. There was a slight stoop of the shoulder,—that bend which is always a characteristic of studious men. But he wore on his countenance a forbidding and disdainful frown, that seemed to tell one that he thought himself better than those about him. His dress did not indicate a man of high rank, and had we been in America, I should have taken him for an Ohio farmer. While I was scanning the features and general appearance of the gentleman, the omnibus stopped and put down three or four of the passengers, which gave me an opportunity of getting a seat by the side of my friend, who, in a low whisper, informed me that the gentleman whom I had been eyeing so closely was no less a person than Thomas Carlyle. I had read his 'Hero Worship' and 'Past and Present,' and had formed a high opinion of his literary abilities. But his recent attack upon the emancipated people of the West Indies, and his laborious article in favor of the reestablishment of the lash and slavery, had created in my mind a dislike for the man, and I almost regretted that we were in the same omnibus. In some things, Mr. Carlyle is right; but in many, he is entirely wrong. As a writer, Mr. Carlyle is often monotonous and extravagant. He does not exhibit a new view of nature, or raise insignificant objects into importance; but generally takes common-place thoughts and events, and tries to express them in stronger and statelier language than others. He holds no communion with his kind, but stands alone, without mate or fellow. He is like a solitary peak, all access to which is cut off. He exists, not by sympathy, but by antipathy. Mr. Carlyle seems chiefly to try how he shall display his powers, and astonish mankind by starting new trains of speculation, or by expressing old ones so as not to be understood. He cares little what he says, so that he can say it differently from others. To read his works is one thing; to understand them is another. If any one thinks that I exaggerate, let him sit for an hour over 'Sartor Resartus,' and if he does not rise from its pages, place his three or four dictionaries on the shelf, and say I am right, I promise never again to say a word against Thomas Carlyle. He writes one page in favor of reform and ten against it. He would hang all prisoners to get rid of them; yet the inmates of the prisons and workhouses are better off than the poor. His heart is with the poor; yet the blacks of the West Indies should be taught, that if they will not raise sugar and cotton of their own free will, 'Quashy should have the whip applied to him.' He frowns upon the reformatory speakers upon the boards of Exeter Hall; yet he is the prince of reformers. He hates heroes and assassins; yet Cromwell was an angel, and Charlotte Corday a saint. He scorns every thing, and seems to be tired of what he is by nature, and tries to be what he is not."

CHAPTER XXII.

> "Fling out the anti-slavery flag,
> And let it not be furled,
> Till like a planet of the skies,
> It sweeps around the world!"

Mr. Brown's name being often brought before the public through reviews of his new book, and different sketches of his life having been published in the London *Biographical Magazine*, *Public Good*, *True Briton*, and other periodicals, he was invited to lecture before literary associations in London and the provincial towns. This induced him to get up a course of lectures on America and her great men, St. Domingo, &c. Thus, during the lecturing season, he was busily engaged, either before institutions, or speaking on American Slavery.

In the spring of 1853, the fugitive brought out his work, "Clotel, or the President's Daughter,"—a book of near three hundred pages, being a narrative of slave life in the Southern States. This work called forth new criticisms on the "Negro Author" and his literary efforts. The London *Daily News* pronounced it a book that would make a deep impression; while the *Leader*, edited by the son of Leigh Hunt, thought many parts of it "equal to any thing which has appeared on the slavery question."

Thus the fugitive slave slowly worked his way up into English literary society. After delivering a lecture before the London Metropolitan Athenæum, the Managing Committee instructed the Secretary to thank Mr. Brown, which he did in the following note:—

"Metropolitan Athenæum,
189 Strand, June 21st.

"My Dear Sir,—

I have much pleasure in conveying to you the best thanks of the Managing Committee of this institution for the excellent lecture you gave here last evening, and also in presenting you, in their names, with an honorary membership of the Club. It is hoped that you will often avail yourself of its privileges by coming amongst us.

You will then see, by the cordial welcome of the members, that they protest against the odious distinctions made between man and man, and the abominable traffic of which you have been a victim. For my own part, I shall be happy to be serviceable to you in any way, and at all times be glad to place the advantages of the institution at your disposal.

"I am, my dear sir, yours, truly,
"WILLIAM STRUDWICKE,
Secretary.
"Mr. W. WELLS BROWN."

FOR FURTHER READING

Primary Sources: Historical and Literary Texts

Ball, J. P. "Ball's Splendid Mammoth Pictorial Tour of the United States." In *J. P. Ball, Daguerrean and Studio Photographer*, edited by Deborah Willis. New York: Garland Publishing, 1993, pp. 237–301.

Banvard, John. *Description of Banvard's Panorama of the Mississippi & Missouri Rivers, Extensively Known as the "Three-Mile Painting," Exhibiting A View of Country Over 3000 Miles in Length, Extending from the Mouth of the Yellow Stone to the City of New Orleans, Being by Far the Largest Picture Ever Executed By Man*. London: W. J. Golbourn, 1848.

Bibb, Henry. "Narrative of the Life and Adventures of Henry Bibb, an American Slave." 1849. In *Puttin' On Ole Massa: The Slave Narratives of Henry Bibb, William Wells Brown, and Solomon Northup*, edited by Gilbert Osofsky. New York: Harper & Row, 1969, pp. 51–172.

Boucicault, Dion. "The Octoroon." 1859. In *Selected Plays of Dion Boucicault*, edited by Andrew Parkin. Washington, DC: Colin Smythe and Catholic University of America Press, 1987, pp. 135–190.

———. *The Octoroon*. 1859. Salem, NH: Ayer, 1987.

Braddon, Mary Elizabeth. *The Octoroon*. New York: Optimus Printing, 186.

Brown, William Wells. *The American Fugitive in Europe: Sketches of Places and People Abroad*. Boston and New York: J. P. Jewett and Sheldon, Lamport & Blakeman, 1855.

———. *The Anti-Slavery Harp: A Collection of Songs for Anti-Slavery Meetings*. Boston: B. Marsh, 1848.

———. *Clotel; or, The President's Daughter*. 1853. Introduction by Joan E. Cashin. Armonk, NY: M. E. Sharpe, 1996.

———. "A Description of William Wells Brown's Original Panoramic Views of the Scenes in the Life of an American Slave, from His Birth in Slavery to His Death or His Escape to His First Home of Freedom on British Soil." In *The Black Abolitionist Papers*, edited by C. Peter Ripley et al. Vol. 1: *The British Isles, 1830–1865*. Chapel Hill: University of North Carolina Press, 1985, pp. 191–224.

———. *The Escape; or, A Leap for Freedom*. 1858. In *Black Theatre USA: Plays by African Americans, 1847 to Today*, edited by James V. Hatch and Ted Shine. 2 vols. New York: Free Press, 1996, pp. 35–60.

———. *Three Years in Europe; or, Places I Have Seen and People I Have Met. By W. Wells Brown, a Fugitive Slave. With a Memoir of the Author by William Farmer*. London: Charles Gilpin, 1852.

———. *The Travels of William Wells Brown: The Narrative of William Wells Brown, a Fugitive Slave, and The American Fugitive in Europe, Sketches of Places and People Abroad*. 1848. Edited by Paul Jefferson. New York: M. Weiner, 1991.

Channing, William Ellery. "On Abolitionists and Integration." In *Racial Thought in America: From the Puritans to Abraham Lincoln*, edited by Louis Ruchames. Amherst: University of Massachusetts Press, 1969.

The Complete Repertoire of the Songs, Ballads and Plantation Melodies. London: Hopwood & Crew, 1870.

Donne, W. B. *Cora; or, The Octoroon Slave of Louisiana Drama*. 1861. Lord Chamberlain Play Collection. London: British Library Manuscript Reading Room.

Douglass, Frederick. *My Bondage and My Freedom*. 1855. Introduction by Philip S. Foner. New York: Dover Publications, 1969.

———. *Narrative of the Life of Frederick Douglass, An American Slave*. 1845. Introduction by Houston A. Baker, Jr. New York: Penguin Books, 1982.

———. *The Nature, Character and History of the Anti-Slavery Movement, a Glasgow Lecture*. London: Anti-Slavery Society, 1855.

———. "What to the Slave Is the Fourth of July? An Address Delivered on July 5, 1852 in Rochester New York." In *The Frederick Douglass Papers*, edited by John Blassingame. Vol. 2: *1847–1854*. New Haven, CT: Yale University Press, 1982, pp. 359–387.

Equiano, Olaudah. "The Interesting Narrative of the Life of Olaudah Equiano, or Gustavus Vassa, the African." 1789. In *The Classic Slave Narratives*, edited by Henry Louis Gates, Jr. New York: New American Library, 1987, pp. 1–182.

Farrison, William Edward. *William Wells Brown: Author & Reformer*. Chicago: University of Chicago Press, 1969.

Hatfield, Edwin F. *Freedom's Lyre; or, Psalms, Hymns, and Sacred Songs, for the Slave and His Friends*. New York: S. W. Benedict, 1840.

Jacobs, Harriet. *Incidents in the Life of a Slave Girl*. 1861. Introduction by Jean Fagan Yellin. Cambridge, MA: Harvard University Press, 1987.

Longfellow, Henry W. *Poems on Slavery*. Cambridge, MA: J. Owen, 1842.

Mattison, Hiram. "Louisa Picquet, the Octoroon: Or Inside Views of Southern Domestic Life." 1861. In *Collected Black Women's Narratives*, edited by Anthony G. Barthelemy. New York: Oxford University Press, 1988, pp. 90–150.

Mott, Lucretia. *Slavery and "the Woman Question": Lucretia Mott's Diary of Her Visit to Great Britain to Attend the World's Anti-Slavery Convention of 1840*. Haverford, PA: Friends' Historical Association, 1952.

Northup, Solomon. *Twelve Years a Slave: Narrative of Solomon Northrup, a Citizen of New York, Kidnapped in Washington City in 1841, and Rescued in 1853, from a Cotton Plantation Near the Red River, in Louisiana*. 1853. Edited by Sue Eakin and Joseph Logsdon. Baton Rouge: Louisiana State University Press, 1992.

Rawson, M. A., ed. *Hymns for Anti-Slavery Prayer Meetings*. London: Jackson and Walford, 1838.

Stewart, Maria W. *Maria W. Stewart, America's First Black Woman Political Writer: Essays and Speeches*. Edited by Marilyn Richardson. Bloomington: Indiana University Press, 1987.

Stowe, Harriet Beecher. *Dred: A Tale of the Great Dismal Swamp*. 1856. Introduction by Robert S. Levine. New York: Penguin Books, 2000.

———. *Uncle Tom's Cabin: or, Life Among the Lowly*. 1852. Introduction by Ann Douglas. New York: Penguin Books, 1981.

Truth, Sojourner. "Address to the First Annual Meeting of the American Equal Rights Association." In vol. 2 of *The Heath Anthology of American Literature*, edited by Paul Lauter et al. 2 vols. Lexington, MA: D. C. Heath, 1990.

———. *Narrative of Sojourner Truth*. 1850. Edited by Margaret Washington. New York: Vintage, 1993.

Warner, Samuel. "Authentic and Impartial Narrative of the Tragical Scene." 1831. In *The Southampton Slave Revolt of 1831*, edited by Henry Irving Tragle. Amherst: University of Massachusetts Press, 1971, pp. 280–300.

Weld, Theodore. "American Slavery as It Is." 1839. In *Black Protest: History, Documents, and Analyses: 1619 to the Present*, edited by Joanne Grant. New York: Fawcett, 1968, pp. 72–75.

Work, John W. *American Negro Songs: A Comprehensive Collection of 230 Folk Songs, Religious and Secular.* New York: Howell, Soskin, 1940.

Secondary Sources: Literary and Cultural Criticism

Altick, Richard D. *The Shows of London.* Cambridge, MA: Harvard University Press, 1978.

Andrews, William L. *To Tell a Free Story: The First Century of Afro-American Autobiography, 1760–1865.* Urbana and Chicago: University of Illinois Press, 1986.

Austin, Allan D. "More Black Panoramas: An Addendum." *The Massachusetts Review* 37:4 (winter 1996), pp. 636–639.

Barrett, Lindon. *Blackness and Value: Seeing Double.* New York: Cambridge University Press, 1999.

Bassard, Katherine C. *Spiritual Interrogations: Culture, Gender, and Community in Early African American Women's Writing.* Princeton, NJ: Princeton University Press, 1999.

Bay, Mia. *The White Image in the Black Mind: African-American Ideas About White People, 1830–1925.* New York: Oxford University Press, 2000.

Bell, Howard H. "National Negro Conventions of the Middle 1840's: Moral Suasion vs. Political Action." In *Blacks in the Abolitionist Movement*, edited by John H. Bracey, Jr., August Meier, and Elliott Rudwick. Belmont, CA: Wadsworth Publishing Co., 1971, pp. 123–133.

Blackett, R. J. M. *Building An Antislavery Wall: Black Americans in the Atlantic Abolitionist Movement, 1830–1860.* Ithaca, NY: Cornell University Press, 1989.

———. "The Odyssey of William and Ellen Craft." In *Beating Against the Barriers: The Lives of Six Nineteenth-Century Afro-Americans*, edited by R. J. M. Blackett. Ithaca, NY: Cornell University Press, 1986.

Blassingame, John W. *Slave Testimony: Two Centuries of Letters, Speeches, Interviews, and Autobiographies.* Baton Rouge: Louisiana State University Press, 1977.

Brody, Jennifer D. *Impossible Purities: Blackness, Femininity, and Victorian Culture.* Durham, NC: Duke University Press, 1998.

Brooks, Daphne A. *Bodies in Dissent: Spectacular Performances of Race and Freedom, 1850–1910.* Durham, NC: Duke University Press, 2006.

Brooks, Joanna. *American Lazarus: Religion and the Rise of African-American and Native American Literature.* New York: Oxford University Press, 2003.

Burnim, Mellonee. "Biblical Inspiration, Cultural Affirmation: The African American Gift of Song." In *African Americans and the Bible: Sacred Texts and Social Textures,* edited by Vincent L. Wimbush. New York: Continuum, 2000, pp. 603–615.

Cruz, Jon. *Culture on the Margins: The Black Spiritual and the Rise of American Cultural Interpretation.* Princeton, NJ: Princeton University Press, 1999.

Cutter, Martha J. "Sliding Significations: Passing as a Narrative and Textual Strategy in Nella Larsen's Fiction." In *Passing and the Fictions of Identity,* edited by Elaine K. Ginsberg. Durham, NC: Duke University Press, 1996, pp. 75–100.

Davis, Charles T. and Henry Louis Gates. "Introduction: The Language of Slavery." In *The Slave's Narrative,* edited by Charles T. Davis and Henry Louis Gates, Jr. New York: Oxford University Press, 1985, pp. xi–xxxiv.

Davis, David Brion. *The Problem of Slavery in the Age of Revolution, 1770–1823.* Ithaca, NY: Cornell University Press, 1975.

Fisch, Audrey A. *American Slaves in Victorian England: Abolitionist Politics in Popular Literature and Culture.* Cambridge and New York: Cambridge University Press, 2000.

Foster, Frances S. *Witnessing Slavery: The Development of Ante-bellum Slave Narratives.* Westport, CT: Greenwood Press, 1979.

Franklin, John Hope. *Runaway Slaves: Rebels on the Plantation.* New York: Oxford University Press, 1999.

Garber, Marjorie B. *Vested Interests: Cross-Dressing & Cultural Anxiety.* New York: Routledge, 1992.

Genovese, Eugene. *From Rebellion to Revolution: Afro-American Slave Revolts in the Making of the Modern World.* Baton Rouge: Louisiana State University Press, 1979.

Gienapp, William E. "Abolitionism and the Nature of Antebellum Reform." In *Courage and Conscience: Black and White Abolitionists in Boston,* edited by Donald M. Jacobs. Bloomington: Indiana University Press, 1993, pp. 21–46.

Ginsberg, Elaine K. "Introduction." In *Passing and the Fictions of Identity,* edited by Elaine K. Ginsberg. Durham, NC: Duke University Press, 1996, pp. 1–18.

Glaude, Eddie S. *Exodus! Religion, Race, and Nation in Early Nineteenth-Century Black America*. Chicago: University of Chicago Press, 2000.

Greenblatt, Stephen. "Resonance and Wonder." In *Exhibiting Cultures: The Poetics and Politics of Museum Display*, edited by Ivan Karp and Steven D. Lavine. Washington: Smithsonian Institution Press, 1991, pp. 42–56.

Grover, Katherine. *The Fugitive's Gibraltar: Escaping Slaves and Abolitionism in New Bedford, Massachusetts*. Amherst: University of Massachusetts Press, 2001.

Hartman, Saidiya V. *Scenes of Subjection: Terror, Slavery, and Self-Making in Nineteenth-Century America*. New York: Oxford University Press, 1997.

Hedin, Raymond. "Strategies of Form in the American Slave Narrative." In *The Art of Slave Narrative: Original Essays in Criticism and Theory*, edited by John Sekora and Darwin T. Turner. Macomb: Western Illinois University Press, 1982, pp. 25–35.

Humez, Jean M. *Harriet Tubman: The Life and the Life Stories*. Madison: University of Wisconsin Press, 2003.

Jefferson, Paul. "Introduction." In *The Travels of William Wells Brown by William Wells Brown: The Narrative of William Wells Brown, a Fugitive Slave, and The American fugitive in Europe, Sketches of Places and People Abroad*. New York: Markus Wiener, 1991, pp. 1–20.

Kent, Christopher. "Spectacular History as an Ocular Discipline." *Wide Angle* 18:3 (July 1996), pp. 1–21.

Levine, Lawrence W. *Black Culture and Black Consciousness: Afro-American Thought from Slavery to Freedom*. New York: Oxford University Press, 1977.

Lovell, John. *Black Song: The Forge and the Flame; The Story of How the Afro-American Spiritual Was Hammered Out*. New York: Macmillan, 1972.

McCaskill, Barbara. "Introduction." In *Running a Thousand Miles for Freedom: The Escape of William and Ellen Craft from Slavery*, by William Craft and Ellen Craft. Athens: University of Georgia Press, 1999, pp. vii–xxv.

McFeely, William S. *Frederick Douglass*. New York: W. W. Norton, 1991.

Meisel, Martin. *Realizations: Narrative, Pictorial, and Theatrical Arts in Nineteenth-Century England*. Princeton, NJ: Princeton University Press, 1983.

Miller, Angela. "The Panorama, the Cinema and the Emergence of the Spectacular." *Wide Angle* 18:2 (April 1996), pp. 35–69.

Olney, James. " 'I Was Born': Slave Narratives, Their Status as Autobiography and as Literature." In *The Slave's Narrative*, edited by Charles T. Davis and Henry Louis Gates, Jr. New York: Oxford University Press, 1985, pp. 148–174.

Pease, Jane H. and William H. Pease. *They Who Would Be Free: Blacks' Search for Freedom, 1830–1861*. New York: Atheneum, 1974.

Price, Richard. *Maroon Societies: Rebel Slave Communities in the Americas*. Garden City, NY: Anchor Press, 1973.

Quarles, Benjamin. *Black Abolitionists*. New York: Oxford University Press, 1969.

Reilly, Bernard F. "The Art of the Antislavery Movement." In *Courage and Conscience: Black and White Abolitionists in Boston*, edited by Donald M. Jacobs. Bloomington: Indiana University Press, 1993, pp. 47–74.

Ripley, C. Peter. "Introduction." In *The Black Abolitionist Papers*, edited by C. Peter Ripley et al. Vol 1: *The British Isles, 1830–1865*. Chapel Hill: University of North Carolina Press, 1985, pp. 3–35.

Robinson, Amy. "It Takes One to Know One: Passing and Communities of Common Interest." *Critical Inquiry* 20:4 (summer 1994), pp. 715–736.

Ruggles, Jeffrey. *The Unboxing of Henry Brown*. Richmond: Library of Virginia Press, 2003.

Saks, Eva. "Representing Miscegenation Law." *Raritan* 8:2 (1988), pp. 39–69.

Smith, Valerie A. " 'Loopholes of Retreat': Architecture and Ideology in Harriet Jacobs's *Incidents in the Life of a Slave Girl*." In *Reading Black, Reading Feminist: A Critical Anthology*, edited by Henry Louis Gates, Jr. New York: Meridian, 1990, pp. 212–226.

Southern, Eileen. *The Music of Black Americans: A History*. Third edition. New York: W. W. Norton, 1997.

Spencer, Suzette. *Stealing A Way: African Diaspora Maroon Poetics*. Diss. 2003 Mar; 63 (9), pp. 3188–3189. University of California–Berkeley, 2002.

Spillers, Hortense. "Mama's Baby, Papa's Maybe: An American Grammar Book." In *African American Literary Theory: A Reader*, edited by Winston Napier. New York: New York University Press, 2000, pp. 257–279.

Stepto, Robert Burns. "I Rose and Found My Voice: Narration, Authentication, and Authorial Control in Four Slave Narratives." In *The Slave's Narrative*, edited by Charles T. Davis and Henry Louis Gates, Jr. New York: Oxford University Press, 1985, pp. 225–241.

Sterling, Dorothy. *We Are Your Sisters: Black Women in the Nineteenth Century.* New York: W. W. Norton, 1984.

Stevens, Charles E. *Anthony Burns: A History.* New York: Arno Press, 1969.

Stewart, James Brewer. *Holy Warriors: The Abolitionists and American Slavery.* New York: Hill and Wang, 1976.

Still, William. *The Underground Railroad.* Chicago: Johnson Publishing, 1970.

Stuckey, Sterling. *Slave Culture: Nationalist Theory and the Foundations of Black America.* New York: Oxford University Press, 1987.

Weinauer, Ellen M. " 'A Most Respectable Looking Gentleman': Passing, Possession, and Transgression in *Running a Thousand Miles for Freedom.*" In *Passing and the Fictions of Identity*, edited by Elaine K. Ginsberg. Durham, NC: Duke University Press, 1996, p. 38.

Williamson, Joel. *New People: Miscegenation and Mulattoes in the United States.* New York: New York University Press, 1984.

Wolff, Cynthia Griffin. "Passing Beyond the Middle Passage: Henry 'Box' Brown's Translations of Slavery." *Massachusetts Review* 37:1 (1996), pp. 23–44.

Wood, Marcus. " 'All Right!': *The Narrative of Henry Box Brown* as a Test Case for the Racial Prescription of Rhetoric and Semiotics." *Proceedings of the American Antiquarian Society* 107:1 (April 1997), pp. 65–104.

———. *Blind Memory: Visual Representations of Slavery in England and America, 1780–1865.* New York: Routledge, 2000.

Yellin, Jean Fagan. "Introduction." In *Incidents in the Life of a Slave Girl: Written by Herself,* by Harriet Jacobs. Cambridge, MA: Harvard University Press, 1987, pp. xiii–xxxiv.

———. *Women and Sisters: The Antislavery Feminists in American Culture.* New Haven, CT: Yale University Press, 1989.

Look for the following titles, available now and forthcoming from
BARNES & NOBLE CLASSICS.

Visit your local bookstore for these and more fine titles.
Or to order online go to: WWW.BN.COM/CLASSICS

Title	Author	ISBN	Price
Aesop's Fables	Aesop	1-59308-062-X	$5.95
The Age of Innocence	Edith Wharton	1-59308-143-X	$5.95
Agnes Grey	Anne Brontë	1-59308-323-8	$5.95
Alice's Adventures in Wonderland and Through the Looking-Glass	Lewis Carroll	1-59308-015-8	$5.95
Anna Karenina	Leo Tolstoy	1-59308-027-1	$8.95
The Art of War	Sun Tzu	1-59308-017-4	$7.95
The Awakening and Selected Short Fiction	Kate Chopin	1-59308-113-8	$6.95
Babbitt	Sinclair Lewis	1-59308-267-3	$7.95
Barchester Towers	Anthony Trollope	1-59308-337-8	$7.95
The Beautiful and Damned	F. Scott Fitzgerald	1-59308-245-2	$7.95
Beowulf	Anonymous	1-59308-266-5	$4.95
Bleak House	Charles Dickens	1-59308-311-4	$9.95
The Bostonians	Henry James	1-59308-297-5	$7.95
The Brothers Karamazov	Fyodor Dostoevsky	1-59308-045-X	$9.95
The Call of the Wild and White Fang	Jack London	1-59308-200-2	$5.95
Candide	Voltaire	1-59308-028-X	$4.95
A Christmas Carol, The Chimes and The Cricket on the Hearth	Charles Dickens	1-59308-033-6	$5.95
The Collected Poems of Emily Dickinson	Emily Dickinson	1-59308-050-6	$5.95
Common Sense and Other Writings	Thomas Paine	1-59308-209-6	$6.95
The Communist Manifesto and Other Writings	Karl Marx and Friedrich Engels	1-59308-100-6	$5.95
The Complete Sherlock Holmes, Vol. I	Sir Arthur Conan Doyle	1-59308-034-4	$7.95
The Complete Sherlock Holmes, Vol. II	Sir Arthur Conan Doyle	1-59308-040-9	$7.95
A Connecticut Yankee in King Arthur's Court	Mark Twain	1-59308-210-X	$7.95
The Count of Monte Cristo	Alexandre Dumas	1-59308-151-0	$7.95
The Country of the Pointed Firs and Selected Short Fiction	Sarah Orne Jewett	1-59308-262-2	$6.95
Daisy Miller and Washington Square	Henry James	1-59308-105-7	$4.95
Daniel Deronda	George Eliot	1-59308-290-8	$8.95
David Copperfield	Charles Dickens	1-59308-063-8	$7.95
Dead Souls	Nikolai Gogol	1-59308-092-1	$7.95
The Death of Ivan Ilych and Other Stories	Leo Tolstoy	1-59308-069-7	$7.95
The Deerslayer	James Fenimore Cooper	1-59308-211-8	$7.95
Don Quixote	Miguel de Cervantes	1-59308-046-8	$9.95
Dracula	Bram Stoker	1-59308-114-6	$6.95
Emma	Jane Austen	1-59308-152-9	$6.95
The Enchanted Castle and Five Children and It	Edith Nesbit	1-59308-274-6	$6.95
Essays and Poems by Ralph Waldo Emerson		1-59308-076-X	$6.95
Essential Dialogues of Plato		1-59308-269-X	$9.95
The Essential Tales and Poems of Edgar Allan Poe		1-59308-064-6	$7.95
Ethan Frome and Selected Stories	Edith Wharton	1-59308-090-5	$5.95

(continued)

Title	Author	ISBN	Price
Far from the Madding Crowd	Thomas Hardy	1-59308-223-1	$7.95
The Federalist	Hamilton, Madison, Jay	1-59308-282-7	$7.95
The Four Feathers	A. E. W. Mason	1-59308-313-0	$6.95
Frankenstein	Mary Shelley	1-59308-115-4	$4.95
Germinal	Émile Zola	1-59308-291-6	$7.95
The Good Soldier	Ford Madox Ford	1-59308-268-1	$6.95
Great American Short Stories: from Hawthorne to Hemingway	Various	1-59308-086-7	$7.95
Great Expectations	Charles Dickens	1-59308-116-2	$6.95
Grimm's Fairy Tales	Jacob and Wilhelm Grimm	1-59308-056-5	$7.95
Gulliver's Travels	Jonathan Swift	1-59308-132-4	$5.95
Hard Times	Charles Dickens	1-59308-156-1	$5.95
The Histories	Herodotus	1-59308-102-2	$6.95
The House of Mirth	Edith Wharton	1-59308-153-7	$6.95
The House of the Dead and Poor Folk	Fyodor Dostoevsky	1-59308-194-4	$7.95
Howards End	E. M. Forster	1-59308-022-0	$6.95
The Idiot	Fyodor Dostoevsky	1-59308-058-1	$7.95
The Iliad	Homer	1-59308-232-0	$7.95
The Importance of Being Earnest and Four Other Plays	Oscar Wilde	1-59308-059-X	$6.95
Incidents in the Life of a Slave Girl	Harriet Jacobs	1-59308-283-5	$5.95
The Inferno	Dante Alighieri	1-59308-051-4	$6.95
The Interpretation of Dreams	Sigmund Freud	1-59308-298-3	$8.95
Ivanhoe	Sir Walter Scott	1-59308-246-0	$7.95
Jane Eyre	Charlotte Brontë	1-59308-117-0	$7.95
Journey to the Center of the Earth	Jules Verne	1-59308-252-5	$4.95
Jude the Obscure	Thomas Hardy	1-59308-035-2	$6.95
The Jungle	Upton Sinclair	1-59308-118-9	$6.95
The Jungle Books	Rudyard Kipling	1-59308-109-X	$5.95
Kim	Rudyard Kipling	1-59308-192-8	$4.95
King Solomon's Mines	H. Rider Haggard	1-59308-275-4	$4.95
Lady Chatterley's Lover	D. H. Lawrence	1-59308-239-8	$6.95
The Last of the Mohicans	James Fenimore Cooper	1-59308-137-5	$5.95
Leaves of Grass: First and "Death-bed" Editions	Walt Whitman	1-59308-083-2	$9.95
The Legend of Sleepy Hollow and Other Writings	Washington Irving	1-59308-225-8	$6.95
Les Liaisons Dangereuses	Pierre Choderlos de Laclos	1-59308-240-1	$7.95
Les Misérables	Victor Hugo	1-59308-066-2	$9.95
The Life of Charlotte Brontë	Elizabeth Gaskell	1-59308-314-9	$7.95
Little Women	Louisa May Alcott	1-59308-108-1	$6.95
Madame Bovary	Gustave Flaubert	1-59308-052-2	$6.95
Maggie: A Girl of the Streets and Other Writings about New York	Stephen Crane	1-59308-248-7	$6.95
The Magnificent Ambersons	Booth Tarkington	1-59308-263-0	$7.95
Man and Superman and Three Other Plays	George Bernard Shaw	1-59308-067-0	$7.95
The Man in the Iron Mask	Alexandre Dumas	1-59308-233-9	$8.95
Mansfield Park	Jane Austen	1-59308-154-5	$5.95
The Mayor of Casterbridge	Thomas Hardy	1-59308-309-2	$5.95
The Metamorphoses	Ovid	1-59308-276-2	$7.95
The Metamorphosis and Other Stories	Franz Kafka	1-59308-029-8	$6.95

Middlemarch	George Eliot	1-59308-023-9	$8.95
Moby-Dick	Herman Melville	1-59308-018-2	$9.95
Moll Flanders	Daniel Defoe	1-59308-216-9	$5.95
The Moonstone	Wilkie Collins	1-59308-322-X	$7.95
My Ántonia	Willa Cather	1-59308-202-9	$5.95
My Bondage and My Freedom	Frederick Douglass	1-59308-301-7	$6.95
Nana	Émile Zola	1-59308-292-4	$6.95
Narrative of Sojourner Truth		1-59308-293-2	$6.95
Narrative of the Life of Frederick Douglass,			
an American Slave		1-59308-041-7	$4.95
Nicholas Nickleby	Charles Dickens	1-59308-300-9	$8.95
Night and Day	Virginia Woolf	1-59308-212-6	$7.95
Northanger Abbey	Jane Austen	1-59308-264-9	$5.95
Nostromo	Joseph Conrad	1-59308-193-6	$7.95
O Pioneers!	Willa Cather	1-59308-205-3	$5.95
The Odyssey	Homer	1-59308-009-3	$5.95
Oliver Twist	Charles Dickens	1-59308-206-1	$6.95
The Origin of Species	Charles Darwin	1-59308-077-8	$7.95
Paradise Lost	John Milton	1-59308-095-6	$7.95
Père Goriot	Honoré de Balzac	1-59308-285-1	$7.95
Persuasion	Jane Austen	1-59308-130-8	$5.95
Peter Pan	J. M. Barrie	1-59308-213-4	$4.95
The Picture of Dorian Gray	Oscar Wilde	1-59308-025-5	$4.95
The Pilgrim's Progress	John Bunyan	1-59308-254-1	$7.95
Poetics and Rhetoric	Aristotle	1-59308-307-6	$9.95
The Portrait of a Lady	Henry James	1-59308-096-4	$7.95
A Portrait of the Artist as a Young Man			
and Dubliners	James Joyce	1-59308-031-X	$6.95
The Possessed	Fyodor Dostoevsky	1-59308-250-9	$9.95
Pride and Prejudice	Jane Austen	1-59308-201-0	$5.95
The Prince and Other Writings	Niccolò Machiavelli	1-59308-060-3	$5.95
The Prince and the Pauper	Mark Twain	1-59308-218-5	$4.95
Pudd'nhead Wilson			
and Those Extraordinary Twins	Mark Twain	1-59308-255-X	$5.95
The Purgatorio	Dante Alighieri	1-59308-219-3	$7.95
Pygmalion and Three Other Plays	George Bernard Shaw	1-59308-078-6	$7.95
The Red and the Black	Stendhal	1-59308-286-X	$7.95
The Red Badge of Courage			
and Selected Short Fiction	Stephen Crane	1-59308-119-7	$4.95
Republic	Plato	1-59308-097-2	$6.95
The Return of the Native	Thomas Hardy	1-59308-220-7	$7.95
Robinson Crusoe	Daniel Defoe	1-59308-360-2	$5.95
A Room with a View	E. M. Forster	1-59308-288-6	$5.95
Sailing Alone Around the World	Joshua Slocum	1-59308-303-3	$6.95
Scaramouche	Rafael Sabatini	1-59308-242-8	$6.95
The Scarlet Letter	Nathaniel Hawthorne	1-59308-207-X	$4.95
The Scarlet Pimpernel	Baroness Orczy	1-59308-234-7	$5.95
The Secret Garden	Frances Hodgson Burnett	1-59308-277-0	$5.95
Selected Stories of O. Henry		1-59308-042-5	$5.95
Sense and Sensibility	Jane Austen	1-59308-125-1	$5.95
Sentimental Education	Gustave Flaubert	1-59308-306-8	$6.95
Silas Marner and Two Short Stories	George Eliot	1-59308-251-7	$6.95

(continued)

Sister Carrie	Theodore Dreiser	1-59308-226-6	$7.95
Six Plays by Henrik Ibsen		1-59308-061-1	$8.95
Sons and Lovers	D. H. Lawrence	1-59308-013-1	$7.95
The Souls of Black Folk	W. E. B. Du Bois	1-59308-014-X	$5.95
The Strange Case of Dr. Jekyll and Mr. Hyde and Other Stories	Robert Louis Stevenson	1-59308-131-6	$4.95
Swann's Way	Marcel Proust	1-59308-295-9	$8.95
A Tale of Two Cities	Charles Dickens	1-59308-138-3	$5.95
Tao Te Ching	Lao Tzu	1-59308-256-8	$5.95
Tess of d'Urbervilles	Thomas Hardy	1-59308-228-2	$7.95
This Side of Paradise	F. Scott Fitzgerald	1-59308-243-6	$6.95
Three Lives	Gertrude Stein	1-59308-320-3	$6.95
The Three Musketeers	Alexandre Dumas	1-59308-148-0	$8.95
Thus Spoke Zarathustra	Friedrich Nietzsche	1-59308-278-9	$7.95
Tom Jones	Henry Fielding	1-59308-070-0	$8.95
Treasure Island	Robert Louis Stevenson	1-59308-247-9	$4.95
The Turn of the Screw, The Aspern Papers and Two Stories	Henry James	1-59308-043-3	$5.95
Twenty Thousand Leagues Under the Sea	Jules Verne	1-59308-302-5	$5.95
Uncle Tom's Cabin	Harriet Beecher Stowe	1-59308-121-9	$7.95
Utopia	Sir Thomas More	1-59308-244-4	$5.95
Vanity Fair	William Makepeace Thackeray	1-59308-071-9	$7.95
The Varieties of Religious Experience	William James	1-59308-072-7	$7.95
Villette	Charlotte Brontë	1-59308-316-5	$7.95
The Virginian	Owen Wister	1-59308-236-3	$7.95
The Voyage Out	Virginia Woolf	1-59308-229-0	$6.95
Walden and Civil Disobedience	Henry David Thoreau	1-59308-208-8	$5.95
War and Peace	Leo Tolstoy	1-59308-073-5	$12.95
Ward No. 6 and Other Stories	Anton Chekhov	1-59308-003-4	$7.95
The Waste Land and Other Poems	T. S. Eliot	1-59308-279-7	$4.95
The Way We Live Now	Anthony Trollope	1-59308-304-1	$9.95
The Wind in the Willows	Kenneth Grahame	1-59308-265-7	$4.95
The Wings of the Dove	Henry James	1-59308-296-7	$7.95
Wives and Daughters	Elizabeth Gaskell	1-59308-257-6	$7.95
The Woman in White	Wilkie Collins	1-59308-280-0	$7.95
Women in Love	D. H. Lawrence	1-59308-258-4	$8.95
The Wonderful Wizard of Oz	L. Frank Baum	1-59308-221-5	$6.95
Wuthering Heights	Emily Brontë	1-59308-128-6	$5.95

ƀ
BARNES & NOBLE CLASSICS

If you are an educator and would like to receive an
Examination or Desk Copy of a Barnes & Noble Classic edition,
please refer to Academic Resources on our website at
WWW.BN.COM/CLASSICS
or contact us at
B&NCLASSICS@BN.COM.

All prices are subject to change.